THE OTHER MOTHER

Also by Seth Margolis

False Faces
Vanishing Act

THE OTHER MOTHER

Seth Margolis

LONDON NEW YORK SYDNEY TORONTO

This edition published 1993
by BCA
by arrangement with Headline Books Ltd.

First reprint 1993

Copyright © 1993 Seth Margolis

The right of Seth Margolis to be identified as the Author of
the Work has been asserted by him in accordance with the
Copyright, Designs and Patents Act 1988.

All rights reserved. No part of this publication may be
reproduced, stored in a retrieval system, or transmitted,
in any form or by any means without the prior written
permission of the publisher, nor be otherwise circulated
in any form of binding or cover other than that in which
it is published and without a similar condition being
imposed on the subsequent purchaser.

All characters in this publication are fictitious
and any resemblance to real persons, living or dead,
is purely coincidental.

CN 3291

Printed and bound in Great Britain by
Mackays of Chatham PLC, Chatham, Kent

For Carole, Maggie and Jack

Prologue

Isaiah moved with cat-like stealth down the long hallway of the Manhattan apartment, ignoring the creaks in the old floorboards, which he never seemed able to avoid, no matter how careful he was, no matter how much he practiced. The power-pack was strapped firmly over his left shoulder; the weight of it made him feel strong and safe. In his right hand was the weapon itself, half as long as his body and as mean-looking an instrument as he'd ever seen. A trace of smile formed on his lips, making his eyes squint. He knew what was coming.

At the end of the hallway he paused before the doorway, placing his back flat against the wall. The smile grew wider – he knew this looked bad, but he couldn't help it, this was his favorite part. Count to ten, he told himself; he'd seen guys do this on television. One. Two. Three. This was as far as he got, as far as he ever got. Gritting his teeth behind his smile, he swivelled round into the doorway, raised the weapon to eye level, and shouted as loud as he could, 'GHOSTBUSTERS!'

He saw his mother flinch on the bed, startled, and he flinched, too. He hadn't realized she was in her bedroom. 'Isaiah, honestly! You know I hate when you do that.'

Isaiah glanced around the room for a few moments before running over to a remote corner on the far side of his parents' big bed. He reached behind himself to adjust a knob on his power-pack, then aimed the Ghostzapper into the corner and began firing. It made a whirring sound that he could feel vibrating through him.

'Isaiah, honey, do you have to play with that thing in here?' His mother was lying on her bed reading the paper, same as she did every Sunday.

'I have to,' he said. 'Ghosts here.' He looked closely at his mother; sometimes she just didn't see things the way he did, especially about the ghosts. 'Slime, too,' he added hopefully.

'But haven't you taken care of them already?'

Isaiah had to smile again. 'One more.'

He saw his mother begin to smile. 'Only one more?'

'One more.' Isaiah walked to the opposite side of the room. He

1

knew his mother was watching, so he used his best step, the one he'd seen the real Ghostbusters use in the movie when they walked down that long hallway to rescue the woman. He crouched and thrust his head forward, the zapper in firing position in front of him. When he reached the corner next to her closet – ghosts always lived in corners, Isaiah thought, don't ask how come – he opened fire. Who you gonna call? he chanted to himself. GHOSTBUSTERS! Who you gonna call? GHOSTBUSTERS! He let the gun do its thing for a long, long time, until he heard the newspaper rustling and knew that she was going to say something that would make him feel bad. So he stopped and turned round, a big, proud smile on his face.

'Ghosts in living room now,' he said, and left the room.

Margaret signed and leaned back on the bed, picking up the paper. It still mystified her that Isaiah had become fixated on Ghostbusters. She would never forget the look in his eye after he'd seen the movie on their VCR for the first time, that gleam of the newly-enlightened she'd seen on some of the religious types who asked for money in subway stations. Of course, on a two-and-a-half-year-old, the gleam wasn't quite so off-putting, but Isaiah *had* been transformed that night, and ever since, all he talked about was Ghostbusters this, Ghostbusters that. It turned out there was a not-so-small industry devoted to producing Ghostbusters this and Ghostbusters that, and now Isaiah lived for his next piece of tacky plastic equipment.

Three months was a long time for a fixation to stay rooted in a two-and-a-half-year-old. Hannah, who was twelve, ran through fads and crazes in about a week. But that's the way Isaiah had always been, Margaret thought, still holding the Arts and Leisure section. Stubborn. Tenacious. Driven. She laughed to herself at this, at the thought that a two-year-old could be driven. But Isaiah had a powerful will; she felt certain that this would be his most salient quality as an adult.

She remembered how he used to howl in the middle of the night, from hunger, because he needed changing, or perhaps only from a bad dream. When Hannah had cried at night, Margaret had been able to calm her down in a few minutes; only once in a while did it take more than a few. But Isaiah would howl half the night, and in those blessed moments when he'd take a break, his chest heaving from exertion, she'd pray the storm was over and begin to relax . . . until she caught a glint in his eyes that told her he wasn't stopping for *anything*. 'It's *okay*, Isaiah,' she'd coo, holding his little body against her, hoping that her growing frustration wasn't obvious to him. 'Let it go,' she'd whisper. 'It's okay to let it go.' But Isaiah made these episodes last half the night, until she could barely hear him. When he stopped crying, the silence filled up his room like water rushing into a chamber, warm, comforting water that washed away her frustration and even her exhaustion, making her feel like they were the only two people in the world. She felt incredibly close to Isaiah in these quiet moments, closer, she hated to admit, than she'd ever felt to Hannah. Perhaps closer even than to Charles, her husband, because when she'd crawl back into bed after placing Isaiah in his crib, she'd do so with a totally unnecessary caution, practically terrified that Charles would wake up and say something to her.

It still amazed her sometimes how much she loved Isaiah. It shouldn't, but it did. Walking around their West Side neighborhood, she made a casual study of mothers and their sons, and what she learned each time was that the reasons for mother love were obvious – these children looked just like their mothers, to varying degrees, of course, but there was always an obvious kinship. How could you not love something that was so clearly an outgrowth of yourself? She remembered, with Hannah, how she'd catch a glimpse of herself in one of her daughter's gestures, in a particular inflection, and feel a surge of miraculous love. It had been inside her, this love for her daughter, since the very moment the tiny girl had been placed on her chest a few seconds after birth, red as tandoori chicken, her face scrunched into an angry, ancient scowl. What she saw in the mothers on the West Side, what she saw in her own love for Hannah, was instinct, the instinct to love and protect your child.

With Isaiah it was something else. He'd been adopted. She'd had to fall in love with him.

When she'd brought him home, already a few months old, she told herself that the fluttering ache in her chest was love. In reality it had been merely pity. She had wondered if Isaiah's being black would prove a barrier between them, but she had quickly put this thought out of her mind, afraid, at the time, of where it might lead her. Now this concern seemed absurd. Now, when she noticed the contrasts in their skin colors, it only served to remind her of how she'd fallen in love with him, slowly but inevitably, since that March day over two years ago when she'd brought him home. No obstetrician had plunked him onto her chest to let the maternal instinct kick in. She'd had to find Isaiah, *take* him. And then he'd won her over.

She still enjoyed running through the whole process of finding and adopting Isaiah, just as she'd gone over Hannah's birth a thousand times afterward. Both had been fraught with pain and fear, but her mind returned to both episodes often, savoring the remembered moments, seizing on the almost-forgotten detail. You never remember the pain, Margaret thought. Never *really* remember it.

3

Isaiah had been screaming when she'd first seen him, his distended mouth practically obliterating his little face. Maybe that's why he continued to scream through the night every so often, because that one time he'd been heard, he'd been rescued. Maybe that's why she'd fallen in love with him, too: she'd loved that quality in Isaiah that wouldn't let go of the screaming, that wouldn't be overlooked. He'd screamed and screamed until she'd heard him, rescued him. And he still screamed, much more than Hannah ever did. I'm not safe yet, he seemed to be saying. Even with my Ghostzapper and my Ghostpopper and my Slimer, I'm not really safe yet.

Yes you are, she would tell him when he screamed into the night. Yes you are.

But he still screamed, and Margaret knew why.

Selma Richards entered the church by the side entrance and walked downstairs, into the basement. Churches are cold enough, she thought. But church basements are meat lockers. Tuesdays and Thursdays, when the literacy program met, she always brought herself an extra sweater, but by the end of the session the cold had penetrated whatever she was wearing. But then, Selma knew there were hidden costs to everything in life. Freezing half to death was the price of learning to read. It's the way things worked. You get sick, you take a day off, you don't get paid. You stop to admire something in a shop window, maybe not even a dress or something nice but some lettuce on sale, you miss your subway and the next one comes so late you can't squeeze yourself onto it. You want to learn to read at the ripe old age of twenty-five, you have to catch your death in some musty church basement in the middle of Manhattan. Hidden costs, that's all. 'For unto whomsoever much is given, of him shall much be required,' she muttered as she navigated the hard, twisting steps, feeling the temperature drop as she went. Scriptures always got it right.

The big room in the basement where the literacy people met had tables scattered all about. Pairs of people and a few groups hunched over the tables, reading out loud, reading silently, writing, just talking. The room always had a strange effect on Selma. No one outside this room knew she couldn't read, not a soul. But every time she walked into this room it was like announcing: I, Selma Richards, can't read or write any better than a first-grader. She'd been coming twice a week for three weeks and still she couldn't get used to it, it was like taking off her clothes for the first time in front of a man.

As she walked across the room to the table where her tutor sat, she cast furtive glances at the other students. You could always tell the students from the tutors. For starters, one group was mostly

4

black – guess which. Some of them looked like real losers, you knew why they couldn't read. Others looked normal, the way she figured she looked. She wanted to ask them, How come you never learned? Course, then they'd ask *her*, and what would she say? Tell them her whole entire life history, be the only way to explain.

She saw Lizzie Kaplan, her tutor. Wearing one of her suits, naturally, with some kind of bow under her chin that made her head look propped up. Lizzie worked for a bank and lived in Manhattan; this was the sum total of everything Selma knew about her. It pissed her off, she knew so little about her when she had to keep explaining over and over about herself. Didn't have to, actually, but Lizzie kept asking, like she was interested. Probably never met anyone like me, Selma thought. Unless she has a black maid, that is. Selma chuckled to herself. She came from work, too, but cleaning house and taking care of someone's child didn't lend itself to wearing suits. No one cared what she wore to work, come to think of it. Specially not the kid. Makes no difference to a baby what it spills its milk on and throws its food at.

'Hey, Selma,' Lizzie called when she caught sight of her. Always cheerful, peppy.

'You always in such a good mood, Lizzie. What's your secret?'

Lizzie smiled, like she was embarrassed. 'How're you doing, Selma?'

'Can't complain.' She took off her coat and sat down on the other side of the small round table. If she arrived first, Lizzie always sat down right next to her, so their shoulders practically touched. Selma hated this. *Hated* it.

'How's your reading coming?'

Selma took her book out of her bag, which said 'The family that prays together, stays together' on the side. Two weeks on the same book and she wasn't even nearly done with it. *A Day in the Life* was the title. It had photographs on every page of two young black people with big afros like people wore back in the seventies. The book was about this couple who meet and get married and look for work. Catherine and George.

'I read another couple of pages,' Selma reported.

'Good. What's happening with Catherine and George?'

'Catherine think she's pregnant. George says he have to get a second job, on account of there's a kid on the way.'

'Does Catherine want to have a child?'

Selma thinks about this. 'Don't say. Guess so.'

'So soon after marriage?'

Selma looked at her. She knew she should be grateful to Lizzie for volunteering to teach her and all, but this woman was hard to warm up to. She looked like someone from a TV show. Stiff, like she's

5

reading lines. 'At least they married.'

Lizzie smiled. 'Good point.'

'You have any kids?'

'Me? I'm not even married.'

'You want kids?'

'Someday.'

Selma could see Lizzie getting nervous. 'When you getting married, then?'

'The sixty-four thousand dollar question.'

'How old are you?'

'Thirty-two. Hey, what's going on? I thought we were reading.'

'We sharing, that's all.'

She saw Lizzie give her a look. *Sharing* was a word Lizzie used all the time. She heard other tutors at other tables use it, too. Selma figured they taught it to all the tutors when they trained them. After they read something, Lizzie'd say, 'Let's share some thoughts on this.' It made Selma's skin crawl, all this sharing.

Lizzie's face was a little red now, which made her look less uptight. Maybe I could learn to like Lizzie, Selma thought. It's hard liking people you're supposed to be grateful to, though.

'We'll read later,' Lizzie said. 'Now I think it's time to do some writing.'

Selma had been dreading this. They told her when she started she'd have to write. All I want to do is read, she said, but no use. They told her she had to learn to read and write at the same time.

'Don't know what I have to write about.' She took out her notebook and turned to the first page, as white as a new diaper.

'Let's talk about it, then.'

At least she didn't say share. 'Nothing to talk about.'

'A good place to start might be why you're here.'

'To learn to read.'

'I mean, *why* you want to learn to read.'

Selma felt her heart clamp up. 'I can't spell the words.'

'That's okay. You leave blank lines for the words you don't know. If you think you know the first letter, put that down.'

Selma picked up her pencil. 'I don't know,' she said.

'Just get your ideas down on the paper. Write why you want to learn to read. That's what's important.'

Selma nodded and looked at the white paper. The pencil felt slippery in her hand. She put the point on the paper and made an I, but when she took the pencil back up she saw she'd barely made a scratch. So she retraced the I harder, then took a second look. Better. A few seconds later she made a W and put a line after it. Lizzie excused herself to get a cup of coffee. When she returned a few minutes later Selma was done.

'Done?' Lizzie asked brightly.

'If you call this chicken scratch done.' They both looked at Selma's page. The only complete word was 'I' , if you could call that a word. All the rest were just single letters followed by a line.

'Would you like to share it with me?'

'You mean read it to you?'

Lizzie just rolled her eyes good-naturedly.

Selma looked down at the page. A sentence. Her sentence. The first sentence she'd written since she was in grade school. It looked a mess, but she knew what it said because she'd said it to herself so many times this past year. Seeing it written down, there on the page, made her feel funny, like now it was a fact, not just a dream.

'Ready?' Lizzie asked. 'You were going to write why you want to learn to read.'

Selma felt her breath start to speed up. She didn't have to look at the sentence, but she made herself follow the words on the page anyway, because she wanted to learn, she needed to learn. Slowly, feeling hope and determination rise up inside her, she read her own words.

'I want to get my boy back.'

PART ONE

Chapter 1

Charles Lewin was not the sort of man to take stock, in fact he half believed doing so could put a jinx on him and his family, a *kinahurra*, his mother would say. But this particular Monday morning he couldn't help it. Things were simply going too well.

So he allowed himself to drift away from the invoices he was reviewing to contemplate all that he had to be thankful for. He knew he should start with his family but he couldn't resist thinking of his business first. Anyway, nothing unusual was happening at home, but business, as he had learned only this morning, was truly booming. LewinArt, the graphic design firm he'd founded five years ago, had just been given the go-ahead on an annual report for the second largest bank in New York – the phone call had come minutes after he'd arrived at his office this morning, and had set him off on this dangerous and uncharacteristic examination of his life. Even though he'd low-balled the estimate for the annual, he figured LewinArt would clear twenty, thirty thousand. And since he, Charles Lewin, *was* LewinArt – though he employed three designers and an assistant, all profits were his – this meant he'd personally clear the twenty, thirty thousand. Not to mention the other work from the bank that LewinArt could expect if they did a good job on the annual.

Charles's office was the opposite of his apartment, and he liked it that way. At home he and Margaret had gone the traditional route – oriental rugs, lots of oak, a congenial clutter of small objects and framed photographs, all of it accented with an advancing plague of children's toys. But his office was serenely modern, even stark. His desk was just a big, thick slab of glass supported by two red trestles. He joked to his assistant that if he could see his knees he knew he was making progress with the paperwork. A Tizio lamp loomed vulture-like in front of him, and he had a futuristic telephone with a panel of buttons he'd still not mastered. A small conference table on the other side of the large room was also glass, surrounded by four spare, modern chairs that were murder on the coccyx. Two windows let in light all day, and there was even a view, through one of them, of the Chrysler Building. In all he rented a thousand square feet in the East Twenties, where all the ad agencies and graphics firms were moving. It cost him three thousand a month for the space alone, plus another six thousand for payroll, and about a thousand more a month for miscellaneous supplies, utilities, whatnot. Once or twice a week he added it all up – ten thousand a month just to break even, never mind paying himself anything. One hundred and twenty a year in expenses. His chest would contract during these calculations, he'd feel an icing of sweat form on the back of his neck, and he'd ask himself, for the ten thousandth time, why he'd left the ad agency to open his own studio.

Mornings like this he knew.

But enough about business, he chided himself. The whole point of it was to make a better life for Margaret and the kids and me.

Charles was a product of the sixties and seventies, or so he considered himself, a protest-marcher, draft-resister, recreational drug-user, and it still vaguely discomfited him to get too excited about making money. Of course you *had* to make a lot of money these days just to live like a human being. He and Margaret talked about this all the time. It wasn't a question of greed. It was a question of getting by. Living was expensive today; somehow it had been cheaper back then in the sixties. Apartments were expensive today, kids were expensive, even education was expensive, what with Hannah's private school tuition and Isaiah's pre-school fees. Yes, there were public schools, but they were awful in Manhattan, dangerous, even – everyone said so – and even in the sixties he and Margaret had agreed that nothing was more important than a good education.

So suddenly they had this hundred thousand dollar a year lifestyle that they'd never planned on, never asked for. It had just settled on them, like an unexpected inheritance in reverse. Once in a while they'd look at each other, he and Margaret, usually during one of their monthly triage sessions with the bills, and ask each other how this had happened, how they'd gotten in so deep. They'd fantasize about chucking it all, moving somewhere cheaper than Manhattan (where *wasn't* it cheaper than Manhattan?), somewhere where the kids could go to public schools and housing didn't cost seventy-five thousand dollars a room. But then they'd shrug and return to the bills, knowing they'd never make the move. They were too caught up in it, really, to escape.

'Got a minute, Charles?'

It was Susannah Foster, one of the designers he employed.

She crossed the room in two long strides. The other two designers, both of them women, needed several more steps to make it from the door to his desk, but not Susannah. She did it in two expansive, resolute strides of her long, long legs. He noticed this

12

each time she came into his office, and it never failed to buoy him, the way she just *took* the office in two strides.

'What do you think?' She placed before him a rough layout for the cover of a mail-order catalog of fancy foods they were producing. 'Maybe you can't tell from this sketch, but it's basically a kitchen counter overflowing with a lot of the stuff inside the catalog.'

Charles looked at the sketch, trying to appear critical. But he was thinking about Susannah. He thought about Susannah a lot. She was attractive all right, but not *that* attractive. Not as attractive as Margaret, for example. Sometimes he thought it was her aura of competence that intrigued him. Where'd you find her? colleagues and clients were always asking, as if she were some superduper new office supply. Can you clone her?

She's married, Charles reminded himself often. Happily married, like me.

'Who would we get to shoot it?'

She named three well-known studio photographers. 'I've put feelers out. They're all available on short notice.'

'You think this is a better approach than focusing on one product?'

'There isn't one product that stands out. I thought it would be better to show the *range* of merchandise.'

She sounded almost evangelical about this point, so he didn't argue, though he knew she wasn't necessarily right. He decided he'd let her present the concept to the client, confident that they, too, would be helpless in the face of her zeal.

'Okay, why don't you refine the sketch a bit, maybe give it to Alice to do, and then we'll fly it by the client.'

Susannah smiled crisply, picked up the design, and reclaimed the office in two more strides.

Margaret had only met Susannah once. She'd stopped by a month ago; her office was only ten blocks away, but she rarely visited. He'd taken her into the offices of the other designers first, unconsciously leaving Susannah for last. That night, reviewing her visit, Margaret had mentioned everyone except Susannah. 'What about Susannah?' Charles had said, against his better judgment. 'What did you think of her?'

'Susannah? Very pleasant. Competent.'

Charles nodded.

'Is she?'

'Is she what?'

'Competent.'

'Oh yes, very.'

'She bites her nails, you know.'

13

He knew. It was the one thing about Susannah he couldn't figure. Sometimes the tips of her fingers were so chewed up there were little specks of blood along the edges. Otherwise she was impeccably groomed, albeit in the casually arty way you'd expect of a graphic artist. He'd always been a bit harsh on nail-biters, inclined to read all sorts of character flaws into this single failing. Susannah's nails repulsed him, but he guessed that if they weren't so badly mangled he wouldn't be so intrigued by her.

Charles wondered how men had extra-marital affairs. Just thinking about Susannah made him feel guilty; if he ever touched her he'd probably have to throw himself out of a high window. He and Margaret had been together for fifteen years, since college, and married for twelve. Endangering what they had together would be like endangering himself.

He picked up the phone and pressed the top button on the memory panel. Margaret answered after two rings. 'Margaret Lewin,' she said loudly and crisply, as if reading her name for the first time off a list. It was the way she always answered her phone at work; he'd never gotten entirely used to it.

'Guess what?' he said, anxious to tell her about the new business.

'Don't you mean guess who?'

'You *know* who. Your husband.'

'Charles, Charles, is that you?'

He had to smile. 'We got the annual.'

'Hey, that's wonderful. Really great.'

'I might clear enough for a down-payment on a country house.'

He heard her inhale, savoring the thought. Isaiah was at the age now where by noon on weekends he had to be out of the house and in a park or he'd combust spontaneously. He'd circle the apartment like a caged animal at ever increasing speeds. The park! he'd shout like a battle cry. The swings! The slide! They dreamed of having a weekend house where they could simply release him out the back door; in the city, going outside meant all sorts of logistical arrangements, not the least of which was the fact that in the city, Isaiah couldn't go outside by himself.

'Let's celebrate tonight, Margaret. Go out somewhere nice sans enfants.'

'Sans Enfants. Wouldn't that make a great name for a French restaurant? Anyway, I'd like to celebrate, but we have the auction at Hannah's school. Remember?'

'Right,' he said dispiritedly. 'The auction.' It was a fund-raising event in which each parent donated something for the other parents to bid on. What the Tilden School, reportedly the second best in Manhattan, never seemed to realize was that, for people like Charles and Margaret, there simply wasn't any money left for such

14

events after paying the $8,000 tuition. Nothing valuable to donate, and certainly no money to bid. This year Charles and Margaret were donating the color TV they'd won at the school's annual raffle last year – they only hoped no one remembered.

'I hate those things.'

'Me too. But we have to go. Hannah's friend Linda's mother is chairman, and Hannah's really excited that we're going.'

Hannah was only twelve, but she already had a fairly keen sense of what it took to make it in the world, and she knew that if her parents missed the auction, their image among her friends' parents, all of them movers and shakers in business and the arts, would be tarnished. He worried, sometimes, how readily Hannah warmed to the lives led by her friends in their Fifth Avenue apartments and summer houses in the Hamptons. Once she'd mentioned that the father of a friend of hers was going into the hospital for a bypass. 'What's he do, anyway?' Charles had asked, just in passing. She named a big insurance company. 'He's the CEO,' Hannah had said casually, sending a shiver down his spine and triggering yet another let's-chuck-it-all-and-move-to-the-country fantasy.

'Then we'll celebrate some other time.'

'I'm so happy for you, really.'

'For us, Margie.'

'Right, for us.'

Margaret hung up and checked her watch, which she did so frequently these days it was practically a tic. Perhaps it was a nervous tic, she sometimes thought, but she never could resist checking the time when it occurred to her to do so, and nowadays it occurred to her to do so every fifteen or twenty minutes. Ten forty-five. She ran through all the things that ten forty-five on a Monday meant to her. Hannah would be at school, of course; the seventh grade. Isaiah would be at the Children's Center for another hour and a quarter. At noon Liv, their au pair, would walk over to the school and pick him up. Charles was at his office. And she had an appointment with an art director in fifteen minutes.

For a few minutes she thought about Hannah at school. She always imagined her walking from class to class, never actually sitting in one. She pictured her surrounded by a large group of girlfriends, never alone. It was a satisfying image, her daughter surrounded by an amorphous mass of friends. True, Margaret wished these girls weren't quite so, well, *chic*, with their expensive haircuts and blasé expressions. Whenever Margaret was out of the city she made a point of noticing junior high school girls; with their anachronistic hair and wide-open smiles, they never looked nearly as stylish as Hannah and her friends. They reminded Margaret of

15

herself and her friends when they were in school. There was something timeless about the look of these small town girls. Hannah's friends, on the other hand, were amazingly, shockingly, up to the minute. Still, Hannah was popular, and very involved in school, and for this Margaret had to be happy.

With Isaiah, at these times, her mental image was also unchanging. She pictured Liv meeting him at the front door of the Children's Center, which was in the basement of a Unitarian church not far from their apartment. She imagined Liv crouching down and extending her arms, into which Isaiah would run, smiling as if he had no idea he was being picked up at school, as if this didn't happen every day. She wondered if Liv did in fact crouch down. She hoped so, but she couldn't be sure; Liv was pleasant and responsive and Isaiah liked her a lot, but there was a coldness to her that Margaret had sensed right away. Perhaps it was only that, after all, Isaiah wasn't her child; she'd be going back to Denmark in nine months (her tourist visa had long since expired), so why should she bother getting too close? Margaret didn't completely buy this; perhaps it was just being *Scandinavian* that made her this way. Certainly there could be no greater contrast than between Liv and Isaiah. Liv had blonde, almost white hair and a pale complexion that tended to fade even further in bright light. Given the promise of her hair, her face was disappointingly plain – angular and somehow crooked. And then there was Isaiah, with his deep brown skin that glowed, it seemed to Margaret, in bright light, making him look warmer, richer. She smiled, picturing him flying into Liv's waiting arms in front of the church. She hoped her arms were waiting, and that Isaiah would fly into them. Charles said that he suspected Liv was warmer with Isaiah when they weren't around, that she was inhibited in front of them, reluctant to express emotion. Just let her arms be open and waiting fifteen minutes from now, Margaret thought. Just that.

Margaret checked her watch again, then chided herself; it was only ten minutes later, ten fifty-five. She'd spent ten minutes making sure that all was right with her world at ten forty-five, and now she was due across town in five minutes and had hardly made a dent in the pile of bills and other paper on her desk. Three photographers' portfolios were stacked on her visitor's chair, waiting to be evaluated. Margaret sighed as she surveyed the unfinished business she'd be leaving behind.

As a photographers' rep she had two constituencies: the photographers themselves, of course, and the art directors who employed them. The photographers were generally pleasant and solicitous at the beginning; but if Margaret succeeded in getting them steady work, they tended to become surly and demanding, never satisfied

16

with the fees she negotiated for them, nor with the number of assignments she managed to secure. The art directors – at ad agencies, magazines, in graphic studios like her husband's – were usually harried and typically gave her only five or ten minutes to present her clients' work. But Margaret had assembled a diverse and original group of photographers – her 'stable of talent' – and more often than not these days her cold calling resulted in an assignment. The work was more salesy than she'd at first anticipated, more pressured, but it didn't seem too precipitous a leap from her training as an art historian to specializing in photography. At least this is how she consoled herself on those hectic days when selling insurance seemed a more appealing, less pressured way to make a living than representing photographers.

Chapter 2

The worst part about weekday mornings was waiting on the bathroom. When Selma dreamed of a better life, sometimes she couldn't get further than just rolling out of bed and into a bathroom, no waiting. Her mind would just stop there in sweet contemplation of not having to stand in that cold hallway every morning, feeling her bladder practically *growing* inside her, while Marie Sherman or her daughter Josette did whatever they did in there for minute after agonizing minute.

Selma rented a room from Marie Sherman, who had a two-bedroom apartment in a city project in the Bedford-Stuyvesant part of Brooklyn. Her kids slept in the living room, Josette on the sofa, Raymond on a cot they set up at night, so Selma could have the second bedroom. She paid Marie $250 a month, which was supposed to include meals. But Selma usually bought her own food, since she couldn't stand the way Marie cooked, when she bothered to cook. It was against the rules for Selma to be there, maybe even against the law, since you couldn't have any 'unrelated parties' living on the premises.

That's me all right, Selma sometimes thought: an unrelated party.

'Hey in there. Some of us got to work.' She rapped on the flimsy bathroom door, which jittered in the frame.

'And some of us got to use the toilet.' Selma recognized Josette's voice and rapped on the door a second time for good measure. She was only ten but fresh as could be. Probably doing up her hair into those pleated braids she liked so much. Pay as much attention to your schoolwork as your hair, you'll go right to the head of the class, Selma wanted to tell her. But she wasn't the girl's mother. No way. So she was careful to keep her mouth shut. Not that it wasn't tempting to step in. Marie sat around all day drinking beer and wine and complaining about this and that, mostly her ailments. She was only a few years older than Selma – maybe thirty, thirty-one? – but she looked *old*. Her face was already puckered, and she sagged everywhere, from her eyelids to her ankles; wouldn't surprise Selma to come home one day and find her in a puddle in the middle of the living room floor. Marie cropped her hair off so she wouldn't have

19

to fuss with it (like she had anything better to do!) but it only made her look worse, like a *bald* old prune. Not that looking this way kept the men away. Uh uh, men didn't care so long as the wine and the sex were free and clear. They were free and clear with Marie.

And now she was pregnant. When she told Selma she sounded embarrassed. And why not? The last thing she needed was another mouth to feed. You got to give up drinking now, Selma had told her. I know that, Marie said, getting her back up. I had two before, you know. That don't make you an expert, Selma almost said, I should know. But Marie kept on drinking, like Selma knew she would. Baby'll come out drunker than a wino, Selma kept thinking. I know I of all people have no right to criticize, but still, it's just not right.

Josette finally opened the door and sauntered out like the Queen of Sheba. She scowled at Selma as she squeezed by. Well, how could you blame her; Selma's room used to be hers and Raymond's. But two hundred and fifty a month was nothing to sneeze at, with only food stamps and welfare to keep the three of them in food and clothing, not to mention beer and wine, and soon enough Pampers and formula. Not that the money didn't run out anyway by the end of every month. Then Selma would notice some of her own food missing. A can of tuna fish, a Coke or two, half her bread, sometimes there'd be a big finger mark in her peanut butter. She didn't complain – how could she, when the kids needed feeding? Not so much Josette as Raymond, who was just three. Sometimes she brought home a carton of milk for him, pretending to Marie it was for her but knowing that Raymond would drink it. Now she would sometimes catch Marie swigging from the carton, and she couldn't very well complain about that either, could she? Babies need milk, even unborn ones.

She made her tea in the kitchen and brought it back to her room. She tried to spend as little time as possible with the others; didn't pay to get too involved in other people's problems, and that's all these three had, problems and more problems. She was getting dressed when her door started to swing open. 'Get outta . . . oh, it's you.'

Still in his pajamas, Raymond looked up at her with that devilish smile that she couldn't ever resist. This kid'll be trouble, she said to herself. 'You want something?'

He shook his head, jumped onto the bed, and sat on it, swinging his legs. Sometimes he would just watch her, like she was the TV or something.

'Good thing I already had my clothes on. You should learn to knock before you come in.'

'Knock knock,' he said, then looked up at her and grinned.

'Very funny.'

'Me go to see fishes today.'

'Fishes? Where you gonna see fishes?'

'Quarium.'

'Day care taking you there?'

He nodded. 'Me see whales, too.'

Kid talks like Tarzan, Selma thought. 'Oh, you'll like that, won't you, Ray?'

'Yes.' He nodded vigorously.

'Maybe you should get dressed now. Don't want to be late today of all days.'

'Mommy not up yet.'

'Oh, now I see.' Since she'd gotten pregnant, Marie slept late a lot. 'Well, come on then.' She took his little hand and led him into the living room, where his clothes were kept in a chest of drawers that had been transferred from the bedroom when she'd moved in. Josette was primping in front of the mirror when they walked in.

'Let's see. Look here, this one's got fish on it.' She pulled a long-sleeved shirt from the drawer that sure enough had little fish all over it. 'You want to wear this one?'

'To the quarium!'

It took her just a few minutes to dress Raymond; she was getting good at it.

'Better wake Mommy up, Ray,' Josette said, still fussing with her hair. 'I can't take you to day care today. Have to be at school early.'

Raymond looked up at Selma, like he was asking, Do I have to? Marie was a monster in the morning, and she was specially hard on Raymond, who just couldn't get it into his head that people who went to sleep drunk needed peace and quiet in the morning. Selma felt this close to saying, No, don't wake her up, I'll take you, but if she did she might be late for work, and this she couldn't risk. 'Go ahead and wake her up, Raymond. Tell her you have to go to school.'

He paused a second before sprinting down the hall to his mother's bedroom, his feet clacking on the bare floor. Not so loud, Selma wanted to call after him.

From her own room Selma could hear his little voice, quaking like he was nervous. 'Mommy? Mommy?' She heard him walk across the room and she couldn't help it, she peeked out of her room and looked across into Marie's. He was standing by her bed now, almost invisible in the dark room. 'Mommy, I have to go to day care now.' No reaction, just a big dead heap under the white sheets. Raymond put a hand on top of the heap and patted it, ever so gently, like it was a polar bear at the zoo. 'Mommy, time to wake up,' he whispered, and what made Selma's heart turn over was the way he

21

said it, almost cheerful, imitating the way a nice normal mother would sound waking up her little boy. Now where did he ever hear anyone wake up a child that way? Selma wondered. Must have been on TV. The heap of sheets rustled as Marie rolled over. Ray looked so little next to the big polar bear.

Selma poked her head into Marie's room. 'Here, Raymond, let her rest. I'll take you to school.'

Now, don't get carried away, Selma told herself on the way to Raymond's day care center. This ain't your kid, this ain't your job. You just filling in, and if you're late for work you'll catch hell.

Oooh, but it felt good, having Raymond's little hand in hers. Like a doll's hand, but warm, and when it moved Selma felt a little shiver up her arm. Thoughts of her own son seeped into her mind like drops of water, leaking. She shook her head when this happened. No way she was going to start confusing Raymond with Isaiah. No way.

It was dangerous getting Raymond tangled up with Isaiah in her mind. Getting too involved with Raymond, like he *was* her son or something. And she couldn't afford that. No sir. She wanted her son back, her Isaiah. She'd already done so much, gotten so much closer to her dream, she couldn't have any distractions. No sir.

'Hell copper! Hell copper.' Raymond pointed up to the sky.

Selma looked up and saw the helicopter. 'You're a smart boy, Raymond.'

'Me smart,' he said in a serious voice.

'Maybe some day you can ride in a helicopter.'

He looked up and took a big breath. 'Next week,' he said with confidence.

'Well, maybe not next week.' Now she regretted putting ideas in his head.

'Soon.'

'Yeah, soon.'

As they approached the day care center he spotted two of his friends and broke into a run, almost pulling Selma over. 'Hey, Ray, aren't you going to say goodbye?'

He looked back. ''Bye, Selma.'

She started to turn towards the subway station but stopped. 'Hey, Ray, come here.'

Reluctantly he left his friends and walked over to her, looking like he knew he'd done something wrong.

'No, I'm not scolding you. I just want something.'

'What?'

Suddenly she turned shy. Shy! In front of a two-year-old. Crouching down, she said softly, 'A little sugar, that's all.'

22

He knew what she meant and didn't hesitate, wrapping his short, skinny arms round her shoulders. She squeezed him for as long as she could before he'd think she'd gone nuts or something, then let him go. He raced back to his friends, and together they entered the day care building.

The hug lasted her for the three blocks it took to reach the Lavonia Avenue station. But when she started up the steps to the elevated platform it began to sour. Then it turned rotten on her. Selma, you're a fool and you know it. A fool and you know it.

The subway ride to the Upper East Side lasted forty-five minutes. Selma hated it. She never got a seat, and she couldn't do what all the other passengers did to pass the time: read something. The minutes crept by, just like the train, more often than not. Still, Bed-Stuy and the neighborhood where she worked were so different, it seemed like it should take maybe a *month* to get from one to the other. So maybe three-quarters of an hour wasn't so bad.

She made it to work just in time. She rang the doorbell at exactly eight o'clock. A few moments later, Mr Fredricks opened the door for her. 'Morning, Selma,' he said as usual. 'Dana's in the kitchen.'

She crossed the hallway, big as her room in Brooklyn, and went to the kitchen. Sure enough there was Dana, sitting in her highchair waving her hands like she was in a parade or something. 'Morning, Dana,' she said. Dana turned and then the waving really got furious.

Selma looked around for a sign of Mrs Fredricks. Probably getting dressed for work. 'Here, let me clean you off.' She took a napkin from a holder on top of the counter and wiped some goo off Dana's face and hands. 'Want a bottle?'

By the time the bottle was ready, so were Mr and Mrs Fredricks. 'There's some leftover pasta in the fridge, Selma. There may be some laundry in the washer to do. Oh, and I may be a little late tonight, not more than fifteen minutes. Drinks with a client.' She shrugged and smiled, like this was something Selma knew all about. 'I'll call if I'm any later.'

Then they both kissed Dana in her chair, the little princess on her throne, and left, like they always did, at eight fifteen exactly. The door shut and Selma let go a big breath, like she always did. 'Okay, Dana, what we gonna do today?' The child actually looked at her for a minute, as if she was thinking of answering. 'Want to go visit Isaiah? You do?' Selma lifted Dana out of the chair and carried her into her bedroom. More toys here than in a toy store, she thought, as she always did first thing in the morning; she just couldn't get used to all the toys. 'Getting heavy in your old age,' she said as she put the child down in the middle of all the toys. She'd been watching Dana since she was born, when Mrs Fredricks went back to her job being a lawyer. Now Dana was a year old, almost walking. Cushy job, Selma had to admit. Not Mrs Fredricks' job, hers. Two fifty a week cash, no one hanging around watching her unless you count little Dana, who wasn't much trouble. 'Easy street, ain't it, Dana?' This time the baby ignored her; she was banging on a miniature piano for all she was worth. 'Will you excuse me please?' Selma asked her, and then left to see about the laundry.

The job was cushy but not all that exciting. Time crawled at the Fredricks', just like Dana. Mornings she'd do the laundry if there was any to do, straighten up, mostly just watch TV while keeping Dana out of mischief. Around noon they'd take a walk, usually to Central Park. The Fredricks lived just off Fifth Avenue in the Eighties, so the park was close by. Can't complain, Selma would tell herself often. Can't complain. If Dana was my own child I'd be doing this for nothing! Seemed strange, but that was the truth.

At eleven thirty she got Dana bundled up. The child always got excited about their walks, started waving around and making bird sounds. Cute little girl, Selma thought. Easier to resist than Raymond, though. Maybe 'cause she was younger. Maybe 'cause she was white. Maybe 'cause her mother was paying Selma to watch her – affection wasn't part of the job. Maybe 'cause she was a girl, and Raymond was a boy, just like Isaiah. Maybe a combination of all these reasons. Probably a combination.

'Want to go see Isaiah, Dana? Want to?' The child grinned at her. Soon she'd start talking, and then these trips over to the West Side would have to stop. Selma could just picture it. Went to school, Mommy. Sure you did, Dana. What an imagination! Saw Isaiah, Mommy. Isaiah? Who's Isaiah? Then Selma would have to explain, probably lose her job. She placed a gentle hand on Dana's fuzzy head. 'When you gonna start talking, little one?' Another gummy smile, hands waving like a traffic cop. 'Just hold off another few months, we got a deal?'

With Dana all bundled up, stiff as a little astronaut, Selma lowered her into her stroller and strapped her in. She made sure she had the keys to the apartment, then rolled Dana out to the landing and locked the door behind her. Only two apartments on a floor in the Fredricks' building. Felt more like a house than an apartment, and big as a house, too, with three bedrooms and three bathrooms and a living room as big as Marie Sherman's whole place.

In the lobby she nodded to the doorman, who made a fuss over Dana, as usual, while basically ignoring her. Outside it was warmer than she'd expected. She worried that Dana would overheat in the pink spacesuit Mrs Fredricks made Selma put on her when they went out. It was six blocks to the crosstown bus over to the West Side. Selma walked the four or five yards to Madison, turned left, and steered Dana onto Madison, heading south.

Seemed like every two minutes she passed a black woman pushing a little white child. Always that same look on their faces, mostly blank but with an edge of anger, like they'd as soon be doing time as looking after these babies. Maybe you couldn't expect them to *like* the work, but you had to feel sorry for the kids, being pushed and shoved up and down the avenues like plows. That's the just the way it is in Manhattan, Selma told herself, all these mismatched pairs. Still, you almost never see a white woman pushing a black kid. Maybe Diana Ross's kids has a white woman looking after them. Maybe Cosby has a white woman for his kids. Seeing that would make my day sure enough, she thought.

The worst part of the whole ordeal was getting onto the crosstown bus. First she had to hoist Dana out of the stroller – always seemed like she swelled up in it after even a short walk. Then she had to collapse the stroller, which she never could get right. Naturally the bus pulled up just as she was struggling with the contraption with her right arm, Dana in her left. The bus driver waited an extra minute for her to figure it out. Thanks, she told him as she put in her token, but she thought the other passengers were staring at her. Look, I didn't design these things, she told them, silently. And as you may have guessed, this ain't my child, neither. Selma was sorely tempted to say this out loud, thought she'd enjoy the startled looks on the people's faces.

Just a thread between me and a crazy person, she thought, laughing to herself. Same as with everyone in this city. Just a thread.

They got off on Columbus and now they had to do the whole thing in reverse. 'Sure will be easier when you can stand up on your own,' she told Dana, who responded by rocking in her arm and kicking her legs, making it even more difficult to hold her and un-collapse the stroller at the same time.

They arrived at the Children's Center right on time. Kids were just starting to trickle out. Their mothers or babysitters were waiting outside – naturally there were a few mismatched pairs in the group. Selma positioned herself on the edge of the group, not wanting to attract too much attention. 'You gonna help me look for Isaiah, Dana? Gonna help Selma find her boy?'

Not that it would be difficult. There were exactly two black children in the Center, and one of them was a girl. So the other had to be Isaiah Richards. Or Isaiah Lewin, as he was known for the time being. Finding him had been another story. Selma remembered from back when Isaiah was born that the family was named Lewin and lived in Manhattan. But when she went to look up Lewin in the phone book (had to ask Josette for help finding the name; then she'd torn out the pages for safe-keeping), there'd been three pages of them. Who would have thought? So she started calling two

Lewins a day from the Fredricks' apartment. Her quota was two a day, case something showed up on the Fredricks' phone bill. May I please speak to Isaiah, she'd say, beginning with Aaron Lewin. There's no such person here, they'd answer. Then she'd hang up, though sometimes the Lewin person would beat her to it. It was stupid, asking for a 2½ year-old, but she knew it would only sound stupid to the Lewin that had Isaiah and knew his age. And she'd know which one that was only by asking for Isaiah.

Good thing it was Charles Lewin that had Isaiah, 'cause at two Lewins a day, weekdays only, it had only taken her two weeks to find Isaiah. She'd had some trouble with the first names, but Charles she recognized – knew a guy named Charles once. 'May I please speak to Isaiah,' she'd said to the person who answered. This was the third Charles Lewin in the phone book, Charles *F*. Lewin.

Usually they responded right away, 'You have the wrong number', and she'd cross off another name on her three phone book pages. This time there was a pause and Selma knew she'd found him. 'Isaiah?' said the voice, a woman's voice, a *young* woman, and foreign-sounding, too. 'He's at the Children's Center. Who is this?'

'Must be a wrong number,' Selma had answered quickly and hung up. But her hand was shaking and the phone slipped from the cradle onto the Fredricks' kitchen floor. Only later, after she'd replaced the phone and sat down and made herself calm by taking big gulps of air did Selma take her pen and circle the name: *Charles F. Lewin. 218 W 75*. Then she had a better idea. She went into the room the Fredricks used as a study and took a piece of paper from a pad on top of Mr Fredricks' desk. Back at the kitchen table, she copied the name and address onto the paper. It took her a while – Selma wasn't used to writing and she wanted this to be neat and totally correct. Charles F. Lewin.

When she was done she stared at the piece of paper for a while. It's begun, she thought, placing it carefully in the pocket of her pants. It's begun.

Isaiah appeared after most of the children had already come out. 'There he is,' she whispered to Dana. Then she noticed that Dana had fallen asleep in her arms. 'Isn't he handsome?' she asked anyway. 'Looks like me, don't you think? 'Cept my face ain't that round, but he's got my eyes, and he's got my small nose.'

Selma watched as Isaiah searched for the blonde girl that always met him. Must be the person answered the phone that time – too young to be the Mrs Lewin from two and a half years ago, though at least she'd let slip where Isaiah was, something Mrs Lewin probably wouldn't have done. When Isaiah finally spotted the girl, he ran over, his little legs pumping in a way that made Selma ache a little.

Then the blonde person did what she always did, she bent over from the waist, a little stiff, like her back hurt, and patted Isaiah on the top of his head and said something to him. Then they walked towards Broadway, Isaiah holding onto the empty stroller and talking nonstop.

I would have bent down and hugged the boy, Selma thought. Even do that for Raymond sometimes. She watched the girl and Isaiah as they walked down the street heading west. When she lost sight of them, Selma felt the usual letdown. Without realizing it she had become the last person at the nursery school, her and Dana. She felt suddenly stranded. She shivered, though it was warm, and gave Dana a long, hard hug. Always huggin' the wrong kid, she thought, and although this struck her as kind of sad she had to laugh.

What a sight I must make, she thought. Standing here with a sleeping baby, laughing to myself. Just a thread between me and a crazy person. Just a thread.

Selma knew it was dangerous, visiting Isaiah this way. *Spying* on him. Dangerous in ways she knew she didn't really understand. But each time she came away reassured. He's okay, my boy's okay, is what she felt, at first.

Later, on the bus back to the Fredricks' side of town, and for most of the next week, until she saw him again, her thoughts were darker. At least I did him no harm, no *physical* harm, she'd think, picturing his perfect little legs pumping as he ran to the blonde person, picturing his big, clear eyes as he spotted her in the crowd of mothers and sitters and whatnot. At least I did him no harm.

Her sins, which are many, are forgiven; for she loved much.

Selma liked this line, which she repeated to herself ever since hearing it a few Sundays ago in church. She'd even managed to find the words in her Bible, and sometimes she traced over them with her finger, saying them out loud. *Her sins, which are many, are forgiven; for she loved much.*

This don't pertain to me, Selma thought, not yet. But I will love, *love much.* I will, and my sins, which are many, *Lord* are they many, will be forgiven, too.

At six thirty, Mrs Fredricks opened the door and said Sorry before she'd even shut it behind her. Not hello, or how was your day. Just sorry. Woman is always running scared, Selma thought. All her money and whatnot and she's always apologizing for something. Usually for being late. She was supposed to be home by five thirty but she almost never was. Most days Selma didn't mind too much, but Tuesday and Thursday were her tutoring nights, and she was supposed to be at the center by six thirty.

'That's okay,' Selma said, like she always did. She knew she should be harder with Mrs Fredricks, but the sight of her always softened her. Selma tried to imagine what must go on at Mrs Fredricks' law office all day. She left in the morning all composed and full of pep and came home at night looking drained, like she was ready to collapse. Mornings, her hair was neatly pulled back or else hanging straight and smooth. Evenings she looked like she'd stuck her finger in an outlet. And she always carried a big mess of papers to and fro; they leaked out of her briefcase and half the time they just spilled out once she put the briefcase down on the hall table.

'Dana's in the kitchen,' Selma told her. 'I just gave her a bottle.'

'Thanks, Selma,' she panted. Another thing about Mrs Fredricks, she always seemed out of breath. She left Selma in the hallway and walked into the kitchen. 'There you are!' she squealed, like she was surprised to find her own daughter in her own kitchen. 'Were you a good girl today?'

Selma put on her coat and gloves and looked into the kitchen before leaving. 'Have a nice evening,' she said.

'Oh, you too, Selma.' Mrs Fredricks was sitting up at the counter with her head leaning back on a cabinet, watching Dana drink her bottle.

Selma was fifteen minutes late for tutoring. Lizzie was already at their usual table, reading the newspaper. 'There you are,' she said when she saw Selma. What is it about that expression? Selma thought.

Selma pulled her notebook out of her bag. From inside the notebook she pulled out a slim book. 'Only read a couple of pages.'

'Good! What's happening in the story?'

Selma looked at the book. 'George found work.'

'Good! Anything else?'

Selma thought for a few seconds. 'I have trouble remembering.'

'You forget what you've read?'

'Yeah.'

'Everyone forgets some of what they read. It's harder for you because you have to concentrate so hard to figure out the words themselves.'

Selma nodded and turned to where she'd left off.

'Let's read together,' Lizzie said.

The two women began to read. 'Catherine found a job as a waitress. It is hard work but she is happy. Now she and George have money for the rent and food.'

Selma enjoyed reading out loud with Lizzie. Made her feel smarter, more powerful than she was. She could hear Lizzie say the words just a second before she did, but even so, it made her feel that she could read better than she did.

'Okay, now why don't you read that same page on your own.'

No problem, Selma thought. My memory's not *that* bad. 'Catherine . . .' How could she have forgotten that word so soon? 'Catherine . . .'

'Found. Catherine *found* . . .'

'Catherine found a job as a waitress. It is . . .' It is what, dammit? 'It is . . . hard . . .' She looked at Lizzie, who nodded. 'It is hard work but she is happy.' This is getting easier, Selma thought. 'Now she and George have . . .' She looked at the next word. It looked so familiar, just like a face you see on the street and know you know but can't place. Let's start this sentence over again. 'Now she and George have . . . mo . . . mon . . . *money*. Now she and George have money for the . . .' She stared at the word hard, like maybe it would talk to her if she looked close enough. But it just wouldn't come to her – some words weren't accommodating that way.

'That's rent,' Lizzie prompted her. 'Rent.'

'. . . money for the rent and . . . food.'

'Very good, Selma. It looks like George and Catherine are going to make it.'

'Yeah. Don't know about me, though.'

'You?'

'I don't feel my reading's improving.'

'Oh, but it is, Selma. When you first came here you couldn't get through that passage on your own.'

'No?'

'Uh uh. Sometimes it's hard to see yourself change. But others can see what you can't.'

Selma looked hard at Lizzie to see if she was slinging the bull. Couldn't tell. Today she was wearing a heavy suit in a checked pattern over a blouse, probably silk. Looking good, Selma thought, though maybe a little uptight. 'You got a boyfriend, Lizzie?'

Lizzie shifted in her big suit. 'Not at the moment, no. Why?'

'Need to know about a person 'fore I can make a fool of myself in front of them.'

'But you're not making a fool of yourself.'

'Oh no? You try reading a baby book like this in front of someone, when you can't even make out half the words. Need to feel comfortable with a person 'fore you do that.'

'I thought we were comfortable together.'

'Maybe you was. I wasn't.'

Lizzie looked defeated, which wasn't Selma's aim. Or maybe it was; pride could be a mean son of a bitch.

'Do *you* have a boyfriend?' Lizzie asked.

'Finished with men.'

'Oh, come on.'

'It's the truth. I'm finished with 'em.'

'But you're only, what, thirty?'

'Not even.'

'So how can you say you're through with men?'

'Only want one thing. My boy back. Like I wrote before. Nothing can get in the way of that, least of all a man. Men got me in the trouble I'm in now.'

Selma turned the page in the book. 'Now how is Catherine gonna keep on waitressing when she's pregnant?'

Chapter 3

Hannah held open the front door and waited with her parents for the elevator. She didn't want to seem too eager, not when they were paying her three dollars an hour to watch Isaiah so they could go to the auction at her school. Actually what Hannah liked best about babysitting for Isaiah, which she'd only been allowed to do very recently, wasn't the money; it was the feeling of power. She was almost never alone in the apartment, which seemed to be getting smaller all the time. It was always Hannah do this, Hannah do that – never time to do what she wanted. God, she'd pay *them* just to leave her alone in the house once in a while. But she didn't want to let on about this. Three bucks an hour times two, maybe two and-a-half hours, was at least six dollars, which would practically buy her one movie, popcorn too if they stayed late at the auction or whatever it was.

So she waited with them for the elevator, trying not to seem like she wanted them out of there.

'Goodbye, honey,' her mother said when it finally arrived.

'Shall we offer greetings to the Alexander Van Camps this evening?' her father said in a fancy voice, making fun, for the millionth time, of her friend Courtney Van Camp and her parents, who happened to be very rich and happened to live on Fifth Avenue.

'Don't bother,' she said, real cool.

Hannah closed the door behind her and felt a sense of power flood over her. All *right*, she whispered. All *right*. She headed straight for Isaiah's room and wasn't a bit surprised to find him playing with his Ghostbusters stuff. 'Look at this place,' she said, recognizing, with a sinking feeling, her mother's voice.

He looked up at her.

'It's a mess.' Hannah's arms waved to encompass the entire toy-infested room.

He still just looked at her. Two-year-olds were so . . . *limited*. Hannah considered asking him to clean up, but decided that this would be stretching it. Why couldn't you be older? she thought. Or

31

younger, even. A real baby could be fun, but a two-year-old was useless. 'Wanna play catch?'

Isaiah sprang from the floor and ran across the room to find the ball.

'How you find things in this room . . .'

He handed her the big inflatable ball and they went out into the long hallway that connected the bedrooms. Isaiah ran to the end nearest their parents' room, she stood outside his doorway.

'Here goes!' she said, and bounced the ball over to him. Isaiah caught it, using both arms. The ball completely obscured his head and neck; holding it, he looked like a cartoon character. Balloon Head, Hannah thought. My brother, Balloon Head.

'Here goes!' he mimicked her, and the ball came dribbling back to her.

Hannah bent over to pick it up. 'Ready, aim, fire,' she said and bounced the ball back to him.

This time he had some trouble and Hannah thought for a moment he was going to fall over backwards, even though the ball was as light as a feather. Isaiah could be so *spastic* sometimes.

'Ready fire,' he shouted when he'd finally got control of the ball. It came rolling back to her.

After two or three minutes Hannah couldn't take it any more. 'Okay, Isaiah, that's all.'

'More?' he pleaded in his high voice.

She tossed him the ball. 'On your mark, get set, go,' she drawled listlessly.

'Set go!' he cried as he shoved the ball back to her.

She left him in the hallway kicking the ball against the wall and headed for the kitchen. As she silently, sullenly inventoried the refrigerator she thought of all her friends who had sisters and brothers near their own age. Not one had a two-year-old. Wait, Penny Rafaelson had a three-year-old sister, but that was a half-sister, from her father's second marriage to some big-deal lawyer in Washington. And even Penny had an older brother, so you couldn't compare her, really. Not counting half-sisters and -brothers and stepsisters and -brothers, she couldn't think of anyone stuck with such a *young* brother.

She had pleaded for a little sister or brother before they brought Isaiah home. Begged for a sibling. After a while she'd gotten the hint not to keep on about it, though. It made her parents sad to talk about having a second child, especially her mother. Hannah couldn't remember if they'd told her or if she'd guessed, but she knew they couldn't have another baby. Then one day, out of the blue, her mother had called her into the living room. Her father was

32

already sitting on the big red couch. She was only ten, but she knew something was up.

'Sweetheart, we have some good news,' her mother had said.

She stopped holding her breath – for a minute she'd thought they were going to tell her they weren't going to the Ice Capades that Saturday like they'd planned.

'We're adopting a little baby boy.'

She didn't know what to say at first. Adopting?

'A little brother for you, Hannah,' her father said.

She was beginning to understand – her mother wasn't *having* a baby. 'Where are you getting him from?'

Her parents looked at each other. 'He's a little, well, a little sick at the moment,' her mother said, not really answering the question. 'But as soon as he's better we're bringing him home.'

'Oh. But what about his parents?'

Another look passed between her parents. 'They don't feel they can take care of him, Hannah. So they're letting us have him.'

'When is he coming?'

'As soon as he's well. A few days, maybe, or a week.'

'What's his name?'

'His name is Isaiah,' said her mother.

'Isaiah?'

'His . . . birth mother named him that the day he was born. We thought we'd keep it. Don't you like the name Isaiah?'

She shrugged.

'Aren't you happy about having a little brother?'

She had been happy, later, but it had taken some getting used to. When they first told her, all she could think of was practical things, like not being able to use his room as her play store, with everything lined up along the wall like shelves in a supermarket and her little plastic cash register near the door. Like having to walk next to his stroller as they did errands on Broadway. Like having to be quiet during his naps.

But once he was home she couldn't help liking him. He was so tiny when she first saw him, with these perfect little hands that she couldn't keep her eyes off, even though they creeped her out, they looked so grown-up and so wrinkled. She had helped change him and wash him and feed him. She was a big help, her mother had said. It was fun, having a little brother. All her friends made a fuss over him, which made her feel special. Even her parents were more fun after Isaiah came, especially her mother, who seemed more energetic, livelier.

Hannah walked into her parents' room and lay down on their big bed. She picked up the remote control and aimed it at the TV. She flipped through maybe fifty stations before shutting it off. Nothing on, as usual. Could do homework, but it was hard doing something like school work when her parents weren't around – seemed like a waste.

At first she hadn't given much thought to Isaiah's being black. Her parents had warned her about this before they brought him home and it only added to the mixture of excitement and dread she'd been feeling. When she first saw him, what was strange was his smallness and his shriveled-up face and those miniature hands, not the color of his skin. It just hadn't seemed like a big deal.

But now it was beginning to matter. Little by little she was becoming aware of the fact that her family was unusual because of Isaiah. They got second looks from people on the street. Once, at her friend Courtney's apartment, she'd mentioned Isaiah in front of Courtney's mother and Courtney had said, for no reason, 'He's black.' Mrs Van Camp had only said Oh, or something like that, but Hannah just knew they'd talk about it later.

But it was in December, at her school's music night, that she truly realized how different her family was from everyone else's. After the show, all the families waited outside the auditorium for the students. Hannah couldn't wait to see her parents. She'd had a solo, she was part of the 'Twelve Days of Christmas' group, and she had had to sing, all by herself, the last section, the twelfth day, which was the longest and hardest. She'd done it perfectly, didn't forget one verse, but it wouldn't be until she'd seen her parents that she'd feel really super.

She'd raced out into the hall to see them but had stopped just before they'd spotted her. There they were: her parents, not too old and okay looking and dressed pretty cool, she thought, and Isaiah, wearing a cute little boy's suit with a bow tie but looking so out of place, so *different*, she'd wanted to die. Why hadn't she ever noticed before the way people looked at them when they were together as a family? Last year, in the drug store, she'd run ahead to the end of a long aisle and then waited for her mother to catch up with Isaiah in his stroller. *That's a switch*, she'd heard one woman whisper to another. She hadn't known then what they were talking about, but something about the tone the woman had used stuck with her. Now she knew: all over the city you saw black women pushing white babies, but you never saw a white woman pushing a black child. Except for her mother and Isaiah. 'That's a switch.' She could hear the woman drawling those words even now.

After music night, her mother had come into her room to say goodnight.

'You were so beautiful, Hannah. We're so proud.' Margaret bent over her bed to kiss her, and for a moment Hannah was overwhelmed just by the smell of her, the sweet, breathy smell of her mother. But as she was leaving, just after she'd switched off the light, Hannah said, 'Mommy, how come you adopted Isaiah?'

She saw her mother freeze at the doorway, then turn around and walk over to the bed.

'We wanted another child, Hannah. We've talked about that.'

'I know. But, well, how come you chose a black child?'

'We didn't *choose* a black child. We . . . we found a baby who needed a home and he happened to be black.'

Hannah nodded, unsatisfied.

'Hannah, is something bothering you?'

'People look at us funny, that's all.'

'I don't understand.'

'Because Isaiah's black, and we're white. They look at us funny.'

Her mother didn't say anything right away and Hannah felt her heart freeze.

'Has anyone *said* anything to you about Isaiah? Anything negative?'

Hannah considered telling her about Courtney and her mother and about the two ladies in the drug store but she decided these weren't necessarily negative. 'No.'

'Well, then, people will always notice what isn't usual, and it is unusual for a white couple to have a black son. But as long as there's nothing negative being said . . .'

'But they notice, they look.'

'Oh, Hannah, it's nice to be special.'

'No, I don't want to be special.' Only after she said it did she realize she had been practically yelling.

Margaret brushed the hair off Hannah's forehead. 'No, I guess at twelve no one wants to stand out. But one day you'll understand. In the meantime, Isaiah's your brother and you should be proud of that. He was so proud of you tonight when you sang. When you started singing he stood up and stared, with his mouth open, and he was squeezing my arm so tightly, I thought he'd break it. When you were done he just collapsed back into his seat. He loves you so much, Hannah, and he looks up to you.'

Hannah could hear him now, playing in his room. You could always hear Isaiah playing because things got banged around and half the time he babbled to himself. She did love Isaiah, and she was proud of him, but that didn't mean she wanted to be looked at like . . . like a freak when they went out together as a family. But she also knew that she couldn't mention this again to her parents. No way. She remembered her mother's eyes when she told her about being looked at funny because of Isaiah. It was an angry look and also something else. Fear? But what was she afraid of?

Whatever it was, Hannah knew she would never talk about this to her parents again. Like when they couldn't have children, before Isaiah, they didn't want to talk about it.

Margaret was swirling with anxiety at the auction. She still wasn't comfortable leaving Hannah home alone with Isaiah; if she weren't penned in by other parents in the auditorium, she'd call home and check up on things. And she never felt very comfortable at Hannah's school. Tilden reeked of money, of course, and this was part of the problem. The Lewins didn't have nearly the resources of most of the other parents, and somehow Margaret always felt that she'd be found out at these parents' events. Found out and ejected. Charles, who'd come from a much more modest background than Margaret, didn't have any such fears, which was ironic, she always thought.

There was something else, too, that bothered her, something other than the money. There was something so competitive about these people, which wouldn't be so bad if they were at the office or on the golf course (where they doubtless spent their weekends) but seemed unsettling in the school environment. They competed over their children. It wasn't enough that their children had already been accepted into the best private school in New York. (Well, some said second best, and maybe that had something to do with all the tension.) Now they fought over whose child was the most accomplished, the most well-rounded, the most likely, Margaret supposed, to succeed.

The school's headmaster, wearing his trademark bow tie, was the auctioneer for the evening. His secretary handed him a succession of objects donated by the parents, and the parents, in the audience, bid on them. The Lewin's color TV had been among the first objects auctioned off. It had been purchased for just a hundred dollars by an attractive couple sitting not far from them. 'Probably for their maid's room,' Charles had said. He deprecated these people, but they didn't make him uncomfortable, or so he said.

The TV was among the least expensive items. There was a Rodin sketch that brought several thousand dollars. Someone had donated dinner for two at the Four Seasons. A weekend at a ski resort in Vermont had been contributed by the resort's owners, who were grandparents of a fourth-grader. But the highlight of the night was the auction of a pair of Tang dynasty cachepots that had been donated by the owner of a chain of three thousand dress shops. He was by far the wealthiest parent at the auction, his wife was easily the most glamorous woman there, with her blonde hair and skeletal figure, and even their daughter, a sixth-grader, was reputed to be nearly perfect. The cachepots were purchased, for forty thousand dollars, by an owlish couple who hardly looked like the types to

36

drop such an amount on a whim, let alone on pottery.

There was a bottleneck at the school's front door when the auction was over, and once again Margaret felt overcome with anxiety. At such close proximity, the other parents would surely notice the vintage of her coat, the scuffs on her re-soled shoes. Once in a while, doing errands on the Upper West Side, which was being simultaneously invaded by hordes of young professionals and hordes of the homeless, Margaret felt conspicuous for her affluence. But here, at Tilden, she felt shabby and fraudulent and in danger of discovery. That was the thing about New York; there was always someone within close range to whom you could compare yourself unfavorably. She caught sight of the owner of the three thousand clothing stores and his glamorous wife: perhaps those two never came up short in their own eyes.

Two mink-coated women in front of her had also caught sight of the retailing magnate. 'Wouldn't you know, he's got a perfect daughter, too,' said one to the other. 'Top grades, plays the cello or harpsichord or something, *and* she's popular.'

The other woman shrugged, sending an undulating wave down her mink. 'She'll probably be anorexic by the time she's thirteen. Happens to all the perfect ones.'

The women exchanged ghoulishly knowing glances and then, as if on a mutually agreed cue, clasped the arms of their respective husbands.

The evening was unusually warm, with a seductive trace of spring in the air. Holding hands, Charles and Margaret walked the short distance from the school to the bus stop.

'Do you think Hannah's happy at Tilden?' Margaret asked.

'I think Hannah's very happy there. Though I worry sometimes that she's absorbing the wrong values.'

'Everyone looks so *rich* there. It almost takes your breath away.'

'We don't look like slobs, Margie.'

'But we don't look like them, either. At least I hope we don't. And the way they talk about their kids, like they were comparing employees.'

'Look, let's not forget that it's the best school in the city . . .'

'Some say second best.'

'. . . and that Hannah's getting a great education there.'

'She asked me about Isaiah the other day.'

'What about Isaiah?'

'About his being black. I think it's beginning to bother her.'

'What exactly did she say?'

'Only that she's noticing that people look at her, at us, funny. She's mortified about feeling different.'

37

'All girls are at her age.'

'Boys too, Charles.'

'Girls and boys. So what else did she say?'

'Nothing else. But I just had a premonition.'

'A premonition of what?'

Margaret shook her head, which sent a light shiver down along her back. 'Nothing specific. Trouble, that's all.'

They walked in silence for a few blocks. Then Charles said, 'When we adopted Isaiah we told each other that it wouldn't necessarily be easy.'

Margaret had to smile, the way he inserted 'necessarily' into the sentence; yes, they had both told each other it wouldn't be easy, but they had both hoped, even convinced themselves, that it would be.

'Sooner or later we'll have to face some things.'

'What things?' Margaret asked, an edge to her voice.

Charles sighed. 'You know what things. The racial thing. The adoption thing. The drug thing.'

'Dr Rosenthal says we don't have to worry about the drugs any more.' Her voice was shrill as she said this; they both heard it.

'What he said was, we were *probably* out of the woods.'

'You can see for yourself that Isaiah's completely normal. He's much more verbal than Hannah was at thirty months, and his motor skills—'

'Margaret, stop it. Just stop it.'

Margaret shut up instantly, but now that he had quietened her, Charles didn't know what to do with the silence. After a few moments he said, softly, 'Our boy was addicted to drugs for the first three weeks of his life. Maybe longer. We'll never know what impact that had.'

'You talk about him like he was a junkie.'

'Not fair, Margaret.'

'He was just a baby.' He turned and saw a frost of tears forming around her eyes. 'He was just a baby.'

What was it about Isaiah, he wondered, not for the first time, that could reduce Margaret so quickly to tears? She was a loving, caring, enthusiastic mother to Hannah, but she *bled* for Isaiah. She bled for him, and probably always would. Since they'd brought him home, Isaiah had had a rather charmed two and a half years, yet Margaret had shed more tears for him, for the tiniest cuts, the smallest disappointments, than she had for Hannah in all her twelve years.

'The impact of drugs on a baby can be even worse than on an adult. Their brains are still developing. Both their intellectual and their—'

'You sound so clinical. He's our son, Charles.'

Another thing about Margaret and Isaiah: she was always hinting,

38

very, very subtly, that he cared less about their son than she did. They both knew how much he loved Isaiah. It was just that he didn't *bleed* for him the way Margaret did. Not often, but occasionally, like right now, this was made to seem a major shortcoming.

'Isaiah will be fine,' he told her, releasing her hand and putting his arm around her shoulder. 'And Hannah will realize how lucky she is to have a brother like him.'

Margaret looked at him and smiled crookedly, her face still streaked with tears. 'We're all lucky.'

He nodded, but he felt that he'd done something terribly wrong in painting so rosy a picture of their future together. No one could forecast so bright a future with confidence today, not without risking a packet of misfortune. Everyone they knew, every family, had their share of calamities. Hadn't they been devastated, eight years ago, to learn that Margaret's uterus couldn't carry a second child? Hadn't a couple they knew quite well just learned that their four-year-old had diabetes? What about that kid at Isaiah's pre-school who had died in a car accident just a few months back? There was *tsoris* everywhere, his mother would say. Everywhere.

They heard stories, all the time, now, about crack babies being returned to foster homes because their adoptive parents couldn't hack it. They'd been warned to look for seizures, mood swings, speech problems. You're the lucky ones, their pediatrician kept telling them. You're beating the odds. Dr Rosenthal had been reluctant to take Isaiah as a patient at first, having had no experience with pre-natal addiction, as he called it. Margaret bristled at this and accused him of betrayal (he'd been Hannah's pediatrician, after all) on account of fear of a malpractice lawsuit. He'd agreed, reluctantly, to take on Isaiah, and had been encouraging about his progress ever since.

Yes, Isaiah had bouts of hyperactivity, and yes, he could gyrate from elation to crying in moments, but who could say it was the drugs doing this to him? Margaret said that Isaiah's birth mother claimed that she'd cut down on cocaine when she found out she was pregnant. Practically gave up the drugs completely. Margaret had repeated this often, in the first year they had Isaiah. Charles wondered if she'd made it up. He wondered if Isaiah's birth mother made it up. Isaiah was short for his age, but then so was Hannah. Isaiah hated changes in routine, and a month ago he'd had a tantrum, a *long* tantrum, when they'd rearranged his room to accommodate a new dresser. Could be the drugs at work, they'd read somewhere; crack babies craved order. Then again, could be just normal two-year-old behavior. A battery of tests performed by a gaggle of specialists confirmed only that he was 'normal', albeit at the low end of the normal range, whatever that meant. Some parents they knew would be devastated to learn that their child was 'just' normal. Charles and Margaret had felt relief so profound it was almost joy.

They had gambled once by taking an infant into their home with a double handicap: he was a black child in a white home, and he'd been born with a drug addiction, the one legacy from his mother, other than his name. Yes, they'd flouted fate once, but with their eyes open. But now, to declare, out loud, as he just had, that all would be fine and dandy down the road, surely this was spitting in the face of fate, or God, or whatever force held their future in its power?

Knock on wood, he found himself whispering. No *kinahurras*, he could hear his mother saying. No *kinahurras*, he heard himself repeating.

Chapter 4

Selma described the latest chapter of *A Day in the Life* for Lizzie, or what she recalled of it. Catherine had her baby, finally, a girl. There was a photograph of her, looking much older than a newborn (the way they always do on TV), lying on Catherine's chest. There's George, too, looking proud.

This was not a scene Selma wished to dwell on. 'Can I read now?'

'Sure, go ahead,' Lizzie answered with her usual enthusiasm.

'The . . . baby . . . is born,' Selma read. That was easy; after looking at the pictures, you knew what was coming. 'It is a . . . boy.'

Selma couldn't help grinning. A boy. Somewhere, in the deepest, densest portion of her mind, Selma remembered hearing the doctor say, 'It's a boy.' Seemed like he was miles away, down there at the other end of her body where she couldn't feel anything on account of the drugs and whatnot. It's a boy. She could hardly hear him, but maybe he wasn't speaking for her benefit anyway. Maybe he was just informing the nurses so they could fill in a chart or something. He hadn't been too friendly, that doctor. Selma remembered he looked tired and ready to snap, and here was another junkie, he seemed to be thinking. Another junkie and her junkie kid on the way. It's a boy.

'Let's turn the page,' Lizzie said.

Okay, let's, Selma almost said. Thinking about having babies was making her snappish. 'The baby's home,' she said, looking at the picture.

'Anything else you see?'

Selma squinted at the page. 'They look happy, George and Catherine.'

'Yes . . .'

'They look kind of nervous, like.'

'What else?'

'There's a crib,' she said.

'Right!'

Selma would bet a week's pay there'd be a crib mentioned in the story. Always worked out that way when Lizzie kept after her until she found something specific in the picture. 'You want me to read now?'

Lizzie nodded.

'The baby is . . . home. It . . . What's that word?'

'That's "sleeps".'

Damn, I knew that, Selma thought. '. . . sleeps in a new . . . crib.'

'Very good,' Lizzie cried. 'Any thoughts?'

Selma looked at her. Thoughts?

'About the story.'

Selma looked back at the page. 'They still don't say how they gonna 'ford the baby.'

'That's true,' Lizzie answered.

'Course there's the food stamps and the SSI. Sometimes it's easier with a baby.'

'Nooo,' said Lizzie doubtfully.

'Yes, the people I live with, they got checks coming and going from the government. No other source of income, 'cept my rent.'

Lizzie shook her head but when she saw Selma noticing she converted to a nod.

'Don't worry, it ain't such a good life.'

'Oh, I wasn't saying that.'

'This morning Raymond – he's three, he sleeps on a cot in the living room – this morning he couldn't get up. Just couldn't. I shaked him and shaked him and he just couldn't budge. The boy don't eat right. Not enough milk, for one thing. No vegetables. And his mother have men traipsing in and out in the middle of the night, wakes the boy up. No wonder I couldn't get him up for school. Had to lift him right off the couch and kind of shake him like a doll. I put him in the shower, like he was hung over or something.'

'That's so sad,' Lizzie said.

'It's terrible. And the girl, Josette, I seen her hanging out with these crack dealers in the back entrance to the building. Shifty characters. And she's only ten.'

'Ten!'

'I'm not saying she's on the crack. Just that I saw her hanging out with these two characters. Wouldn't be surprised if they didn't have her running for them.'

'Running?'

'You know, pick-ups and deliveries. Easier with a kid, less suspicion.'

'How can they use a little girl like that?'

Selma almost told her. She knew how. When nothing matters but the drugs, not even your own baby, you can't see anything wrong with taking advantage of a ten-year-old. 'I'm not saying they already

42

using Josette. But it wouldn't surprise me.'

Lizzie shook her head some more. She had a pretty face, with fine, sharp features, and pale, lightly freckled skin. She really looked shocked, too. Selma felt a small thrill at this. 'Seems like I'm not the only one learning something here,' she said.

Her life was a never-changing pattern, which suited Selma just fine. Work at the Fredricks', two evenings a week at the literacy program, home most nights with Marie and the kids. Too much of her life had been helter-skelter, and now she was getting her life prepared for Isaiah. Sometimes, when she looked over her life, she thought of it as a big comfortable bed she was getting ready for Isaiah, smoothing out the wrinkles, making it soft and inviting. Everything she did, she did to make it possible for Isaiah to join her. She'd never had a purpose before, but lately she was beginning to see that a purpose had its advantages. When you had a reason for doing something, you did it better, and you didn't complain the way you did when you couldn't see the point. Like working for the Fredricks: this was not a job Selma would have thought she'd ever want to do, but now that she had a purpose to life, she didn't mind it so much. It was steady, there was a little bit of flexibility (no clocks to punch, anyway), she was left to herself, unless you counted little Dana, who wasn't exactly a tyrant. She even thought that the Fredricks could help her out some day if she had trouble getting Isaiah back. They seemed powerful, probably knew the right people (whoever *they* were), and wasn't Mrs Fredricks a lawyer?

Whenever Selma thought she needed a refueling of purpose, she took Dana over to see Isaiah. That got her determination going quick enough. Last week they went on a Tuesday. She'd woken up that morning feeling kind of blue, and knew just what she needed. It was the end of April, and the kids who spilled out of the center weren't wearing coats. Selma hadn't seen Isaiah without his puffy little down coat since the fall. Wearing just a light jacket, he looked surprisingly thin, all limbs and jutting angles. He was shorter than the other kids, which upset her a little, since she herself was above average in height. Was this my doing? she worried. Selma had spent the winter picturing him as plump; sometimes, in her bed, she squeezed a pillow and imagined that that was what Isaiah would feel like. Now she'd have to change her way of thinking. Which wasn't such a hard thing to do, but it saddened her how wrong-headed she'd been about her own son. It felt as if even more time had slipped away, more time without Isaiah.

That Tuesday, for the first time, she'd followed Isaiah home. She just had to get used to how skinny he was, never mind the risk of being caught following him. He skipped along with the blonde girl, holding her hand. He never sat in the stroller, which she brought along anyway. Seemed to Selma he was leading the blonde along; she had a lackadaisical way of walking, whereas Isaiah just darted round the corners like a tropical fish in an aquarium.

So this is where he lives, Selma thought when she saw them turn into a large building just off Broadway. Not as fancy a building as the one the Fredricks lived in, but a far cry from a project. For a moment Selma felt a sinking of hope: how could she, living in a project, ever get Isaiah back, when he lived in a place like this? She actually shook her head to stop this thought. 'Hey there, Isaiah,' she heard the doorman call. 'How was school today?'

As she pushed Dana in her stroller past the front door, trying to look as casual as she could, she heard her son say, 'Made finger paints.'

Now she had something else to get used to. His voice. Skinny as he was, she'd expected a high, thin voice. But somehow that skinny body managed a fuller sound than she would have thought possible, like an instrument of some kind, maybe a trumpet. She turned the stroller onto Broadway and headed uptown for the crosstown bus, trying to keep that voice in her head. Made finger paints. Made finger paints. She repeated his words to herself, but by the time they got to the bus stop all she could remember was the words. The voice itself had evaporated, and she was left with the same emptiness she'd had waking up that morning, only a little more bitter, a little more hopeless.

Chapter 5

Charles felt uneasy about the overnight trip to New Jersey. Susannah was coming. The annual report was her project, after all, but the client had insisted at the last moment that Charles come along to supervise the on-site photography. Charles was not happy about this. The way Susannah looked at him lately, the way her frosty blue eyes lingered on him just a moment or two longer than necessary, warned him that this trip would be trouble. Also foretelling trouble, he knew, was the way his own eyes lingered on Susannah's long, long legs as she crossed his office to show him a set of color keys or present a comp for approval.

Isaiah spotted his overnight bag as he was leaving the apartment and tore himself away from *Sesame Street*. 'I come too?' His voice was strained with panic.

'I'm just going to New Jersey for one night, big boy,' Charles said. Isaiah's expression told him this explanation wouldn't do. 'Daddy needs to help photograph some people.'

Isaiah hesitated for a moment, smiled, and left Charles in the hallway. Charles exhaled. Isaiah was hyper-sensitive to change, and disruptions to his routine could trigger tantrums that exhausted all four of them.

Isaiah returned a moment later carrying Charles's camera. 'Don't forget!' he said proudly. Charles started to explain that he wasn't the photographer, only the art director. Isaiah looked mystified (as did many adults, for that matter, when Charles talked about his work), and as Charles continued his explanation he looked as if he might start to cry. So Charles took the camera from Isaiah and put it in his bag.

He began to relax as the dreaded business trip wore on. The Roadway Inn just off the Jersey Turnpike was reassuringly antiseptic – romance had been snuffed out along with the germs – and at an Italian restaurant they had discovered down the road, the dinner conversation never strayed from LewinArt.

But after dinner, back at the motel, Susannah insisted he stop by her room to pick up a copy of the agenda for the next day, which, typically, he'd forgotten. He yawned conspicuously and said he was too tired to think about work, but she insisted. His resistance, never too sturdy anyway, crumbled. He felt himself surrender to Susannah with a comforting sense of relief, as if, after a long trip, he'd just given up the driving to a passenger. When, in her room, she'd stepped up to him and put her arms around his shoulders, he'd been tempted to ask, 'Why?'

But if Susannah weren't so inscrutable, perhaps he wouldn't have given in so easily.

Isaiah wailed that night when he saw the dinner table set for three. 'Daddy will be home tomorrow, darling,' Margaret told him. But Isaiah would not be consoled. He refused to sit at the table, and when Margaret picked him up and placed him in his chair, she felt his body stiffen with – with what? Anxiety? Terror? Rage? Why did these changes in routine send him over the edge? 'What is it, Isaiah? What's the matter?'

'Daddy,' was all he could mutter, the syllables nothing more than guttural sobs.

By bedtime he was still agitated, so Margaret let him stay up later than usual. At nine thirty she dialed the Roadway Inn and asked for Charles Lewin. Isaiah, on her lap, began to shake in anticipation. When Margaret hung up, after seven rings, Isaiah started to pant, always a prelude to hysteria. 'He's having dinner,' Margaret said, holding him to her as if to snuff out the anxiety or terror or rage simmering inside him. 'He'll be back tomorrow.' She felt him trembling in her arms and squeezed him tighter, rocking gently. Fifteen minutes later he was asleep.

Chapter 6

'Look, Gloria,' Margaret said into the phone. 'I've just spent an hour tallying our records. I managed to get you seventy-six days last year at twelve hundred a day. That's . . .' She punched the numbers into a calculator, but hit the minus button by mistake and wished she had never taken on Gloria Rogers as a client. She punched them in a second time, managed to hit the multiply button this time, and saw a figure emerge from behind the tiny screen. 'That's ninety-one thousand two hundred dollars.' She smiled in the solitude of her office; the figure was even larger than she'd thought, weakening Gloria's argument that Margaret hadn't been hawking her work with enough dedication.

'Minus your fifteen per cent.' Gloria's voice was much like Gloria: thin, tense, incredibly irritating.

'Minus my fifteen per cent, yes.'

They were silent for a moment. Margaret, for her part, decided she wouldn't contribute further to this conversation; she had a dozen clients, all successful, thanks at least in part to her efforts, and only one stinker: Gloria Rogers.

'I need more work,' Gloria said at length. 'My maintenance just went up fifteen per cent, and I need a new wide-angle lens, and . . .' Apparently she ran out of reasons. 'I just need more work.'

'I'm always looking out for you. If you're not satisfied with what I'm doing, you can find another agent—'

'Oh, I am,' Gloria said quickly. She always backed down in the end. Margaret could picture her capitulating, her reedy body hunching over the phone like a folding chair.

After hanging up, Margaret made a note to call an art director at *Mademoiselle* to see if there was anything there for Gloria. It was a grim but unavoidable fact of her professional life that the squeaky wheel actually did get the grease; she had other clients more worthy, more talented than Gloria, but it was on Gloria's behalf that she would call the art director at *Mademoiselle*.

She checked her watch. Eleven forty-five. An aerial view of Manhattan formed in her mind, with all the important landmarks standing out like giants: Hannah's school, Isaiah's pre-school,

Charles's office, her own office. Hannah would be getting ready for lunch. Isaiah was still at the Children's Center, but wrapping things up; Liv would be leaving their apartment to fetch him. Charles was at his office – at least Charles could be reached by telephone.

Alice, one of his designers, answered the phone. Everyone at LewinArt always sounded so enthusiastic, so eager. It made a sad contrast to the solitary quiet of her own office.

'Hi,' said Charles when he finally picked up the phone. Even he sounded peppy. 'What's up?'

She wished she had something for him, something 'up'. 'I was thinking we should see my parents tomorrow.'

'Are we due?'

'It's been a while. Anyway, it's supposed to be warm. The kids'll enjoy being outside.'

He hesitated. Margaret could almost hear him deciding whether to protest, whether a protest would be successful. 'All right. But let's not stay for dinner, okay? I gotta run.'

Charles often had to run these days. His business was thriving; she reminded herself of this when she felt his distance from her increasing. He'd already been away three times for photo shoots on the annual report, each time with one of his employees, Susannah Foster. They weren't used to being separated like this, the way most other couples they knew were. When he left, they made a big deal out of the impending separation, saying things like 'I'll miss you, darling' and 'I won't sleep a wink until I know you're safe' – grinning mischievously as they said them. But when he got home their reunions were surprisingly awkward. 'Hi, hon,' Charles would say, grazing her lips with a kiss. Then he'd look intently through the mail, or throw himself into horseplay with the kids. 'How was the trip?' she'd ask. 'Great,' was all he'd say, and when, the first time, she'd pressed him for details, he'd gotten irritable.

If I were another kind of woman I'd be jealous, Margaret thought. And if Charles were another kind of man. She couldn't imagine Charles having an affair with Susannah, though she thought about it fairly often. Susannah was attractive but totally stiff. A schoolmarm in Armani clothing is how Margaret thought of her. Not the sort to inspire extra-marital affairs. Not in Charles, anyway.

The Fredricks were late again. Selma sat on a stool in Dana's room feeling like she would jump out of her shoes if one of them didn't come through the front door soon. She looked up at the clock, as she did every few minutes: it wasn't easy to read, since it had Disney characters worked into all twelve numbers, but she was getting real practiced at it. Six thirty. Damn. Not that she had anything much to get home for. She was thinking of stopping off at church, though.

There was a service every evening, and she liked to attend them once or twice a week, recharge her batteries. Between church and school, she wasn't home much at night, which was how she liked it.

Still, it was Friday evening and it wasn't right to be kept waiting.

Even Dana seemed upset. She was in her playpen, systematically throwing out every toy that Selma had put in there. When she was through, Selma would get up and slowly put the toys back. Then Dana would start over again, only throwing a little harder, a little further. Some job this is, Selma thought, replacing the toys yet again. She hated Mrs Fredricks to come home and find the place a mess, even though some mornings Dana's room looked like a cyclone had just gone through. 'NO,' Dana screeched as Selma put an armful of toys into the playpen. 'NO.'

NO was Dana's first word. 'Are you my boss, missy?' Selma asked the child, dropping another load of toys into the playpen. Dana smiled at her, like she understood the question. Selma had to smile back – the kid was cute, no avoiding that.

Mrs Fredricks finally arrived home at six forty-five, looking harried as usual, her hair flying every which way. Selma wondered if part of being a lawyer was having to put your finger in an electric socket five days a week.

'Sorry, Selma,' she said when she found them in Dana's room.

Selma just shrugged and resisted the urge to say, That's all right. Dana got excited, began shaking the side of her playpen. Mrs Fredricks leaned over and picked her daughter up. 'Did you miss me, sweetheart?' she cooed.

Selma was on her way out but she knew what was coming.

'NO,' Dana told her mother. 'NO.'

Selma's ride home took almost an hour, all of it standing, holding on to the metal straps and trying to keep from falling over every time the train lurched or swayed. She tried to remember what she had back at the apartment to eat and decided she'd have a bowl of whatever canned soup was there. First she'd stop off at church. After dinner she'd read some of her book. Then she'd watch some TV. Then she'd go to bed. It was her Friday night pattern. It didn't bother her one bit. She was getting her life smooth and regular for Isaiah.

Selma heard Reverend Williams's voice from out in the street; when she entered the Brooklyn Pentecostal Church, it engulfed her like a warm, humid breeze. There were only a few dozen people in the large, plain room, which seemed to intensify the Reverend's voice. He was a big, jolly-looking man who, when he preached, was anything but jolly. His voice panted and quaked, he always seemed angry at someone or something, outraged. Hearing him, Selma instantly felt clenched in his grip, as if her mind had been yanked out of her body like an engine removed from a car for repairs.

She sat a few rows from the front and took out her Bible. She usually had trouble finding the right verse but she liked to hold it anyway.

'And then they shall see the Son of Man coming in a cloud with power and great glory,' the Reverend was saying, reading from the Bible. It was his usual theme: Judgment Day, when the good shall be rewarded and the evil punished. He never got tired of talking about it and Selma never got tired of hearing it. The worse things got on the streets, the more it seemed that there just had to be an end – which would be the beginning. Things just can't keep on like this, Selma felt. It kept her coming back to Reverend Williams.

'Behold the fig tree, and all the trees; when they now shoot forth, ye see and know of your own selves that summer's nigh at hand. So likewise ye, when ye see these things come to pass, know ye that the Kingdom of God is nigh at hand.'

Amen, said the Reverend. The word circled the room without fading. Amen, repeated the small but inspired congregation. Selma recognized most of the faces, all black, mostly women. But when the sermon was over, she never stayed to talk with them or the Reverend. She liked to leave with the Reverend's words fresh on her mind, unsullied by conversation; sometimes they even lasted her through the six-block walk back to her building.

When she got home she could tell right away something was wrong. She opened the door and the silence hit her like a cold wind. 'Hello,' she said, softly at first and then louder. 'Who's home?'

She surveyed the apartment, starting with the kitchen and ending with her bedroom. It felt strange being alone in the apartment; she almost never was, especially around dinner time. She felt menace in the air, strong as a bad odor. She spotted one of Raymond's little apple juice cartons and picked it up. He'd barely sipped it, which wasn't like him.

Selma was in the kitchen, thinking about making her soup but too nervous to get really serious about it, when the doorbell rang. The only people who ever rang the doorbell were Marie's boyfriends, and so she was surprised when she opened the door to find a woman standing there.

'I live next door,' the woman said. She was a short, elderly black woman with gray hair; she smelled of cigarettes. Selma had seen her once or twice but didn't know her name. 'I heard you come in and thought you'd want to know.'

'Know what?' Selma said, thinking first of Raymond and then of Josette. 'What happened?'

'They took Marie away in a ambulance.' The woman couldn't disguise her pleasure at being the first to deliver the news. 'Bleedin'.'

The first thing that came to her mind was a fight, one of Marie's men. 'A fight?'

The old lady shook her head; Selma could have sworn she heard something rattling inside. 'Just bleedin' and mumblin' like a drunk.'

'The children?'

'Went with her, in the ambulance.'

Oh Lord, Selma thought. 'Which hospital?'

The woman just shrugged. 'I thought you'd want to know.'

'Thanks,' Selma muttered, feeling no gratitude. She got her coat and set out for the nearest hospital.

The sight of Josette and Raymond in the waiting room almost broke her heart on the spot. They were sitting there, swinging their legs, as quiet and proper as if they were in church, but their eyes were wide with fright and confusion. Raymond jumped off his chair and buried his head in her skirt. Josette just looked up at her without standing.

'I went in her room to see if she wanted dinner,' Josette said, even though Selma hadn't asked her anything. Her voice was flat, trance-like. 'It was getting late. She was laying in bed, mumbling, like, and I thought she was drunk.' Here her voice broke for a second, which Selma found reassuring. 'I could smell the liquor. I was going to leave her be, but then I noticed her sheets looked funny. Darker. I went over to her and saw it was blood.'

Selma felt Raymond's head shaking between her legs. She put her hand over his head and started rubbing it.

'Mama, what happened? I asked her, but she just kept on mumbling. So I called 911 from the kitchen and stayed with her till the ambulance arrived. Seemed like forever.'

'You did good,' Selma said. 'Real good. Where's your mama now?'

'They won't tell us nothing,' Josette said.

'You wait here, then. I'll ask.'

She nodded for Josette to take Raymond from her and then walked down the corridor to the emergency room admitting desk. There was a crowd of people milling around, but Selma managed to push her way to the front. 'I'm looking for Marie Sherman,' she said to the woman behind the desk.

'No visitors in Emergency except immediate family. You immediate family?'

'Sister,' Selma lied.

'Room two eighty. Don't stay long,' the woman said, but she didn't sound like she cared.

Selma hated hospitals, hated walking down those long, cold corridors afraid to look on either side lest you see something you wish you hadn't. She found 280 and poked her head in. The room had four beds. There were three patients, each hooked up to a machine. Marie was in a bed on the far side of the room. Selma crossed the room without looking at the other two patients. Marie was curled up on her side, with a tube in her arm connected to a plastic bag hanging nearby. She looked so scrawny, like she had lost half her weight along with the blood. Selma pulled the covers up over Marie's bare legs. Marie opened her eyes and found Selma without moving.

'I'm here,' Selma said, unable to think of anything better.

Marie closed her eyes, slowly, like two shades being pulled down.

'The kids is out in the waiting room.' Selma didn't know what to do next. 'What happened to you, Marie?'

But Marie said nothing, didn't even move. Selma watched as a drop of clear liquid slithered down the tube from the bag. Other than that drop, nothing moved.

'Gotta tell the kids what's happening to their mama, Marie.' Still no answer, so Selma recrossed the room and went in search of a doctor or nurse.

The nursing station was all the way down at the end of hallway. Selma walked with her head pointed straight ahead. As she passed she could hear moans and other sounds of sickness and death. Too bad you can't point your ears straight ahead too, she thought. 'I need to find out about Marie Sherman in room two eighty,' she told the only person at the desk, a black woman Selma's age who was writing something in a notebook.

'What do you want to know?' the woman asked without looking up.

'What's wrong with her. Marie Sherman.'

'You'll have to talk with the doctor. I'm not authorized.'

'But her kids is out in the waiting room.'

Finally the woman looked up. She reached for a clipboard and ran her finger halfway down it. Selma noticed the blue circles under her eyes, the tired way her face sagged around the mouth. 'Dr Allen is attending her. He'll be back in an hour. You can talk to him then.'

Selma knew better than to count on the doctor returning in an hour. Back in Marie's room she asked her again what had happened. 'Is it the baby, Marie?'

She still got no answer. Marie was how many months pregnant? Four? Five? For all Selma knew she had a little premature baby somewhere in the hospital. They could keep babies no bigger than hamsters alive; Selma had seen a news program about this. 'Marie, I gotta know what to tell your kids.'

Marie's eyes opened and then closed in slow motion.

'I'm leaving then,' Selma said angrily. Getting sick was no excuse to ignore your children. But then Marie had ignored her children before coming to the hospital.

Selma was leaving when she noticed the clipboard at the end of the bed. She lifted it off a hook and looked at it. Nothing recognizable except Marie's name. She tried breaking up the longer words the way Lizzie had taught her but still had no luck. Damn. Right here on this clipboard is the answer to what's wrong with Marie and it might as well be in Chinese, for all the good it does me, Selma thought. Her right hand, holding the clipboard, burned with frustration. Then she had a thought.

She found Lizzie's number in the address book she always carried in her pocketbook. Until now, she'd only called Lizzie twice, both times to tell her she couldn't make tutoring, and both times she'd phoned her at her office. She felt uncomfortable calling her at home on a Friday night, but it seemed the only way to figure out what was going on. Lizzie answered on the third ring.

'It's Selma,' she said. Lizzie didn't say anything, so she added, 'Selma Richards.'

'Oh, Selma!'

She was nervous about having taken the clipboard, so she got right to the point. 'I got something here I need to read but I can't make it out.'

'Sure, go ahead,' Lizzie said brightly.

Always so enthusiastic when it comes to me, Selma thought. 'Okay, here's what it says.' She paused before beginning, because there were two paragraphs of handwriting on the page and she wanted to get to the important part. So she skipped a few lines at the top that had the date and time and whatnot on them and began with a big chunk of words halfway down.

'P-A-T-I-E-N-T.'

'Patient,' Lizzie said 'Like in a hospital or else patient as in, you know, waiting patiently.'

'A-D-M-I-T-T-E-D.'

'Admitted. Patient admitted.' Lizzie's voice lost some of its enthusiasm.

Selma could read the next word. 'With. With . . .' She hesitated. The next word looked familiar too. 'With . . . heavy . . .' The next word started with a 'b' and she knew what it had to be. 'B-L-E-E-D-I-N-G is bleeding, right?'

'Bleeding, right.'

'The next word is "from" and after that it's V-A-G-I-N-A.'

'That's vagina. Patient admitted with heavy bleeding from vagina. Selma, what's going on? Are you all right?'.

'I'm okay. It's a friend.' She heard a clicking and realized her time was up.

'Selma, what's your number there? I'll call you back.'

Selma gave it to her and hung up. This was taking longer than she thought, so she decided to skip to the long word at the end of the second line. She answered the ringing phone and started right in. 'S-P-O-N-T-A-N-E-O-U-S.'

'Spontaneous.'

'A-B-O-R-T-I-O-N.'

'Abortion. A spontaneous abortion is a miscarriage.'

Selma nodded; as far as she knew, this meant there was no premature baby. 'What's T-R-A-N-S-F-U-S-I-O-N?'

'Transfusion.'

She skipped a few words to one that looked important. 'And what's A-L-C-O-H-O-L?'

'Alcohol.'

'Huh,' Selma said. 'Well, that's what I needed to know.'

'Is your friend all right?'

'She's okay. I gotta see to her kids though. You take care, Lizzie. Thank you.'

Selma brought Raymond and Josette into the room and led them over to their mother's bed. Josette walked right over and looked down at Marie, but Raymond backed off as soon as he saw the tube leading into his mother's arm. He stood a few feet from the bed staring at the chair in the corner.

'Mama?' said Josette. 'Mama, you awake?'

Marie managed to open her eyes. 'Hi, honey,' she whispered.

'Selma told us what happened. She says you going to be okay.'

Marie smiled weakly.

'Raymond, you want to say hi to Mama?' Josette asked. But Raymond took a step back. 'He's spooked by the tubes and whatnot,' said Josette to her mother, trying to make things right. 'We'll come by tomorrow, okay?'

But Marie just closed her eyes again, slowly.

'You kids want pizza?' Selma asked as they walked home. The night was so cool and damp, it felt like walking through a giant outdoor cellar. The hooting and howling of Friday night partying could be heard from the bars and clubs in the neighborhood, but Josette and Raymond were silent. 'I know you don't feel much like eating, but you got to anyway. We'll bring some slices home with us.'

They stopped in a pizzeria and waited for their order. 'Can I have a Coke?' Josette asked.

'Sure you can,' Selma answered, pleased to see a spark of life in the girl. 'You want a soda, Ray?'

He shook his head angrily.

'There's juice at home, and milk.'

Another angry shake.

'Okay, let's get on home. Josette, you carry the pizza so I can carry this poor fella.'

Selma bent over to scoop him up, but he wiggled free and started to walk. Outside, he managed to stay a few paces ahead of them, but his feet were dragging and he looked so tired Selma was afraid he'd drop right there on the sidewalk. She caught up to him and took his little hand in hers. He tried to pull away but she wouldn't let him. 'No use resisting, Ray. I'm stronger than you.'

Now he dragged behind her, pulling her shoulder down. At first it was deliberate, because he didn't want anything to do with anybody. But after a few minutes Selma knew it was just exhaustion. She leaned over and picked him up by the armpits. 'Lord, you heavy,' she said. He resisted for just a second. Then he let his head fall into her neck and she felt his little body go limp in her arms. She put her hand under his shirt and rubbed his back as they walked. The smoothness and warmth of it were like balm to her. 'Everything's gonna be all right, Raymond. I promise. I'll look after you till your mama's better.'

She heard a tiny, wheezy snore from him and realized that he'd fallen asleep. Poor little thing, she thought. But she was glad that he'd fallen asleep, because she hated to make promises she couldn't keep.

Chapter 7

Margaret's parents' house in Greenwich hadn't changed since she was a girl. It hadn't changed a bit. Sometimes, during visits, Margaret would walk through the large, meticulously decorated rooms and search for something new, something rearranged. But she never found anything. If a chair needed recovering, Lois Hollander always managed to find a fabric that perfectly matched the original. Likewise with carpeting and drapes and wallpaper. Sometimes, stealthily touring her parents' house (for she always felt vaguely seditious walking around there), Margaret wanted to giggle at the remarkable inertia of the place. Other times she wanted to cry.

It was a warm day for late April. The kids bypassed the house for the back yard, where they enjoyed playing with Lucky, their grandparents' golden retriever. The air had a charged quality, electrified by buds straining against their hulls, bulbs on the verge of piercing through the soil, perennials poised to make their expected reappearance. Margaret knew her parents would be inside, even on this lovely spring day. She and Charles dutifully climbed the front stairs and rang the bell.

'You don't have to ring the bell here,' Lois greeted them a moment later. 'It's still your house.'

'But the door was locked,' Margaret said, neglecting to add that she still carried the key she'd had as a girl.

'Oh!' Lois exclaimed, as if this were a novel state of affairs. 'Yes, of course. Come in.'

Charles placed a kiss on his mother-in-law's powdered cheek, the texture of a fine calfskin wallet. He said he wanted to check up on the kids and headed for the back yard.

If outside all was pregnant spring, inside it was still a barren winter day. The house was chilly and sepulchral, the drapes resolutely closed against the sun. As they crossed the living room, Margaret felt herself sink into the deep pile of the wall-to-wall carpet; it was a bit like walking through a marsh, or a padded cell.

'You haven't commented on the new carpeting,' her mother said when they reached the kitchen.

'I didn't realize it was new.'

'Well, yes, we just had it installed last week. And what a time I had. Do you like the color? Go have a look while I make coffee.'

Margaret obediently returned to the living room and surveyed the vast sea of powder-blue carpet. It appeared to be the same color as its predecessor, but no doubt it was slightly off, and no doubt this had caused Lois no end of consternation. Things change: fabrics fade, carpets wear, paint chips and peels. Even in this house which time seemed to have forgotten, things inevitably decayed. Perpetuating the illusion of timelessness gave her mother a sense of purpose, Margaret supposed. But it also, ironically, made the house feel like the ultimate reminder of time's passage: a mausoleum.

'It looks beautiful, Mother.'

'Thanks, darling. I worried about the color.'

They sat at the kitchen table and drank coffee. Through the large picture window they could watch the children playing with Lucky while Charles sat nearby on a lawn chair, watching.

Lois was rather stiff with the children, which didn't surprise Margaret but still managed, occasionally, to disappoint her. Sometimes she thought that it was Isaiah's color that put Lois off. She'd been bitterly opposed to the adoption and had refused to come and see them until Isaiah was almost one. When Hannah was born there had been a steady stream of baby gifts, but with Isaiah there hadn't been any gifts, and although Margaret had once been a little saddened by her parents' generosity with Hannah, recognizing it as a poor substitute for genuine affection, she had missed the gifts when Isaiah was a baby, had felt resentful on his behalf. Always fair in their bigoted way, they'd stopped sending presents to Hannah as well. So at Christmas, Margaret used to buy a few things for both children and attach cards signed Grandma and Grandpa.

They had come round after a year. Sometimes Margaret wondered why they'd bothered, they seemed so remote from the children, even from Hannah. Perhaps it had to do with some sense of honor, or duty, or a vision of how things were supposed to be with grandparents. Of course, they no longer showed off their grandchildren to their friends and neighbors, the way they'd paraded Hannah around before she had a little brother. Margaret wondered if Lois had even confided to her friends about Isaiah. She had a wide circle of long standing friends but it was hard to imagine her confiding anything in anyone, least of all that she had a black grandson.

Lois and Walter had both been furious when Margaret married Charles. You're too young, just a year out of college, they'd said. How will you support yourselves? He's an artist! But their real objection had been that Charles was Jewish. They never actually said this, except to raise the issue, frequently, of how they would bring up their children. We'll deal with that when we have children, Margaret and Charles had answered. But the funny thing was, they never really had dealt with it. The children were born, they grew up, and the subject of religion was virtually never broached except by Lois and Walter, nonpracticing Episcopalians (was there any other kind?) who claimed that they'd rather see the children raised as Jews than as 'nothing', as Lois called it. Margaret had always doubted the sincerity of this claim. Still, they hadn't boycotted Margaret and Charles after their marriage the way they did after Isaiah entered the family. It was one thing to marry a Jew (their doctor was Jewish, after all, as was the family that lived catty-corner to them) but quite another to adopt a black (they didn't know any blacks socially, professionally, or otherwise). Maybe Isaiah's birth mother was Episcopalian, Margaret had once suggested. I doubt it very much, had been Lois's answer.

'Where's Daddy?' Margaret asked, for usually he made his appearance sooner.

Lois checked her watch, as if she and Walter were on a schedule. 'Why don't you go find him. Maybe he wants a cup of coffee.'

Margaret faithfully went in search of her father. Upstairs the house was even more tomb-like, the air dancing with swirling particles in those few places where sunlight managed to intrude. She found Walter in his upstairs study, looking out the window at the back yard. There was a basketball game on the television, so Walter didn't hear her as she crossed the room on the squishy carpet. He was watching Isaiah and Hannah playing with the dog, an abstracted smile on his face, ignoring his beloved basketball. This surprised Margaret.

As an adult she'd come to realize what had eluded her as a child: her parents, though they could be bigoted and rigid in their thinking, were not without emotion. It was just that they'd been taught along the way to keep these emotions sealed up. Kisses were for bedtimes and reunions, but were never offered spontaneously. Hugs, cuddles – these gestures were as foreign to them as high fives. Margaret had never forgotten how she craved physical contact as a child, and when Hannah was born she promised herself and her daughter that she'd never stifle the urge to kiss or hug. It had been an easy promise to keep, after all, at least until Hannah reached early adolescence and decided that physical contact with the parental units was uncool. Thank God for Isaiah, who never seemed to tire of her touch.

'Hi, Daddy,' she said, reluctantly dashing a scene that pleased her disproportionately.

'I didn't hear you come in,' Walter exclaimed, standing to kiss his daughter. She could tell that he was a little embarrassed to be caught mooning over his grandchildren. She wanted to tell him that it was even okay for Episcopalians to indulge in emotions when it came to grandchildren, but she didn't think he'd understand, or if he did, he'd resent her telling him. 'Mother wants to know if you want some coffee.'

'I think I'll just wait until half-time. I'll be down then.' He replanted himself in front of the television, and Margaret returned to the kitchen.

Charles wondered how much longer he could put off going inside. It wasn't that he disliked the Hollanders. What was there to dislike: a superficial Connecticut matron and her husband the empty suit? No, as in-laws went they were probably not too bad. They only required visits every few months, they would leave behind a hefty estate (though they were not particularly generous while living), and their values were so far from his and Margaret's that even their harshest judgments and criticisms were completely inoffensive. No, he didn't dislike the Hollanders, he just couldn't face them. That was it.

He couldn't face much of his life these days. At dinner lately he'd taken to averting his eyes from Margaret, and he was beginning to think she noticed. At LewinArt he was delegating more and more work to Susannah and Alice, isolating himself in his office, where he indulged in adding up, over and over, the firm's monthly expenses, his payroll, things like that. And now, here in Greenwich, he just couldn't bring himself to go inside and face Lois and Walter, the two most innocuous people on earth.

Charles knew why he was so alienated: he was having an affair, if you could call four sexual encounters an affair. It wasn't as if the affair itself was preoccupying him; in fact, ever since the second time he'd slept with Susannah, on the couch in his office one night after work, the magic had tarnished somewhat.

It was three weeks since it all began at the Roadway Inn in New Jersey. The second episode (for this is how he thought of the affair, as a series of unrelated episodes) took place a week later. He'd been incredibly uncomfortable around Susannah since that first time. Susannah showed no such awkwardness, which he found astonishing. She went about her work (his work!) with her usual energetic efficiency, and fortunately the workload was simply too heavy to allow for intimate talks, let alone sexual encounters. Then, on a Wednesday night, they had all been working late on a brochure layout for a big accounting firm. At eight o'clock Alice announced she was leaving, and when the door shut behind her, a charge went

60

through the office: Charles and Susannah were alone for the first time since New Jersey, and it was immediately clear to both of them that this would have consequences.

They worked diligently for another hour, barely speaking. Charles was painfully torn between his desire to make love to Susannah and an overwhelming sense of guilt that told him to finish the project and go directly home. But at nine, Susannah walked into his office and shut the door behind her. 'Shall I call Andy and tell him I won't be making the ten twenty?' she asked.

Charles found her sangfroid breathtaking and incredibly erotic. All he could do was nod. Once again he felt in the grip of someone so capable, so accomplished, that he believed he could do no wrong. He was her employer, he was powerful, but she was infinitely more efficient, more competent, resolute where he was wavering, decisive where he was hesitant. It was all so . . . erotic.

After that evening there was no urgency to their affair. They simply made love when the opportunity presented itself; so far it had presented itself two more times. When they weren't writhing on Charles's couch, they went about their business as usual, or at any rate Susannah did. Sometimes Charles heard her on the telephone with Andy, discussing dinner plans or vacations, and he couldn't believe that she moved so seamlessly from one life to another. He, on the other hand, dreaded Margaret's calls at the office. They seemed to shake the foundation of the Chinese wall he'd erected inside his head to separate what he thought of as his two lives.

Why am I doing this? he asked himself often, feeling miserable and isolated in his office, taking few phone calls and making fewer still. Why? And yet, if I'm so unhappy, why don't I call it off? God knows Susannah wouldn't miss a beat, would continue to work for me as if nothing had happened. There would be no ugly scenes with her, no recrimination, no guilt. Then again, maybe I'm not so unhappy after all, he thought. Just confused. Just guilty.

Charles crossed the Hollanders' emerald lawn and entered the house through the kitchen door. Margaret and her mother were having coffee at the kitchen table; an air of languor suffused the room, mixing with the damp darkness of the house to convince Charles that he had made a mistake coming inside. Surely he could have delayed a few minutes more, another half-hour.

'There you are, Charles,' his mother-in-law exclaimed, as if she really hadn't expected him to come in at all. 'Would you like some coffee?'

He really wanted a drink, but alcohol wasn't served at the Hollanders' until after six, and even then they indulged only on special occasions, pouring stingy shots of whiskey over too few ice cubes in heavy glasses retrieved from the back of a high pantry

61

cupboard. What good are WASP in-laws, Charles often asked Margaret, if you can't even have a drink with them in the afternoon?

He declined coffee and joined them at the table. 'Where's Walter?'

'Watching basketball upstairs, where else?' Margaret answered.

'Margaret tells me your business is going great guns,' said Lois with forced enthusiasm. Neither she nor Walter considered graphic design a suitable, or even creditable, way to make a living. Most annoying was their habit of referring to him as a 'commercial artist'. It never ceased to amaze them that Charles and Margaret managed to pay their bills. That Margaret, through her own business, managed to contribute at all was beyond their comprehension.

'Too busy,' he answered. 'I may have to add to the staff.'

'Ah, I see,' Lois said. 'That would be nice.'

He smiled weakly and searched for something more to say. Finally he gave up. 'I think I'll go say hi to Walter.'

'Yes, he'll be so pleased to see you,' said Lois.

Hannah and Isaiah were taking turns throwing a stick, which Lucky fetched and returned to them. Hannah used to love doing this – playing with Lucky was about the only tolerable thing about visiting her grandparents – but this time it was kind of boring. She played along for Isaiah's sake; he just didn't seem to get tired of it, he acted like it was a miracle every time Lucky found the stick and brought it back.

After a while Hannah let Isaiah throw the stick by himself, because it had become all gross with Lucky's spit. Sometimes Isaiah only managed to throw it a few feet, and Lucky, who always took a big head start, wouldn't bother running back to get it. So Isaiah would have to fetch his own stick, which meant that they gradually moved away from their grandparents' house toward the neighbors.

Hannah had always been kind of uncomfortable in her grandparents' neighborhood. The houses all looked like fortresses, some even had turrets, and you never saw a sign out front with a name on it. No one walked around the way they did in the city. And everything was perfectly clean and orderly; it reminded her a little of Disneyworld. Whenever she and her parents took walks she felt like any minute someone was going to ask them for passes or something. Come to think of it, she felt a little bit like this *inside* her grandparents' house too.

So Hannah was surprised and even a little frightened when she spotted an older couple watching them from the back yard of the house next to her grandparents'. They both had white hair and wore button-up sweaters, and both had blank expressions, like they were in a trance or something. When Hannah saw them she just froze.

62

She didn't know why, she just froze.

Isaiah, of course, was oblivious. He kept on throwing that dripping stick closer and closer to the edge of her grandparents' property. Hannah, still reluctant to move, feared that he'd manage to get off a good throw and toss the stick right into the neighbors' yard. Maybe it would hit them. She saw the woman pull the sides of her sweater together, as if there was a sudden breeze. She said something to the man, but without turning her glance away from them.

Hannah felt her face grow red and warm, the way it always did when she knew she was being watched. 'Isaiah, let's go back in the house.'

'No,' he said, picking up the stick and tossing it a few yards.

'No really, come on.'

'*More* play.'

He could be so stubborn. She looked over at the neighbors. Once, her grandparents had had a few of the neighbors over to meet her. But that was a long time ago; she barely remembered it, and certainly didn't remember if the white-haired couple had been there. In any case, they hadn't been over since Isaiah. 'Come on, let's go inside.'

This time Isaiah ignored her completely. 'Here, Lucky,' Hannah shouted the next time the dog retrieved the stick. Lucky obediently loped over to her and dropped the disgusting stick in front of her feet. Using only her thumb and forefinger, she gingerly picked it up and ran with it in the direction of the house.

'*More* play,' Isaiah wailed, but Lucky was following her and so he had no choice but to chase after them. When Hannah was near the house she threw the stick onto a row of tall hedges, where it lodged out of Lucky's reach. The dog went crazy jumping up and down, barking and growling.

Isaiah stared forlornly at the frustrated dog. He looked as if he were about to cry.

'You were going to throw the stick at those people,' Hannah said.

Isaiah turned in the direction she was pointing and shook his head.

'They were standing there, watching us.'

He looked at her dumbly, the way he always did, which drove her crazy.

'They were watching *you*.'

Again, Isaiah just stared at her, understanding nothing. The next words just popped out of her mouth like a cough. 'Because you're black.'

Isaiah smiled blankly.

'You're the only black person in this whole neighborhood. Maybe in the whole town.' Hannah didn't know why she was saying this, but she couldn't stop herself. A few yards away Lucky was yelping at the dangling stick.

'No,' Isaiah said defiantly, though he clearly didn't know what she was talking about.

'You are too.'

It occurred to Hannah that, living where they did, on the West Side of Manhattan, Isaiah might not realize that not all neighborhoods had whites and blacks and Spanish people mixed in. 'In neighborhoods like this, they don't expect to see black people, that's all,' she said primly. 'That's why those people were staring at us.' Isaiah opened his mouth to say something but then shut it again and ran into the house.

Now I'm really going to get it, Hannah thought. She wondered if Isaiah would be able to explain to their parents what she had said. She doubted it. She walked over to the hedge and shook it until the stick fell down. Lucky grabbed it and then brought it over to her and dropped it at her feet.

It's true, Hannah reassured herself; those people were staring at Isaiah. Not me: Isaiah. Maybe they're racists. Her parents had told her about racism and bigots and the civil rights movement, and she'd studied it in social studies at school. Maybe the white-haired people were bigots, maybe they weren't. What difference did it make? She just hated their staring that way. More than anything else, she hated being stared at and she hated being different. No one else she knew was different. No one else had a black brother. Only she did.

Hannah kicked the stick a few feet, but Lucky just stood there, waiting for her to pick it up and throw it. She walked over and kicked it again. Then again. Gradually she kicked it back across the lawn. But when she looked up, the white-haired couple had gone. She picked up the stick and hurled it into their back yard. Lucky raced after it, cutting through the shrubbery that divided the two lawns. The sight of Lucky tearing across their smooth, perfectly green lawn lifted Hannah's spirits a bit.

'Good girl,' she said when the dog returned and dropped the stick at her feet. 'Good girl.'

Chapter 8

With Marie in the hospital, Selma's life took on one more dimension: now she had Josette and Raymond to look after. Each morning she got Ray dressed and fed him some breakfast, then walked him over to his day care center. Josette was pretty much able to look after herself, but Selma still felt she should keep an eye on her – she was at a dangerous age, in Selma's experience. Then, in the evenings, on her way home from work or tutoring, she'd pick up Raymond, bring him home, and fix him and Josette some dinner. No time for church, but Selma figured watching the kids was more important. Marie was due home in a few days, but still, she wasn't happy about having this new responsibility. It was a complication, a burden; it was a wrinkle on the big smooth bed she was preparing for her and Isaiah.

It seemed like people in Selma's life were always taking on roles that weren't theirs by right, or by nature. She herself spent half her time looking after kids who weren't hers: first Dana, now Raymond and Josette. Lizzie Kaplan was her teacher, even though Lizzie was just a few years older and God knows Selma didn't feel like anybody's pupil. When she was growing up it had been the same way. Her mother had been no mother to her, and quickly Selma had become no daughter, either. No one played the roles they were meant to anymore. It would be different with her and Isaiah, of course, soon as she got him back.

Selma's mother's name was Annette Richards. She was born in Georgia but had come north as a teenager to work for a white family in Westchester. As best as Selma recollected from her mother's stories, there was this businessman staying at a motel where Annette was working as a maid. One morning he stopped her in the hallway and asked if she wanted to come north and work for him and his wife. Annette hadn't taken but a second to answer. Nothing could be worse than working as a motel maid in Georgia, where the wages were miserable and the black folk walked around all day with their heads bowed down. The white man gave her a train ticket and his phone number. A week later Annette called him from Penn

Station and he told her she had to get herself over to Grand Central Station and onto another train.

It didn't take Annette a week to realize that she'd been wrong about one thing: there *was* something worse than working as a motel maid in Georgia and that was working as a house maid for the Petersons. At least in the motel she never felt she was dusting and scrubbing and picking up for someone *specific*, just a series of anonymous people who sometimes left her some change on the bureau. At the Petersons' she felt her whole life had been given over to these two people whom she found herself hating more and more every day. She hated the way they looked *right through* her when she walked in the room carrying plates or a pot of coffee. She hated the way she was never introduced to any of their friends or relatives. She hated that she didn't even *want* to be introduced to these people. After two years she felt she had to get out of there. She gave her notice and took the train back to the city, where she found a room in an apartment on West 133rd Street.

The apartment belonged to Sadie, who lived there with a daughter and two teenaged grandchildren. They made no effort to get to know Annette, apart from informing her that the rent was due on the first, the bathroom was down the hall on the left. Annette's room was off the living room. It had a small bed and a broken-down dresser and not much else, which was just as well since nothing much else would have fit. The first night, after introducing herself to Sadie and the rest, Annette went into her room and closed the door and looked around the room. So this is what my life has been reduced to: a shoe box. She thought about Georgia, about how even the poor people there had bigger places to live in than up here. And outside even the poorest Georgia windows there was something to watch, even if it was your neighbor hanging the laundry. Here there was another decrepit-looking building not three feet from Annette's window. She pulled down the yellowed shade, sat on the bed, and cried silently, so as not to be heard by Sadie and her grandchildren.

But things began looking up a few days later. She got a job waiting tables at a pancake house near Times Square. It was a tough job but the pay was good, especially the tips, and she could work as many hours as she wanted. Usually she worked as long as she could stand to, sometimes twelve hours straight. There was nothing much to go home for, and she hadn't made any friends. It wasn't much of a life, but it was a step up from the Petersons'.

Then she met Isaiah. She had noticed him around the neighborhood practically her first day there. He was hard to miss. Isaiah was well over six feet and very handsome, with a big, wide grin that made her head go dizzy when he turned it on her. She could tell by the way he looked at her that he liked what he saw, but it was several months before he actually spoke to her.

August was sweltering. Annette was used to heat, but in Georgia you could always find a place with a breeze. Not in New York. There wasn't a speck of breeze in her little room; at night she lay on top of the damp sheets trying not to move, thinking of the swimming hole she and her sisters and brothers used to go to, how they made a game out of forcing themselves into the ice-cold water. When sleeping was impossible, she would pull on a T-shirt and shorts and sit out on the front steps waiting until she was so exhausted she could sleep inside a furnace.

She never forgot his first words. 'Well, if it ain't the Georgia peach,' Isaiah had said, making his voice syrupy slow.

She gave him a look: how do you know I'm from Georgia?

'I know everything around here.'

'Then what's my name?'

'Annette.'

She didn't know whether to feel flattered or nervous. 'What's yours?'

'Isaiah,' he answered. He put the emphasis on the first part of his name: *Eye*-zayah. He was standing a few steps down from where she was sitting, so their heads were practically at the same level. He flashed her a smile that made her breath catch in her throat.

'How come you always out on the sidewalk? Don't you work?'

'My work is on the sidewalk.'

Annette nodded at this. She still felt like a country girl compared to the other people around here. She didn't want to appear even more stupid by asking what kind of work kept a man on the streets all day.

'You want to take a stroll?'

'Now?' Annette hadn't brought her watch but she figured it must be after midnight.

'Don't need an appointment to stroll.'

Annette had to be at work by seven the next morning, but she couldn't let this opportunity go by.

Before long she was seeing Isaiah every night. Usually they just walked around the neighborhood, though sometimes he took her with him into bars and clubs where pool and cards were played. She began spending some of her savings on new clothes and make-up, and got her hair done at a place on 125th Street that she'd heard was the best around. Long after midnight, she and Isaiah would tiptoe through Sadie's apartment and into her bedroom. There they'd make hot, agitated love for what seemed like hours, Annette biting Isaiah's shoulder to keep from crying out and waking the others. Afterwards, Isaiah would tiptoe out and she would fall into a deep, though brief, sleep.

August broiled to the very end, and September simmered halfway through. Then, as she walked to the subway one morning on her way downtown, Annette felt the first chill of autumn brushing against her shoulders. The end of summer saddened her. In her mind, the summer's heat was tied up with Isaiah. She worried how they'd keep things going when they couldn't take walks and sit out on the stoop, talking. She'd asked him to take her to his place, figuring anywhere had to be more private than her little room, but he always had an excuse. 'Ain't polite for a lady to be seen entering a man's apartment,' he said once. He liked to talk formal sometimes. She gave him a look, but he just grinned and melted her.

Then one morning in November as Annette was leaving for work, Sadie let her have it. 'Don't like your bringing Isaiah Reptoe round here.'

Annette wondered if Sadie knew that Isaiah spent the night. 'What I do in my room is my business,' she answered.

'He's a drug dealer,' Sadie said. 'Don't want him round my grandchildren.'

'Isaiah Reptile,' one of the grandchildren piped in from the bathroom. 'Isaiah Reptile,' squealed the other from her room.

Annette's head began to swirl. She was thinking of the times when Isaiah would drop in on a 'friend' during their walks. Just be a minute, peaches, he'd say. Gotta see a friend. Can't I come? she'd ask. Trust me, peaches, you wouldn't like these people. Then why they your friends? Then he'd give her a look that made her feel so stupid, so interfering, that she wouldn't say a word more. And sure enough, he never spent but a minute or two on these visits. He'd come back to her as happy and excited as a kid.

'Isaiah's no drug dealer,' Annette said, but her voice was unsteady.

'No? Then what he do for a living then? How he afford those nice clothes and whatnot?'

Unable to speak, Annette ran out of the apartment. She was heading for the subway when she decided she had to find Isaiah. They never saw each other during the day, except sometimes on weekends. She knew he lived nearby, and she knew who would know his address. There was a small grocery store down the street where they stopped in sometimes to buy beer. This man know everything happening in the neighborhood, Isaiah told her. He meant the owner, a grey old man with watery eyes who kept a big German shepherd with him behind the counter. He just smiled and shook his head when Annette asked him where Isaiah lived, but Annette could tell from his satisfied expression that he knew. She told him it was an emergency. Still he just smiled. 'Here,' she said, putting all the money in her wallet on the counter. 'Now tell me.' He looked at the money like it smelled, but after a few moments he counted it. 'This all you got?' She showed him her empty wallet. He gave her the address. 'Don't tell him I told you, though. Isaiah real private 'bout his address.'

She walked quickly, hardly noticing the stiff, early-morning wind. She knocked on his door and heard some movement. She just knew that when she saw him everything would be better. But when the door opened, there was a woman in a bathrobe standing there, not Isaiah.

'Where's Isaiah?' Annette asked, checking the apartment number on the door.

'In bed. What you want with him?'

The woman had obviously just woken up. She was heavy-set but attractive, with a cocky, knowing look on her face that made Annette want to slap it and then run away. 'Let me see him,' she said. 'I want to see him.'

'Suit yourself,' the woman said and left Annette at the door.

A minute later Isaiah appeared, wearing just his pants. 'What you doing here?' he hissed when he saw her.

Annette had so many questions, she didn't know where to start. 'Who is that answered the door?'

'Never mind who it is, what you doing here?'

'Tell her, Isaiah,' said the woman from across the room. She had lit a cigarette and the smoke swirled about her head in the shadowy room like a swarm of bees.

'You shut up and you,' he looked at Annette, 'get out of here.'

'I'm his wife. Ain't I, Isaiah?'

Isaiah turned to her and then quickly back to Annette; he looked trapped and mean.

'Your wife, Isaiah? That your wife?'

'Who gave you this address?' he asked.

'Why does that matter? You're a drug dealer and . . .' She looked over at the woman; the smoke was devouring her as she stood there, still wearing that knowing look. 'And you're married.'

Isaiah reached out and slapped her hard on the face. He turned round to his wife, then back to Annette, looking remorseful, as if he realized that he'd hit the wrong woman. 'You shouldn'ta come here.'

Annette turned and ran out of the building.

Things went pretty much downhill from then on for Annette. Selma liked to think that if her mother hadn't met Isaiah and fallen in love with him, she might not have become the person she became – angry, unfeeling . . . addicted. Selma often thought that it was her mother's pride that had been wounded more than her heart; she just couldn't stand to be made a fool of, to feel stupid and ignorant.

Then again, if Annette hadn't met Isaiah, Selma wouldn't have been born in the first place. Selma figured her mother was three months pregnant when she went to Isaiah's apartment that day; no doubt that made it worse to find out he was a drug dealer and married to boot. Annette moved out of Sadie's place (probably couldn't stand the humiliation of being the last person in that household to know about Isaiah) and found her own place a few blocks away. She worked at the pancake house until she couldn't bear it any more, then waited at home for the baby to come, seeing no one, doing nothing. Annette dragged herself to Metropolitan Hospital just two hours before Selma was born. Selma didn't know when her mother started taking heroin, she just always knew her mother used the stuff, the way children just know their parents smoke cigarettes without actually ever thinking about it much.

Annette never went back to work after Selma was born. Checks from the government paid the rent and bought them food. Later, Selma would wonder where her mother got money for drugs, but then, after she herself starting using them, she realized that one positive side effect of being addicted was you became amazingly resourceful. She never thought about it then, but now she figured that Annette traded sex for heroin. Other times she'd use her government checks; when food at home got scarce, she'd lift a few items from the store. Even so, things were always pretty lean a day or so before the bi-weekly government check arrived.

Annette used to say she always loved a baby, but Selma had never seen evidence of this. True, sometimes, in a sober moment, she would call Selma over to her and pet her head or sing her a song in her scratchy voice, a song dimly recalled from her own childhood, but always with a somber look on her face, as if she had woken up from a nightmare only to realize that she was a mother. Mostly she ignored Selma, who as a girl quickly learned how to prepare her own meals and make her own way to school. Selma still wondered who had fed her as an infant; all she could figure was that her mother had somehow managed to put a bottle in her mouth every now and then. Or maybe the drugs hadn't affected her so much back then.

Sometimes her mother reminded her of Marie, the way they both favored dark places, the way men came and went like visiting salesmen.

Whole days would pass and Annette wouldn't say a word, not even in answer to direct questions. Other days she'd talk nonstop, with a nervous edge to her voice, like she was afraid she wouldn't get out the words in time. This was how Selma learned all about the Petersons and Isaiah Reptoe. She'd listen to her mother and hope to hear something that would explain how her mother had become the way she was – empty, distant.

'There's bad men you can spot right away and there's bad men who can deceive you with a smile. They're worse. Isaiah was one of those,' she used to say. 'A wolf in sheep's clothing.'

As Selma got older, these conversations used to bother her. 'You talking about my daddy,' she'd say.

Usually this made Annette laugh, a deep, cigarette-stained laugh that made Selma want to run from the room. 'Your daddy, right. Sometimes I forget that.' Then she'd laugh until the laugh turned into a cough and the cough into a wheeze.

It wasn't long before Selma was more at home on the streets than in their apartment. If inside her home all was lonely and depressing, outside it was crowded and lively all through the night. She recognized the dealers but they became invisible to her; she hung out with her friends from school, drinking sodas and eating candy and flirting with the boys they knew.

Once, shortly after Selma joined the literacy program, Lizzie told her that many new students began writing by describing their own lives, starting with childhood. I didn't have a childhood, Selma had said. She'd taken some small, mean pleasure in the way Lizzie had quickly changed the subject. She could tell right away her tutor wasn't prepared to follow up on that.

But it was true enough: she'd been a child, but she'd had no childhood to speak of, not if childhood meant being light-hearted and looked after and loved.

Perhaps if she'd never known what she'd been missing all those years, it might not have stung so bad, even now. But each summer for about six years, starting when she was eight or nine, Selma's mother put her on a bus for Georgia, where she visited her grandmother in a tiny town north of Atlanta called Winfield. During these summers she glimpsed a different life, no lusher than the one she was living, it was true – poverty was different in a small town, but it was still nasty – but at least it offered a child a true childhood.

Lilian Richards had eight children of her own, a few of them not much older than Selma, her granddaughter, plus she was always taking in kids from relatives who for one reason or another couldn't keep them. But when Selma stepped off the bus in Atlanta, she always felt as if her arrival those July mornings, and only her arrival, made Lilian's life worth living. That was Lilian's special gift, Selma always thought, to make each of her many children feel particular and specific.

Lilian was on the short side, and bone thin. Her husband had died years ago and she had survived by taking in laundry and putting her older children to work after school as soon as they were able to lift

71

an iron or push a mower. But you'd think she had nothing to do all year, the way she'd greet Selma and make a big fuss over her. Give me some sugar, she'd say at least half a dozen times a day, summoning Selma from whatever she was doing to plant a kiss on her creased, dark cheek.

The other kids held Selma in awe, since she'd arrived from New York City, a place of mythical evil to the people of Winfield, Georgia. Then, too, Selma had once overheard several of them discussing her mother; the fact that Selma was the daughter of a drug addict only enhanced her standing among her aunts and uncles and cousins. At church on Sundays, the other kids giggled at her ignorance of scripture and ritual, but the fact that Selma never went to church up north reinforced New York's reputation as a modern-day Sodom, and Selma's reputation, even at eight, as a tough survivor.

They were far from idyllic, those summers in Winfield, but they always seemed magical to Selma. She had to start work the day she arrived, ironing or watching the younger kids or cleaning some white person's house. She shared her room with several other kids, shared her bed, too, if the small, ramshackle house was full up, as it often was. To Selma, who at eight was already used to spending long days and nights by herself, it was heaven. And when Lilian turned her glance on her and made her feel particular and specific, Selma felt the possibility of life, the potential. At the bus stop at the end of the summer, Lilian would hug her to her, demand some sugar, and always whisper the same thing: Remember this summer, Selma. Remember your family down here. She never bothered sending greetings to Annette, and she knew better than to promise a return visit the next year. All she asked was that Selma remember.

Those summers had come to an end when Selma was fourteen. In June, she had taken advantage of one of Annette's more lucid moments to ask if she'd be visiting Georgia that summer. She'd grown accustomed to the visits, looked forward to them – lived for them. Not this year, her mother had said with a bitter chuckle. Why not? Selma had asked, feeling a sense of foreboding. You're grandma's dead, Annette had said, then turned away from Selma on some pretext or other. Selma felt the world contract to the confines of her own adolescent body. Dead? Her heart, Annette said flatly. Last month. Selma didn't ask why she hadn't been told right away. Her mother had probably forgotten, like she forgot everything else. All year long, Selma carried with her a vision of that little town completely populated by people she knew, people who knew her. It seemed the flip side of the place she lived in the rest of the year, a place of strangers, and Annette. Now that place was gone, for Selma had no illusion that Winfield would ever be the same without

Lilian at its center. And she knew she'd never visit there again.

But her summers in Winfield stayed with her, no matter how bad things got. They were always there to remind her that there was a flip side to things.

On the stoop one day her friend Esther grabbed her arm and squeezed it. 'Oooh, look at that. Now that's sharp.'

'He's old,' is what Selma said, because that's all she saw, a man at least forty years old.

'He's sharp, though. Name's Isaiah Reptoe.'

Selma looked at him as he passed, feeling her body go stiff with nerves. She half expected him to stop and talk with her, and when he just walked on by with this confident strut he used, she felt horribly let down. Now she had a face to connect with all the stories. Her father's face.

Selma began to follow him whenever she could. Usually he'd end up leaving in his car, so she never got to watch him for more than a few blocks. But it gave her a thrill to be near him. She liked the way people greeted him like a hero or something. 'Hey, Isaiah, what's happening?' they'd shout, and he'd just motion with one of his hands, too cool to shout back or wave. After a few weeks she almost felt she knew him. She felt ready to speak to him. She hadn't intended to tell him who she was, only to speak to him and hear his voice, but when she found herself standing next to him in a bodega on Lenox Avenue, she couldn't help herself.

'Why you staring, girl?' he asked, not angry, just curious, which encouraged Selma.

'Nothing,' she said, but she couldn't stop grinning.

'You calling me nothing?' He threw her a wide grin.

Selma shook her head. He was only joking, but still it made her nervous.

'Then what you staring at?'

After a few moments she just said it. 'I'm Selma Richards.' When this didn't have any effect on him she said, 'My mother's Annette Richards.'

Even then it took him a minute to realize why she was telling him this. Selma flushed with anticipation. But he just stared down at her, studying her. She could feel his hot gaze on her face, on each feature. First the grin went. Then suddenly all the good looks drained from his face. Selma felt herself sink, as if his eyes were driving her down into the floor. He stared, growing uglier each second, his face toughening and puckering. Finally he took the pack of cigarettes he'd bought and stormed out of the store. Selma stood there for a few more moments, too hurt and confused to run. Her mother's stories streamed through her head in fast motion, all the parts about Isaiah blurring in a fast haze until they came to a wrenching halt right there in the store. If the man behind the counter hadn't asked her what she wanted she might have gone on standing there. 'Nothing,' she managed to answer, then hurried back to the street.

Selma saw Isaiah Reptoe every once in a while, but she ducked round a corner or turned away before she could notice if he did the same. She wished, now, that she'd never seen him. He had been a glamorous figure in her mind, despite her mother's criticisms of him, a man who inspired respect, even awe, a man who was loved but wouldn't be pinned down. Now he was just a man who wouldn't recognize her, a father who wouldn't acknowledge his own daughter. That he had recognized at once whose daughter she was, Selma never doubted. She'd seen it in his eyes – in his horror.

Selma had never been much for school, but things really started going to pieces after that incident with Isaiah. In elementary school she'd been attentive and she'd behaved, but she never seemed able to catch on. Especially with reading. When called on to read out loud, she often couldn't make out a word, even when it looked familiar. Spell it out, the teacher would say, her obvious impatience only making it harder for Selma to see straight. U-R-N Selma would answer. Are you sure? the teacher would ask. Selma looked again and nodded. The teacher frowned. Well, it's R-U-N. Run. Say it. Selma dutifully repeated: R-U-N. Run. Why hadn't she seen that in the first place?

The reading just got away from her. She slipped behind with the short words in the early grades and then got buried with the longer words later on. The teachers still let her advance to the next grade, although her report cards were dismal to say the least and always had long comments that Selma couldn't make out and her mother didn't bother with; she signed the cards without looking at them.

After a while there hardly seemed any point to going to school. Every class depended on reading, and Selma just couldn't keep up. It felt like everyone around her knew a secret language except her. It made her head ache to look at a page of words, and the longer she looked, the harder she tried, the worse it felt. Her teachers didn't seem to care if she was there or not; they always got peevish when they realized that she couldn't read, and the other children began to make fun. Annette didn't notice where she went. She was usually just waking up on those increasingly rare days when Selma came home after a full day at school.

Maybe if she could have read better, she'd have stayed in school. Selma still wondered about this, but she always had to think that Isaiah Reptoe had something to do with it. As Annette slipped deeper and deeper into her private drug-clouded world, Selma felt adrift, anchorless; she had no refuge, since her home was a mess and so was her mother. The thought of her father had always bolstered her. She believed that if things got really bad she could always look for him, depend on him. The worse her mother got, the more vivid her image of her father became, a solid, serious man with his life together except for missing his lost daughter. She had never doubted that he missed her. She would picture their reunion over and over, his outstretched arms, the famous smile on his face, tears in his eyes.

When she was forced to give up that dream, she had nothing else to hold on to. Nothing at school, nothing at home, no summers in Georgia to look forward to. Selma's life had never been easy, but things really started to go bad for her that year.

She was fifteen.

Selma knelt down next to Raymond. 'Give me some sugar,' she said. He dutifully planted a warm kiss on her cheek, then teetered off into the day care center. Small as he was, he walked with a kind of grown-up determination, swinging his arms, his head thrust forward, as if fighting invisible forces on all sides trying to knock him over. It made her ache to watch him walk away from her. Another lost kid, she thought, watched after by the wrong person. Like my Isaiah. Like I was. Then she had to laugh: like rich little Dana, too.

Chapter 9

Marie returned from the hospital looking tired and thin, and took even less interest in her kids than she had before her miscarriage. But Selma felt that the time had come to start things moving on the Isaiah front, even if she continued to tend to Raymond more than she cared to. The bed is as smooth as it's going to get, she thought. It's ready for Isaiah.

The problem was figuring out how to start. Sometimes it rankled her that she couldn't just retrieve Isaiah from the Lewins. Just walk into their big building, past the uniformed doorman, up the elevator to their apartment, ring the doorbell, and tell whoever answered that she'd come for her boy, who she'd been too drugged up and just plain stupid to hang on to over two years earlier. But Selma knew things didn't work that way. There were rules and regulations, laws, and she'd have to follow all of them if she was going to get Isaiah back and keep him.

She needed a lawyer. Each week for a year she'd managed to put away fifty dollars, which left her two thousand five hundred dollars in a savings account. This seemed like more than enough to hire a lawyer to fill out the necessary forms. When Selma imagined what getting Isaiah back would involve, she usually imagined a whole stack of forms, none of which she could read, let alone fill out on her own. Occasionally she had a dream in which Isaiah was floundering in a great swirl of papers, but when she went to save him, the papers got in her way, blinding her, choking her. Whatever money she had left over after paying the lawyer she would use to help her and Isaiah get settled in a new apartment. No way was she bringing her boy to Marie's.

She thought about asking Mrs Fredricks to recommend a lawyer. She certainly didn't expect Mrs Fredricks herself to help her. She could tell just looking at her (and her big apartment) that she didn't get herself involved in low-rent things like adoption and custody. But Mrs Fredricks was always so hassled when Selma saw her, either running around trying to get out of the house or else dead on her feet returning to it, always late, looking like one unexpected question would blow her to pieces. And Mr Fredricks was hardly there at all. Selma also didn't want to have to explain to the Fredricks what she needed a lawyer for. They seemed like people who didn't want complications in their life, like they couldn't *handle* complications, and Selma couldn't risk losing her job; she could fill out forms until her hand fell off, no one was going to give her Isaiah unless she had a job.

Pushing Dana down Park Avenue, enjoying the spring warmth which always felt like you were feeling it for the first time – somehow you just never remembered it – Selma would look down the valley of tall buildings, particularly south of Fifty-ninth Street where the offices began, and just know they were stuffed with lawyers who could help her. She had always figured that most of the rich people in the world were lawyers, and in New York these days there were certainly a lot of rich people. So she'd walk little Dana up and down Park Avenue, gazing at the offices in the distance, at the thousands of tiny windows behind which sat thousands of lawyers, and wonder how in the world she was going to find herself one.

Margaret felt a bit guilty as she inserted the cassette of *The Wizard of Oz* into the VCR, but she didn't know what else to do. Charles had phoned to say he'd be late and Liv had the evening off and Hannah was doing homework and Isaiah was just too restless to play by himself while she got dinner ready. So Margaret had resorted to a video.

It did the trick. It always did. 'I'm going to plug him in,' Charles would say when Isaiah was agitated or fidgety. The TV always had a tranquilizing effect on Isaiah, who could watch the same video over and over, mouth agape, rapt.

'Remember when we said we were going to get rid of the TV when Hannah was born?' Margaret asked Charles one night that spring. Charles hated this kind of self-recrimination and just shrugged.

She fast-forwarded to where the film was in color, the better to grab Isaiah's interest and get dinner rolling. He smiled and his round face grew even rounder when the Munchkins appeared. She saw him heave a sigh of contentment from his position on the living room floor and felt a parallel sigh of guilt rise up inside her. After a moment she left him for the kitchen.

Sometimes the obvious things take the longest to figure out. Early in May, at the beginning of a long, warm evening, Selma walked into her tutoring session and realized right away that Lizzie Kaplan could find her a lawyer. It just hit her that day, after months of worrying, when she saw her tutor at their usual table, looking over a newspaper. Lizzie probably knew a dozen lawyers.

'We haven't written in a few days,' Lizzie said after Selma had sat down and retrieved her things from her book bag. 'Why don't we start by writing tonight.'

'Why is it that when you tell me to write I never know what to write about?'

'It happens to all writers.'

'Yeah?' Selma had always figured most people, people who could read, had no trouble finding things to write about.

'You could continue the piece you've been working on.'

Selma opened her notebook to the page with her piece about Isaiah. She looked at it, half a page of her handwriting, messy and smudged. It had taken her a month to write this much, and even so, Lizzie had to help her fill in most of the words. But still, it was her handwriting, her words.

'Pretty impressive, huh?' Lizzie remarked as Selma stared at her own writing. Selma looked across the table at her and smiled. 'I like seeing Isaiah's name written out in my own handwriting. Makes it feel more like he's mine.' At night she sometimes took out her notebook and copied Isaiah's name down on a blank sheet of paper. His name was full of loops and curves, not like hers, which after the complicated 'S' was just a few squat letters bunched together around the 'l'. After a while writing his name was like drawing, and her hand limbered up the way it never did when she was writing with Lizzie. She'd stare at the page full of Isaiahs with the stupidest sense of wellbeing, then pull out the page from her notebook and save it in her top drawer.

'I don't have nothing more to add to it,' Selma said.

'Then maybe we should review what you've already written.'

Selma had been dreading this. You'd figure it would be easy to read what you yourself had written, but Selma had almost as much trouble with her own words as with the books Lizzie gave her. She looked down at the page with a sinking feeling. 'Lizzie, why don't you read it for me? Then I'll know where to start.'

Lizzie looked uncomfortable with this plan, but agreed. 'Only in the interests of getting you writing, okay?' She pulled the notebook closer and began to read. 'My son Isaiah is over two years old. I love him very much even though I cannot be with him yet. Whenever I see him I know he will be back with me and my life will start again.' Lizzie smiled when she finished. 'Do you know what you want to write now?'

Selma couldn't say anything for a moment. She had lived with her dream for so long without sharing it with anyone, sometimes it seemed impossible, like she was one of those crazy people on the sidewalks raving at imaginary enemies. But hearing Lizzie read, she knew she wasn't crazy, she saw that she really could change her life and Isaiah's, make up for past mistakes and start over again. She shook her head. 'I said everything.'

'Are you sure? You never wrote about how you gave Isaiah up. Or about how you're going to get him back.'

Selma contemplated this for a while. 'You want me to write about how I gave him up?'

'I want you to write about what you want to write about.'

Lizzie left her alone to write. Selma smoothed the piece of paper, then picked up her pencil and placed it on the paper, one line below where she'd left off. But the moment the pencil touched the page she realized she didn't know where to begin. How do you begin writing about something like giving away your own child? Should she try to excuse herself by writing about the drugs and how they poisoned her mind and poisoned Isaiah too? But then how do you excuse the drugs? Should she talk about being sixteen and already a user, what that felt like? About ten years of men, men dimly remembered and men immediately forgotten, about thinking at least you can't get pregnant, girl, thank God for that and then . . . Isaiah. Maybe she should begin with her mother and Isaiah Reptoe. But that would take pages, and pages would take her years to write. And in the end, could you ever find enough excuses for giving away your own baby? Selma doubted it. She had never forgiven herself and didn't expect anyone else to, either. All she could do now was try to undo what she had done, to make Isaiah's life as good as it could be, so maybe one day he'd forgive her even if she couldn't.

No, best to start with the birth itself and forget trying to find reasons and excuses that didn't add up to anything anyway. Selma began to write her son's name and realized her hand had clamped up on the pencil so hard her fingers were aching. So she relaxed for a minute before writing. Ten minutes later she'd finished the first sentence. She went to the coffee table to get herself a cup, then returned and looked over what she'd written. 'Isaiah was b——— a dug a———'

It wasn't a pretty sight, her scrawl, but it was the truth and it was where the story should begin; she felt confident about this now. No sense in looking further back, no sense in making excuses. This is where the story began.

When Lizzie returned she asked Selma to share what she'd written. Selma didn't have to look at the page but she did anyway. 'Isaiah was born a drug addict,' she said, then looked across at Lizzie. This time, Selma thought, she better not say 'Good!' the way she always does after I read.

Actually she said nothing, which put Selma off. 'Well?' she asked. 'What do you think?'

'I think you have a lot to write about.'

'True enough.'

Lizzie was silent a second time. Selma was beginning to think her writing had upset Lizzie. It gave her a thrill to think that one sentence could move a person, even a person like Lizzie who read thousands of sentences every day.

'You want to correct my spelling?'

Selma read from her new book for a while, silently, and then talked it over – shared – with Lizzie. Afterwards, she brought up the lawyer.

'Lizzie, you know any lawyers?' They were packing up their books and things, getting ready to leave.

'Yeah, I know lawyers.' She sounded doubtful, like she didn't know whether to admit it or not.

'I need a lawyer to get Isaiah back. To fill in the forms and whatnot and stuff.'

'Let me think about it. Can I give you a name next time? Can you wait a couple of days?'

'I can wait,' Selma said, thinking she would rather get the name right away so she could call him up tomorrow and get things started. 'But you know a lawyer for me, right?'

Again Lizzie seemed uncomfortable. She nodded. 'I'll get you a name. Have you looked into this, this process, Selma?'

'What process?'

'Of getting custody. Have you looked into it?'

Selma shrugged. 'That's why I need a lawyer.'

'Yes,' Lizzie said hesitantly. 'But even so, it may not be easy. Have you thought about that?'

'Yes, I have.'

'Well, good, because if things don't work out, you could be in for a really terrible fall.'

'I've thought about that,' Selma lied. 'I'm prepared.'

They left the church and said goodbye on the corner, heading for separate subways. Selma tried to think about what Lizzie had said, but her spirits were too high to dwell on anything negative. By Thursday she'd have a lawyer. It was foolish, she knew, but she already felt as if someone else was on her side. A lawyer. Her lawyer. How could she lose with a lawyer? Just by asking Lizzie, she had started things rolling. Now it was only a matter of time – what had Lizzie said? a *process* – before she had Isaiah back.

Chapter 10

Charles had to work late again.

Margaret found that by six o'clock she was already bored and restless. She wasn't used to not having Charles around in the evenings; even in the past, when he didn't make it home by six, the prospect of his imminent arrival gave shape to her evenings. Without that prospect, Margaret felt unequal to the evening, even if it included only microwaving dinner for her and the kids. So she decided to take a walk in Riverside Park.

Isaiah's eyes widened at the idea, but Hannah was unenthusiastic and begged off.

'I wish you'd come, honey,' Margaret said, and she meant it. But Hannah was firm.

The evening was warm and breezy, and the entire West Side, it seemed, had taken to the streets. Only a month earlier they'd huddled in steam heating, and in a few weeks they'd nestle in air conditioning, but for the moment nature was pacific, even in New York, and people thronged the streets in grateful celebration.

Isaiah trotted along next to Margaret, reaching up to hold her hand. He had brought along his Slimer gun, and occasionally fired it at something or someone, narrowing his eyes and making a sputtering sound. 'Yeah,' he'd say when the target was destroyed. 'Take that.'

Margaret hated the Slimer gun, and had almost refused to allow him to bring it. She and Charles had agreed long ago that they wouldn't let their children play with toy guns, but Hannah hadn't shown any interest in weapons anyway, and by the time Isaiah became fixated on Ghostbusters they had lost their resolve, telling themselves that these silly green plastic concoctions weren't really guns anyway. But clearly Isaiah thought the Slimer was lethal, and Margaret couldn't help thinking that Isaiah's walking around firing his Slimer left and right somehow reflected badly on her, particularly here on the West Side, where people still held convictions about things like playing with toy guns.

They reached the park as the sun began to sink into New Jersey with a syrupy effusion of orange. 'Isn't it beautiful, Isaiah,' she said.

He dutifully nodded but without looking up at the sky across the Hudson; he was intently stalking a particularly devious ectoplasm.

They passed through the tunnel under the West Side Highway and then walked along the path by the river. When Isaiah saw the playground twenty yards ahead, he squirmed out of Margaret's hand and ran towards it.

Margaret found a seat on a bench with a view of both Isaiah and the sunset. Naturally he'd headed right for the treacherous jungle gym. He'd managed to pull himself nearly to the top of it, the Slimer gun strapped around his shoulder. Margaret's heart lurched each time he let go of one bar to grab another. Physically he was a little smaller than the other kids and definitely more active. But his motor skills seemed about average, which comforted her in a big way, since when they'd brought him home over two years ago, she and Charles had been warned to look out for developmental problems stemming from his ghastly birth. Still, it took all her willpower to keep from running over and hovering beneath him, arms outstretched to catch him.

She tried concentrating on the sunset. The sun was exploding in deep scarlets and crimsons now, but Margaret found it difficult to watch the display, which seemed to demand more appreciation, more gratitude, than she could muster. She wished Hannah had come to distract her from the frightening visions of Isaiah plunging onto the concrete and the sun plunging into darkness. But Hannah was retreating from her. All twelve-year-olds do this, she reminded herself – at twelve she herself had been mortified even to be seen in public with her parents. But she couldn't help thinking that Hannah was retreating from the very life they led, from the very *idea* of them. She spoke so wistfully these days about her friends' apartments on the East Side, using words like 'duplex' and 'foyer' with chilling fluency. She spent at least half her weekends visiting country houses, and Margaret still couldn't get used to hearing Hannah ask if she could spend the weekend with so-and-so 'in the Hamptons'. A few weeks ago Hannah had spotted a grey hair on Margaret and asked her when she was going to start dying it, as if letting her hair turn grey naturally wasn't even a consideration. Mostly what bothered her was Hannah's uneasiness about Isaiah. Margaret noticed that she tended to walk a few yards ahead of them when they were out as a family, something a lot of twelve-year-olds do, true, but with Hannah the rejection felt more profound, more total.

'Isn't it magnificent?'

Margaret looked at the woman next to her. She recognized her from the neighborhood, and smiled. It took her a few seconds to realize that she meant the sunset. 'Yes,' she agreed. 'Spectacular.'

'Lovely.'

Margaret briefly considered continuing the exchange of adjectives. Instead she turned back to focus on her son risking his life on the jungle gym.

'Is that your daughter playing with mine on the seesaw?' Margaret actually located the children on the seesaw before shaking her head. 'Mine's on the jungle gym.'

The woman dutifully looked at the jungle gym. She was the type of young, fashionable, affluent person buying up all the big old apartments on the West Side, no doubt delighting in telling friends on the East Side how much she preferred the West Side, although, thanks to people like her, there really was no longer much difference, as far as Margaret could tell, between the two neighborhoods. Margaret and Charles had lived on the West Side for fifteen years and couldn't help resenting those who were now moving in, buying apartments that had long since become unaffordable for them. True, their own apartment had gone co-op while they lived in it, enabling them to purchase it for less than half its real value, so they really shouldn't complain, but the sight of all those kitchen-and-bath contractors' vans doubleparked outside all the pre-war buildings along West End and Riverside was aggravating. There was simply no getting used to it.

'On the jungle gym,' the woman repeated, squinting unnecessarily in its direction. 'Oh, a boy!' she said brightly.

You mean a *black* boy, Margaret was tempted to correct her. Instinctively she ran through the questions she knew the woman was dying to ask: Is your husband black? Is the boy adopted? What's it like, having a child who looks so unlike you? A sudden surge of anger caused her to take a deep, involuntary gulp of air. But the anger wasn't directed at the woman but at herself. 'His name is Isaiah.'

'Mine's Emma, she's almost three.' A moment later the woman started to laugh. 'I like to think I'm a feminist, and here I'm introducing myself through my child, as if I had no separate identity. I'm Charlotte Mellor.'

'Margaret Lewin.'

'What is it about being in a playground that makes us regress? Another five minutes of that and we'd be trading brownie recipes.'

'You have a good one?'

'With crème fraîche instead of milk. Unbelievable.'

Margaret smiled.

'We're new here. My husband was transferred from Los Angeles a month ago. We bought a place on Riverside and Eighty-Fourth.'

'Welcome to the neighborhood, then. How do you like it?'

'I've never lived in an apartment before. I miss my garden and the privacy.'

'At least you have Riverside Park.'

Charlotte nodded. 'I miss my family and friends,' she said a few moments later.

Surprised by the emotion in the woman's voice, Margaret searched for something comforting to say. 'Sometimes the idea of uprooting myself and my family and moving across the country sounds very appealing.'

'I was thrilled by the idea. The reality is harder, though. And Rob, my husband, is working much longer hours here than in LA. He's an attorney. Somehow I don't think people work quite so hard on the West Coast as they do here.'

A little girl came running over to them and buried herself in Charlotte's lap. 'Emma, say hello to Mrs Lewin.'

'Oh, please. Margaret.'

'Say hello to Margaret.'

'Hello, Margaret,' the girl said shyly, looking up from her mother's lap. 'Is she your friend, Mommy?'

Charlotte looked a bit startled but turned to Margaret and said, 'God I hope so.'

When Hannah was a baby, Margaret used to read her stories every night until she fell asleep. She had amassed a considerable library of children's books, but when Hannah outgrew them Margaret donated them to a hospital, believing that Hannah would be their last child. When Isaiah came along she purchased many of the same books she'd read to Hannah, plus the Sendaks and Seusses that hadn't been available then. But she also began to make up stories for him, or, more commonly, to summarize the plots of novels and movies she had recently read or seen herself.

It had started a year ago. They were renting a house on Cape Cod for two weeks in August, and she had forgotten to take Isaiah's books out of the car the night they arrived. It was raining, so she decided to improvise by inventing a story. But her imagination failed her; she couldn't even remember any of her old standbys, the ones Hannah had liked to hear over and over. Desperate not to let Isaiah down, and feeling rather foolish being mute in front of him, she began to tell him the story of *Gone With the Wind*. It wasn't such an unlikely choice, really. She couldn't recall a more recent film, since they rarely went to the movies any more, not since Isaiah; *Gone With the Wind* simply jumped to mind as she flailed about for a story.

'There was this beautiful lady, Isaiah, named Scarlet. Princess Scarlet. She lived in a castle.' Isaiah had been fixated on castles ever since they'd walked by the Belvedere Castle in Central Park a few weeks back and she'd explained that castles were houses for princes and princesses. 'Scarlet loved a man, a prince, named Ashley. But he was already in love with another woman. Isn't that sad, Isaiah?'

Her son nodded gravely.

'Princess Scarlet lived in a huge white palace. It had white columns in front and peacocks on the lawn. Do you know what a peacock is, Isaiah?'

He shook his head.

'They're birds with huge tails. When they want to show off, they lift up their tails so they look like beautiful rainbows.'

'Ooooh,' he purred.

'Then there was Rhett Butler. He was the handsomest man in the kingdom, almost as handsome as you.' She smiled at Isaiah and he smiled back. 'He was also very gallant and brave. He went to war and returned a hero. He was in love with the beautiful Princess Scarlet, and they got married. But Scarlet was still in love . . .'

Isaiah had closed his eyes.

'. . . in love with Ashley. Don't ask me why, don't ask me why she didn't love Rhett. No one understands. No one.'

She kissed Isaiah gently and pulled the covers up to his chin.

'You'll never believe what I just did,' she told Charles after leaving Isaiah. 'I just told Isaiah the story of *Gone With the Wind*.'

'You did?'

'Well, part of it.'

'I hope you left out the part about Mammie and Prissy. I don't think he'd ever forgive you for that.'

Margaret read several books during those vacation weeks, and she began to summarize them for Isaiah. He seemed to prefer this to actual books, since he was usually too tired to look at the pictures anyway. He'd lie back with a dreamy half-smile on his face as Margaret whispered highly-edited versions of *The Great Gatsby* ('There was this very wealthy man who lived in a castle by the sea . . .'), or watered-down accounts of the most recent mystery she had read, in which murder was replaced, often with considerable difficulty, with the theft of something like a bicycle.

Tonight, though, after returning from Riverside Park and throwing together a pasta-and-salad dinner, Margaret found herself unable to think of a story for Isaiah, not even a plot summary. 'I'll get a book,' she told him, getting up from his bed.

'New story,' he pleaded, which was how he referred to the stories Margaret 'made up'.

Someday he'll realize that I'm not very imaginative at all, she thought, sitting down again. Will it be traumatic the first time he reads *Anna Karenina* and discovers that Tolstoy, not his mother, was its author? Will he think me a fraud? Will he remember at all? Probably not, she reassured herself, though the thought that Isaiah wouldn't remember these wonderful bedtime hours was hardly comforting.

Margaret hadn't done much reading lately. A chill had descended on her relationship with Charles, a chill fanned by his frequent absences at night, and she found herself too restless for books. It was much easier to watch the television; you could do that and think about a thousand other things at the same time, or just let yourself become anesthetized. So nothing came to mind that evening when Isaiah asked for a made-up story. She smiled at him, he smiled back. Sometimes it simply astounded her how handsome he was becoming. Isaiah had a full, round face with a small nose and large, perfectly symmetrical lips. His barber, without instructions, clipped his hair into a kind of rectangular helmet that accentuated his sharp features. The result was that Isaiah seemed to jump out from whatever background he was in. He seemed much more vivid than other children, more of a contrast to the world he lived in. Margaret loved this about him, the way he popped out of his environment as if he'd been painted into it at a later date with fresher colors. She'd once tried to describe this feeling to Charles, but he had said that she saw him this way only because she loved him so much. He said this was the way all mothers felt about their children. I suppose you're right, Margaret had said, but she hadn't really agreed. There was something about Isaiah that stood out, and she felt certain that she wasn't the only one to notice it.

'I know,' she said. 'I'll tell you about the lady and the tiger. Okay?'

'Lady tiger,' Isaiah repeated.

Margaret didn't know how she'd come up with this story, nor was she sure how it went. One advantage of making up stories for Isaiah was that he invariably fell asleep before they ended. Thus she was able to tell him the most tragic stories – she'd told him *Doctor Zhivago* for example – and never have to worry about upsetting him with the unhappy ending. This also meant that she didn't have to be too clear on plots. 'Once there was a prince and a princess and they were deeply in love.'

'In a castle?'

'Yes, Isaiah, they lived in a beautiful castle. They had a huge room full of nothing but toys, another room with ice cream and candy, and a whole other castle just for their pets.'

Isaiah glowed, thinking about this place. 'Tiger?' he asked.

'No, the tiger wasn't their pet. But they had dogs and cats and birds.'

'Hamsters?' His voice was limp with sleepiness, which was just as well, because Margaret couldn't remember how the story continued.

'And hamsters. Seven of them. One for each day of the week. One day the king became angry with the prince. The prince had misbehaved very badly.' Margaret paused here. What could the prince have done to justify being sent into an arena to face a tiger? She noted with relief that Isaiah's eyes had closed. 'So the king decided to punish the prince.'

Isaiah's eyes opened. 'Why?'

Inspiration rescued her. 'He didn't do his homework, and he didn't listen when the king spoke.' This hardly justified the tiger, so she quickly added, 'And he didn't take his vitamins and he forgot to feed his hamsters.'

Isaiah let his head roll over so that he briefly faced his hamster cage. Then his eyes closed.

'So the king devised a punishment. The prince would have to go into the country's huge stadium and there would be two large doors. Behind one of the doors was a beautiful lady. Not his princess, mind you. Another beautiful lady. Behind the other door was a mean tiger. If he picked the right door he would spend the rest of his life with the beautiful lady. If he picked the other door . . .' She could tell by his breathing that Isaiah was asleep now, so she didn't have to worry about upsetting him. 'If he picked the other door he'd be devoured by the tiger. On the day of the punishment, the princess signalled to the prince to pick the door on the right. She must have found out which door concealed the tiger. The prince, however, didn't know whether to trust her or not. What if she was jealous of the other beautiful lady and so had pointed to the tiger? What if she'd rather see her prince dead than with another woman? How could the prince be sure?'

Margaret ran her hand over Isaiah's dense crop of hair. She loved the way it felt, soft yet defined, protective. She kissed him on his forehead, inhaling deeply so she'd have the scent of him to take away with her. 'Sleep tight, Isaiah.'

Hannah was talking on the telephone in the kitchen, in the hushed voice she used lately with her friends when her parents were around. Margaret would have liked some company but had to settle for the television. She walked to her bedroom and turned it on. Channel 3 automatically appeared on the screen. Channel 3 never showed anything of interest to Margaret, which was unfortunate, since lately she had taken to turning on the set without changing the station. Tonight there was a panel discussion taking place, Margaret didn't know the topic. All she noticed, once she'd settled onto the bed, was how confident the people looked sitting round the table, how pleased they seemed to be there. She checked the bedside clock: nine thirty.

Of course the princess pointed to the door with the tiger, Margaret thought, surprising herself, for the outcome of the story had always, in the past, seemed deliciously uncertain. Of course she'd pointed to the door with the tiger.

Chapter 11

Selma's appointment with Arthur Golderson was at six o'clock. He wasn't eager to meet her at this hour, but she had explained to him that she couldn't get away from her job before five thirty, and even then she might have trouble if Mrs Fredricks didn't get home on time.

Selma didn't like the way Arthur Golderson sounded on the phone. His voice was pinched, like he was rushed or annoyed or both. Like he wasn't eager to take her on. When she told him who she was he didn't even recognize the name. She mentioned Lizzie Kaplan and he knew *her* right away, but it still took him a while to figure out who Selma was and why she was calling. 'A custody case, am I right?' he'd said after a long silence. 'That's not exactly my specialty, but, uh, if you want to come in and talk about it, sure.' Don't do me any favors, Selma wanted to say. She almost mentioned the $2,500 she had in the bank but then thought, hell, *I'm* hiring *him*. Selma wasn't used to hiring people.

On the Thursday of the appointment, Mrs Fredricks was even later than usual. Selma didn't arrive at Arthur Golderson's office, on the twentieth floor of a medium-sized Madison Avenue building, until after six thirty. She recognized the name Golderson on the glass door to the reception area. It was followed by two other names she couldn't read. There was no one at the receptionist's desk behind the glass doors, and when she tried to open one of them she found that it was locked. Selma knocked on the door but could tell that no one past the reception area would hear her. Most likely they'd all gone home. Selma knocked again anyway, thinking: I work for one lawyer who can't pull herself away from the office; now I'm trying to hire a lawyer who won't *stay* in his.

She was getting ready to turn round and leave when the door inside the reception area opened. A tall man in a suit carrying an enormous briefcase appeared. He crossed to the outside doors and spotted Selma. 'Selma Richards?' he said through the glass. He sounded like he was under water. She nodded. She could see his face fall a little; he must have been looking forward to getting out of there. 'I'd given up on you.' He opened a glass door and checked his watch. 'I was on my way home . . .'

Selma didn't know what to say to this. 'Mrs Fredricks was late. I couldn't leave Dana by herself.'

Arthur Golderson just looked at her.

'Dana's only one year old.'

He nodded, still looking confused. 'Maybe we can reschedule.'

'Won't be a better time.'

He checked his watch again. Arthur Golderson wasn't bad looking, Selma noticed, but he looked frazzled, too, as if he'd just been spun round on a Ferris wheel or something. His hair was a pile of black ringlets, his nose was kind of sharp, and he wore round, very serious black glasses. Selma wished he'd smile, just once; she felt sure he'd look less frazzled then, handsomer, too.

'It's after six thirty, Selma . . .'

'I know that,' Selma answered sharply, surprising herself. 'Lizzie Kaplan said you was the best in town, but if you don't have time for me, that's fine. I'll ask her for the second best in town.'

'Selma, one thing you should know right up front about the client-attorney relationship.'

'What's that?'

'It requires absolute trust and honesty. Now, I would bet a year's salary Lizzie did not tell you I was the best lawyer in town.'

Selma didn't know what he was getting at so she just stood there.

'I'm not the best lawyer in town by a long shot, and Lizzie knows that.' Arthur actually looked kind of downcast saying this.

'She said you could help me.'

He smiled. 'Now that's more like it. Come on in.' Arthur led Selma along a long corridor lined with offices. They passed a large, glass-walled room full of big, thick books, many of them with identical covers. Desks in the hallway held big typewriters or computers, stacks of papers, empty coffee mugs. The place was eerily quiet, as if it had been abandoned in haste just a moment ago.

He brought her into a large office and motioned for her to sit down. Outside his window Selma could see the Empire State Building and a bunch of other tall buildings she didn't recognize. The sky was turning purple. Arthur sat down behind his desk, opened a drawer, and brought out a pad of yellow lined paper, which he placed in the center of his desk. He took a silver pen from inside his jacket, clicked it, and held it just over the paper. 'Now,' he said, 'why don't you tell me why you're here.'

Maybe it was the sight of that pen, poised over the yellow paper. Or maybe it was just the idea of having to explain to someone, to a stranger, about Isaiah, about the only reason she had been living these last few years. Maybe it was just a case of nerves. Whatever.

Selma didn't know how or where to begin. She opened her mouth but it felt more like she was about to yawn than to speak; her mouth tasted dry and grudging.

'You have a child,' Arthur offered.

Selma nodded. 'Isaiah.'

He wrote the name down on the pad. 'You gave him up for adoption.'

'That's right. About two and a half years ago.'

'And you want him back.'

Selma's voice caught in her throat. She could only nod.

'What was . . .' He looked at the pad. 'What was Isaiah's birthday?'

'How come you want that?'

'It's important to know everything there is to know about the circumstances of the adoption.'

'November, 1989.'

He started to write this down and said, 'November what?'

Selma felt something happening to her. It started in her chest, a tightening, a clamping, and then it rose up into her face like a shiver. It wasn't a shiver, though. It was a sob. For the first time in memory, Selma was crying. Her whole body was getting into the act, heaving and shaking and shuddering. She didn't want to be crying in front of Arthur Golderson, but here she was, bawling her eyes out and feeling almost glad of it. It had been so long since she'd let herself cry, it was practically a relief to find that she still could. She felt the pressure of the last few years leave her body with the tears. It felt like sitting down after a long walk. Like waking up after a long sleep.

When she was finally able to look up, Selma had to laugh. Arthur was holding out a tissue for her, looking like he'd rather be sitting across from someone having a heart attack than from some crazy lady having an attack of the sobs. When she took the tissue he looked so grateful, she had to laugh a second time. Sometimes there wasn't a whole lot of difference between crying and laughing; the same situation could bring out both, the difference depending on how you were feeling to begin with, or on one single detail. Like now: Selma had been so agitated about meeting her lawyer and getting the . . . the *process* underway, she could easily have commenced crying or laughing. She had cried because Arthur Golderson mentioned Isaiah's birthday.

'I don't recall his birthday. I was in such a haze when Isaiah was born, one day just blended with the next. It was like that all the time, even before he came along. I slept during the day, went about my business at night. Except for the times I slept twenty-four hours straight. Or the times I didn't sleep for forty-eight. When Isaiah was born it just mixed things up more. I never could remember what day it was.'

Even upside down she could see him write a question mark next to November. It killed her to see him do this. 'It kills me, not knowing his birthday. Sometimes I wonder how I'm going to find it out, after I get him back. I can't just ask him and I can't ask anyone else. Maybe he'll just—'

'I'll have my secretary check the hospital records,' Arthur interrupted her. 'Where is Isaiah now?'

'He's with a family on the West Side. The Lewins.'

'An address?'

She gave it to him.

'Are you in touch with them, the Lewins?'

'No.'

'Or with your son?'

'I see him from time to time.'

'See him?'

'I see him when he leaves his day care center.'

'Is he aware of this? Are the Lewins?'

Selma shook her head. 'It's just something I do.'

He smiled dimly at her, nervously, like he knew that one wrong word from him and she'd start to cry again. She thought about reassuring him, but decided not to.

'Do you have any reason to believe that Isaiah's not happy with the Lewins?'

'No,' she said. The word swelled in her mouth. 'No,' she repeated. Good thing she hadn't reassured him about not crying anymore.

'Did you bring the papers with you?'

'Papers?'

'You know, adoption papers, birth records, that sort of thing.'

'Don't have any papers.' Selma's heart started racing. 'What papers?'

'There must have been papers.'

'None that I remember.'

'Didn't the agency—'

'Wasn't no agency.'

'How about a lawyer.'

'No lawyer, neither.'

'You're sure of that?'

Something in the way he said this made Selma feel better. 'I'm sure.'

'Maybe you'd better tell me how it went then. From the beginning.'

So Selma told him her sad, sinful story. She started at the same

94

place she had with Lizzie. 'I was a drug addict, and when Isaiah was born he was too.'

Having said this, she felt she'd manage to finish the story. This was the worst part, the worst thing she had done to her little boy. Worse than giving him up.

When she realized she was pregnant she pretty much cut out the drugs. That's why Isaiah wasn't badly damaged, maybe not damaged at all, because she'd managed to stop. But once he was born she had no reason not to smoke crack and she couldn't wait to get out of that hot, stifling hospital and back to the streets. So she had checked herself out the morning after he was born, even though they had wanted her to stay in the hospital.

She hardly remembered giving birth. It's a boy, the doctor had said in a flat, critical voice, as if what she'd made was a mistake and not a new human being. A few hours later she woke up and remembered a dream. A baby was crying, a sharp, gargling sound that made her vibrate. She felt her belly, still swollen, and wondered if giving birth had been a dream. It's a boy. A boy. Boy. Boy. Boy. The word echoed in her head till it lost all meaning. Boy. Boy. Boyboyboyboy. She was leaving that hospital *now*.

Sometimes, over the next few days, she'd have a clear moment. She'd feel her belly going down and remember that she had a son and realize she should visit him. But she only managed a couple of visits to the hospital. The delivery room nurse had warned her that the baby might be born with a drug addiction and would need special care until the drugs worked their way out of his system. After the birth, she'd been told that Isaiah would need to stay in the neo-natal intensive care unit for a while. There were some drugs still in him after all, and he'd been born early, and small. She had watched people shrivel up, shrieking, from wanting a fix. Now, every day or so, she watched her baby do the same thing. He turned bright red and tensed every muscle in his tiny body, making miniature fists. He closed his eyes and opened his mouth and screamed for dear life. Selma worried that he'd pull himself away from all the tubes and plugs attached to him. The nurses had encouraged her to pick him up but she'd been too afraid that she'd harm him. Harm him more than she already had. So she'd stand over his little plastic bed and pet him, her hand practically covering his entire body. She'd stand there and pet him between the tubes and cords and whatnot until she couldn't stand it any more.

Selma didn't think she'd ever be much use to the child. She knew she'd already handicapped him once, by giving birth to him, and she wasn't going to make matters worse by hanging around. Hell, she hadn't even managed to get herself an abortion. Sometimes, because of the crack, she'd miss her periods for months at a time.

Then they'd return, for no reason she could figure. And then they'd disappear again. She was never very careful about birth control anyway, and until the last time, she had never gotten pregnant. She figured she couldn't have children. So when she realized she was pregnant, by the time it *sunk in*, Selma was too far along for an abortion. She'd blown it, she really had. How was she going to manage a child?

But these were her thoughts in lucid moments. Most of the time she wasn't clear-headed at all and never gave her boy a second thought. That was the magic of drugs; you could handle anything, *anything*, because you just forgot.

'What became of the child's father?'

Selma saw the silver pen balanced over the yellow paper, set to write down a name. 'I don't remember his name. Don't even know for sure who he was.'

Arthur Golderson tapped the pen on the pad, looking thoughtful.

''Bout three weeks later the hospital called. The baby was ready to be released. Truth to tell, I hadn't given much thought to this. I didn't think they'd let me keep him. They were stupid to think that I could take care of him. Least I managed to drag myself over there on the right day and bring him home. At first I was almost happy. I'd sobered up for a few hours and I kind of enjoyed just watching him sleeping. I remember how his mouth would go like he was chewing, and the way his eyes would roll around behind his lids. I was scared this meant he was still wanting the crack. Now that I have experience with kids I know they all chews and rolls their eyeballs when they sleep. Back then, I thought my kid was still addicted.'

'You say you have experience with kids.'

'I take care of a little girl. She's a year old but I been watching her since she was six weeks.'

Mysteriously, Arthur Golderson made a note of this and told her to continue.

'Things was okay until that night. I mean, I fed him and I changed him and I thought maybe things was going to work out. But came eleven or twelve at night and I needed to get out. You know what I mean? I had to get *out*. And here was this infant needing watching all the time. I'm thinking, Selma, what business you have with a infant to care for? What made you think this was going to work out? So I left him and went out.'

Selma took a breath and reminded herself that she was a different person now.

'I shouldn'ta left him, but I did. And when I got back towards morning he was crying so loud my neighbors was out in the hall complaining. Your baby been keeping us up all night, they told me.

Can't leave a baby alone like that, they said. Didn't I know it!

'Sometime that day, I don't know exactly when 'cause I slept more than the baby I bet, I had a visitor. I was in such a fog I didn't catch her name or nothing. The hospital told me they would be sending over a social worker to visit, maybe later the city would send a home care attendant or something to help me out. I guess they weren't such fools after all. So I figured this lady was from the hospital. She wanted to see Isaiah. She picked him up and held him and I tried to act as good as I could. Motherly, you know, responsible. She asked me about my plans for the baby. She asked me how I was planning on taking care of it. She asked me its name, too. I hadn't even thought of one. It shocks me now to remember this but it's true, I hadn't even thought of what to call him. But I knew this wouldn't look too good so I told her the first name that came into my head. Isaiah.'

'Isaiah?'

Stick to this one story Selma warned herself; don't get into the other one. 'Like I told you, the name just popped into my head. So this lady tells me that if I was interested in giving Isaiah up for adoption, she could arrange it. She says there might even be some money for me, to pay for expenses and whatnot. I told her I would think it over and she said she'd be back the next day. Well, true to her word she came back. Have you thought about what I said? she asked me. Truth was, I hadn't given it one moment's thought because I knew the minute she mentioned adoption that I had to give him up. I like to think that I was acting in Isaiah's best interests, you know, but truthfully, it was the drugs telling me to give him up, not my mother's instincts.' Selma had to laugh here, bitterly. She saw this made Arthur Golderson uncomfortable, so she moved on.

'The drugs wanted no part of a infant. No part of responsibility. So I said yes, I gave it a lot of thought and I would give him up. And that's when she told me she wanted to adopt Isaiah herself.'

'That was Margaret Lewin?' He sounded surprised.

'That's right. Margaret Lewin.'

'Did she tell you how she came to see you?'

'Like I said, it's all a blur. I think she said she met Isaiah at the hospital. Maybe she was a nurse or something. Can't say.'

'What happened then?'

'What happened?'

'That's right. How did the adoption proceed?'

Selma shrugged, trying to remember what, if anything, *proceeded* back then. 'She came back the next day, to visit Isaiah. Maybe she came back the day after that. Once I agreed to give her Isaiah, I kinda let myself go. With cocaine, I mean. Then one day she came with a man, her husband, I guess, Charles Lewin, and they took Isaiah away.'

'They took him? I mean, there were no papers?'

'I might have signed something.' Selma shook her head to clear it. Outside, the sky was darkening between the tall buildings. Muffled traffic sounds drifted up twenty stories and seeped through the closed window. 'Yeah, I guess I signed something.'

'But you don't have a copy of it?'

'No.'

'And you're sure there was no agency involved? No attorneys?'

'I'm sure. Only person I saw was Mrs Lewin. And her husband, just that once.' Selma had a flash in which she vividly recalled Margaret Lewin's face for the first time since that awful, hazy period: a pretty woman, thin and nervous looking, trying hard not to look around her at the mess in Selma's small apartment, trying hard not to look too shocked and superior.

'What about the money?'

'They gave me some money.'

'How much money?'

Selma had to force herself to say the amount; she knew this wouldn't sit too well with Arthur Golderson. 'Twenty-five thousand dollars.'

'Twenty-five thousand dollars!'

Selma felt a sob taking shape in her throat. 'It didn't last but a short time. I had a expensive habit back then.'

'Did you negotiate for this amount?'

'You mean, did I ask for it? No, she was the one brought up the money.'

'And she mentioned twenty-five thousand dollars right off?'

'What difference does it make?'

'Selling a child is illegal, Selma.'

Without thinking, she started to get up. What was she going to do? Hit him? Walk away from him?

'So is buying a child,' he said quickly.

'I never sold my child.'

He nodded with his eyes closed, to show he understood. Selma eased back into the chair. 'I never sold Isaiah.'

A moment of silence passed before Arthur patted his desk and said, 'Okay. It's a tough case, Selma, as I'm sure you know.'

'Tough?'

'The adoption may have been illegal – technically there might not even have *been* an adoption – but the courts will be concerned more with the child's best interests than with the circumstances of the adoption.'

Selma felt her whole body go heavy, like she could crash through the floor at any time, taking the chair with her. 'Courts?'

'We have no reason to expect that the Lewins won't put up a fight.'

'But he's my child. True, I gave him up, but that don't change the fact—'

'You should understand right now,' he interrupted her, sounding stern all of a sudden, 'that if you want to pursue this matter it could be messy.'

'*If* I want to pursue it? I want my boy back any way I can.'

'As long as you understand up front that it could be very trying.'

'I understand,' Selma said, though she really had only the vaguest notion what he meant.

'Good. Give me a few days to review the facts, do a little digging, and then I'll let you know if I think we have a case and if I'll take it for you.'

More ifs, Selma thought. More ifs.

'I will call you, let's say after the weekend. Can I reach you at your work number?'

Selma gave him the Fredricks' number.

Chapter 12

Charlotte Mellor was one of those people who thrust themselves into someone else's life as unselfconsciously as other people insert themselves at the head of a long line. After their brief meeting in Riverside Park, Margaret hadn't given Charlotte Mellor another thought. If she had thought of her she would have concluded that she'd never hear from her again, unless they happened to bump into each other a second time. But a few days after their initial meeting, Charlotte called and asked Margaret over for lunch. This struck Margaret as such a bizarre thing to do – who 'lunched' any more? The only reason she was at home that day was that Isaiah was sick with a cold and it was Liv's day off – that she accepted. 'Except,' she added, 'you'll have to come here for lunch. Isaiah's home sick.'

Charlotte arrived at twelve thirty and, without invitation, immediately embarked on a tour of the apartment. 'What a fabulous place,' she exclaimed. She remarked on the french doors in the living room, on the ceramic tile floor in the kitchen, on the patchwork quilt hanging in the master bedroom. In each room she went straight to the window and raved about the view.

'It's just rooftops,' Margaret felt obliged to point out.

'Oh, but it's such a *New York* view,' Charlotte answered. When she found Isaiah playing in his room, she said, 'Here's the handsome boy I remember from the park,' as if he were just another appropriate furnishing.

Margaret showed her to the dining table, which had been moved to the living room in order to convert the dining room into Isaiah's bedroom, and then went to the kitchen to get the tuna fish sandwiches she'd prepared earlier. She felt as if an invasion were underway, as if some protective seal around her life were being punctured by this unbelievably presumptuous woman. And yet, oddly, she didn't feel defensive at all.

'I'm afraid all I could muster was tuna fish,' Margaret said as she sat down at the table.

'I love tuna fish,' Charlotte said.

'Actually, I usually have lunch at the office.' Margaret felt

101

compelled to make it clear at the outset that she didn't usually *lunch*. 'I'm a photographer's rep.'

'That sounds interesting.'

'I'm not sure interesting is the word I'd use. It's a sales job more than anything. This morning I called seven art directors, looking for work for my photographers. Only three took my call and none of them had anything. It's not a job I'd recommend for someone who can't deal with rejection.'

'Then it's not for me, that's for sure. Back in LA I almost had a nervous breakdown when Emma didn't get invited to a neighbor's birthday party. Good tuna. Did you adopt Isaiah?'

It took Margaret a few moments to catch up with Charlotte. 'Yes, when he was a few weeks old.'

'What's it like, raising a black child?'

'For Charles and me or for him?'

'Both, I guess.'

'For us it's really not an issue. For him it probably will be, but not until he's older.' Margaret knew this must sound incredibly pat. 'Actually, the one who thinks of Isaiah as an "issue" is Hannah, our twelve-year-old. She's at the age where she wants very badly to conform, and Isaiah is so obviously different.'

'Twelve is a gruesome age. Could I have some more club soda?'

Margaret returned with the soda. 'Did you have a career before Emma?'

'After Emma, too. I worked as an assistant manager at an art gallery in LA. Part-time, actually. But since we moved here I just don't see how I can do it. Rob works such incredibly long hours. I mean, Emma wouldn't see either of us if I worked. At least with me home she sees one of her parents. Maybe if someone dropped a part-time, fabulously stimulating job in my lap I'd consider it. I don't see how I can go out and look for it, that's all.' A seam of vulnerability appeared in the way Charlotte shrugged, shook her head, blinked her eyes.

Margaret nodded sympathetically and then asked, 'Do you want some wine?'

In the middle of her third glass, Margaret returned rather unsteadily from Isaiah's room, where she'd administered children's Tylenol, and put her hand on Charlotte's arm. 'My husband is having an affair,' she said, surprising herself.

'How do you know?' Charlotte responded with complete equanimity, as if Margaret had just told her she'd bought a new dress and Charlotte was asking what color it was.

'What difference does it make *how* I know? He's having an affair.'

102

This silenced Charlotte for a bit. 'Have you asked Charles about it?'

Margaret shook her head.

'Do you know who it is?'

Margaret shrugged. 'I have an idea.'

'Do you have any evidence?'

'Jesus, I just told you my husband is having an affair and you're cross-examining me.'

'It's just that you have to be sure. There are nights when Rob rolls in at midnight and I'm just frantic that he's seeing someone. I mean, how much can a person work in one day? But by the next morning I feel more reassured.'

'Why? What makes you feel reassured the next morning?'

'Just a feeling I have. Trust, I suppose.'

'That's it!' Margaret said, louder than she'd intended. 'I don't have that feeling anymore. Only a few days ago I couldn't imagine Charles with another woman. I was fooling myself. He's changed and I know it's because of this woman at work. Susannah.' Margaret said the name and felt her body freeze. It was one thing to tell a comparative stranger that you think your husband is having an affair, and another to actually name the woman. Saying the name brought the whole situation into greater focus, took it one step further from speculation and one step closer to reality.

'Who's Susannah? Is there any more wine left?'

Margaret emptied the bottle into Charlotte's glass. 'Susannah works for Charles. She's beautiful, I suppose, if you like that long-legged fashion-model look.'

Charlotte rolled her eyes. 'I haven't been this drunk, this early, in years. Are you positive?'

'Have I seen them together? No. But I'm positive.'

'Have you confronted him?'

Margaret shook her head. 'I'm afraid to. I'm afraid he'll say I'm right.'

'Then you're *not* sure.'

'It's one thing to know something internally.' She placed her fist melodramatically on her chest. 'And another to hear it from someone else. From Charles.'

'You want my advice?'

Margaret nodded. There was something comfortably assured about Charlotte Mellor; she took control of situations, Margaret could tell.

'Get the facts and then confront him. Follow him around, hire a private detective—'

'Oh, Charlotte, you must be—'

'I'm serious. Get the facts and then confront him with them.

103

Then, if he confesses, cut his balls off with a dull nail file. That's what I'd do.'

Margaret started to laugh before realizing that Charlotte was quite serious.

'I could never forgive Rob, never.'

'I used to think I'd be that way too. But that was when I couldn't conceive of Charles actually having an affair. Now that I know he is, I can tell already that I'll forgive him. What are my alternatives?'

'I told you, the dull nail file, and there's always—'

'No, really. Do I throw him out? File for divorce? We can't afford to live separately, you know. It's just not feasible. And what about the kids?'

'What about you?'

'I love him.'

This silenced Charlotte.

'You know what's really maddening?' Margaret asked after a while. 'I find myself inventing excuses for him, for Charles. I tell myself that I'm the only woman he's ever been with, that it's only natural that he'd want to, I don't know, experiment. I tell myself that he's under a lot of pressure, what with his business and the kids and the expenses. I tell myself he needs to break away, you know, temporarily.'

'Don't make excuses for him, Margaret.'

'I won't,' Margaret said quickly. There was something very compelling about Charlotte. Perhaps it was this that had encouraged Margaret to confide in her, though they had only recently met. 'But what should I do then?'

'Get the facts first. And get another bottle of wine.'

'What's it tonight, big guy? A real story or a made-up story?'

'Made up,' Isaiah said eagerly, as Margaret knew he would. Whenever she was extra tired, or had a headache, or, as now, felt drunk on the verge of being sick, Isaiah inevitably asked for a made-up story. 'Let's see . . .' Margaret rifled through her memory for a story. 'Ah,' she exclaimed after a minute, having found one that suited her mood perfectly. 'Ready?'

Isaiah nodded earnestly. He looked so darling tonight, the way he always did when he was sick. Isaiah seemed to glow when he had a cold, he radiated a warmth that had more to do with vulnerability and determination than with fever. Margaret had to resist the urge to keep pulling him to her, holding him to feel his warmth. He had been sick when she first saw him, in Metropolitan Hospital. He had glowed then, the way he did now. She had felt the warmth of vulnerability and determination then. She had never stopped feeling it.

'There was a very wealthy man who lived in a big house,' she began.

'A castle?'

'That's right, a castle. He was very lonely, Isaiah. People were afraid of him.'

'Why?'

'Because he was gruff and irritable.' Margaret knew these words would mean nothing to Isaiah. 'He was mean. Nasty.'

'Like Mr Sackman?'

Mr Sackman was an astoundingly unpleasant man who shared the landing with them. 'That's right. Like Mr Sackman.' Margaret felt her temples pounding from the wine, which she'd only stopped drinking a few hours earlier. 'One day a beautiful young lady arrives at the castle.'

'A princess?'

'No, not a princess this time. A servant. Jane was her name. She was charming and sweet and before long she found her way into the old man's heart. He fell in love with her.'

Isaiah's eyelids started to flutter. Good, thought Margaret, he won't be awake for the fire. 'They soon made plans to marry. But then one day Jane did something that she was told not to do. She went up to the attic. There she found . . .' Isaiah had fallen safely asleep. 'There she found an old lady, a hag. It didn't take her long to figure out who this person was, Isaiah. It was the old man's wife. Insane. Insane and old and ugly, but still his wife.' Inexplicably, Margaret felt her eyes fill with tears. 'Well, you can imagine what Jane did when she got an eyeful of this! She ran right out of that house and never came back. Well, she did come back, but not for a long time, Isaiah. When she did finally return, the house had been burned to the ground. Seems the old hag had accidentally started a fire. Or maybe she burned the place on purpose. In either case, there was nothing left of the castle, Isaiah. Nothing.'

Margaret swallowed hard to keep from sobbing. In the quiet room she could hear Isaiah's raspy breathing. She sat on the edge of his bed for a few minutes, listening. Soon her own breathing was keeping time with his.

When Charles returned an hour later, at nine thirty, after dropping Susannah off at Grand Central, he found Margaret lying across the end of Isaiah's bed, one hand draped over his body. He could smell the wine from across the room. He could hear Isaiah's scratchy breathing. The scene unsettled him, and yet he was loath to disturb it.

I am a man having an affair, he thought, reluctantly crossing the

105

room to rouse his inebriated wife from his son's bed. I am a man having an affair.

Chapter 13

It didn't seem right. Selma had two and a half thousand dollars ready to hand over to a lawyer, but the lawyer wasn't sure he'd even take her as a client. Who's hiring who? Selma wanted to ask.

She woke up the Saturday after her appointment, still not knowing if she had a lawyer or not, and knew she had to keep herself busy that day or she'd drive herself mad with wondering. 'You kids want to go to the zoo?' she asked Raymond and Josette, who were having breakfast: some sort of brightly-colored cereal barely covered with the little bit of milk left in the refrigerator.

'The zoo!' Raymond shrieked, jumping off his chair.

'Now hold on, we ain't going yet,' Selma said. She turned to Josette. 'You want to go too?'

The girl raised her shoulders, then slowly lowered them. 'I don't care.'

'Well then, decide one way or the other,' Selma declared as she left the room. This *attitude* of Josette's was beginning to get her down. It was like living with a simmering coal: wherever Josette was, it was too warm, you felt like a fire could start any minute.

She was getting Raymond dressed later that morning when Marie made an appearance. Selma was so surprised to see Marie at this hour that she almost jumped when she heard her voice. Even Raymond gave a start, which made Selma ache for him. 'What you doing?' Marie asked hoarsely. She had lost a lot of weight after her miscarriage, and hadn't put any of it back on. She looked like she could just collapse into herself, like Dana's folding stroller. She'd stopped having men over, though, Selma had noticed. Now the only thing she did in bed was sleep. And could she sleep! Marie slept most of the day and a lot of the night, too. She was like a ghost in the apartment, appearing infrequently and unexpectedly to haunt them with her dim, unhealthy presence.

'Going to the zoo,' Selma said, feeling herself getting nervous and defensive.

'You all going to the zoo, Raymond?' Marie squinted at her son as if she couldn't quite make him out from across the room.

The boy nodded solemnly.

Marie just stood there for a few minutes, so Selma continued dressing him. 'Here, I'll do that,' Marie said after a while. She crossed the living room to where the kids slept and edged Selma away from Raymond. She began buttoning his little shirt, struggling. Raymond stood there kind of stiffly; like Selma, he knew something was happening.

'Didn't I tell you I had plans for them, Selma?' she asked matter-of-factly when she'd finished with Raymond's shirt.

Selma handed her his sneakers. 'Never said nothing about plans.'

'We're going shopping today. Ain't that right, Raymond?'

'I want the zoo,' he piped in.

'Some other day.'

'Selma said today.'

'Selma has no business messing with my plans. We going shopping.'

'No.'

'I said, we going shopping. Then maybe visit your grandmother.'

'No.'

Selma could see something coming. 'Raymond, I shouldn'ta said nothing 'bout the zoo. I forgot your mother planning on taking you shopping,' she lied.

'Will you shut the fuck up,' Marie spat at her.

Selma froze. Marie was usually too drugged or too tired to carry on this way. This morning she'd woken up with the devil.

Marie turned back to Raymond and said over her shoulder, 'Just pay your rent and mind your own fucking business.' She pushed Raymond onto his bed and then shoved sneakers onto his feet.

'I want the zoo,' he protested.

Just be quiet, boy, Selma wanted to cry out. We'll go to the zoo soon enough. Just keep quiet.

'I told you, we going shopping.'

'No.'

The slap made Selma flinch more than Raymond, even though it was his face that took Marie's open hand. 'One more word from you and . . .' She stopped herself and turned round. 'Selma, didn't I tell you to get the fuck out of here?'

'Ain't right to hit the boy,' Selma said calmly.

'Whose kid we talking about? Yours or mine?'

'Any kid.' Selma knew there was nothing left for her to do, so she turned and left the room.

'What's the matter?' Josette asked her in the kitchen.

'Your mother taking you shopping.'

'Yeah?'

'So we ain't going to the zoo.'

'So what?'

'So nothing,' Selma answered.

She didn't know if Marie would actually take the kids shopping. She doubted it. But she knew she couldn't stick around to find out. One look at Raymond's face and she might do anything. She decided to do some shopping herself. She kept to her room until the moment she was ready to leave. Then she hurried out of the apartment without saying a word.

Silently, though, she absolved herself: I'm not your mother, Raymond. No way. You're stuck with the one you were born with. And that ain't me. Isaiah's my son, not you.

But she felt no absolution as she rode down the elevator and left the building. She was reminded of how a few weeks of kindness down in Georgia could make up for a lot of stuff back in New York. Remember this summer, Selma, she'd been told. And she had. So she promised herself that she'd try to do something for the kids, something they could hold onto, too.

It was less than an hour until the end of the Saturday morning session at the Children's Center. Isaiah and two friends, Jordan and Kyle, both three-year-olds, were carefully piling multi-colored blocks one on top of another. They had had several false starts that morning, the tower of blocks tumbling down onto their laps. But this time things were going well, the tower was almost as tall as Kyle, the tallest of the three of them. 'My, you boys sure look serious about this building project,' said Darlene, the teacher. The boys ignored her, intent on their work.

'No more,' Jordan said a while later when the tower started to teeter.

'One more,' Kyle said, delicately placing a yellow block on top. All three held their breath; the tower teetered but didn't collapse.

'Now *really* no more,' Jordan said.

'Just this,' Kyle insisted, holding up a red rectangle.

'*No*,' Jordan said. He stood and placed himself between the tower and Kyle.

'One more,' Kyle shouted.

The two boys began to argue, their faces turning red. Isaiah stayed out of the fight, but he looked even more upset than his two friends. Suddenly he stood and, with a single chop of his right arm, brought the tower tumbling down around his friends.

'Isaiah!' they shouted.

Jordan was almost in tears. Isaiah was panting, as if he'd just run round the room, and there was a determined look on his face. He stood there for a few moments, then darted across the room to where two girls were playing with a doll house. He kicked the house, making the tiny furniture rattle inside it.

109

'Stop, Isaiah,' the girls shouted at him.

He kicked it again, then again. Some of the furniture fell out. The girls started to cry. Darlene came running over, picked up Isaiah, and brought him to a quiet corner.

'Why did you do that?' she asked. He shook his head. 'You're out of breath, and the top of your head is drenched. Why, Isaiah?' He looked at her for a moment. She placed her hand on the side of his head, caressing him. After a moment's hesitation, he buried his face in her lap and began to cry.

Isaiah was very much on Arthur Golderson's mind that weekend. He wanted to take the case. He didn't think they could win it necessarily, or even that there was a case here at all, but he wanted to take it. So much so, in fact, that he did something he hadn't done in a long, long time: he called Lizzie Kaplan and invited her to dinner for Saturday night.

It was close to seven on Saturday when Arthur returned from his gym, having stopped into a gourmet take-out store on the way home and purchased a complete dinner: hors d'oeuvres, entrée, dessert. He knew Lizzie would be prompt. Lizzie was prompt in the way other girls he knew were charming or earnest or promiscuous; promptness wasn't just a personality trait, it defined her in some way. So he hastily straightened up his apartment, which was on the thirty-seventh floor of the second tallest building on the Upper East Side. His doorman buzzed Lizzie's presence at precisely seven thirty.

'Do you know, I tried to be late,' Lizzie said peevishly when he opened the door.

'You look lovely,' he said, leaning over to kiss her on the cheek. And she did. Her light brown hair was swept back off her face, accentuating her most positive features: the sharp angularity of her face, with its high cheekbones and long, even nose, her deepset eyes with their long, dark lashes, her wide mouth and gently upturned lips. Her skin was pale in a healthy way, the complexion of someone who spent a lot of time outdoors in all kinds of weather but never deliberately tried to get a tan.

'How long has it been?' he asked as he wrestled with a recalcitrant cork in the bottle of white wine Lizzie had brought.

She was standing by the wall-sized window at the far end of the living room. In the distance, planes took off every few minutes from LaGuardia Airport. Occasionally a helicopter floated into view like a surreal insect. 'Two years last April. Your last words were "I'll call you".'

'Famous last words.'

'Still at your father's firm?'

He hated it when people called it *his father's firm*. 'I'm still with Golderson, Schaeffer and Pollack, if that's what you mean. Actually, I'm a partner now.'

'Congratulations. Are you happier there?'

'I can't complain.' He finally extracted the cork, in several chunks, and poured two glasses.

'That's a switch.'

'Did I complain that much?'

'Incessantly.'

'I don't anymore.' Which was true. He still hated working at Golderson, Schaeffer, and Pollack – hell, at *his father's firm* – but he had begun to see the futility of complaining. Now he was a believer in strategies, schemes. He knew that being the son of the most famous, most successful trial lawyer in New York was a mixed blessing, but he had recently begun to realize that to most people, the blessing appeared undiluted. So Arthur had stopped complaining. But he never stopped looking for a way out of his dilemma. He was resigned to the fact that he was stuck in the law and stuck in Golderson, Schaeffer, and Pollack – *his father's firm*. But that didn't mean he had to continue gratefully taking the cases his father and the other senior partners couldn't be bothered with. God, how he hated the expressions on the faces of clients when his father told them, sounding just a bit too enthusiastic, that his son Arthur would be handling their case; they looked like they'd just been told that their surgeon was too busy for their bypass and had assigned it instead to a first-year resident – or perhaps an operating room nurse. No, Arthur knew he'd have to prove himself in an arena in which his father didn't compete. True, it would have to be the law, but the law was an enormous territory indeed, and growing. And this week Arthur had found his promised land. He'd found it in Selma Richards and her son Isaiah.

'Tell me about Selma Richards,' he said over the veal Marsala he'd warmed up in his microwave.

'What about her?'

'I don't know. Is she serious about getting her boy back?'

'It's all she thinks about.'

'But will she do *anything* for him?'

'Huh?'

'What I mean is, would she go to court? Would she allow herself to be grilled in cross-examination? How would she feel about being asked about not being able to read? Would she go through that for her son?'

'She's determined to get Isaiah back. It's what she's been living for.'

Arthur nodded contemplatively. 'What if the case became public?

She's such an attractive woman. Dynamite-looking, actually. I wonder how she photographs?'

'Arthur, what are you talking about? It's a custody case, not one of your father's mobster trials.'

'Exactly.'

'What's that supposed to mean?'

'Nothing, really. How's the veal?'

'Delicious. I didn't know you could cook.'

'I don't very often. But sometimes I find it relaxing.'

Lizzie sat on the living room couch while Arthur clattered around in the kitchen. Why am I here? she asked herself for the fiftieth time that evening. Arthur Golderson is bad news. Real bad.

They had dated for almost two years. It hadn't been anything serious, as he'd reminded her almost every time he saw her. We're just friends, right? he'd ask hopefully. I don't sleep with my friends, she'd told him the first time. For two years she convinced herself that she was having a good time. And it was nice to have a regular date on Saturday night, a regular sex life. But it was all too hollow, too insubstantial for her. Then, two years ago, he'd stopped calling, and though she'd told herself (and all her friends told her) that this was all for the best, she couldn't help feeling cut adrift, rejected.

Since that time she'd almost forgotten what it was about Arthur that had so appealed to her. He was good-looking, of course, in an intense way; his personality was like his hair, she'd always thought: dark, tensely coiled, unmanageable. But it wasn't his looks that had kept her coming back for two years. It was – she hated to admit it – it was his unhappiness, or rather the prospect he seemed to offer, deliberately offer, she sometimes thought, that she could help him out of it. There was something about Arthur that suggested that the right word, the encouraging gesture, the perfect caress in the just the right spot would make all his problems simply evaporate. He seemed that close to being a full, contented person.

But when he called her that Friday, insultingly last minute, she had been unable to refuse him. Maybe he's changed, she'd thought, inwardly recoiling from the dishonesty of this.

Did she still love him?

Probably not, she realized with a great sense of relief.

Would she sleep with him tonight, if, as expected, he asked her to?

Probably, she realized with an even greater sense of disappointment.

Chapter 14

There were days when Margaret wished she had a job she could perform on automatic pilot, the kind of job she could do while sick, or depressed, or simply bored. But calling around to art directors, peddling the work of the photographers she represented, simply required too much enthusiasm, too much confidence to be performed when feeling less than one hundred per cent. On such days she yearned for the circumscribed challenge of piles of paperwork. But she was in a 'people business', as she was often reminded. That's what makes it so exciting, she was told. That and dealing with art.

This was one of those days when Margaret wished she had bills to pay, invoices to write, forms to fill in. She was only mildly depressed, but still, she simply couldn't rouse herself to make any calls.

Mid-morning, she decided to take down the photographs hanging on the short wall of her office, a small, sunny room which she rented from a large photo archive house. This struck her as the kind of unimportant yet consuming project that perfectly suited her mood.

The current photos were by one of her more successful photographers, a young woman who double-exposed her prints to create surreal, sometimes violent images that a growing number of women's magazines seemed to think suited their fashion layouts. But Margaret was tired of looking at her pictures tacked to the wall. Grateful for a distraction, she began untacking them, carefully stacking the proofs on her desk.

But she found the empty walls even more oppressive than the photographs. Dusty outlines were visible where the prints had been; the bare walls looked almost reproachful. She mentally reviewed her client roster, trying to decide which photographer's work would best suit her mood. None of them would do, however. She realized with a mental shudder that all the people she represented achieved a kind of hyper clarity in their work. In their own unique ways, they managed to capture their subjects, almost always people, at their most vivid, so that they seemed to assert themselves through the photograph, proclaiming their singularity, their separateness. This was no small accomplishment, Margaret had to admit, given that many of the subjects were professional models.

Today this clarity, this singularity, felt like an encroachment, a threat, so Margaret finally abandoned the idea of displaying any of her clients' work for a time. Then she remembered some proofs she had of Hannah and Isaiah. A grateful client had volunteered to shoot them free of charge, he was one of the top studio photographers in New York, with a daily rate of fifteen hundred. Margaret found the eight-by-ten proofs in a desk drawer and began tacking them to the walls. One of them, a shot of both children, she recognized as the photo she kept in a frame in the living room at home. The others seemed curiously unfamiliar to her, though she'd gone through them, a year or so ago, quite carefully. Again, the photographer had succeeded in capturing the individuality of his subjects, those traits, not all of them physical, that set the kids apart. They were black and white prints, shot against a white, heavily shadowed background. Margaret recalled the Saturday morning when the photographer arrived at their apartment to take the photos. He'd brought his own screens to use as backdrops, and had an assistant on hand to carry in the heavy lights. Hannah had been thrilled by all the attention, by the dozens of shots the photographer had taken. She'd really played to the camera, adopting sultry poses that she no doubt thought made her look like a professional model. Later, Margaret had heard her on the phone with various friends, describing the experience in breathless detail. Isaiah had been miserable, though, squirming in the bright lights and refusing to hold still for more than a second or two.

Now, a year later, Margaret could see how the children's response to being photographed was revealed in the photos themselves. There was Hannah, eleven, opening up to the camera in print after print, like one of those fast-motion composite shots of an unfolding plant. And there was Isaiah, closing up, revealing a distrust of the camera – and the world behind it – even through his big, automatic smile.

Margaret tacked up the last picture and then sat down to survey her accomplishment from her habitual position behind her desk. She was surrounded by Hannahs and Isaiahs, ten of each, she counted. It was an eerie feeling but oddly comforting, too. Margaret had always wished she had more children, even after Isaiah. Now, in her office, she was encircled by twenty children, and she felt prolific and safe. The feeling that she'd had lately, that her world was spinning out of her control, that everyone she loved and cared about was moving away from her, couldn't touch her here. Yes, changing the photographs had been a smart idea, and replacing them with these particular shots had been especially shrewd.

Margaret checked her watch: eleven forty. The map of Manhattan appeared in her mind, with all the important sites jutting out disproportionately. Isaiah's teacher would be getting him ready to go home in a few minutes. Hannah was at school, also looking forward to lunch. Charles was at his office, overseeing his burgeoning business – or perhaps screwing his able assistant. Margaret took a deep breath; everyone was accounted for. She thumbed through her Rolodex until she found the card for the art director of a direct mail catalog she'd been pitching for almost a year. Yes, she'd call him now.

'Haven't you noticed any change in your relationship with your husband?' Charles asked Susannah one night over Chinese food in the office. They had just made love on his couch and, still ravenous, had ordered in dinner.

'I'm spending more time at the office, if that's what you mean.' She'd grinned provocatively. 'But Andy knows I'm compulsive about work. If I were home at six he'd be suspicious.'

She manoeuvres her chopsticks like an artificial hand, he thought. 'That's not really what I meant.'

'Then what do you mean?'

'We're not close anymore, Margaret and I,' Charles said, and felt a tightening, a clotting, in his throat, for he realized that he'd grown distant from everyone he knew; he wasn't close to anyone now, not even Susannah. Having an affair had given him a new-found heady sense of independence, but it had isolated him emotionally. 'We do make love now and then,' he said.

Susannah nodded, as if this was to be expected.

'Do you and Andy? Make love?'

'Charles, please.'

'No, I mean it, I want to know.'

'Yes, of course we do.'

'Okay,' he said peevishly, 'that's all I wanted to know.'

'You're incorrigible,' she said, reverting to a kittenish voice.

'What's in this for you, Susannah?'

'In this? You mean, what do I have to gain by sleeping with you?'

Charles nodded.

She pincered a piece of chicken and inserted it daintily into her mouth. Still chewing, she shrugged. 'One thing I do know. I'm not in it to have long, guilt-ridden, analytical sessions with my lover.'

Life was so easy for Susannah, she sought pleasure the way a plant seeks sunshine. But for Charles the affair – if you could call a series of almost purely anatomical encounters an affair – had proven less of an escape from his life than an ever-present, irresistible opportunity to evaluate it. He'd allowed himself to be drawn into it

115

as a way of losing himself, but now realized that he was discovering himself anew at every turn.

'So you see, social service agencies discourage interracial adoptions, but that doesn't really have anything to do with the Family Court. I'm no expert, but I don't think . . .'

Arthur Golderson held the phone away from his ear, which was throbbing. He was listening to a woman at the New York State Social Service Agency. A lawyer in his office knew her, and she had agreed to talk with him without requiring actual names. Arthur had long ago realized that there were always people available whose brains you could pick without fee or obligation; someone he knew always knew someone. But this woman had gone on far too long. He'd already learned what he needed to know: ultimately the courts, if the case ever went to trial, would decide Isaiah Lewin's fate on what was best for him. That his adoption was illegal would be an important consideration – shredding light on the morality of the Lewins, say – but it would not be decisive. This was not great news for Selma Richards, or Arthur Golderson.

'Great. That's what I needed to know,' Arthur interrupted her. 'You've been a big help.'

'Oh, well, I'm glad,' she said, sounding a bit put off. 'If you'd like I could—'

'No, I've got a handle on the facts now. Thanks again.'

'Hey, before you hang up . . .'

'Yeah?'

'Are you any relation to Abe Golderson?'

'He's my father.'

'*The* Abe Golderson?'

'The one and only. Goodbye.'

Arthur was feeling decidedly pessimistic about Selma Richards' case when his secretary informed him that Sal Fishman was on the phone. Sal doubtless had more bad news re the Isaiah Lewin case (or non-case, as Arthur was beginning to think of it), but he took the call eagerly. Sal Fishman was a private investigator, and just the notion of this man's profession made talking to him mildly thrilling for Arthur. A private investigator. PI. Arthur liked to imagine the man in a dingy, smoke-filled office one flight up over a barber shop somewhere. But in reality Sal Fishman worked for a large investigative agency that specialized in corporate work. Arthur's firm retained Fishman when they needed to track down a witness.

'Sal,' he greeted the man, 'how goes it in Sleuthdom?' Arthur liked to adopt a jocular tone with Sal Fishman, aspiring to the kind of banter he enjoyed in the old detective movies.

'Good, good,' Fishman replied. 'How're things with you? How's Dad?'

This reference to 'Dad' was a bit deflating. 'Did you find anything?'

'Everything there is to find. You want it over the phone, or should I have my girl write it up for you?'

'Tell me now.'

He recited the Lewins' names, ages, and their address. 'A pre-war luxury building,' he added. 'Father works at his own company, called LewinArt. Mother is self-employed as a photographers' representative. The black kid goes to a day care center mornings, in the afternoon they have a Danish live-in for him. Older girl's in seventh grade at a snooty school on the East Side. You want the name?'

'That's all right,' Arthur said glumly. This wasn't looking too interesting.

'Father's Jewish, parents deceased. Mother's Protestant or something, parents live in Connecticut. They're loaded.'

'Great.' Things were looking even worse.

'They owe two thousand on their Visa card, fifteen grand on a home equity loan, plus the mortgage, which they've paid down to about one forty-five. Bank accounts and brokerage accounts are harder to get to, you understand. They have accounts at Merrill Lynch and Shearson, though.'

Arthur was hardly listening. He was wondering when another case would come along that would give him the lever he needed to pry himself away from his father. This one was evaporating before his eyes.

'That's it . . .' Fishman paused dramatically. 'Unless you're interested in the fact that the father's banging one of his employees.'

Arthur sat up in his chair. 'I'm interested, I'm interested.'

Arthur Golderson's secretary called Selma on Tuesday at the Fredricks and asked her if she could come into the office that afternoon at two. Selma said she could, though she'd have to bring Dana along with her.

The reception desk had someone behind it this time. The woman looked at Dana and smiled. 'Whose little girl are you?' she said, leaning over her desk to look at her in the stroller.

'I'm here to see Mr Golderson,' Selma said.

The receptionist looked up at her. 'Senior or junior?' she asked, sounding suspicious.

'Arthur Golderson.'

'I see. And your name.' She looked at Dana and smiled.

'Selma Richards.'

Selma had always thought she'd like to work as a receptionist. To sit behind a desk all day and answer the phone seemed the most comfortable kind of job there was.

A young woman with bushes of hair cascading from her head came to the inside door and told Selma to follow her. 'You can leave the stroller out here if you want.'

Arthur stood to greet her when she entered his office. He looked puzzled when he saw Dana. 'I couldn't just leave her,' Selma said.

'Oh, that's right. This must be the little girl you take care of.'

'Well, she doesn't look like my baby, does she?'

Dana turned to Selma and began to cry, as if she'd understood. Selma patted her on the back but felt helplessness coming over her. She didn't like fussing with babies in front of other people. 'Come on now, Dana, be nice.'

'Maybe my secretary can take her,' Arthur said. 'Lenore!' A moment later the woman with the cascading hair appeared in the doorway. 'Lenore, how are you with babies?'

Lenore only shrugged, but she glanced at Dana as if she were a rabid squirrel.

'Good, then why don't you show her around while Selma and I discuss business.'

Selma handed Dana over to her and thought that if Mrs Fredricks saw her give her girl to a stranger she'd be fired on the spot. Dana's crying turned to hysteria as she was taken from the office by this stranger. Selma listened as the wailing receded back down the hall.

'Alone at last,' Arthur said, smiling uncomfortably.

Selma smiled back at him.

'I've agreed to take your case,' he said, leaning back in his chair and locking his hands behind his neck. Selma noticed dark blotches of sweat spreading out under his arms. 'I think we have an uphill battle, though.'

'Why's that?'

'Do you think it's easy to take back a child you gave up for adoption? Have you thought about what's best for your son? Because the Family Court will think about it.'

He was sounding awfully unfriendly, considering he was her lawyer. 'The best thing for Isaiah is being with his natural mother.'

'Maybe, but it may not be easy to prove. Let me tell you the problems I foresee.'

Selma nodded.

'First, he's been with the Lewins for over two years. He knows them as his parents, not you. Second, they're a nice middle-class family. A *nuclear* family. They can offer him a lot in the way of material things that you can't.'

Selma started to say something but he put his hand up to stop her.

'Third, you have a history of drug abuse—'

'I haven't touched—'

'Fourth, you work full-time, you're unmarried, and you're illiterate.'

Selma felt her face flush at the last word.

'I'm sorry, but those are the facts.'

'Then why bother with me?' Selma said faintly, barely able to speak.

'Ah, now for the plus side. The adoption was completely illegal. They basically bought Isaiah from you. From a purely legal standpoint, the Lewins have no right to Isaiah. If we can show that they coerced you into giving him up, when they knew you were in a weakened state, we may have a chance. Then there's the race issue. The social service agencies don't like mixed families. They just don't. We'll have to play up this point a lot, get experts to testify about the alienation your son will feel growing up black in an all-white environment. Finally, it seems that the Lewins aren't the solid, middle-class family they appear to be. Both parents work, so Isaiah is relegated to a day care center and an au pair. This will help if they try to show that you won't be able to take care of him. There's no religious observance there . . . By the way, are you religious at all?'

Selma nodded.

'Good, that's great. Finally, and here's the real killer, Charles Lewin is having an affair. This'll blow the judge away.'

'I don't understand. Why do we have to *attack* the Lewins?'

'Attack them? Do you have any idea what they're going to say about you? The drugs, the illiteracy. Selma, the best defense is a good offense. We've got to show that the adoption was illegal to begin with, and then that Isaiah has been brought up in a bad environment. That's our only hope.'

'I don't like the idea of hurting nobody. They mean well, the Lewins.'

'Yeah? Well then, why don't you just let them keep Isaiah?'

'He's my son.'

'That may be beside the point.'

Selma just looked at him. She didn't like Arthur Golderson, she decided. Something told her that the nastier this whole thing got, the better he'd like it.

'Now, seeing you with that baby gave me an idea. Will your employers testify to how good you are with children?'

'I guess they would. Tell the truth, they don't see me much with her. I just hand her over to Mrs Fredricks when she come home.'

'But they're pleased with you?'

'I guess.'

'Good. I'll get their names and numbers from you before you go. I mentioned the religion bit. Maybe there's a minister or priest we could call in? How about your living situation? Do you rent your apartment?'

Selma described her living arrangement.

'That's not good, not good at all. Why don't you start looking for your own place? Preferably something with a separate bedroom for Isaiah. How much did you say your salary was?'

'I didn't say. It's two hundred a week.'

This seemed to take the wind out of Arthur Golderson's sails. 'Two hundred a week. Shit.'

'It's cash,' Selma offered hopefully. 'No taxes taken out.'

'That won't exactly thrill the court. Let me see what I can do.'

'Do?'

'About your living situation. Maybe I can pull a few strings. Now, the next step is I'll serve notice on the Lewins that we are starting proceedings to claim custody of Isaiah. This we should be able to do next week. Assuming they decide to put up a fight, which I'm sure they will, a court date will be agreed to. In custody cases they like to move quickly, so we should have this matter resolved by the end of summer, early fall at the latest.'

All of this sounded very expensive to Selma. 'How much is your fee?'

'Oh, that's okay. I'm doing this *pro bono*. Free.'

It took Selma a few moments to absorb this. 'No, I want to pay you.'

'Uh uh. Save your money for your son.' His eyes briefly scanned her black sweatshirt and stretch pants. 'And you'll want some good clothes for the trial.'

Selma wasn't feel pleased about this. If she didn't pay him she didn't really control him, she was thinking. It was her case and her son and she wanted to be in control. On the other hand, if she needed a new place to live and some new clothes . . .

'You think I got a chance?' she asked.

'There's not much precedent for your situation, Selma. I really don't know.'

Chapter 15

Emma Mellor's birthday party was the first Saturday in June. Do you think anyone will come? Charlotte had asked Margaret anxiously. Isn't everyone in New York supposed to be away on summer weekends? Margaret had assured her that plenty of people would come. But will they hate me for making them miss a weekend in the country? Not the three-year-olds, Margaret had told her.

But the day was warm and clear, and even Margaret regretted that they couldn't spend it at the beach, or visiting friends who lived out of the city. It was the kind of day that inevitably made her and Charles rethink why they chose to live in the city. It was the kind of day that caused Isaiah to gyrate agitatedly about the apartment until someone, usually Charles, got it together to take him out to the park. Saturday morning sessions at the Children's Centre were a welcome refuge, but they ended after Memorial Day. Only Hannah had managed to do the right thing; she was visiting her friend Alexandra, whose parents had 'a place', as Hannah called it, in East Hampton.

That morning she and Charles had woken up before Isaiah. This happened very rarely, and when it did they usually took advantage of the situation and made love, quietly, furtively, knowing that they might be interrupted at any moment. It was part of the pleasure, straining to be silent and quick; these stolen moments had been a satisfying ritual with them ever since Hannah was born.

Charles heard Margaret roll over to check the clock and asked her what time it was. She told him it was six thirty and fell back into bed, too tired to get up but unable to fall back asleep. Their eyes met and they both knew what was expected of each other. Charles dutifully put an arm on Margaret's shoulder; it felt unusually heavy to her. Then he shimmied over and began kissing her. She wondered if he'd made love to Susannah in the past few days. She tried to recall which nights Charles had been home that week. He pulled away from her. 'Aren't you interested?' She could feel his erection against her leg, and marvelled at his desire. Didn't they say, however, that having an affair actually increases your sexual desire with your spouse, the way repeated overeating increases your appetite for food? Margaret felt sure she'd heard this somewhere.

'Margaret, what's going on? Do you want to or don't you?'

The strange thing was, she wanted to. She wanted to hit him, castrate him, strangle him – and make love to him. All of these impulses were wrapped tightly together, and while ordinarily, during the day or at night, waiting for him to come home, they made her dizzy with anger and pain, right now they made her want to have sex with Charles with an avidity that astonished and infuriated her.

But she couldn't answer him in words, she just couldn't, somehow. So she pulled him back over to her and indulged herself in Charles's familiar morning mustiness. As always in the morning, it took Margaret a long time to reach orgasm. But Charles was as diligent as ever, holding back until just after she came. They limited their vocal accompaniment to a few stifled groans; afterward, Charles held her the way he always did and she felt safe and loved, the way she always did.

But by the time Isaiah made his morning whistle stop in their bed, about seven o'clock, the old demons had returned: the doubts, the anger, the hurt. Isaiah crawled into the middle of the bed, pulled the covers up to his chin, and, with his parents cuddling him on either side, Margaret saw him take a big, reassuring breath.

Charlotte held the birthday party on the roof of her building. It was not a 'roof garden'; there was no astroturf, no potted trees, but a three-foot wall made it safe, and the view it afforded was thrilling. To the west, New Jersey unfolded neatly, like a Breughel painting, if you overlooked the hideous high-rises sprouting on the opposite shore. Directly below, Riverside Park looked spongy-green and spotless. Charlotte and Rob had brought tables from their apartment up to the roof, on which they'd taped down brightly-colored paper cloths. Chairs had also been brought up. A clown had been hired to entertain the children with gags and by making fantastic sculptures from balloons. Rob grilled hot dogs for the children, who ranged in age from two to six, and of course there was birthday cake. For the adults there was beer and wine.

The children were captivated by the clown and happily forgot their parents, who congregated under the shade offered by the raised entrance to the roof. The adults were having more difficulty socializing than their offspring. Most didn't know each other, particularly the husbands, and their only common ground seemed to be their children. The conversations tended to be formal and strained.

'Isn't it amazing how the boys act just like boys, and the girls just like girls?' Margaret said to the woman standing nearest her. It seemed an appropriately harmless thing to say, given that the boys were using their sculpted balloons as instruments of war, bashing each others' heads with them, while the girls demurely cosseted their creations, displaying and comparing them.

'It's all television's fault,' the woman said somberly, a trace of bitterness evident in her voice.

'You think so?' Margaret said. 'I'm beginning to think it's something instinctive.'

'We don't own a television,' the woman said, as if she hadn't heard Margaret. 'Does your child watch much TV?'

'Not too much,' Margaret replied, thinking of the Ghostbusters cartoons Isaiah had just watched that morning, and of the arsenal of Ghostbusters apparatus he'd only reluctantly let her stow in a corner of the roof while he watched the clown. 'Excuse me,' she said and gratefully headed for Charles. All the men, though, were huddled together just like their boys. This annoyed her, somehow, so she turned and searched for Charlotte.

Her friend looked like she could use some reassurance. 'Great party,' Margaret told her.

'You really think so? You never know how far to go with these things. That woman there . . .' She pointed to a thin woman with perfectly straight black hair who looked slinky and fashionable in a white, clingy sun-dress. 'She and her husband,' Charlotte pointed to a balding, jowly man who looked squat and unfashionable in checked trousers, 'threw a party for their four-year-old at Windows on the World. They bused everyone down from the Upper East Side and had actors there dressed up as Disney characters and a caricaturist and of course a clown. The parents got to order anything they wanted from the regular menu.'

'That's going too far.'

'*I* know that, but do they?' Charlotte gestured to the guests.

A moment later the clown approached them. 'Well, that's that,' he said through the tiny mouth that peeked out from inside the huge painted-on mouth. 'Seventy-five dollars, please. Made out to "Humorous".'

Charlotte nodded. 'Humorous.'

'That's two words without the "o", as in "Humor us".' the clown enunciated. 'Get it?'

Charlotte smiled weakly and called her husband over. 'Do you have a check, darling?'

He pulled out his wallet and handed her one. The clown produced a two-foot yellow pen from one of his over-sized pockets. 'Some people add a little extra if they're really pleased with my work,' he said helpfully.

Charlotte made out the check for eighty dollars. 'Thank you,' she said, handing it to him along with the pen. He looked at it before placing it in his huge pocket. 'De nada,' he said buoyantly, turned, and left.

The door to the stairwell had barely closed behind him when Margaret heard a collective gasp from the guests. She turned and quickly located the cause. One of the children, a little boy, perhaps Isaiah's age, had pulled a chair over to the far end of the roof and climbed up on it. Apparently frustrated at being too short to enjoy the view that so thrilled the adults, he'd somehow managed to pull himself onto the protective ledge, which he was now straddling. His legs were so short, however, that the slightest movement would send him plunging fifteen stories.

'Don't move, Matthew!' a woman cried. She walked quickly and deliberately towards him, taking long, exaggerated strides. Matthew turned to her and grinned, but in doing so he disturbed his balance and began to teeter. Margaret felt her heart start to race and fought the impulse to turn away. Even the children were silent.

As Matthew swayed, his mother began tearing across the roof. A moment later she had him in her arms. He was wailing now, suddenly aware that he'd been in danger – or at any rate, the center of unwanted attention. Charlotte ran over to the mother, leaving Margaret by herself. For a moment she couldn't find Isaiah and panic reclaimed her. She dashed around the roof, searching. When she ran into Charles she practically shook him. 'Have you seen Isaiah?' He shrugged, then caught her panic and began looking himself. A few seconds later they found him, standing rather forlornly in a corner of the roof, obviously still shaken by the panic that had temporarily overtaken the party. 'There you are,' Margaret said. He ran to her and hugged her legs. Margaret leaned over and caressed his head with both hands. Her eyes locked with Charles's, and for a moment they were just parents together – not spouses, not lovers, not friends. Even fifteen stories above the menacing city, whose clamor reached them, muted and benign, on an unexpectedly cool June breeze, life was inescapably perilous after all, and the best they could be was allies, expediently joined for a cause, nothing more.

Later that week, Selma arrived at the literacy center on time and was greeted by Lizzie's usual enthusiasm. She got down to business right away. 'Let's work on your sight words first today, okay?'

'Fine by me.' Selma dug through her tote bag and extracted two packs of index cards, one much fatter than the other. Each card contained a word, written in large, neat letters by Lizzie, that Selma had had trouble with during her reading.

'You don't have to keep bringing the retired words, you know,' Lizzie said.

Selma looked at the pile of cards that she'd already mastered. 'I know. I just like to remind myself what I learned.' Which was true. Just holding the fat wad of words she'd memorized made her feel accomplished.

Lizzie took the thinner pack and began holding the individual cards in front of Selma one at a time. The first one always threw Selma; she had to get into the rhythm of the exercise. She shook her head in frustration; she recognized the word, the distinctive pattern of letters, but somehow she just couldn't bring her lips to say it. 'I know it,' she said irritably. 'I know it. Even, right? No, *every*! Right? Every?'

Lizzie nodded and showed her the next card. This one took Selma only a second. 'Would.'

'Give me a sentence with "would".'

Selma paused. She knew there were two words that sounded like would. Wood like in furniture, and the other one. 'I would like to read better,' she said. Lizzie smiled and flashed another card.

The exercise continued until the entire deck was exhausted. 'I think we'll retire a few more words,' Lizzie said. She removed three cards and handed them to Selma. 'Rest in peace.'

'Amen,' Selma said as she added them to the fat wad of mastered words. She couldn't help smiling.

Later, as they were leaving, Selma said, 'Lizzie, can I ask you a question? Why is Arthur Golderson taking my case for nothing?'

'He's taking it for nothing?'

'Uh huh. I told him I had money saved, but he wouldn't take it.'

'I guess he thinks it's a good cause.' She sounded doubtful.

'I don't like getting something for nothing. Don't sit right with me.'

'Trust him,' Lizzie said, sounding doubtful again.

That night Selma put Raymond to bed. His mother had started going out again, which was a relief. Even though she came home so drunk she often slept half the next day and didn't see her kids until they came home from school, at least she wasn't hanging about all the time, haunting them like some half-starved ghost. Thirty minutes later Raymond walked into Selma's room (which used to be his room – Selma thought of this every time he came in) and said he couldn't sleep. He looked so small and helpless, wearing only his tiny white jockey shorts; his legs looked spindly and unsteady, like a new-born colt's. Selma got up from her bed, where she'd been watching television, and walked him back to his room. She heard Josette in Marie's room, talking on the phone. Selma put Raymond into his little fold-up cot and pulled the covers up.

'Read me a story,' he asked.

Selma felt her heart sink. 'It's late,' she told him.

'I can't sleep.'

Selma could see she'd have to do something to get him to sleep. She looked around the room and noticed a few books scattered about. It burned her up that Marie, who could read perfectly well, was out carousing. It burned her up just that Marie could read. She thumbed through a few books, feeling the tension she always felt when she held a book, until she found one that looked easy. It was just pictures of animals with a single word underneath. She brought it over to Raymond and sat on the edge of the cot. Selma opened the book to the first page. 'Here's a cow, Ray,' she said. She hadn't had to actually read the short little word at the bottom of the page; the picture told her what it was. 'And here's a pig.' This time she made a point of noticing the word. P-I-G pig, she said to herself. 'And here's a sheep.'

'That's a lamb!' Raymond said with some distress.

Selma looked at the word. Kid's right, she thought, the word begins with an 'l' not an 's'. 'I mean a lamb.'

Raymond fell asleep towards the end of the book. When Selma saw his eyes close she felt the silliest, strongest sense of accomplishment. She'd read him to sleep. She continued through to the end of the book just for good measure, and because it felt good to finish a book, even a child's book like this one. She'd read him to sleep – another wrinkle smoothed out of the big bed she was preparing for Isaiah.

Chapter 16

Lizzie felt very conflicted about seeing Arthur. He'd called her the Monday following their dinner in his apartment, which surprised her, and asked her out for later that week. Then they'd seen each other the next weekend, and now they were having dinner on a Wednesday night. Even at the height of their relationship (or the depth of it, as Lizzie preferred to think of it), they rarely saw each other except on weekends. Worst of all, Lizzie was falling back in love with him. Or, at any rate, that old feeling that Arthur needed her was reappearing, that groundless conviction that she alone could make him feel at peace with himself. Lizzie was all too aware that she often confused feeling needed with being in love; what was painful about her current relationship with Arthur Golderson was that she suspected that the need itself was something she'd invented.

They were having dinner at an outrageously expensive French restaurant in Lower Manhattan. 'I'll write it off,' Arthur had assured her, but the prices still made her uncomfortable. Arthur made a point of ordering the most expensive items on the menu: *foie gras*, a chocolate *soufflé*, a hundred-dollar bottle of wine. Since Arthur knew he didn't have to impress Lizzie, and since he'd never expressed much interest in either food or wine, Lizzie had to conclude that the real pleasure in ordering up this storm would come when he submitted the bill to the firm. His father's firm.

The restaurant was extraordinarily beautiful and romantic, painstakingly decorated to achieve the look of a rustic French inn. But it was filled with expense-account types: tables of men, or tables of three men and a single woman, all dressed in suits, all relating to each other with the delicate and uncomfortable blend of familiarity and formality that marked them as colleagues rather than friends. On the whole, Lizzie wished they had stuck to a neighborhood place uptown. This was overkill, and it wasn't even effective.

'This is fabulous,' Arthur said, biting onto a wedge of toast heaped with *foie gras*. But his voice was unenthusiastic.

'Delicious,' Lizzie agreed, and she meant it, although the food seemed somehow unimportant. 'I still don't know why we're here, though.'

'Why not? I'm in the mood to celebrate.'

'Celebrate what?'

Arthur waited for a few seconds. 'Our reunion.'

'Is it cause for celebration?'

'You're not glad we're back together?'

'I'm not sure we *are* back together. Every time you say "I'll call you" I get a knot in my stomach.'

'Can't you take things one step at a time?'

'I'm too old for one step at a time, Arthur. And since when do you take anything one step at a time? You're always scheming.'

'Me? Scheme?'

Lizzie smiled and took a five-dollar sip of wine. 'For instance, why are you representing Selma Richards for nothing?'

'Haven't you ever heard of *pro bono publico*?'

'Answer the question.'

He thought about it for a moment. 'Because this case is completely different from anything my father's ever done. It's a way for me to break away, make a name for myself. It'll probably infuriate the old man, which is another plus.'

Honesty didn't come easily to Arthur Golderson; Lizzie noticed that he was slightly out of breath.

'But does she have a chance of getting her son back?'

'A small chance.'

'Then isn't it . . . *wrong* to lead her on just to make a point to your father? Have you thought of her feelings?'

'She knows it won't be easy. I warned her that this could get ugly, that the publicity could be hurtful.'

'Publicity? Arthur, what do you have in mind here?'

'I don't have anything *in mind*. These matters have a way of becoming public. And this particular matter has all the elements.'

'All the elements of what?'

'All the elements of a story that the media would be interested in.'

Lizzie felt herself flush. 'But only if someone tips them off.'

'Publicity could only help Selma's case The poor illiterate domestic fighting for her son against the have-it-all yuppies.'

'The poor, illiterate domestic . . . Is that how you think of her?'

'She's all three of those things, isn't she?'

'She's a lot more than that,' Lizzie said softly, feeling suddenly very sad and regretting that there were three more courses to get through.

'I know that, Lizzie,' Arthur said. He took her hand and began gently massaging it. 'I know that.'

Lizzie already had a mild hangover headache by the time the taxi pulled up in front of her building that night. 'I need to sleep,' she said, losing her nerve at the world 'alone'.

'I'm beat too. We'll sleep together,' Arthur proposed.

'Not tonight. But thanks for dinner. It was lovely.'

'Are you sure I can't come up?' His look was more incredulous than hurt. 'Well, I'll call you later in the week.' Their eyes met just before Lizzie closed the door and they both laughed at the probable dishonesty of this. But Lizzie's stomach did not get knotted this time, which, she reflected sadly, walking into her building, was progress. Undeniably progress.

Margaret flipped through the small stack of mail on Monday evening and put it down without opening anything. The mail held little interest for her, and few surprises; she didn't correspond with anyone, received few invitations, and she was not the sort to open up bills as soon as they arrived to survey the damage. Nowadays, important news, good or bad, came over the telephone; the mail had been rendered innocuous.

It had been a long day, and as was always the case when she arrived home late, Isaiah had worked himself into a feverish commotion, practically hurling himself at her when she walked through the door. Even Hannah seemed relieved to see her. 'Where've you been?' she asked, strolling to the door holding a can of Diet Coke.

'At the office, where else?'

'I don't know, you're later than usual.'

'Do I need a note?'

'Dad called.'

'How late?'

'Eight or eight thirty. He said not to hold dinner.'

'Nice of him.'

'He can't help it,' Hannah said with surprising bitterness.

'So I'm not allowed to be an hour late but your father can miss dinner entirely?'

'Oh, Mother,' Hannah said. She turned and walked to her room.

Isaiah had been watching this exchange with grim fascination. Suddenly he darted from the hallway, ran to his room, and returned with a large drawing. His eyes widened as he handed it to her and waited for her reaction.

'It's beautiful, Isaiah. Did you make this all by yourself?'

He nodded, smiling.

'May I bring it to my office to hang up?'

'Okay.'

Margaret crouched to give him a kiss. She inhaled deeply as she hugged him, savoring the familiar smell.

In the kitchen Liv was making spaghetti with meat sauce, one-fifth of her repertoire. 'Almost ready,' she greeted Margaret.

'There's some wine in the refrigerator.'

Margaret poured herself a glass and took it with her into her bedroom. On the way she grabbed the pile of mail. There were some catalogs she thought she'd flip through in the few minutes before dinner. She changed into a sweatshirt and jeans, tossing her work clothes onto the bed. Then she turned to the mail again, this time quickly segregating it into two piles: the catalogs, which she'd deal with now, and the rest. But an official-looking letter caught her eye. She'd noticed it before and figured it had to do with their city taxes. Since she was self-employed and Charles owned his own business, their taxes were very complicated, and they were always getting unfathomable missives from federal, state, and city tax collectors, which they promptly turned over to their accountant. She picked up the letter and studied it more carefully this time. It was from the Department of Social Services. Margaret figured it had something to do with installing child-proof window guards or registering for school, but she decided to open it anyway. The catalogs, on second glance, weren't all that exciting.

The name was her first clue that something was wrong. Selma Richards. It jumped off the page and stopped her heart. It was a name that she'd expunged from her memory over two years ago. Now it had been typed by hand on an official-looking form and sent to her. This could only be trouble.

'Mommy, dinner.' He was standing in the doorway to her room; Liv had already put his bib on. Isaiah always hated to eat without her; even as an infant he'd stop drinking formula if she left the room to fetch something or answer the phone, no matter who was feeding him. When she'd return to the room he'd be anxiously staring at the doorway, frozen in anticipation.

'I'll be right there, darling. Liv will put you in your chair.'

'Coming?' he asked.

Margaret looked at him and the face of Selma Richards, puckered with drugs, hard and yet fragile, flashed in her mind. 'In a minute, Isaiah. One minute.'

He just stood there, sensing her nervousness the way he always did.

'Please, Isaiah, I need to read this before dinner.' She waved the letter at him.

He took a step closer to her on the bed.

'It's just a letter. Liv!'

'It's dinner,' he protested, sounding cranky all of a sudden.

'Liv!' A moment later she appeared. 'Liv, please get Isaiah started on dinner. I'll be there in a moment.'

Isaiah started to protest as Liv picked him up and carried him away. Margaret tuned him out instantly, turning to the letter that

130

had already become wrinkled from the pressure of her hand.

The letter was addressed to her and Charles – and to Selma Richards. They were asked to appear at a court building downtown in two weeks time for a preliminary hearing on 'the custody of the child known as Isaiah Lewin, aged two years, six months'.

Margaret remained absolutely still for a moment. Perhaps if she did nothing, she could somehow arrest time until this absurd matter was eradicated. She knew instantly that this was all a grotesque mistake, at worst some sort of bureaucratic rigmarole. And yet the name Selma Richards . . . Where had the city even gotten hold of that name? The adoption had been . . . private, off the books. How would the city even know that Isaiah's mother, his *birth* mother, was a person named Selma Richards?

When Margaret could sit still no longer she stood up in a burst of nervous energy. Only then, when standing, did she realize that there was nothing for her to do just then. Her instincts were to do something defensive, to fortify their battlements. But what could she do? What action could she take? Whom could she call?

She dialed Charles's office with little expectation that he'd be there. She let it ring at least ten times, finding the sound oddly soothing. When she hung up she felt a sense of isolation so powerful, so like a cold, powerful wind, that she had to sit down again on the bed lest she be blown over by it. There she sat until Hannah came to see why she wasn't joining them. 'Mom, what's the matter?'

Margaret looked at her, almost surprised to see a familiar face. 'Hannah,' she said pointlessly.

'Mom, you look, like, weird.'

Margaret stood up abruptly. 'What?'

'Mom, we're practically done with dinner. What's the matter?'

'Oh, I'm not hungry, that's all.'

'Are you all right?'

Margaret felt weak and dizzy. 'I could use a hug.'

Hannah looked horrified, but after a moment she crossed over to Margaret and put her arms round her. Margaret barely held her at first, but very quickly her arms tightened into a strong, quivering embrace. 'This is too weird,' Hannah said.

'Yeah,' Margaret agreed, still holding on. 'I agree.'

Later, Isaiah asleep, Hannah in her room, waiting for Charles to come home, Margaret convinced herself that no one and nothing could take Isaiah away from her.

Who else knew the precise and unvarying configuration of pillows and stuffed animals he insisted on before he'd even lie down on his bed at night?

Who else knew that while he liked his toast cut into bite-sized pieces, he'd have a tantrum if his frozen waffles were tampered with?

Who else knew that 'Bushell and a Peck' was his favorite song, the way he laughed every time she got to the 'doodle-oodle-oodle' part at the end?

Who else could translate his evolving diction, in which 'wheeze' was please, 'ryenow' was right now, and 'wuffu' was I love . . .

Margaret squeezed her eyes shut. To give in to tears would be to accept the reality of what was surely a bureaucratic snafu. Isaiah wasn't a piece of equipment that came with instructions. It had taken over two years to learn how to be his mother. No letter, nor any court, could take that away from her.

PART TWO

Chapter 17

Life got harder for Selma once Arthur Golderson agreed to take her case. The notion of getting Isaiah back was sometimes overpowering; she'd try to picture her life with another person in it and would feel her entire head grow heavy, as if such thoughts were too much for it to contain. Other times she'd ponder the idea of losing the fight that she knew lay ahead; this she felt in her chest, a tightening, as if her heart were swelling to twice its normal size. These opposing thoughts, life with Isaiah, having to face life without him, crowded her mind night and day, making going about her life that June very difficult.

One Wednesday evening, after Raymond and Josette were asleep, Selma decided to step outside the building for some air. Her room was hot and close, and thoughts of the upcoming 'process' kept her awake like a ticking clock. She put on a pair of slippers and rode the elevator down to the lobby. Hers was one of six nondescript brick buildings collectively known as the Marcus Garvey Residences. They were connected by a series of paved paths that cut across dirt lawns. Graffiti covered the first-floor walls. Though the project itself was quiet, the city ranted and raved all around her. Cars tore down Livonia Avenue, sirens of all kinds sliced through the humid evening air, and the unbridled shouts of men and woman occasionally drifted above the mechanical din. She closed her eyes and thought that with all the noise, it could just as well be the middle of the day, or early Saturday night.

When she opened her eyes there was a man standing by her. Her heart gave a start until she realized that he meant no harm. You get good at making such determinations in a half-second. 'Summer's here,' he said somberly.

Selma nodded and got a better look at him. He was about forty or so, on the short side with light brown skin and a perfectly round bald spot on the back of his head. He had a distinguished air to him, somehow, like he didn't really belong here in the projects.

'Thought I'd have a smoke.' He removed a pack of Kools from his shirt pocket. He held the pack out to her, flicking it so that three cigarettes emerged in a perfect configuration, just like on the subway ads. Selma said no thanks. She had given up smoking when she'd given up drugs and booze and all the rest, including men. 'I gotta get back upstairs,' she said.

'Got kids?'

'Not really.'

'Not really?' He laughed with his whole body, a kind of dance step.

'The woman I live with has two kids. I look after them sometimes.' He took a deep drag on his cigarette. In the orange glow Selma saw his eyes taking in the scene. 'You new here, right?'

'Visiting my sister. From Boston.'

Selma nodded appreciatively. Her knowledge of geography was very sketchy, and the only place she'd ever been, other than New York City, was Winfield, Georgia. New York struck her as so big and confusing, she was always impressed when people managed to find their way into it from somewhere else.

'I'm Calvin Hughes. You?'

Offering her name would commit her to a conversation with this man; she hesitated before telling him. 'You here on vacation?'

'Suppose you could say that. Mostly to see my sister and her kids.'

'Guess this ain't much of a vacation spot,' Selma said, glancing around.

'No, it is not,' Calvin agreed.

'What kind of work you in?'

'Me? I'm an electrician. I do new construction mostly. You work?'

'I work for a family,' Selma said. This wasn't a perfect description of what she did, but he nodded.

They didn't speak for a bit, just listened to the chaotic roar of Brooklyn for a while. 'Would you be interested in having dinner with me tomorrow?'

Selma was taken by surprise. It was so long since she'd let herself get interested in men, she just assumed they weren't interested in her. 'I can't,' she said quickly, without thinking.

'Busy?'

Selma almost told him about Isaiah and the big bed she was smoothing out for him and how a man in her life would mean a new complication, a new wrinkle. 'Yeah, busy,' she answered.

'Then maybe another night? I'm here till Sunday.'

Selma looked at him. There was something inviting about him, something soothing. Perhaps it was his voice, smooth as water and deep, vibrating. What harm could there be in seeing him? He'd be back in Boston before the hearing.

'Maybe I could find time,' she told him.

★　★　★

When Charles finally got home and Margaret gave him the news about Selma Richards, his first thought was that this was all a mistake. No way they'd have to give up Isaiah. Didn't the city have better things to do than break up perfectly happy families? Well, complete families, at any rate. This led to his second thought: he'd have to break off with Susannah. That's it for Susannah and me, he told himself. Finito. Caput. The family would have to draw closer now, form a protective mass. No chinks in the Lewin family armor could be tolerated now. Adios, Susannah. Oh don't you cry for me.

'Well say *something*,' Margaret had said.

'We'll have to get a lawyer.'

'You think this is serious.' A statement. She slapped the paper, which he still held in his hand.

'It's probably some kind of bureaucratic screw-up, but we have to treat it seriously anyway.'

'You think there's a chance that . . . that this woman could get Isaiah . . . back?' Margaret's voice was quivering with panic.

'This wasn't the most kosher adoption in the world, Margie.'

'Because of a technicality they're going to take our son away from us?'

'I'm not saying they're going to take him away. I'm just saying that it won't be cut and dried. For either party,' he added glumly.

Hannah and Isaiah knew something was up that night. Hannah left the self-imposed exile of her bedroom, in which had been installed, much to her parents' regret, a telephone extension, and followed her parents around the apartment. 'I *know* something's wrong. I can't *believe* you won't tell me. I'm twelve years old, you know. Like, I'm old enough to be included?'

'It's a financial thing,' Margaret told her, exasperated, thinking that this would put Hannah off.

'Are we poor?' Hannah said with horror, and Margaret was dismayed to see that she had just confirmed, rather than alleviated, Hannah's worst nightmare.

'No, we're not poor. Just angry at ourselves for making a poor investment.'

'What kind of investment?'

Margaret turned and looked at her twelve-year-old daughter who was interested in investments. 'In the stock market.'

'But I thought the market was up.'

'The market is up but the one particular stock we bought is down. Honestly, Hannah, it's none of your concern.'

'Alexandra's father says we're headed for a recession.'

'Do you always talk about the economy with your friends' parents?'

'Mom, he was on *Wall Street Week*. The special guest?'

With Isaiah, the inquiries were less direct, unconscious, in fact. First he stalked Charles with his Slimer gun, zapping him in the kitchen, the guest bathroom, and finally in the master bedroom. 'Isaiah, you've got me three times,' Charles complained. 'Enough already.'

So Isaiah pursued Margaret. Lying in bed, holding a magazine in front of her but not reading, she was too easy a target, so he put down the gun and joined her on the bed, where he began playing with her hair. 'Isaiah, I'm trying to read.'

'Read me a story.'

He never asked for a story except at bedtime. But the atmosphere was charged this evening; he knew things were different. 'Later, okay? I'll tell you a story when you're in bed.'

'Now,' he peeped.

'Later,' she answered and before he could say another word she added, 'Please, later.'

'I called Steve,' Charles told her. Steve was a friend of theirs from college, a lawyer. 'He gave me the name of a lawyer who specializes in litigation. I'll call him tomorrow.'

'Why not tonight?'

'I think tomorrow will be fine.'

'Don't patronize me, Charles. I want answers tonight.'

'I'll call him first thing. If we pester him at home he'll think twice about taking our case.'

'If we can't feel comfortable calling him at night, then I don't want him representing us.'

Charles raised his arms and dropped them, letting his hands slap against his hips. Then he left the room. 'Glad we're all in this together,' Margaret shouted after him. 'As a team.'

A few moments later Hannah came in. 'In what together, Mom?'

Selma saw Calvin three times that week. The first time, the night after they met, he picked her up in Marie's apartment wearing a tie and jacket. He was greeted at the door by a wide-eyed Raymond and a suspicious Josette. Selma figured they weren't used to men appearing at their door while it was still light out. Calvin joked with the children while Selma got ready. She had a very limited selection of clothes, none of them, she thought, right for a date. Well, it's not a date, really, she decided. He'll be back in Boston in a few days after all. But when she saw him in a coat and tie she was touched (no man had ever picked her up dressed like that) and wished she had something nicer to wear than the white blouse and black skirt she'd put together.

He drove her in a borrowed car to Sheepshead Bay. The air was damp and salty there, dense with the promise of far-off places. 'Takes a man from Boston to bring me to a place in Brooklyn I never been to before,' she told him.

Over dinner in a seafood restaurant, Calvin told her that he'd been married and divorced, had two teenaged kids. Now that the building boom in Boston was slowing he decided to take his first vacation in three years. Selma glanced over the long menu and found few words that looked familiar. 'I'll just have the fillet of sole,' she told Calvin, the only fish she could recall just then. She closed the menu.

'They got sole fifteen different ways,' Calvin said.

'You pick one for me then,' she said as lightly as she could, pushing the menu away from her as if she couldn't be bothered opening it up again.

Calvin looked at her strangely, like he could read her mind, and said, 'Have it broiled with lemon, that's my recommendation. Now tell me about your work.'

Selma wasn't fooled any more than he had been, but his kindness made her want to sob with pleasure.

She told him about her 'work' in three sentences. She wasn't used to talking about herself; no one ever asked her to. Later in the evening, feeling comfortable with Calvin, she almost told him about Isaiah. But she held back, since there was no telling what she might do if she got started on that subject.

He took her up to Marie's apartment and kissed her lightly on the lips. 'You're a beautiful woman, Selma,' he told her. When she shook her head he caught it between his big hands. 'A beautiful woman,' he repeated. 'I'll be by for you tomorrow night.'

On Saturday, they returned to Marie's past midnight. This time Selma quietly led Calvin into the apartment and back into her bedroom. They undressed in the darkness, careful not to make noise. 'Marie's out, but the kids is asleep and you can hear everything through these walls,' she whispered. But in truth she was glad they had to be silent. It had been a long time since Selma had been with a man. The darkness and the silence made her feel safer, more confident.

They made love slowly and quietly, as comfortable as if they'd been with each other a hundred times before. Afterwards, when Calvin started to move off her, Selma held him tight. She wanted to fall asleep with the warm, dense weight of this man blanketing her; she hadn't felt this secure in ages. But when, towards morning, she forced herself awake in order to ask him to leave before the children got up, he was lying next to her, sprawled across two-thirds of the bed, and the entire evening seemed unreal as a dream, as unreclaimable as a passing breeze.

Chapter 18

Margaret had insisted on an appointment with David Elliot, the lawyer they had been referred to by their college friend, the next morning. Charles seemed content to wait until the afternoon, or even the following day, as David Elliot had suggested, which infuriated Margaret. She knew she'd have no peace, and no sleep, until she'd discussed the situation with an attorney and been told that there was no chance, not even the slightest possibility, of losing Isaiah.

David Elliot was a partner in Busby, Stephens, and Risely, a large firm specializing in litigation. The offices occupied two full floors, connected by a sweeping spiral staircase, of a new midtown sky-scraper. Margaret felt reassured by the oriental rugs, the mahogany furniture, the rich upholstery. How could they lose with this kind of firm behind them?

'I don't know if this is the place for us,' Charles said while they waited.

'If you're worried about the cost—'

'Not the money, Margaret. I just think we might need a more, I don't know, a more scrappy firm. This isn't Ford versus General Motors.'

'It's just as important to me,' Margaret shot back.

Charles took a deep, steadying breath. 'It just feels wrong, okay? I'd be happier with a less conservative firm.'

A chilly silence settled in while they continued to wait for David Elliot. He finally appeared, fifteen minutes late.

'You must be the Lewins. I'm David Elliot.' He extended a hand to both of them. 'Have you been waiting long?'

'No,' Margaret said, eager to ingratiate herself.

'Yes,' Charles said.

Elliot looked momentarily puzzled. 'Come this way.'

David Elliot was tall, handsome, and, Margaret thought, feeling reassured, utterly bland. He could be a politician, a soap opera star, chief executive of a steel company, or what he was, a partner in an important law firm. He could be thirty-five or forty-five, perhaps even fifty: he had probably gone from boyish to distinguished in a matter of hours, no doubt at the opportune moment.

He directed them to the small couch in his office and then sat in a side chair, crossing his legs. They discussed their mutual friend for a while, Charles with somewhat more enthusiasm than Margaret could muster.

'Now,' he said after a few minutes. 'Tell me why you're here.'

'There's this woman . . .' Margaret began, feeling the words pour out of her mouth like escaping steam.

Charles leaned forward. 'Two and a half years ago we adopted a little boy. Now his mother . . .'

'His birth mother,' Margaret interjected.

'. . . wants to reclaim custody.'

'Does she have any grounds?'

Margaret was about to shake her head when Charles said, 'The adoption wasn't exactly legal.' He looked at Margaret; it was the first time either had mentioned this fact to anyone else since the day they brought Isaiah home. At the time, it had seemed irrelevant: they were rescuing him from squalor and neglect, they were giving him a *life*.

David Elliot must have sensed their discomfort. He smiled encouragingly, revealing surprisingly crooked teeth that bespoke a less privileged childhood than one would have imagined for him. 'When you say "not exactly legal", what exactly do you mean?'

And so they told him, rehashing events that had seemed unreal at the time, and now seemed not only unreal but ancient, buried; calling up fear and pain long since converted to love.

'We put off signing papers until it was too late,' Charles explained. 'We felt the child was in some danger – danger of abuse, of neglect – and so our first thought was just to get him away from his . . . from Selma Richards. We kept meaning to begin an official adoption, but we were distracted, understandably . . . And we were, well, worried about Selma Richards having second thoughts, maybe even asking for more money, which we didn't have in any case. A few months went by and I finally had the necessary papers drawn up. But it was too late. She'd disappeared. We tried to locate her and couldn't. She wasn't listed in any New York City phone books. We figured it was the last we'd hear from her. Actually, we were relieved.'

As Charles spoke, Margaret pictured Isaiah in his little hospital layette, tubes emanating from all parts of his tiny body, his mouth distended in rage and pain, covering half his face. If you survive, she had whispered to him, holding him gingerly so he wouldn't come loose from any of his mechanical props, if you survive I'll take care of you always. Just make it through these next few days and I'll help you after that. Forever.

When they finished, Margaret was crying. She usually cried whenever she thought of Isaiah as a newborn. The whole adoption still struck her as miraculous as an actual birth, and it still fazed her that the great joy in her life that was Isaiah might never have happened had events not transpired exactly as they had two and a half years ago. It was the fragility of life, the tenuousness of connections between events and people, that made Margaret cry each time she thought of Isaiah back then.

She glanced over at Charles. His eyes, too, were reassuringly damp. They had shared the experience of bringing Isaiah into their lives every bit as much as they'd shared the birth of Hannah, when Charles had held her hand and towelled her forehead and endured her agony-fueled invective, finally crying along with her at the outcome.

David Elliot was still for a few moments. Margaret felt she was waiting for a verdict.

'Would you say the boy, Isaiah, is a well-adjusted child?'

'Perfectly,' Charles said.

'And there are no lingering effects of the drugs?'

Margaret shook her head but Charles leaned forward and said, 'He's a little small for his age, which might be a symptom, but since we don't know his genetic make-up, it's hard to say. During his first year he was much more . . . agitated than normal . . .'

'But what's normal?' Margaret said.

'. . . and his attention span is very short, which may or may not be a symptom.' Charles could feel Margaret's warm gaze on him. 'His motor skills are pretty average, I'd say, but it's too soon to tell about things like reading and school work. He talked later than average—'

'But that's always the way with second children,' Margaret interrupted, shrugging with forced casualness. 'Especially with boys.'

The lawyer nodded. 'Are there any other grounds, other than the illegality of the adoption, that would tend to strengthen this Richards woman's claim? Anything happening at home that would lead a judge to consider you . . . unfit?'

Charles turned to Margaret with a look that told her, for the first time, that he knew she knew about his affair. The look told her not to say anything, but Margaret also knew that she could no longer avoid a confrontation.

'Nothing,' she said, turning back to the lawyer. 'We're basically normal.' She giggled nervously.

'It looks like we'll have to argue about protecting the boy's best interests, then. They'll be counting on the illegality of the adoption, so we'll counter by describing the benefits to Isaiah of the life he has with you. The more we can contrast your home life with that of Miss

143

Richards, the better. Is she married?'

'We don't think so,' Charles said. 'Her name's the same as it was back then.'

'Good, good. Any notion what she does for a living?'

They both shrugged.

'Well, we'll bring that up in court. Something tells me her income won't quite match yours.' He smiled indulgently at them. Margaret squirmed in her chair.

'As to the drug problem, I'm going to assume she's over that. If she weren't, no lawyer in New York would take on her case. And she's managed to find herself a rather prominent firm.'

'But she doesn't have Abe Golderson,' Margaret said eagerly 'She has his son, Arthur.'

'I know that. But he's no two-bit ghetto lawyer, even if he isn't in his father's league.'

'So you've agreed to take this case?' Margaret said, changing the subject.

'If you'll have me.' David Elliot grinned broadly, warmly, revealing his hearteningly crooked teeth. The grin quickly evaporated, though. 'My fees are two hundred and fifty an hour, plus out-of-pocket expenses.'

'Fine,' Margaret said quickly.

Charles sat up in his chair. 'Have you had experience in this sort of case?'

'As a matter of fact I have. You may recall the Brody case a few years back?' When neither Charles nor Margaret said anything, he looked slightly crestfallen. 'It was covered in the papers. Steven Brody sued his wife for custody of their two children, claiming that she was having an affair with an alcoholic.'

Margaret nodded approvingly.

'We won that case. Then there was the matter of an obstetrician in Westchester who gave a newborn to a couple seeking to adopt without going through the proper channels.'

'What happened there?' Charles asked.

'The physician was found guilty, unfortunately. But we managed to have his sentence commuted to a hundred hours of community service, and he didn't lose his license.'

Neither Charles nor Margaret knew what to make of this. 'But have you handled anything exactly like this?' Charles asked.

'Like this case? I think you have to admit this is pretty unique.'

Charles leaned forward to speak but Margaret pre-empted him. 'Okay, what do we have to do between now and the hearing?' Charles looked reprovingly at her.

'Just go about your life as normally as possible. I'll do whatever I can by way of preparation, but in all honesty, that's not much. We'll

144

wait for the hearing and see what evolves then.'

'How are we going to afford that guy's rates, tell me that?' They
were heading downtown toward their respective offices. The afternoon was oppressively hot, a milky haze had settled over the city,
but neither could help walking at a fast pace.

'If you don't think it's worth spending a few dollars—'

'Go to hell, Margaret.'

They were silent for half a block. 'We have our savings,' Margaret
offered while they waited for the light to change. She felt sweat
forming on her back; every once in a while a tiny bead would break
lose and drip down to her waist, an awful sensation.

'Our savings? Margaret, we haven't saved a dime in years. I think
our savings account has all of twelve hundred in it.'

'Our IRA accounts, our Keogh's.'

Charles said nothing.

'And my parents, of course.'

'Somehow I don't picture them forking over money to keep Isaiah
in the family.'

They walked, silently.

All we have, now, is our children, Margaret thought. Nearly a
decade and a half of marriage has come down to this: as a couple,
we perhaps owe nothing to each other, but we owe so much to our
children. Margaret held Charles's hand. He looked at her briefly as
they walked, as surprised, at first, as she at the gesture. But he
quickly understood.

Chapter 19

The phone rang just as Selma was putting Dana down for her nap.
The baby's eyes, which were nearly closed, sprang open at the
sound. 'Now you just relax,' Selma told her. 'I'll see to the phone.'

She went to the kitchen to answer the phone. 'Fredricks' residence.'

'Is this Selma?'

She knew immediately it was Arthur Golderson calling. Even if
she hadn't recognized his voice right away – a tense, woundup voice
that came at you like gunfire – she knew it had to be Arthur because
no one else called for her at the Fredricks' place. 'This is Selma.'

'I found a place for you, an apartment.'

Selma took a moment to digest the fact that he hadn't introduced
himself, nor asked how she was doing. Then she got to the part
about an apartment. 'A place?'

'An apartment. In Manhattan,' he said brightly, as if this would
please her. 'In the west nineties.'

'Manhattan? But I live in Brooklyn.'

'Don't you want to live in Manhattan?'

Selma didn't answer because she didn't know what to say.

'You'll be closer to your job, closer to my office. Closer to
everything.'

'How much is this place?'

'That's the incredible part. A guy I know actually *owns* the
building. So he's giving it to us at the previous rent, with no vacancy
increase. It's six hundred a month.'

'How much?'

'I know, it's incredible. Six hundred a month. I'm tempted to
move in myself. I forgot to ask if that includes any utilities. My guess
is it includes gas but not electric. You got a pen? I'll give you the
address.'

'I can't afford six hundred a month.'

A long pause, then, 'This isn't a slum, Selma. It's a one-bedroom
in a decent building. I'm sure I could get my friend to throw in a
paint job. Since there's no vacancy increase he's not required to—'

'I don't care how nice it is. I can't afford six hundred a month, I already told you how much I make.'

'If it's a question of stretching,' Arthur forged on, 'then you'll have to stretch. You'll be laughed out of court if you don't have your own place.'

'I can't afford six hundred.'

Selma heard Arthur exhale slowly, almost whistling. 'How much can you afford?'

'Right now I pay two fifty a month, and I'm saving almost fifty.' Selma nearly said that she was saving the fifty for lawyer's fees. 'So I guess I could pay three hundred if I had to. But that doesn't include child care costs, which I'll have to pay once I have—'

'Wait a minute, you can afford *three hundred*? Selma, there aren't apartments for three hundred in the whole fucking city.'

'Don't curse at me for something I didn't do.'

Another slow, hissing exhale. 'You sure you can't go higher?'

'I could take a second job, but how would that look?'

'Bad, real bad. Okay, let me think. Let me think. Okay. Okay. Right. Right. Selma? Are you still there?'

'Got nowhere to go.'

'Okay, I've been thinking. I'll subsidize your rent to the tune of three fifty a month. Okay? That leaves you with two fifty to pay. Okay? How does that sound?'

'I don't want nobody paying my way.'

'Just till this matter's settled. Then you and . . . you and Isaiah can find a cheaper place somewhere else.'

'I don't know.'

'You want your boy back?' He sounded angry. 'Then take this apartment. It's even accessible to the day care center he currently attends, which might be a plus, who knows? And you'll be able to get home from work earlier, which is also something to consider.'

'All right, then,' Selma said, and at that moment she felt control over her life break lose from her and slip away, the way a branch breaks loose from where it's caught on the side of a river and floats helter-skelter downstream. Selma felt she could watch control over her life slip away from her the way you could watch a branch drift downriver.

You got to learn to trust people, she reminded herself. Trust.

But is Arthur Golderson someone to trust?

'You can move in the first of July, okay? That okay with you?'

'Yeah, sure. Okay.'

Charles didn't take this custody thing too seriously. How could Isaiah possibly be better off than he was now? And wasn't this, the child's welfare, the criterion the courts would use to determine what to do with the boy? From the day they'd brought Isaiah home,

148

Margaret's eyes had been closed to the possibility of anything going wrong. Her love for him was fierce and determined, so different from the soft, gentle love she'd shown for Hannah. But Charles had always looked for trouble. Isaiah had not exactly had the ideal pre-natal environment. Far from it; he was born a drug addict.

He remembered how Margaret had given up coffee and alcohol a month before she even tried to get pregnant, and how she wouldn't let him smoke around her once she was pregnant with Hannah. After Hannah was born she upped the pressure on him to stop smoking altogether, and eventually he had. Selma Richards hadn't concerned herself with what she was doing to her unborn child. Charles remembered how scrawny Isaiah had been, the yellow bruises on his arms and legs and even on top of his head where all the needles and tubes and probes had been attached. Even now, two and a half years later, he still looked for the long-term effects of the drugs. Every time Isaiah had a doctor's appointment he expected to hear that something was developmentally wrong with him. When Isaiah's first birthday came and went and he hadn't started walking, Charles had stayed awake nights wondering if he had a developmental disorder of some sort. He'd always suspected that Isaiah's distorted birthright would come to haunt them all. He'd just never thought it would come in the form of Selma Richards and her pointless, her *cruel* bid for custody.

In the three weeks that had elapsed since receiving notification of the custody suit, life at home had grown increasingly tense. Margaret was behaving as if the whole world had turned against them, as if everyone they passed in the street harbored a determination to break up their family. Every time the phone rang, she stiffened visibly, and she'd taken to picking up Isaiah herself from the Children's Center. Though there seemed no point to telling Isaiah what was happening – he was too young to understand – they'd had no choice but to tell Hannah; she'd pestered them from the start to find out. Her angry response had touched them both. She immediately became much more considerate to Isaiah, smothering him with attention and hugs and kisses to the point where he became irritable. But she'd actually withdrawn further from her parents, isolating herself in her room even more than usual. Charles suspected that she knew that this custody thing, no matter how it turned out, would drag the whole family even further away from the normalcy she so coveted. In a way he felt sorrier for her than for Margaret.

Charles knew the confrontation with Margaret about Susannah was coming, and he correctly guessed it would erupt over something trivial. It was always the way with them.

The decisive moment occurred on a Saturday afternoon in June.

The entire population of New York, it seemed, had fled the city for the beach or the country. The sense of being stranded weighed as heavily as the hot, humid air. Isaiah was more irritable and restless than usual. Charles took him to the playground in Riverside Park shortly after breakfast and let him exhaust himself on the swings and slides and seesaws. Unfortunately, even Isaiah wasn't immune to the heat. He was peevish with the other children at the playground, and after fifteen minutes he straggled over to Charles, who was sitting, with the other parents, on a bench, reading the *Times*. 'Too hot,' he said in an injured voice, as if he held his father personally responsible for the weather. Then, in one of his uncannily accurate imitations of an adult that always delighted Charles and Margaret, he wiped his tiny hand across his forehead. 'Too hot.'

So they walked home not long after leaving it, Isaiah agreeing uncharacteristically to being pushed in his stroller. He was limp but not asleep by the time they returned. The apartment was cool, thanks to air conditioners in the bedrooms and in the living room. 'Ahh,' Isaiah cooed as he entered the apartment, another adult imitation. He revived almost instantly and went into the living room to watch his favorite Saturday television shows. His mastery of the remote control wand, at least, was precocious.

Charles found Margaret in their bedroom, though he wasn't looking for her. It was amazing how two people could avoid being alone together in even a modest-sized apartment. 'Back so soon?' she said without interest.

'Isaiah didn't like the heat.' Charles had decided to take a shower and began to undress.

'Did you get the milk?'

Something in her tone, in the falsely casual way she posed the question, told him that this was the moment. His failure to remember to stop for milk on the way home was the excuse she'd been looking for – the assassination at Sarejevo, the sinking of the *Lusitania*. He wished he hadn't undressed. 'I forgot. I'll get it later.'

'Never mind, I'll go,' she snapped.

'No, Margaret. I said I'll get it.'

'You don't do a fucking thing around here anymore.' Her back was to him, she was rooting through her underwear drawer, but Charles saw her lean on the top of the dresser as if for support.

'That's not true.'

'Isn't it? You're never here enough to even know what needs doing. When was the last time you helped Hannah with her homework? When was the last time you picked up the cleaning? Even this morning you couldn't manage to spend more than ten minutes in the park with Isaiah. I guess your time's become too precious.'

150

'He was hot. He wanted to leave.'

'Oh, fuck off, Charles.'

She said this so dismissively, with such weary disinterest, that he felt anything he said would be worthless, pointless. The only thing he could think to do was put a robe on.

'Once this thing with Isaiah's settled, then you can move in with Susannah Foster.' She pronounced 'Susannah Foster' with a tense shudder, as if the name itself held the key to the woman's adulterous attraction. 'I don't really care. But until then, as long as you're living here, I expect you to behave like a . . . like a partner.'

Charles didn't know what to deal with first: the part about moving in with Susannah – something he had no intention of doing, even if she weren't already married, for God's sake! – or the part about not pulling his weight around the house, which he felt was totally unfair. 'I don't want to move out, Margaret,' he said, taking the issues in descending order of anxiety.

'No? Why not?' She said this lightly, but with an edge.

'Because . . .' How could he explain how little he really cared for Susannah, and how little, in all probability, she cared for him? How could he explain why he'd risked his marriage for a woman he was in awe of, perhaps, but certainly not in love with? And how, in the heat of battle, when everything he said would sound defensive and false, could he assure her that the love he'd always felt for her had not vanished but merely been suppressed, buried, relegated? 'Because this is my family, my life.'

'And she's what, your lover? Is that how it is? You have your family, your lover, all in separate compartments?'

That's exactly how it is, Charles answered silently. 'I'll stop seeing her.'

'You're damn straight you'll stop seeing her.'

'Immediately. Right away.'

'If Selma Richards ever got wind that you were having an affair, neglecting your family, *your son*, for some other woman—'

'I have not been neglecting—'

'If she ever got wind of this it might hurt our chances.' Margaret's voice cracked for the first time. 'I'd never forgive you.'

'I'll stop seeing her, I promise.'

'You'll fire her.'

'I don't know if I can do that, Margaret. For the sake of the business, I need her. And it wouldn't be fair.'

'Fair? Hah. That's a laugh.' But she said this dryly, without humor. 'She has to go, Charles. For Isaiah.'

Put in these terms, he didn't really know how he could protest. 'All right. I'll talk to her next week.'

'Monday.'

'Okay, on Monday.'

Margaret crossed the room, and as she brushed by him he thought, momentarily, that she was going to put her arms around him, tell him all would be forgiven. The thought buoyed him. But she breezed past him, and he felt overcome by a disappointment of disproportionate, even absurd, intensity.

Chapter 20

For once Selma didn't have to think about what she was going to write. 'The pencil's got its own mind today,' she told Lizzie, who nodded encouragingly.

'Just leave blank lines for the words you can't spell, okay?'

Selma hunched over the paper and could already feel herself gripping the pencil like it was going to fly away or something. Sometimes writing even one sentence would make her hand cramp up.

Lizzie went to get a cup of coffee and then browsed through the Center's library. When she returned Selma had finished.

'Wow, you're getting pretty good at this,' Lizzie told her, looking at Selma's notebook. She'd managed to fill nearly half a page.

'Getting faster, anyways. Wish my handwriting'd improve some.'

'What it looks like doesn't count. You should see my handwriting.'

Selma had, as a matter of fact, and it looked a whole lot better than hers.

'You want to hear what I wrote?' She pulled the notebook closer and began. 'It feels like I am in the center of a hurricane. Everything around me is changing fast. On Saturday I move out of Marie's and into a place in Manhattan that I can't even afford on my own. Pretty soon I am going to be in court asking for my child back. Calvin called and ask can he come down for a weekend. Help.'

Lizzie put her hand on Selma's. 'It must be frightening to have so much going on.'

'I know I asked for it, but I just don't like this feeling that I'm out of control, you know?'

Lizzie nodded, then grinned. 'Calvin?'

'He's a fella I met. From Boston.' Selma decided to change the subject. 'The apartment I'm moving into? Your friend Arthur Golderson's paying half the rent for me.'

Selma saw Lizzie flush. With her pale skin, it was like watching a glass fill up with punch.

'I don't like it neither, but he says I need a place of my own for the sake of Isaiah.'

'I'm sure he knows what he's doing,' she agreed, but her voice said otherwise. 'Should we go over your piece?'

Selma slid the notebook across the table. More than half the words were just blanks, or blanks with a few letters filled in. If the lines were straight and if it weren't so full of erasing smudges, it would look like a government form or something.

It took Selma about an hour to pack up her things. How little time it took to pack up a life! How sad. Raymond watched her as she worked, sitting up on her bed with his legs dangling off, banging them on the side of the bed with a steady rhythm that would have driven her crazy if she weren't feeling bad already about leaving him.

'I'll come get you soon and we'll go to the zoo. Okay, Ray?'

He nodded solemnly. Did he think his mother would prevent the zoo trip from happening a second time? Marie was still sleeping. Though she didn't work, she tended to sleep later on weekends, as if recuperating from a hard week. Selma hoped that she'd find a new tenant quickly, someone who'd be willing to get Raymond dressed and off to school. 'Who could resist you?' she said, pausing to look at him.

Raymond looked at her quizzically. He *is* a beautiful boy, Selma thought. He had a triangular-shaped head – a narrow, pointed chin, a wide, smooth forehead. His broad forehead and big eyes made him look smarter than his years, wiser, and his small mouth made him look judicious, wary. He looked like a survivor and a victim at the same time. A winner and a loser. You want to hold him close and protect him, Selma thought, and at the same time you want to stand back and give him room to grow strong on his own. 'You'll need to be strong, Ray, that's for sure.'

'I am strong,' he said, jumping off the bed and standing before her in a military pose.

'Strong here,' Selma said, tapping her head. 'It's a lousy world. You gotta be strong to survive.'

Two large suitcases held all her belongings. When she'd lived in Harlem she'd collected some furniture and things. But she'd left them behind with the drugs. Best to start fresh, she'd thought, wanting no reminders from that time. Now here she was going back to that place. Manhattan. It made her shudder.

It's not Harlem, Selma, Arthur Golderson had told her. Oh no, this is a hot neighborhood now, you'll see. Lots of things happening. Co-op conversions, restaurants. You'll see.

Selma didn't want anything to do with a hot neighborhood. Especially a neighborhood she couldn't afford without help from Arthur Golderson. If West 110th Street wasn't Harlem, it was close enough. Too close for comfort. I'll live there till I've got Isaiah back, she reassured herself. Then we'll find a place we can afford on our own.

West 110th Street may have seemed to her like a thousand miles from where she was now, but to poor Raymond it must have felt like she was leaving for a different planet. She tried to make light of it but he wore a mournful look all morning as she packed. Even Josette looked sad, though she tried to seem unconcerned. 'Long as we get somebody else for the rent, and quick,' she'd said a few days ago. 'Meantime, I'll have my own room back.'

But when Selma had finished saying goodbye to Raymond, promising to come see him soon, Josette shrugged off Selma's hug. Instead she picked up one of the large suitcases.

They were silent as they walked, pausing every few yards to change the suitcases from one aching hand to another. Josette went with Selma up to the platform and put down the suitcase.

'Thanks a lot,' Selma said. 'I'm very grateful.'

Josette just shrugged and turned away.

'I'll say goodbye then.' Selma stepped forward to hug Josette, but she stepped back quickly.

'See ya,' she said, then turned and ran down the steep steps back to the street.

Waiting for the train, Selma looked down Livonia Avenue and caught sight of Josette walking home. She wasn't running anymore. In truth, she was barely walking, just kicking pebbles and things off the sidewalk into the street with listless swings of her left foot. She looked so small and specific down there, Selma was glad when the train pulled in and blocked her view.

Selma found her new building with no trouble. She had to admit it wasn't bad. It was made of red stone and was only six stories high, with fire escapes running up the front. She peeked in the small lobby and thought that it may have been recently painted. She noticed a table with some flowers on it – probably fake, but they wouldn't have lasted ten minutes on Livonia Avenue. She put her bags down and waited for Arthur Golderson to arrive with the key. A few minutes later a man left the building dressed in shorts and a T-shirt, a radio strapped on his hip and earphones round his head. As soon as he hit the sidewalk he turned west and started to jog. Something else you didn't see on Livonia Avenue: he was white.

Arthur arrived a half-hour late. He was wearing a blue polo shirt tucked into blue jeans. He looked leaner than ever, Selma thought, more coiled up. The sunglasses he had on looked like they belonged on someone driving a convertible.

'Not bad, huh?' He gestured to take in the street, which was lined with buildings very much like the one she was going to be living in. Selma decided she wouldn't comment one way or another about the neighborhood or the building.

Arthur produced a pair of keys and, after some difficulty, managed to unlock the front door. 'You're in 3D,' he said. Scanning the row of mailboxes, he found the one for 3D and pointed to it like a new discovery. 'This is yours, Selma.'

They climbed two flights of stairs and found the apartment. Another struggle with the keys and they were inside. The front door opened directly onto the living room, a rectangular room that smelled of fresh paint. Sunlight streamed in from two windows on the far end. The floors had been polished to a high shine.

Selma was reluctant to move around the apartment. Freshly painted and polished, it felt uninviting, like it was waiting for someone else. 'Here's the kitchen,' Arthur shouted from a room off the lounge. His voice sounded hollow and nasal in the empty room. She took her first step into the apartment, almost surprised that the floor didn't give out underneath her, opening up into a dark and bottomless chasm where people who tried to live beyond their means, people who were willing to live on the charity of others were forced to spend their lives. Maybe if I was paying for this myself . . .

The kitchen was tiny but it had everything a kitchen should have and it had been painted bright white like the rest of the place. Arthur called her into the bedroom, which was a smaller version of the living room. Here, too, light poured in through two identical windows, but there was nothing to cast a shadow, so the light seemed to just whirl pointlessly around the room, making Selma dizzy. If there'd been a chair handy she'd have sat down.

'So, pretty nice, right? A one-bedroom in Manhattan, not bad, right?'

Selma's lack of enthusiasm was clearly unnerving Arthur. She managed a weak smile. 'Nice,' she said quietly; the word bounced off the walls a few times before dying.

'Your furniture on its way with a mover?'

'I don't have furniture.'

Arthur took a few steps away from her, as if she'd slugged him. 'What are you talking about?'

'Don't have no furniture. I been renting a furnished room up till now.'

Arthur's taut, tense face began to uncoil. 'Where were you planning to sleep, Selma?'

'Truth is, I thought this place was furnished.'

'Well, it's not.'

Foolishly, they both looked around the empty room, as if what Arthur had just said needed proving.

'You'll have to buy furniture, then, starting with a bed. Do you need money for that?' He sounded weary all of a sudden.

Selma shook her head without thinking. Then she remembered the money she'd put away for her lawyer's fee. 'I can buy a bed and whatnot.'

'Good, good. But what about tonight?'

'I'll be all right.'

'You can't stay here without furniture.' A few seconds of silence passed. 'You could stay at my place until the bed arrives.'

This was offered with so little enthusiasm, with such reluctance, that Selma just had to laugh. 'Maybe we should get married. That would impress the judge, right?'

Arthur laughed nervously. 'I bet I could get one of those bedding places to deliver a bed immediately. I'll slip them a few bucks . . .' He reached into his wallet and thumbed through the folding money section. 'Come on, Selma. Let's buy a bed.'

By five that evening Selma had a double bed in the bedroom and a convertible sofa and a color television in the living room. Arthur had been at his best that day, hustling the people at the mattress store to send over the bed right away, cajoling the salesman at the sofa place to have the couch delivered immediately, too. Anything was possible for Arthur Golderson, Selma realized. He expected things to go his way and so they did. She was filled with an uncharacteristic feeling of optimism. If this man can buy a bed and get it delivered in an hour, he can get me my son back, too.

There'd even been time to buy sheets and a few pots and pans. Arthur had volunteered his credit card for all these purchases, Selma promising to pay him back as soon as she got to her bank on Monday. He called the phone company for her, Con Edison. 'You want cable?' Arthur asked her. He didn't call the cable company. By five she was a thousand dollars poorer, bone tired, and in possession of the most decent place she'd ever lived. 'Not bad for a day's work,' Arthur said, surveying the living room. 'Not bad for a day's work.'

Selma didn't appreciate the look he wore as he glanced around. A landlord's look.

'Let the judge come here and see the kind of life you and, uh, Isaiah, will have. Let him come.'

When the front door closed behind Arthur, Selma felt suddenly very isolated. She'd lived alone before, true, but she felt as if she'd been pushed into this new life against her will. She thought of Raymond and Josette, but they seemed a thousand miles away; already their faces were dim in her mind. She stood next to the front door for a while, contemplating her situation. Being in this new place, a place of her own, should have made her feel more secure, but she couldn't help remembering that she couldn't afford the rent here, that she was at the mercy of Arthur Golderson, whose interest in her situation still confused and unsettled her. Selma felt she had nothing to grab on to, nothing secure that she could grip to withstand the powerful wind she felt blowing her way, a wind that she knew would only get stronger as the summer passed and fall approached. This sense that she was floating was so vivid, she grabbed onto the doorknob to steady herself.

A few minutes later, feeling more secure, she picked up her set of keys and left the apartment. Her fingers shook as she struggled to lock the door. She descended the steep flights of steps two at a time, and when she reached the front door, opened it, and felt the warm evening air, she felt better already. At the corner of Amsterdam she saw a pay phone and hurried towards it. She just prayed Calvin Hughes would be home when she called.

Chapter 21

Margaret was painfully aware that her behavior towards Isaiah had changed since this custody thing, as she thought of it, had come to pass. She watched him more, as if he might disappear from her life if she weren't vigilant. And watching him, of course, she found things to comment on, fuss over, do something about. It was almost as if he had developed a disease and she was waiting anxiously for the symptoms to appear; she watched him that closely.

Everyone in the family reacted to Margaret's new vigilance in their own way. Charles treated her as if she were neurotic, unbalanced. Their relationship had developed into a kind of cold war, but the pressure of unspoken issues and unexpressed emotions reminded them both that warmer hostilities were just an ill-judged word or two away.

Isaiah alternately reveled in and shrugged off her solicitousness. He knew, in an unconscious way, that something had changed. He still stalked the apartment looking for Slimers, but now he tended to avoid rooms that Margaret occupied. More alarming was his new habit of biting other children at the day care center. Twice in July the head of the center had called to alert her to the situation. 'It's just biting, for God's sake,' Margaret had said defensively. 'He's only two and a half.'

'It's Isaiah I'm concerned about. The other kids are starting to avoid him because of this.'

Margaret felt her chest contract. Avoid Isaiah? *Ostracize* him? 'I'll talk to him,' she managed to say.

'That would be helpful, I'm sure. Is there anything happening at home that might account for this change in behavior?'

The director had the careful, deliberately modulated voice of a professional counselor, with the vaguely syrupy overlay of someone who specialized in children. 'Nothing,' Margaret got out, hoarsely, feeling a gasket of sweat form between her hand and the receiver.

'Well, then, most of the time these things pass in a few weeks. We'll just keep a closer eye on Isaiah, okay?'

So poor Isaiah now had two women keeping a closer eye on him.

That evening Margaret brought him into her room and talked to

159

him about biting. 'You wouldn't like someone to bite you, would you?' she asked him.

He shook his head, making a face of disgust.

'The other children feel the same way.'

He stared at her, apprehensive.

'When you bite them they hurt.'

Now Isaiah looked terribly sad and Margaret briefly considered leaving off there.

'So please don't bite anymore, okay? When you feel like biting someone, give them a hug instead, okay? A big, gentle hug.'

Isaiah nodded solemnly and said, 'Okay.'

'Isaiah, do you know why you bite?'

He looked at her with an expression that was eerily adult-like: Are you crazy? I'm not even three.

'Never mind. Some things are mysterious, right?'

He repeated the word mysterious, jumbling its syllables.

'Exactly, Isaiah, mysterious.' She pulled him over to her and hugged him until he began to squirm. Lately she'd had trouble knowing when to end a hug.

But it was Hannah she really worried about. Hannah was spending as much time as possible away from the apartment, staying late at school under some unconvincing pretext or other, visiting friends for weekends out of the city, or else simply hanging out with friends at their apartments. In the past, she and her friends had often chosen the Lewins' apartment to spend time in. Margaret had always been privately proud of this, congratulating herself on having created the kind of atmosphere kids felt comfortable in. Now she never saw Hannah's friends, and she missed them. She saw little of Hannah, too.

When she did see her daughter she looked gloomy and petulant. She'd convinced Margaret to let her get her hair cut at an outrageously expensive salon on Madison Avenue ('*Mom*, all my friends go there') and had returned with a cut that was a decade too sophisticated for her. A lot of the girls at Hannah's school looked this way, bored beyond their years, world-weary, but with a flash of irony in their expressions, a cynicism.

And even this wouldn't have been worrisome in itself if she hadn't also become angry and sullen. She was unhappy, and Margaret knew it must have something to do with this custody thing and the way she, Margaret, was reacting to it. She wished she had insisted that Hannah go to sleep-away camp for the summer. At least she'd be absent during these high-pressure months. But Hannah had refused to consider camp, choosing instead an 'enrichment' program at her private school, which offered students courses in film, crafts, psychology.

Midway through July, Margaret made a lunch date with Hannah. 'Just the two of us,' she'd said, a line from which Hannah cringed visibly. 'No, really, we'll go somewhere special, just us.'

Reluctantly, Hannah agreed. She picked a sleek and fashionable place on Third Avenue that was convenient neither to her school nor to Margaret's office. Done up in post-modern pastels, with Doric columns and pediments lining the room and rock music blaring, even at noon, from invisible but potent speakers, it seemed a more fitting place for complaining about a mother than actually talking to one. From the moment they sat down, Margaret felt at a disadvantage.

Hannah ordered a Diet Coke and Margaret asked for a club soda. They both concentrated on the menu for a while, getting comfortable; it had been a long time since the two of them had been alone together.

Margaret was surprised to find that the menu was Italian; the decor was so generically modern (or post-modern), she had expected a more generic cuisine.

'How did you hear about this place?' she asked Hannah from behind her menu.

'It's very hot,' Hannah answered nonchalantly without looking up from her menu. Margaret considered mentioning that this wasn't really an answer.

They both ordered pasta and a green salad. When the waiter took their menus away, Margaret felt suddenly defenseless. 'We've never really discussed this custody thing, Hannah. That's why I thought it would be nice to have lunch together.'

Hannah smiled weakly. 'Surprise surprise.'

'And also because, I don't know, I may be a little distracted lately. Not paying as much attention as I should.'

'I don't need a lot of attention.'

'I know that.' Margaret took a big sip of club soda and wished she'd ordered wine. 'How do you feel about what Isaiah's birth mother is doing?'

'It sucks.'

Margaret had to laugh. 'God, are you right. It sucks.'

'She doesn't have a chance, does she?'

Margaret shook her head back and forth. 'No, no, of course not.'

'So then what's the big deal?'

The arrival of their salads released Margaret from having to answer. The big deal, she would have said, reluctantly, was that when someone wants to take your child away, even if they don't really have a serious chance of succeeding, you feel terrorized and helpless, you feel under siege from an enemy you can't defend against, at least not in the physical, neck-wringing way you'd like to.

161

Alas, there was only so much attention one could pay to a green salad. 'Remember, once, we talked about how you felt about having a brother who's black.' Why, Margaret wondered for the millionth time, did the word 'black' stick to her tongue when she used it in reference to her son?

'Mom, don't do this to me.'

'Do what?'

'Like, make me feel guilty because I once said something about Isaiah being different. That doesn't mean I want him taken away from us.'

Margaret saw Hannah's sophisticated veneer start to dissolve. A glaze of tears formed at the outer edges of her eyes. Margaret felt a huge throat-clogging sob rising inside her, from deep down, inexorable as a yawn. 'Oh no, sweetheart, that's not what I meant at all.' She reached across the table and put her hand on top of Hannah's, which lay there, inert, like the hunk of Italian bread next to it. 'You know that's not what I meant.'

But things were very complicated, Margaret was beginning to realize. She could see that there was a part of Hannah that wanted this whole mess to go away and leave her life normal. Sometimes this desire included Isaiah himself – didn't every big sister at some point wish her little brother would simply vanish? Margaret saw this furtive longing in her daughter's eyes, she'd heard it in her voice a moment ago. But she'd also heard the pain, the guilt.

Things were getting very complicated indeed.

Hannah said, 'I wish it were September and everything was back to normal.'

Was everything so abnormal now? Margaret wondered. 'What do you mean by everything?' she asked nervously.

'Like, you weren't all bent out of shape about Isaiah, and you and Dad weren't, like, at each other twenty-four hours a day.'

'Oh, Hannah, we're not *at* each other.' Actually, we don't talk at all, she finished silently.

Looking unconvinced, Hannah turned to her pasta.

'It's true, the strain of this custody thing has taken its toll on our relationship,' she said.

Hannah speared a tube of pasta and inserted it in her mouth. The sophisticated mask was back.

'Every marriage has its ups and downs, you know. And when something like this happens, you're bound to hit some bumps.'

'You doth protest too much, Mom.'

Margaret sat back in her seat and shook her head.

Hannah cracked her first smile of the day. 'We saw Olivier's *Hamlet*. In my film class.'

162

Chapter 22

Selma was at work when Arthur Golderson called about the interview. She was getting Dana ready to go to the park. The child was already in her stroller, and when the phone rang Selma had to leave her, stranded, in the small vestibule by the elevator. The sound of the door closing behind Selma caused Dana to scream in terror, and by the time Selma picked up the phone she was a little frazzled.

'Selma, Arthur. Listen, there's a reporter from the *Times* who's dying to talk with you. Can we arrange an interview?'

Phone calls from Arthur Golderson always made Selma feel that she'd just climbed over a wall and landed, breathless, in some strange new country. The best she could manage, what with Dana screaming out in the hall, was repeating what she could remember of what he'd just said. 'Reporter. Interview.'

'Yeah, right. All he needs is a half-hour.'

'I don't think I want to talk with—'

'Listen, Selma, it'll be no sweat. Just answer his questions honestly.'

'But I don't want—'

'It'll help our case.'

'It will?'

'Sure it will. Everyone will sympathize with you.'

'I don't want sympathy.'

A brief, uncharacteristic silence. Then, 'I didn't say they'll feel sorry for you, Selma. They'll feel bad about your not having your kid with you.'

'Isaiah,' Selma said.

'Yeah, Isaiah.'

Dana's crying had deteriorated into a hacking, gasping wail. 'I need to think about it.'

'No time for that, Selma. He wants to meet you at your place on Saturday. By the way, how is the apartment? Fixed it up at all? It'd be great if you had a nursery or something all ready for, uh, Isaiah.'

'Nursery? Kid'll be almost three by the time he's back with me.'

'Well, just make sure it looks homey, know what I mean? We

163

want to show that you don't live in some project or slum. This article could be very important to us.'

Something in the way he said this, some tensing of his voice, set off an alarm in Selma. 'I just don't know.'

'Selma, you've got to trust me on this. Speak to the reporter, please.'

Next he'll be reminding me he's not getting paid for this, Selma thought. From out in the hallway she could now hear a dull, rhythmic sobbing, as if someone was trying to start a car with a very, very weak battery. 'All right, I guess. You tell him where I live, okay?'

Selma's latest book was called *Getting By*. Selma read it while riding on the bus down Lexington Avenue towards the tutoring site. It embarrassed her, sometimes, to read on the bus, since her books just didn't look like the kind other adults read. They looked like kids' books, really, even though they were meant for adults. Selma told herself not to be embarrassed – Lizzie kept reminding her that there was no disgrace in being unable to read – but she couldn't help feeling self-conscious.

'Are you enjoying it?' Lizzie asked her when Selma took *Getting By* out of her book bag.

Selma looked down at the book. When she read, she concentrated on getting the words straight; it just didn't occur to her to *enjoy* it. 'It's okay.'

'Let's read a few paragraphs out loud. Start with Chapter Two.'

Using her finger as a pointer Selma began to read 'Maria worked in a store . . .' Damn. Stuck, and right in the first sentence.

'Downtown.'

Damn, she should have known that. 'Maria worked in a store downtown. She was . . . happy to have a nice job. She gave . . . most of her money to her mother, who she lived with.'

'Good, Selma, I think you're reading a lot better.'

'You think so?'

'Don't you feel it?'

'Sometimes.'

Selma continued to read aloud. When she came to the end of the next chapter, Lizzie told her she could stop. 'Let's work on your flash cards, okay?'

Selma retrieved her cards from her tote bag. 'You ever been interviewed by a reporter, Lizzie?'

'Me? Never.'

'Arthur Golderson called today and asked did I want to be interviewed by a reporter. I said no, then he tells me I have to. For Isaiah's sake.'

'A reporter from where?'

'He said the *Times*.'

Lizzie considered this for a moment. 'Are you nervous about speaking to a reporter?'

'I'm nervous all right.'

'Then my advice is, don't do anything you're uncomfortable with. Trust your instincts.'

'That's almost funny, Lizzie. Since beginning this custody case I haven't felt comfortable about anything.'

Another reason she didn't want to be interviewed by the *New York Times*: Calvin Hughes was coming to visit for the weekend. She hadn't explained to him about Isaiah. It seemed important to keep him separate from that part of her life. Why this was so, she didn't know.

On Friday, before Calvin arrived, Selma took the subway to her old church in Brooklyn. Only a handful of people were there; never was much of a turn-out on Fridays. 'Jesus said, "Where two or three people are gathered together in my name, there am I in the midst of them." ' Reverend Williams always dredged up this line when attendance was low. That's why Selma spent an hour on the subway each way getting there: not too many things in life were predictable. Reverend Williams was one of them.

Calvin rang her front doorbell just before eight that evening. All day long, even in church, she'd worried about seeing him again. They'd only been together that one week back in June. Now it was a month later and she felt she was letting a stranger into her apartment, her life. But when she opened the door for him all the worry left her. Just seeing him standing there, wearing a bright blue shirt and white pants with a straight, dark crease running down them, she remembered why he was the person she had called the day she moved in, when she felt so lonely and confused she could hardly stand it. She remembered. 'Hey, baby,' he said, and pulled her toward him. 'You're a sight for sore eyes.'

She made dinner for him – nothing special, just chicken and rice and spinach, but it was the first real meal she'd cooked in a long time; certainly the first in this apartment. He was as grateful as a military man on leave. 'Don't nobody ever cook for you, Calvin?'

''Fraid it's a bachelor's life, sweetheart.'

She loved when he called her things like sweetheart and honey and baby. It took the hard edges off her life, if only for a brief moment. She thought: A man like Calvin must have women throwing themselves at him all the time. She wanted to ask him about other women, past and present, but didn't want to spoil things. Since giving up drugs, Selma hadn't had much to do with friends, male or female. Once she'd sobered up there just didn't seem to be enough energy left over for other people. Not much reason to be with other people, either, considering what Selma had seen of them. She had her church, her job, and her dream about Isaiah. Nothing more. Now there was a man in her life, at least for the weekend, and it seemed too beautiful, too unbelievable to risk spoiling with prying questions.

'Calvin, you got anything you want to do tomorrow, you know, by yourself?' She saw his eyebrows shoot up, so she quickly added, 'There's something I gotta do tomorrow morning, and I was just thinking, maybe there's something you want to do.'

Dinner was over and they were both fidgeting around, filling an awkward period before settling into romance.

'Nothing special. Whatever you got to do, we'll do together.'

Selma crossed the living room and sat down next to him on the couch. 'Few years ago I had a baby boy, Calvin.'

He just shrugged, like what did having a baby have to do with tomorrow?

'I gave him up, and now I'm trying to get him back. I have to go to court. There's this reporter who wants to write about my situation, see? My lawyer says if I talk to this person, maybe it will help me get Isaiah back. That's my boy, Isaiah.'

'Isaiah. Nice name.'

Selma couldn't help smiling: a name was the one thing she'd given him. 'The reporter's coming here tomorrow morning, and I just think I should—'

'No problem,' he interrupted her. 'I'll make myself scarce.'

'You don't mind?'

'Why should I mind? You gotta do everything you can to get your boy back.'

A while later, in bed, Selma asked him' 'You don't want to know why I gave my son up?' Her head was on Calvin's chest; she could feel his heart beating, his chest rising and falling. It felt like being plugged into life itself.

'You must've had a powerful motive to give up your own child. You must've had your reasons.'

Later, 'Calvin, you think it's possible to start over, to make things right?'

He ran his big hand along her back, making her feel small and protected. She asked him in general, but he answered in particular: 'I know you can, lover. I know you can.'

Chapter 23

Charles just couldn't find a way to break off with Susannah, let alone fire her. He ran a thousand scenarios through his head and none of them worked. There just didn't seem to be a way to do it. He needed her. LewinArt needed her. He was trapped.

Trapped! The very notion made him laugh. Hadn't he taken up with Susannah to feel free, to indulge himself in something that was solely for his benefit, for his enjoyment alone? Hadn't the very selfishness of the affair been its chief appeal? Now he was screwing Susannah to accommodate her, employing her to accommodate his clients, and facing the prospect of having to get rid of her to accommodate his wife.

Trapped! Sometimes he had to laugh out loud.

Laugh he might, but he still couldn't find a way to fire her. Margaret had only mentioned her once after their initial confrontation. 'If she's not gone by the time we go to court, I'll kill you,' she said with menacing solemnity. 'Hear me, Charles? I'll kill you.' Perhaps she was relishing the idea, Charles thought, because even though he continued to come home late, though not as frequently, she never said a word. Just looked up from her book when he appeared in their bedroom door and then returned to it a moment later, silently. She must know I've been with Susannah, he thought. Perhaps it's the thought of killing me that's sustaining her.

As for Susannah, she'd only once referred to the fact that he wasn't spending as much time with her as he used to. I mean *quality* time, she said, annoyed, when he pointed out that they worked together at least forty hours a week. He looked at Susannah and a feeling of loathing, *self*-loathing, came over him. How had he become involved with someone who talked about *quality* time? Pressures at home had been his excuse, and he almost told her about Isaiah and Selma Richards. But he didn't. It seemed important for all concerned that Susannah Foster be quarantined from anything to do with Isaiah.

The irony was, business was booming at LewinArt, requiring at least one or two legitimate late nights at the office, and making Susannah's continued employment all the more critical. Through a contact, he'd picked up one of the big accounting firms whose partners, it seemed, had an insatiable appetite for brochures and very, very deep pockets from which to pay for them. A tiny but growing computer firm on Long Island, whose business Charles couldn't begin to fathom, had retained LewinArt to develop an entire corporate identity program, along with a series of four-color brochures.

With all this work, Charles knew he needed Susannah more as an employee than as a lover. But he couldn't see how to end the physical relationship while retaining the business connection. Sometimes, when he mentioned the awkwardness of their situation to Susannah, a glint in her eye, a tiny upturn of her lips caused him to suspect that she savored the awkwardness, was turned on by it, the power it gave her over him.

'Charles?' It was Margaret on the phone, and the way she said his name, the fact that she said it at all, told him something was wrong.

'What's up?'

'There's a reporter,' she said, practically gasping for air. 'He's writing an article. For the *Times*. About us.'

'About us?'

'About this custody thing. I just spoke to him. He's interviewing Selma Richards tomorrow and he wanted to meet with us next week. I told him to forget it. I told him please not to write the article but he said he couldn't do that.'

'Take it easy, Margaret. This isn't the end of the world.'

'No? Then I'd like to know what is.' She paused to catch her breath. 'Charles, this could be dreadful. Don't we have a right to privacy? Who do we know at the *Times*? Maybe my parents know someone. Didn't they once mention they knew someone at the magazine section?'

'Maybe we should speak to him.'

'My father?'

'No, the reporter.'

'Are you serious? Open up our lives to some stranger, for all the world to see?'

'We haven't done anything wrong, Margaret. And it's always best to talk to the press. That way you have some control over what's reported.'

'No, I won't be interviewed about our private affairs.'

'Fine, we won't be interviewed.'

'But they're doing an article! Charles, they're going to write about us and Isaiah and I don't think I can face it.' She sounded breathless.

'How did they find out about this, I wonder.'

'Who cares how they found out? They're going to attack us.

168

They're going to help take Isaiah away from us.'

'They, they! Who's they? The *New York Times*? Come on, Margaret. Nobody's after us.'

'Oh, no? You just wait.'

Selma used to get this feeling when the drugs started to wear off. It was like being hungry but not for food. Not for breakfast, lunch, dinner, or dessert. It was like being tired but not wanting to sleep. It was like wanting sex but not with anyone you could think of, not even in your dreams.

When the reporter for the *New York Times* left her apartment on West 110th Street, she felt a shadow of that old feeling, a nameless, faceless desperation that made her legs go wobbly. Now she knew, literally, what it meant to feel drained; she had to resist the urge to check to see if her skin had been punctured and her sustaining juices were pouring out of her.

Not that the reporter had been so hard on her. He'd just ask about Isaiah, about her life, and then interrupt her to ask for details. Hadn't she had to go through the same thing with Arthur Golderson? Yes, but this time it felt different, and a few minutes after the reporter left she knew why: he wasn't on her side, not necessarily, anyway. At best he was neutral, like the judge would be. And neutral was frightening, because in Selma's mind her position was the only fair one. Anything else, even neutrality, was a threat.

The reporter, Martin Vandenberg, was a small, tense man whose feet had barely touched the floor when he sat on Selma's sofa. His fingernails were bitten down to jagged stubs, and what little of them remained was dirty, Selma concentrated on this whenever she felt nervousness about to overwhelm her. Arthur said he'd found Martin Vandenberg through a PR firm he used. Selma didn't like the sound of this. She'd sat next to him on the sofa since there had been nowhere else to sit, and he'd placed a small tape recorder between them. 'You don't mind, do you?' he'd asked. Selma looked at it like it was a mouse or something. Yes, she minded, but who was she to object?

The reporter reminded her of Arthur, even though he was about a head shorter and much paler. It was the intensity, the feeling they both gave off of being all wound up and ready to blast off. Being with them was like being with an animal that was tamed but still capable of springing on you.

The interview had lasted longer than she thought, so Calvin arrived just a few moments after the reporter left. At first she felt too uptight to want to be with him. How could he understand what it felt like to lay out your life to a person for all the world to judge?

169

But when he put his arms round her she felt the tension drift out of her in one long, easy sigh.

Yes, Selma, she thought, reminding herself, things are different now. When you're hungry you can eat. When you're tired, you can sleep.

They were in bed when the phone rang, watching the sunlight retreat in orderly fashion across her bedspread as evening came on.

'So how'd it go?'

'Hello, Arthur,' she said, insisting on the greeting.

'So?'

'It went okay.'

'Okay? Did he ask you much about drugs?'

Selma thought about this but Arthur jumped in before she could answer. 'Did he dwell on why you gave him up, or did he concentrate on today, on how well you're doing?'

'Both.'

'Okay, we can deal with that. They'll be a photographer over sometime next week.'

'A photographer?'

'I'm being interviewed on Monday.'

'You are?'

'And here's a piece of good news. The Lewins aren't talking to him at all. Refused.'

'He asked to interview the Lewins?' Selma hadn't considered the fact that the reporter would want to report both sides. She hadn't considered that there *were* two sides.

'Yeah, but if they're not talking, there's no way he can get their side.' Selma pictured Arthur walking round in small circles as he talked: he always sounded like he was in motion. 'I'm hoping the story appears next week. That way there'll still be a month before we go to court, and maybe they'll be follow-up publicity. I have a contact at the *Voice* who says he . . . who was that?'

Calvin had asked if she wanted something to drink. 'Calvin.'

'Who's Calvin?' His voice had lost all its enthusiasm, gone flat.

'A friend who's visiting.'

Calvin pointed to himself: Me? A friend?

There was a long silence on the phone. Selma could picture her lawyer frozen for once, but still standing: Arthur just didn't sit for long. 'Was your *friend* present during the interview?'

'No.'

More silence.

'Did you mention him to the reporter?'

'Why would I do that?'

'You never mentioned to me that you had a boyfriend.'

170

Selma looked over at Calvin and had to smile. 'Boyfriend' just didn't do him justice. 'Never thought it mattered.'

'It might matter, Selma. It might.'

The way he said this, the words coming out slowly, reluctantly, like the last drops of water wrung out of a dry sponge, made her heart go cold. Suddenly Selma didn't think she could handle being on the phone with Arthur Golderson while Calvin was with her; it felt wrong, impossible. 'I gotta go, Arthur.'

'Yeah, right,' he said, sounding flatter than she'd ever heard him before. 'If the reporter calls back for a follow-up interview, don't mention your friend, okay? In fact, I wouldn't mention him to anyone until this thing's over, right? He's not living there, is he?'

Selma answered by hanging up.

Chapter 24

Dana Fredricks was one of those kids who never could sit still. Even when she slept she rolled around her crib until she was nearly strangled in a tight cocoon of sheets and blankets. Then she'd wake up, damp, and scream with frustration.

Selma liked an active child. When she pictured Isaiah she always imagined him in motion, running, jumping, even eating, but never sitting down or sleeping, although she did like to think sometimes about putting him to bed, reading him a story from one of the books she'd buy him. But it was August now, and unbelievably hot, and in the playground in Central Park the other kids had slowed down; they tired out faster than usual and dragged themselves over to their sitters, collapsing onto their laps. Not Dana. Only recently able to walk, she seemed unaffected by the heat, whirling from slide to sandbox to seesaw to jungle gym as if it were still spring. Her face glowed with perspiration. As far as Selma was concerned, the only problem with this was that by the time they got home, Dana was as moist and slippery as a seal. For all her activity, she was a plump little girl, and small rivers of sweat settled in the little folds of skin along her legs and arms.

So it was that when Mrs Fredricks got home the first Wednesday in August, a few minutes early for a change, she found Selma in the bathroom giving Dana a bath.

Dana greeted her mother by clapping her hands, sending a spray of bubbles onto Selma's blouse. 'Hello, darling,' Mrs Fredricks said, bending over the tub and kissing the air over her daughter's head, keeping just far enough away to protect her suit. 'Hello, Selma.'

She left the bathroom and returned a moment later carrying a newspaper. 'I assume you've seen this,' she said, holding out the paper.

Selma shook her head.

Mrs Fredricks handed it to her. It was folded into thirds, and there in the center of the part that showed was a picture of Selma on her couch. Selma took the paper but quickly put it down when the water from her hands started spreading over the article, obliterating it.

'Don't you want to read it?'

Selma felt her heart freeze, the way it always did when she was asked to read something. 'I know what it's about.'

'Why didn't you tell me about this, Selma?'

Selma looked up at Mrs Fredricks. From this angle she was a steep mountain of red suit topped by enormous ledges of shoulder pads. Selma decided she had to stand. Then, eye to eye, she said, 'I didn't think it made a difference.'

Mrs Fredricks grabbed hold of her thick jade necklace and started kneading it. Her hair was pulled back, which didn't make her look as frazzled as she usually did at the end of the day. Instead, she looked wide-eyed, astonished, like she'd just heard some very bad news. Softly, hardly moving her lips, she said, 'It matters, Selma. Very much.'

Selma looked down at the newspaper, lying stupidly between them. What could it possibly say that would make a difference to Mrs Fredricks?

'For one thing, you never told us you were a drug addict.'

'I'm not.' Selma felt a rush of blood on its way up to her head.

'Not now, perhaps, but in the past—'

'I ain't gone near drugs in two years.'

Mrs Fredricks nodded, unconvinced. 'And then there's this custody case. When you're with Dana I expect you to give her your full attention.'

At the sound of her name Dana began to churn the water, causing some of it to spill onto the floor. Selma bent over and rescued the newspaper.

'With your mind preoccupied with getting your son back, how can you devote full attention to Dana?'

'Dana!' repeated the bather. 'Dana!'

'That's right, darling,' Mrs Fredricks said sweetly. 'Be a good girl.' Then, more sternly, 'Will there be other articles? Reporters calling here for information? Will *we* be involved? Our co-op board won't take kindly to having reporters traipsing in and out.'

Selma didn't know what to say. Everyone has a private life separate from their work; why couldn't she? 'I won't let none of this get in the way of tending to Dana, Mrs Fredricks.'

'That's what you say, Selma. But how can I be sure?'

This was the longest conversation Selma had had with Mrs Fredricks since she was interviewed by her. She'd never noticed before the way her throat tightened, frog-like, when she spoke. 'I won't let nothing interfere.' And I won't bother asking you to testify for me, she continued silently.

Mrs Fredricks frowned and shook her head, as if Selma had just

174

told an obvious lie. She looked at Dana, who must have sensed the tension in the room and was now staring up at the two women with a look of amazement.

'See how we've upset Dana already?'

They both stared at the child, Selma half hoping that she'd come to her defense. Dana looked more enthralled than upset.

'This mean I'm losing my job?'

'I don't know, Selma. I just don't know.'

'If I don't have a job, I won't get my boy back.'

'And if you *do* get your boy back, what then?'

Selma just looked at her, not understanding.

'How will you take care of him and still hold down this job?'

'I'll find someone to look after him.' Same as you're doing with Dana, she added silently.

Selma bought a paper before getting on the Lexington Avenue bus. It took her almost ten blocks to find the article, which was on the front page of one of the inside sections. She looked at the photograph for a while, trying to absorb the reality that it was her, Selma Richards. She looked stern and kind of unfriendly, Selma thought. She supposed it was just as well that she wasn't smiling – this was serious, after all. But, she wondered, panicking, would people see this as the face of a woman who should raise a little child? Is this a mother's face? She held the paper away from her, then brought it back closer, squinting. A terrible thought occurred to her and she quickly looked around the bus. Had anyone recognized her?

Selma puzzled over the headline until the bus reached her stop. But the words were simply too long and unfamiliar. And she was far too unsettled, about the article, about the photograph, about possibly losing her job, to do any serious concentrating.

Lizzie was waiting at their usual table. 'Hi, Selma,' she said in a voice that told Selma she'd seen the article. 'I guess we know what the lesson is today.'

'Couldn't even read the damn headline,' Selma said as she sat down. She felt a sense of defeat coming over her like the first treacherous sign of a cold that's bound to get worse. Something told her that the article wouldn't please her one bit.

'We'll go over it now, then.'

Selma handed Lizzie the paper. 'What did you think of it, Lizzie?'

Lizzie hesitated before answering. Selma held her breath. 'I think the reporter was sympathetic to your case. But . . . I don't know. It made me want to protect you.'

Their eyes met, startled.

'I don't need protecting.'

175

'I know that,' Lizzie said quickly. 'You want to take a crack at the article?'

'Not this time.'

'Okay, then follow along as I read.'

Using her finger as a guide, Lizzie began with the headline: 'Custody Case Poses Ethical Dilemma for Courts'.

Lizzie looked up at Selma, who wasn't sure what this meant, exactly, but nodded for her to continue anyway.

In her small but comfortable apartment on Manhattan's Upper West Side, Selma Richards waits for a judge to decide whether the child she gave up for adoption over two years ago should be returned to her care.

Just twenty blocks to the south, Charles and Margaret Lewin are also awaiting the judge's decision. Two years ago they adopted Selma Richards' son. Soon, a judge will decide whether or not they can keep him.

It's an emotionally charged case that pits two very different parts of the city against each other. Though separated by just a mile or so, Selma Richards and the Lewins inhabit totally separate worlds.

Ms Richards is a babysitter for the child of a wealthy East Side couple. She was raised in poverty and lives on its fringes even today. The Lewins are well-to-do professionals, he a graphic artist, she a photographers' representative.

Ms Richards lives in a two-room walk-up on a marginal block. The Lewins inhabit a sprawling apartment in a doorman building in one of Manhattan's most gentrified neighborhoods.

Ms Richards is black. The Lewins are white.

The case also brings into focus the dark underworld of illegal adoptions, a world in which babies are bought and sold like commodities. And it raises the issue of whether a child can live a happy life in a family whose race is different than its own.

Selma Richards was a cocaine addict two-and-a-half years ago when she gave up her son, Isaiah, for adoption. So was Isaiah.

It was while Isaiah was struggling for life in a neo-natal care unit at Manhattan's Metropolitan Hospital that Margaret Lewin first met the infant. She was a volunteer 'holder' – someone who spends a few hours a week cuddling children who are born addicted. These children are often abandoned by their drug-addicted mothers and risk perishing without periodic physical affection.

Mrs Lewin who, with her husband, declined to be interviewed for this article, developed a special attachment to Isaiah

176

and continued to visit him even after he was released into his mother's care. It was during this period, roughly two months after Isaiah was born in November 1989, that Mrs Lewin offered to adopt Isaiah in return for $25,000.

'I was starving for drugs,' Ms Richards recalls. 'I knew I couldn't take care of my boy, and I knew I had to have some crack or I'd die. Even so, it took me a few days to decide.'

'The adoption was illegal, pure and simple,' claims Ms Richards' attorney, Arthur Golderson. 'It was never registered with the state, and the payment of $25,000 was a blatant case of baby buying.'

But it won't be a cut-and-dried matter. 'Ultimately the case should be decided on what's best for the child,' says Betty Logan, a child psychologist. 'And clearly what's best for the child is to remain with the family.'

Arthur Golderson, however, contends that the long-term difficulties of growing up black in a white family and in an all-white environment will far outweigh any temporary trauma of separation. 'Look, someday this kid is going to ask about his adoption, and if his parents are honest, they'll tell him that it wasn't legal, that they paid his mother cash for him, and that when he was two years old his mother wanted him back and they prevented it. Talk about trauma.'

The issue of mixed-race adoption is a particularly thorny one right now. Thousands of black babies languish in hospitals and foster homes waiting for 'suitable' homes. 'Suitable is often a euphemism for racially compatible,' according to Betty Logan. 'There is an unwritten policy among social service agencies to place babies with parents of their own race.'

Bruce Althorp of Brooklyn Children's Services denies the existence of such a policy, written or unwritten. But he does acknowledge that 'when possible' children are placed in families of the same race.

'There's a resentment among child welfare professionals about this attitude that a black child is always better off in a middle-class home, regardless of the race of the parents,' Althorp says. Asked about the Isaiah Lewin case, he claims that the short-term trauma of separation might well be outweighed by the long-term benefits of being raised by his birth mother. 'It's terrible to admit, but we've had kids in foster homes for this period of time [two years] and have placed them permanently after that. There are ways of smoothing out the transition, such as visitation rights.'

The issue could come down to who would be better parents for Isaiah, the Lewins or Selma Richards.

'The Lewins will undoubtedly make the case that Ms Richards' background as a drug addict, her low wages, and her poor education make her less suitable,' says Frank Spears, an attorney who specializes in custody issues.

Apart from the drug issue, the material advantages offered by the Lewins might have an impact. 'They're educated, cultured people,' asserts Charlotte Mellor, a family friend. 'Their oldest child, Hannah, goes to one of the best private schools in the city. Isaiah will have every advantage. Not just financial,' she quickly adds. 'Emotional advantages, too.'

As for the inter-racial issue, Ms Mellor is unconcerned. 'Sure, there are tensions now and then. But it's just not a big deal to them.' Asked about these 'tensions', Ms Mellor shakes her head dismissively. 'Nothing serious.' She refused to elaborate.

Then there's the issue of single parenthood. 'A judge will always look more favorably on a married couple than a single parent,' Frank Spears points out.

'I don't buy that,' argues Ms Richards' lawyer, Arthur Golderson, whose father, Abe Golderson, is a prominent Manhattan trial attorney. 'Do you know who takes care of Isaiah during the work week? A day care center. And when he's done there, the Lewins have hired a nanny to pick him up and bring him home. They're both professionals who work long hours, even weekends. At least my client has regular hours, nine to five. In terms of quality time, she'll probably spend more of it with Isaiah then they do.'

The case is scheduled to go before Family Court in early September. In the meantime, Selma Richards is preparing her home for the return of the son she hasn't seen in over two years. 'Everything I do, I do to prepare for Isaiah coming home. I just bought him a bed last week, and now I've saved enough for a dresser for him. I'm getting that on Saturday.

'I used to think you couldn't help the way things turn out,' she says, emotion thickening her voice. 'But now I think you can. I think you do get a second chance. I'm going to make it up to my son.'

Whether she gets that second chance to make it up to Isaiah will be decided by the courts next month.

When Lizzie finished reading, Selma felt dizzy, as if someone had been spinning her round and had stopped abruptly. She hadn't enjoyed hearing the story read to her, but at the same time she didn't want it to end. Because then she'd have to think about it, *feel* it.

'The reporter obviously took your side,' Lizzie said. 'That came through even more the second time I read it.'

'You think so?'

Lizzie nodded vigorously.

Selma pulled the newspaper across the table towards her and stared at it. Lord, how she wished she could read it! It probably would do her spirits no good, but she wished she could read it again, maybe a third time. This was her life, and she couldn't even read it.

'You want me to read it again?' Lizzie asked.

Selma looked at her, surprised. 'You wouldn't mind?'

So Selma listened to her life a second time, concentrating to hold on to the parts that mattered. This time, when it was finished, she felt less dizzy but no less unhappy. 'I might not get him back,' she said quietly.

'Oh, Selma, I wouldn't jump to that conclusion. This article is very biased in your favor. The Lewins didn't even talk to the reporter, you know.'

Selma could hear the doubt in Lizzie's voice, and it hurt her to hear her tutor fooling herself as she tried to fool Selma. 'All I want is my boy back. I don't want no picture in the paper. I don't want no publicity. Look at this.' She slapped the offending *Times*. 'Drugs and the poverty and selling babies. Why would a judge let me raise a kid, tell me that? Why would he?'

'Because you'll be a good parent. A loving parent.'

Selma shook her head and gathered up her things.

'Selma, don't leave. That article can only help, I promise.'

Selma looked at her. '*You* promise? What can you promise?'

She waited a few seconds for an answer, then turned and, for the first time since joining the literacy program, left before her session was over.

'Lizzie! How'd you like the article!'

Lizzie placed a hand on the door of the phone booth to steady herself. 'How could you do that to her?'

'Do what to her? The article's perfect. True, I wish they hadn't gotten so explicit about the twenty-five thousand, and mentioning my father was kind of gratuitous . . .'

'The article's perfect for *you*, Arthur. But Selma just walked out of her tutoring session miserable. She's never done that before. It's like she's giving up.'

'I don't get it. This is just the kind of publicity we need.'

'*You* need, Arthur. Selma can't even read the fucking article.'

'I never said this was going to be easy.'

'But you didn't have to do this.'

'Pre-trial publicity can't hurt.'

179

'It's already hurt Selma.'

A poisonous silence lingered between them, broken by Arthur. 'You want to have dinner?'

His insensitivity was magnificent. 'Not if you were the last single man in Manhattan.'

Which, she thought, hanging up, you might well be.

Chapter 25

Hannah answered the phone when Charlotte Mellor called the morning the article appeared in the *Times*. 'I don't want to speak to her,' Margaret called from the kitchen, where she was straightening up before leaving for her office. 'She says it's important,' Hannah shouted impatiently. Margaret stopped what she was doing and tried to think calmly, rationally. Charlotte hadn't said anything truly damaging in the article, except for the part about tensions surrounding the race issue, and even that hadn't been too bad.

But how dare she speak to the reporter at all! How dare she!

Margaret's rage over the article had been building all morning. Charles had read it first, then handed it to her saying, 'It's not too bad, all things considered.' Once she'd read the article, Charles's equanimity added another dimension to her rage. Margaret found the article devastating, humiliating, *threatening*. And with no better target available, her rage and fear had taken aim at Charlotte Mellor.

'You have a lot of nerve calling,' she said the instant she picked up the receiver.

'Margaret, I had no idea—'

'You didn't know he was a reporter?' Margaret's spirits lifted momentarily. If the reporter had deceived Charlotte, their friendship could be resuscitated, and might not retaliatory action against the reporter be possible?

'I knew he was a reporter . . .'

Margaret's spirits deflated.

'. . . but I had no idea you'd refused to speak to him. I thought I was helping you. I didn't know the part about "tensions" would sound so bad, especially when I refused to say anything more about that. The way he wrote it, it sounded like I was covering something up.'

Charlotte sounded so frantic, Margaret began to soften. Then she remembered something. 'How the hell did he find you?'

'In the playground in the park, where you and I met. He was asking some of the mothers a few days ago. I think I talked to him for all of two minutes. I was going to call you about it. I thought I was being helpful, Margaret.'

Rage was dissolving into panic. 'I'm going to lose him, Charlotte. I'm going to lose Isaiah.' Margaret found herself whispering the words, the way people of her parents' generation used to whisper *cancer*, as if enunciating the word would make it more real.

'Don't say that, Margaret. The article won't have any effect on the judge, and anyway, it wasn't so bad.'

'It was awful. I feel like a criminal.' She lowered her voice. 'I can't even look at Hannah. She didn't know we'd paid Isaiah's . . . his birth mother. Thank God Isaiah can't read yet.'

'You've been a super mother to him. You saved that child, Margaret. You rescued him.'

'I'm going to lose him,' Margaret whispered hoarsely into the phone, tightening her grip on the receiver. In her mind, she replayed the scene that had haunted her for a month: standing in some dimly-lit corridor, she reaches out, holding Isaiah, and thrusts him into the darkness. When her arms are completely outstretched, Isaiah simply vanishes into the shadows. Each week the scenario grew more distinct, though Isaiah's birth mother remained a shadow; only her emotions, and the look of terror on Isaiah's face, grew more vivid. 'It's happening, I can feel it. I'm losing him.'

'I think I better come over. You shouldn't be alone.'

'Hah,' Margaret spurted. 'That's a laugh. I shouldn't be alone. My husband's having an affair, my daughter barely speaks to me, and now some stranger is trying to take my son away. You're right, I shouldn't be alone.' Margaret actually began to laugh out loud.

'Please let me come over.'

Margaret took a second to catch her breath. 'Thanks, Charlotte, really. I'm okay. I'm going to go to the office now and pretend that none of this is happening.'

Charles, too, felt like a criminal that day, though for a different reason. He'd never mentioned the Isaiah situation to Susannah, and now he felt sure she'd see the story in the *Times* and feel cheated, deceived. He felt guilty, keeping this important part of his life from her. He had begun this whole mess by cheating on his wife; now he was cheating on his lover too. Not that a man was expected to share intimate details of his family life with his lover, Charles consoled himself. But this was different, he had to admit. This was different.

Susannah was at the office when he arrived, which was always the case, no matter how early he got there. He greeted her without stopping and walked directly into his office. The temptation to close his door was strong.

She waited a full half-hour before confronting him, which he

182

hadn't expected. It would have been more in character for Susannah to have charged in after him.

'I was sorry to read about Isaiah,' she said.

'Thanks,' Charles replied. Then, to his dismay, she closed the door and sat down across from him.

'We have to talk.'

He only nodded.

'Do you have any idea what it felt like to read that story in the paper this morning?'

'I'm sorry, Susannah, I should have told you about it, it's just that . . .' He didn't know how to finish the sentence, so he let it die.

'Even if we weren't lovers, Charles, we're colleagues. This is clearly the most important thing happening in your life now . . .' Her voice faltered here, triggering a sympathetic tremor in him. '. . . and you never even mentioned it.'

It surprised Charles, and reassured him, to discover genuine emotion in Susannah. He'd begun to doubt it existed. 'I didn't want to burden you with it.'

'Get off it, Charles. You didn't tell me because you didn't take me seriously as a . . . a person.' Her old composure, her directness, had returned, which heartened Charles, though he was aware of being rebuked. 'I was an employee and a lover – make that sexual partner. You weren't interested in any other dimension of me at all. Reading that article on the train this morning, I saw this clearly.'

Charles was astonished at the depth of her feelings. He'd never believed that she cared for him in any profound way. She'd entered the affair, he'd always felt, purely for the pleasure of manipulating him, and perhaps her husband, too. Now she was learning that she'd been manipulated as well.

'I'm going to look for another job. I'm sure you understand why. I'd quit today except we can't afford it.'

Charles nodded, hating himself for immediately gauging the impact her departure would have on LewinArt.

Reading his mind, she said, 'Don't worry, Charles. I'm sure you'll find someone competent to replace me.'

At the door she turned and said, 'I didn't even know he was black, not even that.' Then she left him with his degradation.

Later, when Margaret called, suggesting a two-week vacation before the hearing, he jumped at the idea. 'I need to get away from here,' she told him.

'We all do,' he answered.

When Margaret went to Isaiah's room to get him ready for bed, she found that Hannah had beat her to it. She was sitting on the edge of his bed, reading him a story in a voice that had a schoolmarmish singsong to it, the voice she always used when in charge of Isaiah.

Margaret could have stood in the doorway, watching her children, for an hour or more. For a moment it seemed almost possible that things would work out. How could anyone, let alone a judge, allow these two children to be taken from each other? Surely such affection was as binding as nuclear fusion.

But then Hannah spotted her. She must have recognized Margaret's doting expression, and she recoiled from it.

'I'm just reading him a story,' she said.

'*Engine That Could*,' Isaiah piped from the bed.

'I used to read that to *you*, Hannah.'

Isaiah looked at Hannah but Hannah looked away from both of them, back at the book.

Margaret crossed the room and kissed Isaiah goodnight. 'Sleep tight,' she said, as she always did, and then overcame a momentary but intense urge to linger in the room. 'Thanks, Hannah,' she said as she left. But Hannah just shrugged it off, and waited for Margaret to leave the room before resuming the story.

The evening was unusually cool for August. The air conditioner was turned off for the first time in weeks, and a dispirited but welcome breeze found its way into the master bedroom through the open window. But when Charles got up off the bed, where both he and Margaret were reading, and turned on the air conditioner, Margaret knew why. The apartment was stifling, though not warm, and the drone of street noise was intrusive. They both wanted a barrier, a *barricade*, and the air conditioner would have to do.

Margaret was rereading the article, which she'd been doing all night, it seemed to Charles. 'You can't let that article get to you, Margaret. Here,' he said, reaching for it, 'let me get rid of it.'

Margaret pulled it towards her in an almost protective motion. 'I'm not finished.' Actually she was staring at the photograph of Selma Richards, trying to see in it the emaciated, shivering woman who had handed her Isaiah over two years ago. If she could only make the connection, she thought, then Isaiah would be hers forever. But the Selma Richards in the photograph was undeniably healthy looking, her straightened hair neatly, even fashionably arranged, her face strong and resolute, anything but the diseased color she recalled.

Worse than Selma Richards' robust appearance was the resemblance to Isaiah that peeked through, try though she did not to see it. But it was there, like a shadow in the photograph. It was there in the roundness of the face, in the large, almond eyes that drooped ever so slightly on the outside. It was there in the extra-wide mouth and in the unexpectedly narrow nose. It was there.

'What I want to know,' Charles said, 'is how we became the

villains?' He got into the bed next to her. 'I mean, how did we become this symbol of the acquisitive middle class? I'm a fucking graphic artist, for God's sake. We don't live on Park Avenue. We don't have ten cents left over at the end of the month. But suddenly we're Simon Legree out to rob Miss Ghetto of her son.'

Margaret continued to stare at the photograph, squinting now and then to alter it. The closer she looked, the more Isaiah's face came through.

'We smoked pot in college, we marched in civil rights demonstrations, anti-war rallies, you name it. Now suddenly we're acquisitive, selfish, careerish, mean-spirited baby snatchers. I don't get it.'

'We're symbols,' Margaret said. 'We're *yuppies*.'

'God, how I hate that word.'

'But I guess that's what we are. Everyone always accuses everyone else of being a yuppie, and never considers that they could be one, too.'

'We're not, though,' Charles insisted. 'Our values are different. We're not into material things.'

'Then how did we get all this?' Margaret said, taking in, with a sweep of one arm, the new over-sized Sony television, the patchwork comforter on their bed, the mahogany highboy they'd purchased at an antique store in New Hope, the silver frame on their dresser holding a family photo, the two closets overflowing with clothes. 'Where did all this come from?'

'This isn't so much,' Charles said, looking around the room as if for the first time.

'But it is a lot,' Margaret answered. 'It is, it's just that we never set out to acquire.'

'The highboy nearly bankrupted us.' They looked at each other and almost smiled. After writing a check, they'd raced back to New York and emptied two savings account to cover it. They'd had to wait three weeks until they had enough money to afford to rent a van to transport it back to New York.

Margaret felt a choking sorrow rising up from deep inside her and wanted to hold onto Charles until it subsided. But she felt suddenly, sadly, bashful. 'I couldn't bear to lose him, I couldn't stand it.'

Charles heard the stifled plea in her whisper and reached across the bed. 'We're not going to lose him.'

'But what if we do?' In Margaret's mind her arms were outstretched and Isaiah rolled off her fingertips into a kinetic void the color of the backs of her eyelids.

In the old days when they argued, before the trouble with Isaiah and before Susannah, the only way to cement a reconciliation was to make love. Nothing short of this ever stuck, nothing but sex ever completely dissipated the tension or anger or hurt. Charles felt his

185

hand massaging Margaret's familiar breasts and decided to trust his instincts. Margaret squirmed and started to turn away, but he held her and kissed her forcefully on the lips. Her resistance evaporated a moment later; Charles felt her body relax in a single movement. She held him on top of her with both hands clenched around his back. She squeezed him until she came, then squeezed even harder until he came as well. But when she finally released him and Charles pulled away, her face did not reveal the satisfied calm he'd come to expect at such times. Instead, she looked panicked, threatened.

It didn't work this time, her spooked eyes said to him. It didn't work.

Chapter 26

One Friday evening in early August, shortly after Calvin's arrival, Selma found herself talking about Josette and Raymond. 'Sometimes I think I abandoned them,' she said. She had made spaghetti and a salad, which they were eating at the small plastic 'butcher block' table she'd placed outside the kitchen door. Selma wasn't very hungry but she liked watching Calvin, who was, devour the food she'd prepared. Such feelings of accomplishment were rare in life. 'Don't they feed you in Boston?'

'Who's "they"?'

Selma smiled and looked away. Calvin seemed too perfect to her; she was always searching for the flaw, the fatal defect, like a secret wife, or girlfriends.

'I'll get you some more.' Selma went into the kitchen and spooned more spaghetti onto Calvin's plate, thinking she should have made more. When she returned to the table, she told him about a dream she'd been having.

'There's this little boy. He's in a room full of bright light, a glow, so bright the little boy's just a shadow, a dark spot. He's stuck there, in the middle of the room, sitting on a chair, and the light pouring in on him makes him tired, makes him weaker and weaker. I try to get to him but I can't, the light is so bright it burns my eyes. But when I close them, I can't find him. I just stumble around in the dark, searching for him, feeling the hot light on me.'

'That's your boy, Isaiah, you're dreaming about.'

'I used to think that, the first times I had that dream. But then one day it hit me, like a chill or something. Last Saturday afternoon I came into the bedroom to put the laundry away, and the sun had just poked round the building across the street. It looked like the room was on fire. I stood there, kind of scared, since it was like the dream was coming true or something. 'Cept in my vision it was Raymond I saw sitting in the middle of the room. Raymond, not Isaiah.' Selma heard her voice falter. Calvin must have heard it too. He put down his fork and wrapped his big hand round hers.

'Why don't we pay them a visit tomorrow? How 'bout it?'

Selma looked at him, feeling almost faint with relief. 'You serious?'

'Sure I'm serious.'

'I once told them I'd take them to the zoo . . .'

'Then we'll go to the zoo.'

A sudden thought clouded over. 'Their mama won't like that. Might not let us take them.'

'We'll see about that,' Calvin said, returning to his dinner. Looking at him, strong and sure in the way that only men over forty ever really are, she knew he'd manage it.

Selma hated looking back, hated even thinking about the past. But the look on Josette's face when she opened the door made up for any uneasiness she felt about revisiting her old apartment. Selma had forgotten how big the girl's smile was, the way it took over her face. 'Selma!' she cried, and then gave her a big hug. 'Raymond, come see who's here.'

Selma heard Raymond's little feet scuttling from the kitchen. When he saw her he stopped dead in his tracks, though. 'Ray, don't tell me you forgot me this soon?'

He shook his head.

'Then how about a hug like the one your sister just bestowed.'

He moved towards her and let her take him in her arms. 'You're getting so big, I can't hardly get my arms round you.' When she let go he almost fell away from her.

'He gets like that,' Josette said quickly, nervously.

'I understand,' Selma said. And she did. Adults liked to think that kids were trusting and forgiving, but a child can detect a betrayal the way a dog sniffs out fear. Only when you get older can you get suckered. ''Member I told you I'd take you to the zoo?'

Josette's eyes widened. Raymond just nodded solemnly.

'How 'bout today?'

A reluctant smile broke out on Raymond's face, and Selma felt something break out inside her, too.

'You remember Calvin, used to come for me sometimes?'

The children nodded.

'He's going with us to the zoo, if your mama says we can.'

'She's sleeping,' Josette said scornfully.

'Well, I'll just go tell her we're going then,' Selma said with much more confidence then she felt.

Marie's room was almost entirely dark, lit only by a faint yellow glow from behind the drawn shade. It smelled dusky and sharp, too, the way rooms get when someone sleeps in them for too long. Like a cellar, Selma thought, only warm.

At first Marie was indistinguishable from the sheets and blanket

188

heaped around her. She was so thin, she made more of a crease than a mound. Selma stood over her for a moment, reconsidering. Let sleeping dogs lie, she thought, listening to Marie's whiskey snore. Then she bent over and shook her gently. 'Marie? It's me, Selma. Are you awake, Marie?'

Marie opened her eyes without moving, reminding Selma of a turtle.

'I come to take the kids to the zoo. That okay by you?'

'What time is it?' Marie moaned.

''Bout ten.'

Marie shut her eyes, slowly.

'Okay, then, we'll be back 'fore dinnertime.' Selma tiptoed from the room, shutting the door behind her.

They took the A train back through Manhattan and into the Bronx. Selma couldn't help thinking how much they looked like a family, the four of them, sitting in a row on the subway. She had to smile, thinking how deceiving looks could be; only Josette and Raymond were related. This was no more a family than she and Dana.

'Which animals are your favorites?' Calvin asked the kids.

'Elephants,' Josette said quickly. 'And giraffes.'

'Elephants and giraffes,' Raymond agreed, swinging his legs against the seat in anticipation.

'Then we'll start with the elephants.' Calvin looked at Selma and they smiled. An hour later they got off in the Bronx.

It was a hot and muggy Saturday. The animals in their cages and enclosures barely moved, as if the air itself were too thick to maneuver through; some seemed to have collapsed with exhaustion, though they had little to do other than look presentable for the people. Only the children, the *human* children, were active that day, darting from one exhibit to another, shrieking in delight or fear, poking at the animals, hassling their parents for food.

Raymond and Josette were no exception. As soon as they arrived at the zoo they shifted into high gear, making a strange contrast to the languid animals. 'There are the hippos,' Josette would squeal, and off they'd go, hanging over the wall surrounding the hippo pond, momentarily fascinated by the inert hunks of gray flesh, until Selma and Calvin caught up with them a minute later, at which point some other beast would lure them away.

'Some of these animals look like they stuffed,' Selma told Calvin as the children raced ahead to the giraffes.

'Being cooped up makes you lazy,' he said. 'And the heat don't help the situation.'

There was one creature that put on a display. It looked like a tall, very thin deer to Selma, with twisted horns on its head. It leapt around its enclosure like the ground was giving off electric shocks. It seemed lighter than the air itself. 'What's that, Selma?' Josette asked, leaning into the fence to get a better look.

Selma just shook her head.

'Here, this tells what it is.' Josette had moved to a plaque, but it was too high for her to read. On it Selma could see a few paragraphs and a picture of the animal that was dancing about before them.

Selma looked for Calvin to rescue her, but he and Raymond were buying a pretzel from a snack stand. She leaned toward the plaque and squinted at it, as if having a hard time making it out. She guessed that the big green letters spelled the animal's name. She also guessed that the map told where it came from. But she couldn't make out any of the words, no matter how hard she concentrated.

'What is it, Selma?' Josette persisted.

'I guess it's a deer,' she offered weakly.

'A deer? Is that what it says?'

Selma made a show of looking closely at the plaque. 'Not exactly, Josette.'

'Then what does it say?'

The deer or whatever it was had hopped behind some trees and Selma found herself envying its grace and ease; she felt heavy and useless.

'What is it, Selma? What's its name?'

'I'm studying it, child,' she answered testily. She felt Josette's hungry gaze on her, hotter than the sun.

When Calvin joined them, Josette continued her inquisition. 'What's the name of this? Selma won't tell me.'

Selma looked up at Calvin, hotter and more flushed than before. She avoided Calvin's eyes but she felt his stare, too. She took a step away from them, fixing on the animal that had caused all the trouble. Calvin looked down at the plaque and then back at Josette. 'Maybe if you'd asked her politely, she'd told you it's a antelope,' he said sternly.

'Antelope,' Josette said with satisfaction, ignoring his reprimand. 'Look, Ray, there's the antelope.'

Selma continued to avoid looking at Calvin, even when she felt his hand on her shoulder. She wished they could leave the zoo right away; now it struck her as an unfriendly, even hostile place, a place full of things she alone couldn't understand. It felt, suddenly, a lot like the world she was always trying to escape from, a world where you couldn't improve yourself, a world where the only thing you knew for sure was how little you knew, a world where the past kept you captive like these animals, imprisoned by walls and cages and glass. Selma took one last, longing look at the antelope, stationary for the moment but full of grace and potential. Then she followed the kids to the elephant enclosure.

They had lunch in a large, echo-filled cafeteria. The kids loaded a tray with sandwiches and cakes and drinks, but Selma couldn't eat. The place reminded her of one of the exhibits; it had the same earthy smell, the same stifled, pent-up atmosphere.

'So tell me how your mother's doing,' Selma asked them as they ate.

'The same,' Josette said between bites of her tuna fish sandwich. Raymond nodded automatically.

'She feeling better?'

'I guess.'

'Didn't look like she filled my old room.'

'Mary lived there,' Raymond offered through a mouthful of peanut butter and jelly.

'Mary?'

'Mary came about a week after you left,' Josette explained. 'But she left a few weeks later.'

'How come?'

'She and Mama didn't get along.'

'How didn't they get along?'

'Sometimes they would fight. Mary was real religious, always reading her Bible and talking to Mama about sin and hell and damnation and whatnot.'

'Oh, Lord,' Selma said, laughing in spite of herself. 'I can see where they wouldn't see eye to eye.'

Josette nodded agreement but looked sadly down at her plate. Selma felt bad that she had laughed; Mary must have seemed like a refuge to the kids, whatever her faults. 'You liked Mary, didn't you?'

Josette shrugged. 'She was okay.'

'She was okay,' Raymond echoed.

Later, walking back to the car, Selma said to Calvin, 'It's hard on the kids, having people come and go. Any of them must seem like an improvement over what they got.'

'Don't blame yourself, Selma.'

'Oh, I had to move out. Even if my lawyer hadn't told me to, I'd had to move out once I got Isaiah back.' Selma thought of her grandmother, of the lingering importance of those summers spent in Winfield, Georgia. 'At least if I keep on visiting with them, maybe I can do some good.'

They walked in silence for a few moments. Then Calvin said, in a hesitant voice, 'Selma, you ever stop to think how you'll take it if you don't get him back?'

'I don't stop to think. But sometimes it flashes through my mind. Like a sharp pain.'

'You got your life together now. You got to keep it that way no matter what happens in September.'

'I won't fall apart, if that's what you're afraid of,' she told him. She wasn't really sure if this was true. Maybe Isaiah, the thought of him, was the glue that was holding her together. If she didn't have to run from the past, then what was to prevent her from falling back into it?

'You started over once, you'll start over again if you have to.' But Calvin sounded more hopeful than sure.

They found Marie sitting at the tiny kitchen table, drinking a glass of tomato juice. She looked gaunt and unhealthy. And there was something contagious about the way she looked, Selma thought. You didn't want to get too close, let alone touch her.

Josette walked directly from the front door to the back room that used to be Selma's. But Raymond ran over to his mother and began telling her about the zoo.

'We gave peanuts to the elephant,' he said, recounting a highlight of the afternoon. When Marie failed to rise to his enthusiasm, he told her about the seals. 'They jumped in the air to get the fishes. And they honked like buses.'

'You got no business taking my children,' Marie said in a somber monotone. Raymond turned and looked at Selma and Calvin.

'We just borrowed them for a few hours,' Calvin said brightly. Then he added, quickly, 'So's you could rest.'

'I asked you about it earlier, and you said okay,' Selma told her.

Marie took a contemplative sip of tomato juice. Next to her bloodless skin, the tomato juice looked gaudy and loud.

'I didn't give permission to take the kids nowhere,' Marie said.

'I thought you did,' Selma said. She glanced down and saw Raymond looking up at her through darkening eyes. Not wishing to tarnish his day further, she took Calvin's arm and said, 'Let's go.'

At the front door she shouted goodbye to Josette, who called back to them. "Bye, Selma. 'Bye, Calvin.' She sounded like she was crying out from inside a cave. Selma felt awkward about kissing Raymond in front of his mother, but fortunately he followed her to the front door. She squatted down and took her in his arms. 'How 'bout we do that again real soon?' she said, squeezing him. He had that flimsy feel that little boys have, yet at the same time there was a weighty solidity about him that was incredibly satisfying. 'Maybe we'll go to the beach,' she offered. She felt him nod into her shoulder.

But when she released him and he stepped back, she saw that he'd

192

reverted to the same distrustful look he'd worn that morning. I won't be deceived, his eyes were telling her. Not this time.

'We'll go to the beach, I promise,' Selma said, but Raymond had already withdrawn into the apartment.

Chapter 27

By the time they were ready to vacate Manhattan for their two-week rental on Fire Island, Margaret felt an almost frantic need to get away. This need grew as the departure date approached, but it wasn't a pleasant feeling of anticipation; it was desperation. The *Times* article had ruined New York for her, turned the whole city against her, in her mind. She felt watched, judged, violated. This feeling was most intense when she was out with Isaiah. She had never noticed the second glances when she pushed Isaiah in his stroller or walked with him, holding his hand. When Hannah had pointed out to her that people stared, she'd been quite surprised; it really hadn't occurred to her that they made an unusual pair. Now she felt the double takes as keenly as darts. Once, New York had seemed heterogenous, accepting, the kind of place where no one cares what you do, or whom you do it with. The kind of place where no one notices. But New York was a changed place now, a hostile, judging, cruel place.

She'd finished packing two days in advance. When Charles came home that Wednesday to find bulging suitcases lined up in their front hall, she'd been embarrassed. I don't want to be crazy tomorrow and Friday, and I had some free time this afternoon, is what she'd told him, but his thin, indulgent smile told her he was no more convinced than she was. As a child she'd often thought about families who had to flee together for one reason or another: Jewish families in Germany, pioneer families outrunning Indians, pilgrims escaping persecution in England. Perhaps it was the stifling sameness, the cold impersonality of her own family's life that made her fantasize about families united by a common enemy, and their need to elude it. She'd picture her parents huddled over her in some dark alleyway as storm troopers marched by. Or she'd imagine them cowering in a covered wagon as Indians circled. She'd read the diary of Anne Frank three times as an adolescent, relishing the thought of her own family in similarly tight quarters. Later, she'd wondered why such fantasies appealed to her, when her reality was as secure as any girl's. To make heroes out of her parents, who were anything but heroic? No, it wasn't that. It was the huddling itself that had

195

appealed to her, Margaret figured, the drawing in of the wagon train.

Now she was feeling this all over again, but the enemy this time was more real, closer. Her need to huddle with her family, even Charles, was acute. They had to escape, together, as a family, to remain a family. That's why she packed the bags two days in advance, causing no end of inconvenience to the family, who spent those two days complaining, a bit excessively, Margaret thought, of inaccessible clothes and toiletries. The truth was, she'd had to force herself to hold off packing even earlier, the need to be prepared to flee at a moment's notice was that strong.

The enemy was at the door.

Only on the ferry to Fire Island did Margaret relax. Now there was a palpable distance, a barrier between her family and the forces that would tear them apart. Margaret didn't even like to *think* the name Selma Richards. She sat on top of the ferry and watched the shoreline of Long Island recede and felt her tension and fear recede along with it.

They'd rented a three-bedroom house directly on the beach. Charles had been appalled at the rent, but Margaret wanted as little interaction with other people as possible, and on Fire Island, the only way to ensure privacy was to face the ocean; at least there'd be no neighbors on one side. The house was perched, somewhat precariously, on stilts, jutting out over gentle mounds of sand that had once been dunes but had been severely eroded over time; it shook when two or more people were in motion. But it was nicely furnished and the view of the Atlantic never failed to captivate Margaret, no matter how many times a day she opened the sliding doors from the living room and came upon it. The ocean's vast impersonality acted as a balm on her tender nerves. As Charles and the children swam and played in the sand, she would stand at the railing of their deck and stare out over the bathers with their brightly colored towels and umbrellas to the infinite emptiness of the sea. By the end of their first weekend, she was feeling restored.

The Fredricks, too, were on vacation. They were spending the last two weeks of August in the Hamptons, visiting Mrs Fredricks' parents. Selma learned this only a week before they were going. 'So I guess you can take your vacation then too,' Mrs Fredricks had said brightly.

'I wasn't planning on taking a vacation,' Selma had told her. In the back of her mind she wondered if her employer was setting her up to take the two weeks off without pay.

A loud crash in the living room had interrupted them. They both raced from the front hallway (or 'foyer', as Mrs Fredricks called it) to find Dana standing, stunned, over a broken crystal vase. Mrs Fredricks cast an accusatory glance at Selma, whose eyes widened in immediate protest. Unsuccessful in pinning the blame on Selma, she reluctantly turned to Dana. 'I've told you not to play in here,' she said in a tightly controlled voice. Dana waited a moment (Selma recognized her expression – calculating which response to give) and then burst into loud sobs.

'Oh, sweetie,' Mrs Fredricks said, squatting down with her arms open. Dana waited another second before scrambling into her mother's arms.

'Sometimes the best vacations are the ones you spend at home,' Mrs Fredricks said over her daughter's head. Selma stood over them, feeling awkward. 'You know, sleeping late, doing little projects around the house.'

'Is this a paid vacation?'

'I don't think so,' Mrs Fredricks said in an innocent voice, like this wasn't her decision, like this hadn't occurred to her before. Which, Selma thought, perhaps it hadn't. 'I mean, this custody suit of yours does complicate matters, after all,' Mrs Fredricks added, her back to Selma. 'Frankly, I'm a little surprised that you'd ask a favor of me, given the situation.'

Selma was tempted to reply that a paid vacation wasn't a favor. 'I need this job, else I'll never get my boy back.'

'Oh, you'll have the job,' Mrs Fredricks said bitterly. 'Frankly, I don't like the idea of such a . . . distraction. Dana must be your first priority.'

Like she's your first priority, Selma thought.

'And if I'd known about the drugs . . .'

Selma forced her teeth together.

'But I wouldn't want the *New York Times* to report that we've been insensitive to your . . . needs,' she said with obvious distaste. 'That's the last thing we want. It was very clever of you, getting that article written, and in the *Times*, of all places.'

Selma made herself ignore this and deal with the issue at hand. Dana's sobs had subsided into muffled gasps into her mother's left shoulder pad. When she looked up for a moment, Selma refused to smile at her. 'The custody hearing? My lawyer says it will last two or three days. I'll be needing that time off, but I don't expect to get paid.'

'That's very generous of you, Selma.'

She ignored the sarcasm. 'But the two weeks you going on vacation – I wasn't planning on taking no vacation. If I'd a known about it, maybe I'd a planned something. This way, I lose two weeks salary and—'

'All *right*, Selma,' Mrs Fredricks interrupted, motioning to Dana, as if this conversation would upset her. 'I'll talk to Mr Fredricks this evening and let you know.'

As it turned out, Selma did get paid for her two weeks off, but she wasn't really enjoying her vacation. For one thing, she was too nervous about the upcoming hearing to enjoy anything; at least taking care of Dana would have kept her occupied. For another, she had been hoping to take a week or two off when she got Isaiah back, just to get acquainted. Would Mrs Fredricks allow her to take two more weeks off, never mind the pay? Selma didn't think so. And another thing: Calvin wasn't free to take time off with her, which struck her as kind of a waste. Selma spent the first week doing just what Mrs Fredricks said she'd do – not the part about sleeping late (Selma rose at six thirty on the dot, seven mornings a week), the part about little projects around the house. She'd never taken much interest in fixing up, but she was expecting Isaiah in just a few weeks, so she thought she'd try to make it more welcoming for a little boy.

She found an enormous toy store on Broadway and bought a huge stuffed giraffe, remembering how much Raymond had liked the giraffes at the Bronx Zoo. At a furniture store she found a miniature chair and table, which she bought without hesitation. When she placed it in the bedroom, the whole room seemed suddenly immense, out of proportion; she had a momentary sense of what it must be like to be Isaiah, and what it would be like to leave his family for this strange woman. She wondered, briefly, if she were doing the wrong thing. Sometimes this thought slipped into her mind like leaking water. Then she'd have to stop what she was doing and argue it out with herself. The boy would feel some pain, being separated from the Lewins. But in the long run he was better off with his real mother, a mother of his race who would understand him as he grew up. She'd let Isaiah visit with the Lewins; this wasn't about getting revenge or anything. It was about restoring what was right, making up for past sins, guaranteeing the best life for a little boy. How will Isaiah feel down the road when he realizes he's a black boy living in a white world? He should be with his own kind; Selma had no doubts on this score.

Still, staring at the tiny table and chair, Selma had a glimpse of the world the way Isaiah saw it. For the thousandth time she rebuked herself for giving him up; for the ten thousandth time she promised she'd make it up to him.

Another reason Selma would just as soon have been working was that the city was beginning to heat up, the air was thickening with sour humidity, and Selma's apartment, unlike the Fredricks', was not air-conditioned. She woke up in the morning stuck to her sheets. Showers helped, but not much, and her towels never quite dried.

Calvin looked cool, though, when she opened her door to him Friday night. 'Don't you feel the heat?' Selma asked him, marveling at his dry forehead, his crisp blue shirt.

'Now I do,' he said with a sly grin.

Selma just shook her head as he walked past her into the apartment. 'Don't it get this hot in Boston?'

'Oh, it gets hot all right.'

She hesitated. 'Maybe I should pay *you* a visit sometime.' She held her breath and regretted moving to such a dangerous topic so early in the weekend.

'You'd come up to see me?'

She slowly let out her breath. 'Course I would.'

'I'd show you a real nice time, Selma. Next time, okay?'

'Next time I might have a little boy with me.'

'I'm looking forward to meeting him.'

Selma was beginning to believe that things could work out for the best. How else to explain Calvin Hughes, who entered her life when she thought love was something other people felt, a luxury other people could afford, and showed her otherwise? On Monday she took the big step, the frightening step, of telling him she loved him.

'I love you too, sugar,' Calvin answered, almost matter-of-factly.

They were walking, practically in slow motion, in Riverside Park. The heat was almost visible; waves of damp air came at them down the long, grassy promenade as they strolled, holding hands. 'You do?'

'Course I do. Why else would I be here?'

Living seemed so easy for Calvin. Loving, too. Selma saw life as a struggle, an obstacle course. Calvin had come too easy to her, she hadn't had to chase him, cajole him, plead with him. Could it really be so easy?

'Tell me about your ex-wife, your divorce,' she asked him, surprising herself and him.

'What you want to know about that for?'

'I just do, that's all.'

'She was a beautiful woman, Lonnie was, tall with these big wide eyes and this big, wide smile. We had three kids together and then one day she told me she was in love with someone else. I felt like someone had punched me in the stomach. Like she had punched me. She and this other fella been together ever since. Now I sometimes think my own kids think of that man as their father. When I see them it's like they meeting an uncle or something. A distant uncle.'

'Wouldn't think you'd want much to do with women after that,' Selma suggested.

'That's the truth.'

'Then how come . . .'

''Cause I could see from the start, right there in Brooklyn, that you wouldn't do to a person what my wife did to me.'

'You could tell that?'

'Uh huh. You learned your lesson, Selma. 'Bout what happens when you let someone down. You won't do it again.' They walked without talking for a while. 'Plus, you happen to be the prettiest thing I seen in a month of Sundays.'

'Did I tell you lately I love you?'

'Five minutes ago.'

The phone was ringing when they got home. Calvin went into the bedroom to start packing while she answered it.

'Selma, hi. I tried you all day at the Fredricks. You sick or something? Listen, I had a thought.'

'How you doing, Arthur?'

'You think the Fredricks would want to testify on your behalf? You know, describe how loyal and hard-working you are, and how good you are with kids?'

Selma told him about her conversation with Mrs Fredricks. 'They don't want no trouble, Arthur. They already upset 'bout the article.'

'That's a shame. With one of them on the stand, we could show how stable you are *and* how experienced you are taking care of kids. You know, they could bring the kid to court, show how close the two of you are.'

'Selma, you see my sunglasses?' Calvin called out from the bathroom.

She cupped the phone with her hand and told him they were in the bedroom.

'Selma, who was that?'

'Calvin Hughes,' she said evenly.

'Same guy as last time?'

'Yes,' she hissed into the phone, getting irritated.

'He living with you or something?'

'He lives in Boston.'

'He planning on marrying you?' His voice sounded more hopeful now.

'None of your business.'

'Oh yes it is. If you were married . . . What does this guy do for a living?'

'I'm hanging up.'

'Okay, okay. About the Fredricks.'

'Forget it. Only reason they letting me keep the job is they don't want to look bad firing me.'

Selma was shaking when she hung up. Calvin appeared in the

200

living room holding his bag, ready to go. 'Wish I didn't have to leave.'

'Me too,' she said, but in her heart she was suddenly glad he was going. Arthur Golderson's voice echoed inside her; the way he talked about Calvin, the way his thoughts worked, made her dizzy. She wanted to sit down and think things over. She wanted to be alone.

Calvin could see something was wrong. 'That your lawyer?'

'Yes.'

'Everything okay?'

Selma nodded.

'Then it's goodbye.' He kissed her on the lips, then pulled away. 'You sure everything's all right?'

'I'm sure,' she lied. But when the door shut behind him, a terrible feeling of dread came over her. She ran to the door and leaned over the banister. She could see the top of Calvin's head moving down the stairs. 'I love you,' she shouted after him. He looked up and smiled.

'You talking to me?' he said.

'Yes, you,' she answered, and, for a moment, just his big, easy smile reassured her. Then he continued on down the stairs and the dread returned.

Chapter 28

Most days, Margaret stayed up on the deck that cantilevered over the flattened dunes. From this vantage, Isaiah and Hannah and Charles were satisfyingly visible as they played or rested by the ocean's edge, but distant enough to retain an aura of perfection. It helped, too, that she could see hundreds of yards down the beach in either direction; this made her feel protective, reassured her that her family was basically safe.

Yes, it was worth the unthinkable rent to be on the beach. Worth even the humiliating trek up to Greenwich to ask her parents for the money. Legal fees had wiped out their savings, leaving nothing for a vacation, let alone a house on the beach. So Margaret had driven up to Connecticut one Wednesday to ask her parents for the four thousand dollars their two-week rental was costing them.

'Four thousand dollars,' her mother said, repeating the figure. 'I've never heard of paying that much for two weeks.'

'I haven't either,' echoed her father.

They were having lunch on the terrace behind the Hollanders' house. Connecticut was at its suburban best that afternoon, the greens of the grass, trees, and shrubbery especially lush, thanks to a wet spring and summer, but perfectly behaved, nonetheless, thanks to the well-compensated efforts of the Hollanders' gardener. Lois had made roast beef sandwiches. The moment Margaret bit into hers, she was brought back to her childhood; no one made a more meager sandwich than her mother. As she chewed a mouthful of quality white bread surrounding a thin slice of roast beef glazed with mayonnaise, she reminded herself that they needed the vacation, and that four thousand was in fact the going rate for two weeks at the beach, directly on the ocean. She bit her lower lip until she felt composed, then said, 'That's what the houses go for. If we didn't have the legal fees . . .'

Her parents smiled uncomfortably at this and concentrated on their sandwiches for a bit. They mentioned the case as little as possible. Lois, after the *Times* article, had remarked only that twenty-five thousand dollars seemed like an awful lot of money for an illegal adoption. I mean, Margaret, if it had been on the up and up, that would have been one thing. But it wasn't even legal! For twenty-five thousand, I'd have insisted on a *legal* adoption. Margaret had bit her lip then, too.

'I always thought Fire Island was for queers,' Walter offered after a few minutes of silence. 'Didn't you, dear?'

'Homosexuals,' Lois whispered to him anxiously, as if she were worried that one was lurking behind their privet hedge.

The subject of the four thousand dollars wasn't discussed further, and Margaret just didn't have the heart to bring it up again. She felt suffocated by the futility of her expedition. She spent the remainder of the lunch thinking of alternatives: a home equity loan, borrowing from friends, perhaps a less expensive house. Her parents spoke intermittently on their favorite topics: the high cost of home maintenance, cholesterol, the misfortunes of friends.

As Margaret was getting set to leave, her father gave her a kiss on her cheek and then pulled himself up short. 'I almost forgot,' he said, slapping his hip in annoyance. 'I won't be a minute.'

Margaret hadn't the slightest idea what he meant, but Lois smiled indulgently at the memory lapse. A few minutes later Walter returned with a check for four thousand dollars. 'Where's our memory going?' Lois asked goodnaturedly, as if it had been decided hours ago that they were going to give Margaret the money. Perhaps it had been.

Margaret had years ago memorized the twists and turns of the Merritt Parkway. It was her favorite road because it made her feel like an accomplished driver; she loved passing frightened looking drivers in station wagons as she negotiated the curves that had thrilled her since she was sixteen. She reminded herself how glad she was about the check – at one point, she even took it out of her wallet to look at it. She reminded herself because in fact she was terribly saddened by it. She recalled her mother's expression as her father ran upstairs for the check, a look devoid of pleasurable anticipation. Where was the eager, pleased expression of a parent about to present a daughter with a generous gift? Where was the look of enjoyment at what their material wellbeing enabled them to do for their daughter?

They're cold and emotionally inept even in their generosity, Margaret thought. They might have been presenting a check to the United Way.

If she felt more relaxed the second week of their vacation, she was anything but truly calm. The trial loomed ahead like painful and risky surgery. Wednesday morning she broke down and called David Elliot. It was only after he answered that she realized she had nothing to ask him. 'I was just wondering how things are going,' she offered weakly.

'Oh, fine, fine,' he answered with maddening serenity.

'Well, is there anything new?'

'New?'

'You know, any new developments.'

She heard him take a deep breath. 'This isn't the kind of matter that requires a lot of research, if that's what you mean. I believe the custody laws favor our side, but beyond familiarizing myself with these laws, there's not much to be done until September seventh.'

The children and Charles burst into the house at that moment, probably hungry for lunch. Margaret tried to end the conversation without giving away whom she was talking to. 'Great,' was all she said. 'That's just great.'

'Is there anything else I can do for you?'

'No, nothing. Thanks. 'Bye.'

She hung up and immediately busied herself making tuna fish sandwiches.

'Who was that?' Charles asked her when Hannah was briefly out of the room.

Margaret wanted to lie. She hated being the nervous one, the panicked one; it had never been her role in the past. She'd always been as level-headed as Charles, maybe more so. When they got lost while driving, Charles was the one to freak out, Margaret the one calmly to consult the map and determine their location. When Hannah had fallen on Broadway many years ago and split open her lip, they both handled the situation calmly, but it had been Margaret who stood by in the examining room while Hannah's lip was stitched up, squeezing her hand and wiping the sweat and tears off her face. Charles said his presence would just overcrowd the room, but Margaret knew, and hadn't even cared, that he was simply frightened. Now she was the hysterical one, and she hated it.

'It was David Elliot,' she said as casually as she could.

'Did he call?' Margaret was gratified to detect a note of alarm in his voice.

'No.'

Charles went to the refrigerator and got out the lemonade. Margaret had squeezed a dozen lemons that morning. 'Anything happening?'

'No.'

Hannah had wandered back into the room, so Charles whispered, 'If you're feeling concerned about things, why don't you talk to me? I can help you more at this point than a goddamn lawyer.'

'*If* I'm feeling concerned?' she hissed. 'Jesus Christ, did you think I just forgot about the whole thing?'

Isaiah, with his uncanny ability to detect tension between his parents, ran over and asked for juice. Margaret went to the refrigerator and got out a cardboard container of orange juice. 'Apple,' he said when he saw it.

'We only have orange, sweetie,' Margaret said. 'Here, I'll put the straw in for you.'

'I want apple,' he insisted.

'I have lemonade. Homemade.' She picked up the pitcher and lowered it to Isaiah's eye level.

He inspected it for a moment. 'Apple.'

'There is no apple, Isaiah. Have orange juice.'

'No,' he said with unexpected firmness.

'Then sit down and I'll pour you some water.'

'No,' he said again, and this time Margaret could detect tears forming.

'I put some tuna fish in a bowl for you, Isaiah, the way you like it.'

'No toofish.'

'Please sit down, Isaiah,' Margaret insisted.

'*No.*'

'I'm asking you.'

'*NO.*'

The sight of Charles sitting at the table with Hannah, calmly eating his sandwich, was the last straw. She took two big strides across the kitchen, picked up Isaiah, who began to flail in her arms, and jammed him into a chair at the table. When his knee hit the edge of the table, his whimpering escalated into hysterical crying.

She stood there dumbly for a moment or two, aware that Charles and Hannah were staring. I've overreacted, she told herself. That's all. I've overreacted. She picked a napkin and began dabbing Isaiah's face, which was a mess of tears and mucus. 'I'm sorry, darling,' she said. 'I'm sorry.' The words triggered something in her, some internal thermostat stopped functioning; she knew right away she had to get out of the house. She took a deep, steadying breath and announced in a tremulous voice that she was going to the store for apple juice.

Charles had said nothing to Margaret about ending his affair with Susannah. He still hated talking about it, even about the end of it. And there was a part of him that harbored a nasty guilt that in fact it had been Susannah who ended the relationship, not him.

Perhaps it was being on vacation, but he didn't miss her. He called the office every other day, and Susannah briskly ran down the current projects, reassuring him that things were under control at LewinArt. When he thought about missing her he thought about missing her cool professionalism, not her personality or even her

206

sexually. He thought of the loss to LewinArt, not to Charles Lewin.

Charles wished he could help Margaret feel better. Yes, he felt anxious about the upcoming trial, and he couldn't imagine life without Isaiah, let alone Isaiah's life with that Richards woman. But he could handle his anxiety in a way that she couldn't. It was a part of him that he could set aside when helping Isaiah build a sandcastle, when flying a kite with Hannah. Margaret couldn't put it aside. Grief and pain were blinders that hung always before her eyes, limiting her vision to the ordeal they were facing. In the mornings she waited until he started to get out of bed and then pulled him on top of her, kissing and fondling him in a frantic, loveless, but ultimately successful seduction that always left them both panting and sweating in the humid August heat, more aware than before of the terrifying limits of love.

Sometimes Hannah looked at Isaiah and couldn't believe how *strange* he looked. There were a lot of little kids on the beach, and they all tended to bunch around the edge of the water, digging in the wet sand and getting themselves all filthy. Isaiah was the only black kid in the bunch, which the other kids didn't seem to notice or care about. But to Hannah he just looked so different, especially wearing nothing but this tiny bathing suit. The other day, while he was sleeping in his room back at the house, Hannah had bent over and examined his skin real closely, like a scientist. She'd looked so close her eyelashes brushed against his arm; she could even make out the tiny pores. Then she'd done the same thing with her own arm. When you get that close, she realized, there really isn't much difference. Both arms looked like maps or photographs of the surface of the moon or something. But from a distance, like on the beach, she just couldn't get over how different Isaiah looked. Different from her. Different from her parents. Different from *everybody*.

Hannah had met this girl on Fire Island. Mara. Mara's parents owned a house on their walk, a few houses in from the ocean. Mara had been coming to Fire Island all her life, and knew everything about everybody. She had a story about everyone who walked by on the beach. I saw him snorting cocaine last summer in his living room . . . Her brother is married to a cousin of Michael J. Fox . . . She had a nose job over the winter. Mara was the perfect friend because Hannah wasn't in the mood to talk much and all Mara did was talk about other people. They'd set up their beach towels as far from their parents as they could without moving into the next town. Hannah would lie on her back, concentrating on her tan, while Mara chattered on and on about this one and that one.

Then, during the second week, right out of the blue, she

mentioned the *Times* article. 'My parents read it, I didn't. They said Isaiah's adopted.'

'Brilliant.'

'They said you might have to give him back to his real mother because the adoption was illegal.'

'His *birth* mother.'

'Yeah, right.'

Hannah wondered if Mara would talk about them next summer if they returned to Fire Island. 'Look, those are the Lewins. They almost lost the black kid, he was illegally adopted. They PAID his mother $25,000 for him.' Or maybe she'd say, 'See those people. The Lewins. They used to have this kid. A black kid. Only now he's back with his real mother.'

Hannah sat up and looked at Isaiah. Sometimes it made her crazy that he had no idea what was happening. It was unfair in a way. Back in the city she'd once tried to feel him out about the whole color thing. Look, Isaiah, she'd said, speaking softly so her parents wouldn't hear. She put her hand next to his on the couch in the living room. 'What do you notice different about our two hands?' He'd just looked at her, like she was nuts or something. 'Well, which is bigger, my hand or yours?'

'My hand,' he'd mimicked with a big smile. He *loved* guessing games.

'Wrong, *my* hand. Now, which is darker, yours or mine?'

He studied the hands intently for a while, then looked at her dumbly.

'Darker, Isaiah. Like . . .' She searched the room. 'The couch is darker than the curtains. Darker in color.'

'Darker,' he repeated, slapping the couch.

'Right. Now, look at our hands. Which is darker, yours or mine?'

'Yours,' he said with a satisfied grin.

She hadn't even bothered to correct him. What was the point? How could a 2½-year-old know what was what?

Hannah sat up, suddenly uncomfortably hot. Behind her she could see her mother, standing on the deck of their house like a security guard or something. Hannah couldn't even bear to look at her these days. Her face was so tense, you could see the worry on it just like a rash or something. Her father was down by the water, digging a long trench from the ocean to a sandcastle he and Isaiah and a couple of the other kids had made. So that was how it stood: her mother wringing her hands all the time, her father acting like a jerk all week, never sitting still, always digging in the sand, flying kites, jogging down the beach, hunting sea shells. And Isaiah, just as ignorant as a puppy. 'Can you believe she has the nerve to wear that bathing suit?' Mara was saying.

Hannah was beginning to feel dizzy from the sun. 'I'm going in,' she said, hoping Mara wouldn't come with her. She ran into the ocean without stopping, diving under a huge wave and emerging on the other side of it, surprised to find that the water was only waist high; it felt as if the ocean floor had risen up to meet her.

Chapter 29

Hardly a day went by that Selma didn't regret not being able to read and write. Some days just walking down Broadway made her head ache from all the signs shouting out at her in a language she didn't understand. Music, any kind of music, sounds too loud when you don't like it; words are like that too, they scream louder, they're more jarring, when you don't know what it is they're saying.

But on Thursday of the second week of her vacation, Selma thought she'd trade her entire future of reading and writing for the ability to write just one letter. If I could just write this one, she thought, I'd never ask to write another.

'Something's wrong,' Lizzie greeted her Thursday evening.

Selma put her book bag on the table and sat down across from Lizzie. 'I need your help.'

'Sure, anything,' Lizzie said. Selma heard the worry in her voice, though. It's always risky promising something before you know what it is.

So Selma told her about her conversation earlier that week with Arthur Golderson. As usual, he'd started in without introducing himself: 'Listen, Selma, I've been thinking.'

'Good, Arthur,' she said. A week and a half on vacation had made her kind of sassy.

'This thing, uh, with your boyfriend . . .'

That's when Selma's heart froze. 'Calvin,' she said, making her voice as forceful as she could.

'It's no good, Selma. If the Lewins find out about him, we're finished.'

'Ain't I allowed a social life?'

'As far as the court's concerned, you're the Virgin Mary.'

'Little late for that, Arthur. This is about getting my *son* back.'

'I'm sorry, Selma. If you're serious about getting him back . . .'

'Of course I'm serious,' she hissed into the phone.

'Then stop seeing Calvin.'

'I don't see why I can't have a man in my life.'

'A man is one thing, not great but we could live with it. A married man, forget it. I can just hear Dave Elliot now, making fucking mincemeat of us on that.'

Now Selma's whole body froze. 'He's divorced.'

'No, he's not.'

She waited, and then asked, 'How do you know?'

'Look, Selma, I couldn't take any chances. I have this detective, Sal Fishman . . .'

In a flash, Selma absorbed the possibility that Calvin really was married. The thing was, the person she was angriest with was Arthur Golderson. Not herself, not Calvin. Arthur Golderson.

'You understand why you can't see him, don't you? You've got to show the court that you'll make a super mother. We're going to try to bring down the Lewins and their yuppie values with them, but we can't do this if you're carrying on with a married man. We might as well drop the case right now.'

Selma never could predict with Arthur what it was that pushed her over the edge from annoyance to fury. This time it was the words *carrying on* that made her hang up on him. She would have preferred to wait a few minutes, but she was afraid Arthur would call back, so she picked up the receiver again and dialed Calvin's number up in Boston. There was no answer, which meant he'd already left for work. Waiting for the long day to end so she could try him again, Selma consoled herself with the fact that at least no one else had answered – like a wife, for example.

When she did finally get him, early that evening, she froze at the sound of his voice. Sometimes, just accusing someone of something, just doubting them, is enough to choke off love. 'There's something we gotta talk about,' is how she started.

'Shoot,' he said with such unconcern, she began to feel better.

'My lawyer, the one who's helping me to get my boy back, he says he had you investigated, and that you're married.'

Selma held her breath during the long gap that followed.

'Well, you got yourself a good lawyer, Selma.'

She couldn't think of anything to say.

'My wife and I haven't lived together for ten years. That part is true. And she is living with another fellow that's like a father to my children. That part's true, too. We just never made it official. We kept meaning to, but never did. After a while there didn't seem much reason to do it, we been living separate so long.'

This last part hurt: Ain't I reason enough?

'Selma, say something.'

'Nothing *to* say.'

'This don't change nothing, does it?'

Selma felt her throat tighten up. Everything had changed, was the problem. 'Goodbye, Calvin.'

'Selma, you still coming up to Boston next weekend?'

She knew she wasn't but said, 'We'll see.'

When she hung up she felt dizzy with loneliness. As alone as she'd ever felt in her life, and she'd been through some rough, isolated times. She walked to the bedroom to lie down but stopped when she saw the giant stuffed giraffe. Everything has its price, the giraffe scolded her through a leering smile. How come I never noticed that ugly smile before? Selma wondered. Everything has its price.

Lizzie looked as grim as Selma felt. 'So, the thing of it is, I got to write him a letter. I got to tell him I can't see him no more.'

'But Selma, it's not as if he's living with her.'

'But he's married.'

'Technically, yes. But in spirit he's—'

'He's married,' Selma interrupted, 'and I can't be caught with a married man. Bad enough having a boyfriend, according to Arthur Golderson. If he can track down Calvin up in Boston, then so can the Lewins. And what if they ask me about him on the stand? I can't lie, can I? I got to give him up.' Selma surprised herself with the firmness of her voice.

'Until the hearing, then. After, you can resume your relationship.'

'Uh uh. If I do get Isaiah back – ' when did I start thinking *if* I get him back? Selma wondered, stifling a sense of panic – 'when I get him back, they'll still send around social workers and whatnot. I got to be on my best behavior, and seeing a married man's not nobody's idea of best behavior.'

Even if it weren't for the social workers, Selma knew things would never be the same with her and Calvin after the trial. The question had been circling over her mind like a vulture all week. How do you tell a man to get lost until the most important event of your life was over, and then tell him, okay, now you can come back? How do you say that to a man?

'I feel just terrible for you,' Lizzie said. Her pale cheeks seemed to grow transparent, letting a reddish color come through.

'You'll help me with the letter?'

'Of course I will, but don't you think you'd rather talk to him in person, or over the phone?'

Selma shook her head. 'I can't get my thoughts together on the phone. I can't think right when someone's arguing back at me.'

'Okay then,' Lizzie said. 'Do you know where you want to start?'

Selma got out her notebook. 'I know where, at the end.'

'Then why don't you start, I'll leave you alone, and then we'll go over it, okay?'

'Just this once, I'd like you to write the letter.'

213

Lizzie started to say something.

'My words,' Selma quickly added. 'I'll speak them to you, like we used to at the beginning when I dictated and you wrote down what I said on those big sheets of paper.'

'Language experience exercises,' Lizzie said dispiritedly.

Selma had to smile. 'Yeah, language experiences.' Then she said, 'When I write myself, I get too tangled up in the spelling and I forget what I want to say. If you write it, I can copy it over tonight and send it in the morning. Just this once.'

Lizzie pulled Selma's notebook over to her, flicked the end of her ballpoint pen, and said, 'Shoot.'

'Dear Calvin,' Selma began, then felt a cold vacuum envelop her. After a few minutes of silence, Selma shook her head. 'Truth is, it's the words themselves that's hard. Getting them down's not half as hard.'

'That's what I've been telling you all along.'

'Yes, you have,' Selma admitted.

After another minute of silence she found the beginning. 'It pains me to write this . . .'

Lizzie raced home that night propelled by rage. She didn't bother picking up her mail from the lobby. She let her apartment door slam shut behind her, something she never did. She walked right over to the phone. 'I only have one question for you,' she said when he answered.

'Lizzie,' Arthur Golderson said. The way he pronounced her name – pleased but not in the least surprised to hear from her – fueled her anger.

'One question. Does she have a chance?'

He hesitated for a moment. 'I wouldn't have taken the case if I didn't think so.'

'Yes you would have.'

'I'd take a case with long odds, Lizzie. But not one with no odds.'

'So she has a chance?'

'She has a chance.'

Lizzie hung up.

PART THREE

Chapter 30

The trial was scheduled to begin at nine thirty, but Selma and the Lewins had both decided to arrive early. Selma, however, had more trouble finding the appointed room in the massive court building; the words on the signs were difficult to read, particularly while walking down a dimly lit, echoing hallway, and even the numbers were confusing, extending as they did to four digits. So she arrived about ten minutes after Charles and Margaret Lewin. When she opened the big, heavy door to room 1204, they were already seated at one of the tables in front of the room. They turned to see who it was, and then, spotting her, turned quickly away.

Selma remembered Mrs Lewin the way she might remember a specific photograph she used to have, rather than the way she'd remember a living person. Margaret Lewin looked attractive and not unkind. Still, Selma had been able to look into her eyes in the split second they connected. They spoke of fear and anger and determination; they were a mirror of Selma's own feelings. She hadn't bothered noticing Charles Lewin; from the beginning she had thought of this as a dispute between her and Margaret, not Margaret and Charles.

After a long moment, in which she resolved to fight her desire to wait outside, Selma walked quickly down the aisle and sat at the table opposite the Lewins. She had bought two outfits for the trial, figuring it would take two days; this morning she had on a pale blue suit over a white blouse, with a string of fake pearls round her neck. She'd felt conspicuous getting on the subway dressed like this, but once the train hit Manhattan she realized she fitted right in – she might be going to a desk job in any one of the big skyscrapers, absorbed in a big, fat bestseller, her child in day care.

She was aware of the Lewins whispering, and felt outnumbered. In her pocketbook was the book she was reading for her literacy program. She considered taking it out. It was called *Tomorrow*, about a guy, Angel, who gets kicked out of school and can't find a job. The words were as big as a newspaper headline, however, and each page had a black and white photograph of Angel looking for work or hanging out. Selma decided not to take the book out, though she could have used the distraction.

Nine thirty came and went and still no lawyers, no judge. Every few minutes a different guard would look in, sometimes one of them would stroll lazily down the aisle, turn around, leave. Only the Lewins' presence reassured Selma that she was in the right place.

Arthur arrived at quarter to ten. The moment he entered the high-ceilinged room he seemed to fill it up. He walked quickly to the desk where Selma sat, taking long, noisy strides. He had on a vest that made him look self-important and a little offbalance, as if he were in danger of tumbling forward. He sat down next to her and said, 'Quiet this morning. How ya doing, Selma?'

'I was afraid you weren't coming.'

He gave her a puzzled look, then opened his big briefcase and pulled out some papers. 'You're up first this morning, like we discussed. Nice suit. And the pearls, nice touch.'

Whenever Margaret thought of Selma Richards, in the weeks preceding the custody fight, she'd think of a shriveled, jittery woman with enormous, drug-swollen eyes, sitting on a sofa next to her newborn son, who might have been a pillow, for all she bothered to look at him. She thought of a dark, airless room heavy with the odor of old upholstery and yesterday's perfume. She thought of the urge she'd had, an almost physical craving, to simply grab Isaiah and take him away.

But in the moment when their eyes locked just now, Margaret had the dismaying realization that she would have to discard her memories, or at least update them. For here was a tall, even dignified woman, heavier than she remembered, but not at all overweight, her eyes less protruding now, her skin healthy, rich. An attractive woman, a capable looking woman, with Isaiah's nose and his high, wide cheeks. His birth mother. Her nemesis.

The judge, a woman, appeared before David Elliot arrived. David had mentioned that Family Court judges were often women, but Margaret, vaguely ashamed of herself, had still been expecting a man. She couldn't help thinking that a woman would be more sympathetic to their case, but then she noticed Selma conferring with her attorney and wondered if they might not be thinking along the same lines.

'Good morning,' the judge said in an unexpectedly deep voice. 'I'm Renata Champion. And this is . . .' She looked down at some papers. 'This is the matter concerning Isaiah Lewin, am I correct?'

Arthur jumped to his feet. 'That's correct, your honor. My client is Selma Richards.' He nodded down towards her. 'I'm her attorney, Arthur Golderson.'

The judge smiled, not unkindly, at his enthusiasm. 'Thank you, Mr Golderson. Would you by any chance be related to Abe Golderson.'

'Yes, your honor.' His words rang out in the empty courtroom. 'He's my father.'

The judge nodded and turned to the other side of the room. 'You must be Margaret Lewin. And you are?'

'Charles Lewin. Our attorney isn't here yet.'

'I see. Well, we'll give your attorney a few more minutes.'

With that, Judge Champion turned her attention to the papers on her desk. She was a homely woman who looked to be in her fifties, her gray hair pulled back inexpertly into a large bun. The hair, her sallow complexion, her black robe, and the fact that she was elevated several feet above the rest of the courtroom, combined to give her an intimidating, almost lugubrious demeanor.

They waited five more minutes for David Elliot, during which time Arthur Golderson shuffled papers, made notes, conferred with Selma.

'Let's call David,' Margaret said in a nervous whisper.

'He'll be here,' Charles said evenly, but he too snapped round every time the door to the room opened.

Finally, David Elliot appeared. He walked calmly down the aisle, apologized to the judge, then sat down next to the Lewins. 'Did you catch her name?' he whispered to Charles.

'Renata Champion.'

He took a legal pad from his briefcase and wrote down the name.

'Are all parties present and accounted for?'

'We are, your honor,' Arthur Golderson shouted. David Elliot nodded.

'Then, Mr Golderson, why don't you begin.'

Selma watched her lawyer circle round to the front of their table. 'Your honor, this is not a complicated case.'

'Thank the Lord for that,' said Judge Champion with a smile. Arthur Golderson hesitated a moment, then smiled back at her.

'But it *is* an emotionally charged situation. More than two years ago my client, Selma Richards, under the influence of drugs, gave her son to this couple.' He pointed behind him to the Lewins, without turning round. 'Tired, sick, desperate for money and unable to see her way clear to raising the child in the manner it deserved, she accepted twenty-five thousand dollars from this couple in what amounted to an illegal adoption.' Here he paused to turn to the Lewins. 'An unconscionable adoption.'

He allowed the phrase to resonate in the courtroom a moment, then faced the bench. 'We will not attempt to excuse the actions of my client, your honor. We will, however, show how this couple

219

preyed upon her desperation and her inherent love for her child to cause her to act in a way that was counter to her own best interests and those of the child.'

Selma couldn't believe what she was hearing. She hadn't realized Arthur was going to paint her as a victim. She'd figured he'd focus on the twenty-five thousand, and on the fact that, when all was said and done, she was the child's real mother. She'd never forgiven herself for giving him away, and she certainly didn't expect the judge to.

'I will also demonstrate how that first act of turpitude, that twenty-five thousand dollar payment, was just the beginning of a succession of illegal, even immoral acts perpetrated by the Lewins, thus rendering them unfit as parents to Isaiah. I will not seek to deny that returning the child to his rightful – his only – parent will be wrenching for him. But I will show, through expert testimony, that his continued residence with this family is neither morally nor legally justified. Isaiah deserves better than Margaret and Charles Lewin. He deserves Selma Richards, his mother.'

As Arthur returned to his seat, Margaret began to clench and unclench her fists. What was this man, this *lunatic*, talking about? Then David Elliot rose to address the court.

'Your honor,' he said from behind the table. 'We will not deny that the adoption was not legal. But we will maintain that it was done for the right reason – to rescue a child born to a drug addict from a life of misery and poverty and suffering.'

Margaret stole a look at Selma and felt these last words fall flat.

'We will also show that Isaiah Lewin has a warm, loving, and supportive home. An older sister who adores him, loving grandparents, a caring community. We will question the ability of Selma Richards to care for the child, and we will question her motivation as well. Both parties were wrong, two and a half years ago, to enter into this adoption. But the Lewins acted out of love and generosity. Selma Richards acted out of greed, pure and simple.'

Walk up to the bench, Margaret wanted to tell him. Why are you standing back here? He sounded so dispassionate. Maybe Charles was right, maybe they should have shopped around for a lawyer. Someone less classy, less corporate. Someone scrappier.

'Finally, we will show the court that taking Isaiah Lewin away from his family, the only family he's ever known, could cause long-term psychological damage. Irreversible damage. Damage that would be unspeakably cruel.'

Judge Champion took a deep breath and leaned forward on her elbows. 'These are very serious accusations, the more so because a child's future is at stake. So before we begin, I want to make it very clear to all involved that I'm not going to tolerate slander and abuse

220

in this courtroom. We are here as sensible adults to decide the fate of a child. If both parties are sincere in their intentions, then they will consider only the child's welfare. Which will *not* be served by seeking to defame the other party. It *will* be served by a reasoned, accurate presentation of the facts. Am I clear?'

'Yes, your honor,' said Arthur, half rising from his chair.

'Yes, your honor.' David Elliot hardly moved.

'Then we can begin. Mr Golderson, would you like to call your first witness?'

It seemed to Selma that Arthur let her sit in the witness box for a long time while he walked slowly back to the table and looked over some notes. She got more and more annoyed watching him, but she was afraid to look anywhere else in the room. What if her eyes fell on the Lewins? On the judge? On the handful of spectators who'd migrated in over the past hours? Who *were* these people? She watched Arthur and hoped the judge wasn't as annoyed as she was.

'Ms Richards,' he said at last. The 'Ms' had a buzzing sound to it that was bound to irritate the judge. 'Let's start at the beginning, shall we?'

Selma nodded.

'You were born here in New York. In Harlem, is that correct?'

She nodded again.

'Please articulate your answers, Miss Richards,' the judge interjected.

'That's correct.' She hoped 'articulate' meant pronounce.

'Your parents were?'

'Separated.'

'I was getting at their professions.'

'My mother did housework.' Well, it was the last job she could recall her mother doing.

'And your father?'

'Don't know what he did.'

Selma had a sudden, compelling vision of Isaiah Reptoe coming to the trial, taking a seat in the visitors' area and watching, silently. Isaiah's grandfather, she thought, wondering for the first time ever if the Lewins had parents alive. Hadn't their lawyer mentioned grandparents? *Living* grandparents?

'So it's fair to say that you were not raised with a silver spoon in your mouth.'

David Elliot rose to his feet and objected. 'What does this have to do with the matter at hand, your honor?'

'Objection sustained,' the judge said evenly. 'Please restrict your questioning to issues that bear directly on the custody question.'

'Yes, your honor,' Arthur said respectfully, but Selma saw lines of anger form round his mouth. 'I was only trying to demonstrate the milieu in which my client was raised.'

'I don't see how that relates to this matter. I think you would be safe in skipping to the child's birth, Mr Golderson.' Her tone was patronizing. Selma saw Margaret Lewin look at her husband with satisfaction.

Arthur waited a few seconds, took a deep breath, and started over again. 'Ms Richards, what hospital was Isaiah born in?'

'Metropolitan Hospital.'

'Were there any complications?'

'You mean the birth?'

Arthur nodded.

'No, no problems.'

'But afterwards, there were problems?'

Selma nodded.

'Please speak up, Miss Richards,' the judge admonished.

'Yes,' she said, and found herself almost winded from the exertion of getting out this one word.

'Can you describe for the court what these problems were?'

'I was using drugs.'

'And the child?'

'He was born frail.'

'You mean, low birth weight?'

She nodded again, sensed the judge about to scold her, and said, 'That's right.'

'Was the child put on special medication, special equipment?'

'Yes, they kept him in the hospital for almost a month.'

'And did you visit him during that period?'

'Yes, I did.'

'And how did you feel, seeing him there in the hospital?'

Selma looked at him, wondering what she was expected to say. 'Felt terrible,' she muttered.

'Louder, Selma,' Arthur whispered.

'I felt terrible,' she said loudly, hearing her voice choke on the end of the word.

Arthur let the courtroom digest this for a while. Then he said, 'You brought him home after almost a month. His health was improving?'

'Yes.'

'You were planning on raising him?'

Selma shrugged 'I guess so.'

'But you had a visitor. A frequent visitor.'

'Yes.'

'Who was that visitor, Ms Richards?'

'Margaret Lewin.'

Arthur turned to face her, then back to Selma. 'How did she come to know you, can you tell us?'

'She used to take care of Isaiah at the hospital.'

'Took care of him,' he repeated. 'Was she a doctor?'

'No.'

'A nurse?'

'No.'

'I see. So she "took care" of Isaiah at the hospital, then started visiting you at home once he was released. What did she do when she visited?'

'She held him. Asked me questions.'

'What type of question?'

Selma tried to remember. All she could recall was the *feeling* of being questioned. ''Bout different things, like how Isaiah was getting along.'

Arthur walked over to her and put an arm on the railing. 'Things weren't so great, were they, Selma?' he said gently. Still, Selma wanted to turn away from him. 'Were you still using drugs at the time?'

'Yes.'

Selma expected more questions about this but Arthur suddenly moved away from her. 'About how many times would you say Margaret Lewin visited you?'

'Four or five.'

'Over a period of how long?'

'Two weeks, maybe three.'

'At what point did she mention the possibility of adopting Isaiah?'

Selma thought about this. 'I'd say the second or third visit.'

'How did she bring up the subject?'

'She asked did I think I wanted to raise Isaiah.'

'And how did you answer?'

'I said yes, I did.'

'What happened next?'

'Nothing. She kept on asking if I thought I was fit to raise him, and I said yes.'

Selma saw Margaret lean over to her lawyer and say something.

'I never said I couldn't take care of my baby,' Selma insisted, looking first at the Lewins, then up and behind her, at the judge. 'I told her I didn't like her coming round, interfering. But she kept coming.'

'What happened next?' Arthur said calmly.

'One day she ask me if I would let her raise Isaiah. I said no.' Her voice had trailed off.

'You said no?'

'That's right. Then she mentioned the money.'

'In what context did she mention money?'

Selma just looked at him.

'*Why* did she mention the money?'

'She said this would . . .' Selma searched for the word. 'She said this would make up for my baby.' She knew this sounded bad; it *felt* bad.

'How much money did she mention?'

'Twenty-five thousand dollars.'

'Did you agree right away?'

'No, I didn't. She came back the next time and we discussed it some more. That's when I said yes.'

'Did you hand over your son then and there?'

'No. She came back with her husband. They brought the money.'

'Was this cash?'

'Yes.'

'Were there any papers to sign?'

'No.'

'Were there any city officials there?'

'No.'

'Any government or social welfare officials?'

'No.'

'Any adoption agency officials?'

'Objection, your honor,' said David Elliot wearily. 'I think we've gotten the point that the Lewins acted on their own behalf.'

'Sustained. Counsel will kindly move on.'

Arthur seemed pleased by this. 'Was that the last time you saw your son?'

Selma thought about watching him leave his daycare center but kept this to herself. 'Yes, it was.' The lie sent a shiver through her.

Arthur turned and walked back to the table, then pivoted on one foot. 'What was your state of mind in the weeks between giving birth to Isaiah and turning him over to the Lewins?'

'I was on drugs. When I found out I was pregnant, I cut back. Truth is, I practically stopped altogether. Didn't have the stomach for them anymore, and I knew they wouldn't do my baby no good. But after Isaiah was born, I went right back. Like my body was telling me, okay, Selma, you had your break, now get us some more stuff.'

'I was asking about your state of mind following the birth.'

She could tell by his expression that she'd been wandering into dangerous territory. 'My baby boy was in the hospital, sick. And still I couldn't help myself. I needed the drugs same as my son needed me.'

'Did you feel . . . Let me rephrase that. How did you feel about your son's condition?'

'I felt terrible, like it was my fault.'

'Did this cause you—'

'It *was* my fault,' Selma broke in.

Arthur nodded. 'What would you say your habit was costing you back then?'

'It varied. Maybe a hundred, two hundred a day. But sometimes I traded for it.'

She saw Arthur's eyes flash and the Lewins' lawyer write something down at the same time.

'Did you have a job at the time?'

'No, I didn't.'

'I see. So you had a two ʰundred dollar a day habit, a child to support, rent, I presume.'

'I was getting welfare,' Selma added.

His eyes flashed again, and again, David Elliot made a notation.

'With all these expenses, these *desperate* expenses, twenty-five thousand dollars must have been quite tempting.'

'Objection,' said David Elliot, half rising from his chair. 'Leading the witness.'

'Sustained.'

'In light of your expenses,' Arthur continued, 'how did you look upon the twenty-five thousand dollars?'

'Like it was salvation.'

Arthur at last looked pleased with something she said. 'Were you ever so desperate for drugs, you acted against your best interests? Did you ever do anything that you knew was . . . damaging . . . just to get drug money?'

'Drugs was damaging.'

'Yes, but was there anything . . .'

Selma saw what he was getting at. 'You mean, like, did the drugs make me give up my son?' He nodded. 'Yes, they did. I was half crazed. I wasn't feeling nothing, neither. Just kind of numb, and wanting to stay that way. When I gave Isaiah away, it was like there was pain, but I wasn't feeling it. Somebody else was feeling it.'

Selma looked around the courtroom. There were ten people in the room, give or take, and there was something kind of thrilling, talking about herself this way in front of an audience. She wasn't enjoying it, but it did feel electrical in a way, like she was wired. When the judge suggested a recess, she felt the energy drain out of her, a let-down. When she stood up, her legs were like soft rubber; she held onto the railing until she felt steadier, then crossed the courtroom to the table. 'Okay, Selma,' Arthur Golderson told her. 'The worst is over.'

This made her feel good until she looked over and saw David Elliot writing furiously on a yellow notepad. He looked like the kind of person she would never get along with, with his perfect hair and his perfect pink skin and this attitude, like he had all the answers. She could imagine sitting down with the Lewins and having a cup of coffee, but not David Elliot. When Selma imagined the kind of people who ran big corporations and the government, she imagined people like David Elliot. Unapproachable people. The sight of him writing on his pad – writing about *her* – made her legs go rubbery again. 'I don't think the worst's over yet,' she said. 'Not yet.'

Chapter 31

'Wait till the cross-examination,' Charles said over lunch. They'd found a tiny Chinese restaurant on the fringes of Chinatown that was decorated entirely in Formica. 'David will make mincemeat of her.'

'I don't want to make mincemeat of her.'

'It's a little late for second thoughts.'

They concentrated on the food for a while.

'I'd convinced myself she was evil,' Margaret said, as if this were a continuation of a conversation. 'I never expected to *like* her.'

'You *liked* her?'

'Well, I mean, I don't actually know her. But there was something strong about her. She's been through so much, you have to admire her.'

'She took drugs while she was pregnant. Today they're putting women in jail for that.'

'But she basically stopped when she found out she was pregnant,' Margaret insisted. 'For Isaiah's sake we have to be glad for that. And she's recovered, don't you see?'

Charles just shrugged. 'I suppose.'

'Also, I keep seeing Isaiah in her. The way she squints when she doesn't understand something, that's just what Isaiah does. I wouldn't have thought that kind of thing was inherited.'

'I think you're imagining it.'

'What about her cheeks, then? You can't deny they have those in common.'

'Cheekbones are genetic. Squinting isn't.'

Margaret thought about this for a while. 'What I kept thinking,' she said when her plate was empty, 'was that she'd probably make a good mother.'

Charles just looked at her like she was the most exasperating woman alive, and didn't change the look, even when tears began falling down Margaret's cheeks. He put a few dollars on the table, stood up and walked to the cash register. He paid the check and went outside to wait.

★ ★ ★

A hundred blocks uptown, Isaiah Lewin and Emma Mellor played in separate corners of the Mellors' spacious living room. Charlotte had suggested the afternoon playdate, which always sounded better in principle than in practice. The two children, though close in age, rarely played together, and when they did, it usually degenerated quickly into a turf war. This was normal for kids their age, both mothers knew. But it didn't stop them from bringing the children together, hoping for some sort of positive interaction.

While Emma chattered enthusiastically into a toy phone, Isaiah repeatedly jumped off a small stool onto the couch, then shimmied back down onto the stool. Across the room, Charlotte tried to concentrate on a magazine, keeping a wary eye on Isaiah but refraining from asking him not to jump on the furniture. She kept thinking about what was happening downtown. It didn't seem fair to scold him, not today.

Emma tired of the phone sooner than Isaiah tired of his gymnastics. She stood, inventoried her arsenal of toys, and selected a small plastic dump truck which she began to push round the room. This immediately caught Isaiah's attention. He stopped jumping and ran over to her. For a moment he just stared. Charlotte had to smile at his look of wonderment; there was something about his face, those big, feline eyes, that large, wide mouth, and something else, something less obvious, in the richness of his skin color, perhaps, that enabled him to give full, nearly perfect expression to emotions like wonder, awe, surprise, puzzlement. Emma was quicker to laugh, and perhaps to cry as well, but she didn't have nearly his capacity for being simply dazzled.

After a few minutes observing Emma, Isaiah decided to get more physically involved. He reached out towards the toy. Emma pulled the truck away from him and looked at him defiantly. He seemed more mystified than upset by the rebuff, and took a step towards her. 'No,' she shouted, yanking the truck even further from him. Undaunted, Isaiah reached out and grabbed the toy truck. He didn't pull it towards him, but he didn't let go of it either when Emma tugged at it a second time. 'My truck,' she wailed, then looked over at her mother, as if for verification.

'Why don't you share it with Isaiah?' Charlotte suggested.

'*No*,' Emma shouted, giving the truck another yank. This one caught Isaiah off guard, jerking him forward and almost toppling him.

There was a moment of silence. Isaiah's face was frozen, but it looked almost swollen, as if about to erupt. Charlotte stood, crossed the room. Before she'd taken two steps Isaiah burst into tears, giving vent to loud, explosive sobbing. Emma backed away in alarm. Charlotte put a consoling arm on Isaiah, but he recoiled from the touch, standing in the middle of her living room, wailing.

'Emma, tell Isaiah you're sorry,' she said as calmly as she could.

Emma managed a garbled apology.

'Isaiah, did you hear Emma say she was sorry for not sharing?'

He refused to acknowledge either of them. His sobbing persisted, arms flat against his sides, his body rigid, cheeks molten with tears. Charlotte heard whimpering from Emma and figured she had to do something right away before both children were hysterical. She scooped up Isaiah and held him to her. His sobs were muffled somewhat by her shoulder. He felt hard and rigid and surprisingly heavy, since he made no effort to wrap his arms or legs round her. If he'd only hold on, she could let go with one arm and pat his head, stroke his back. But without his help, she needed both arms to hold him up. Charlotte had never held a child who didn't instinctively cling to a familiar adult.

His sobbing abated, but his body continued to vibrate. 'It's only a stupid dump truck,' she told him. Emma retrieved the truck and held it up towards Isaiah, a peace offering. Isaiah was too agitated to notice. And besides, Charlotte knew the gesture was futile, if well meant.

'It'll all be over soon, little guy,' she whispered into his damp brown ear. 'Real soon.'

'Tell me, Selma,' said Arthur Golderson offhandedly, as if he and his client were having coffee and not appearing before a judge. 'How long have you been off drugs?'

'Two years.'

'Two years. Never gone back?'

'No.'

'Never been tempted?'

'No.'

'What do you do for a living now?'

'I take care of a little girl, Dana.'

'You take care of her. You mean while her parents work?'

'Yes.'

'How long have you been doing this?'

'Over a year. Since the baby was born.'

'So the baby is now, what, almost two years?'

It was tempting to just say yes, make Dana and Isaiah the same age, which is what Arthur wanted. 'She's just over a year,' she said instead.

'You have full responsibility for this child?'

'That's right.'

'Changing her diapers, feeding her, that kind of thing?'

'Yes.'

Margaret saw what Arthur Golderson was getting at. She wished she could stand up and tell the court that raising a child was more than changing diapers and feeding it lunch. She'd seen these black babysitters on Park Avenue with their white charges, their faces utterly blank, uninterested. Even the children looked blank, uninterested. Charlotte said that she assumed the babysitters gave the children a drug that made them sit still while they pushed them. 'Whenever I take Emma out, she squirms so much I end up carrying her and pushing an empty stroller. I wish I knew their secret.' Margaret wished she could take the judge on a tour of the Upper East Side sometime. Then she'd know that taking care of someone else's child had nothing to do with mothering. But perhaps the judge had children and already knew this. Margaret hoped so.

Arthur returned to his chair. Selma started to rise but the judge motioned for her to stay put. 'Mr Elliot, would you like to question Miss Richards?'

'Yes, I would, your honor.' He stood up and circled the table. 'Miss Richards, you told the court earlier today that you were using drugs at the time of your pregnancy. Could you specify what type of drug you were using?'

'Cocaine.'

'Could you speak up, please?'

Selma had spoken softly, but she knew he'd heard her. 'Cocaine,' she repeated.

'Thank you. How did you take the cocaine, Miss Richards?'

Arthur stood up. 'Objection, your honor. My client has already stated for the record that she is no longer taking drugs. She's already submitted a blood test to the court.'

'Your honor, I am only trying to establish the relationship between Miss Richards and the child from the moment it was conceived. If Miss Richards was negligent toward her unborn child, then it has grave—'

'Objection overruled,' the judge interrupted. 'Continue.'

'Miss Richards, how did you take the cocaine?'

'I smoked it.'

'So we're talking about crack, am I correct?'

Selma hesitated. The word sounded so ugly now. 'Yes,' she answered.

'Crack,' he repeated ominously, stretching the word into two syllables: Ker-ack. 'I see. Now, did your drug use change at all during your pregnancy?'

'I already said, when I realized I was pregnant, I cut back.' The lawyer seemed about to pounce on this so she added, 'I practically stopped.'

'*Practically stopped*,' he aped. The words just dangled there.

Selma wished she had something to say to cancel them.

'When Isaiah was born, he was gravely ill, is that correct?'

'Yes.'

'Do you recall what was the matter with him?'

'It was the drugs,' Selma answered.

'Yes indeed, it was the drugs. But do you remember what the symptoms were?'

'He was too small.'

'Low birth weight, it's called. That was one symptom. Anything else?'

Selma thought for a while. She remembered the tubes and wires and the plastic bubble over his tiny body, but not what they were for. She shook her head.

David Elliot walked over to the table and returned with a folder. He removed a piece of paper and handed it to her. 'Perhaps this will refresh your memory.'

'Please enter it into the record, Mr Elliot,' cautioned the judge.

He retrieved the paper from Selma and handed it up to the judge. 'Your honor, this is the chart from the neo-natal intensive care unit at Metropolitan Hospital. It covers Isaiah Lewin's hospital stay over two years ago.'

The judge scanned it, then handed it back to him. 'Thank you, Mr Elliot.'

He gave it back to Selma, who let it rest on her lap.

'Now, Miss Richards, if you'll look down to the section called "Diagnosis".'

Selma scanned the document. It appeared to be a form that had been filled in with different colored pens. There were several styles of handwriting, all very small. Selma couldn't make out a word of it.

'Do you see the "Diagnosis" section, Miss Richards?'

Selma looked down, stared at the paper as if reading it, then looked up. 'I can't find it,' she said softly.

'Let me help you.' He walked over, took the paper, then returned it. 'Here,' he said, indicating a section at the top with his finger. 'Why don't you read this section for the court.'

'Objection, your honor,' shouted Arthur. Selma had been wondering when he'd rescue her. 'My client is not a medical expert. She's being asked to comment on matters of which she has no knowledge or expertise.'

'Nobody's asking her to comment, Mr Golderson,' said the judge. 'Only to read. Overruled.'

Arthur sat down slowly, looking at Selma with fresh alarm. Selma looked at the paper. She saw Isaiah's name on top, and her own name, but that was all she could make out. She looked up at the lawyer.

'Please, Miss Richards. Read the Diagnosis section for the court.'

Selma just stared at him.

'I understand that this might be painful for you, Miss Richards.'

Selma looked down at the paper; maybe a miracle would happen and she'd be able to read it.

'Your honor,' said David Elliot, sounding peevish, 'witness is being uncooperative.'

The judge leaned over and told Selma to read.

Selma felt suddenly warm. 'I can't.'

'Excuse me?' said David Elliot.

'I can't read it.'

'Why not?' He looked genuinely surprised.

'I can't read.'

'You already said you can't read it. I asked you why not.'

'I can't *read*,' Selma said loudly. The word echoed in the silence that followed.

The lawyer looked at her for a few moments. 'You can't read anything, Miss Richards?'

'Nothing hard,' she answered. She saw the Lewins look at each other. She saw Arthur slump in his seat.

David Elliot paused for a few seconds. 'Could you read a children's book, for example?'

'Objection. What does a children's book have to do with the matter at hand?' shouted Arthur.

'Your honor—' David Elliot began.

'Overruled. Witness will answer the question.'

Selma didn't know how to answer. She was tempted to lie but what if they brought a book in for her to read to the judge? In the state she was in she didn't think she could read more than a word of anything. She felt like an animal surrounded by hunters. 'Some books,' she answered.

'Some *children's* books?'

'That's right.'

'But not all children's books.'

'No, not all children's books.'

David Elliot let this sink in before continuing. 'Okay, well, back to the document.' It was clear that he could hardly contain his satisfaction at this course of events. He took the paper from her and waved it before the judge. 'Your honor, since the witness is unable to read this on her own, may I read it aloud for the court?'

'Proceed,' the judge told him. But she was looking at Selma.

'That was a bonus,' David Elliot told the Lewins during a recess.

'What was?' Charles asked.

'The illiteracy thing. I mean, this woman wants to raise your child

232

and she can't even read it a bedtime story.'

'Not *it*,' Margaret corrected, 'him.'

'Right him. Now, if you'll excuse me, I have to make a call.'

The hearing resumed at three o'clock on the longest day of Selma's life. 'Miss Richards, who is the child's father?'

'Objection,' shouted Arthur. 'What relevance—'

'Overruled,' the judge interrupted impatiently.

'I repeat. Who is the child's father?'

'I don't know that,' Selma answered.

'But surely you must have some idea who it is?'

'But I don't remember.'

'Was he a steady lover, a casual acquaintance?'

'A casual acquaintance.'

'Did you have sexual relations with him on several occasions?'

The truth was, Selma really didn't know. At that period in her life, she'd have done anything for drugs. She was sleeping with anyone who offered her a toke or a few bucks. Often she didn't remember the next day who she'd been with. 'Several occasions, yes,' she answered.

'And yet you can't recall his name.'

'No.'

'Did you sleep with many men at that time Miss Richards?'

'Objection.'

'Sustained. I think you've established that Miss Richards does not remember the name of the child's father.'

David Elliot allowed himself a moment to shift gears. Then he started asking Selma about giving up drugs.

Charles hadn't liked the part about 'Isaiah's father'. I'm Isaiah's father, he thought as David Elliot grilled Selma Richards. It actually occurred to him to stand up and object! Wasn't 'birth father' the accurate phrase, or was 'birth' only used with the mother, the person who *gave* birth? What about 'natural father'? No, that would make him the 'unnatural' father.

Sometimes, in the period leading up to the hearing, an ugly demon raised its head inside Charles and whispered that perhaps it would be better for all concerned simply to give up Isaiah without a struggle. It's nothing but trouble down the road, the demon whispered. Isaiah's black and you're white. Think of the drugs he was born with – do you think they won't have any long-term effect? Do you think his mother is going to roll over and die, even if you do retain custody? Charles never shared these thoughts with anyone, least of all Margaret; for her, he knew, there was no whispering demon.

233

But here in the courtroom, face to face with Selma Richards, hearing some unnamed, *unnameable* stranger described as Isaiah's father, Charles felt a strengthening resolve. This woman had no right to their son. She once had a right, but she'd lost it two and a half years ago. Not when she accepted $25,000. No, she'd lost the right when she continued to take drugs after she was pregnant. She lost it when she failed to visit her child more than once or twice in the weeks he was in the neo-natal ICU, where they had to call in volunteers like Margaret just to hold him, stroke him. And he and Margaret had assumed the right to raise him not because of the $25,000, but because they'd made an oath to take care of him and love him and they were keeping that oath. The money had nothing to do with it. The judge *had* to see it that way.

Arthur Golderson hadn't counted on Selma's illiteracy coming to light in the trial. This couldn't be helpful to them. He'd have to re-examine her to get out the fact that she was in school. He wondered if he should ask Lizzie to testify about Selma's progress, assuming she *was* progressing. The thought of calling Lizzie down to testify was devilishly satisfying. She was being so holier-than-thou about this thing, as if he were hurting Selma instead of giving her maybe $30,000 of free legal help. Maybe if she saw him in action, here in court, she'd see how serious he was about helping Selma. She'd see that Selma stood a decent chance of winning back her son. She'd see what a dynamic lawyer he was . . .

One thing had gone right that day. Martin Vandenberg, the reporter for the *Times*, had showed up. He was sitting a few rows back, scribbling furiously the entire day. Arthur had re-introduced himself during the break, while David Elliot was making phone calls. 'I keep forgetting you're related to Abe Golderson,' Vandenberg had said. 'I cover a lot of court cases, so over the years I've seen him operate.' Arthur had paused a moment to enable Vandenberg to add that his performance that morning had been every bit as good as his father's. But the reporter had kept this observation to himself, so Arthur, allowing himself an additional few seconds to recover, asked him if he needed any information for his story or if he wanted an 'exclusive' with Selma Richards. Vandenberg, however, seemed uninterested in anything Arthur had to offer, and actually sat back down on his chair while Arthur was mid-sentence. Arthur had returned disappointed to his table, reflecting on the general inadequacy of journalists.

'Miss Richards,' David Elliot began, as he always did, 'you say you haven't used drugs in two years, is that correct?'

Selma felt on firmer ground here, where only she was involved and not her son. 'That's right.'

'Did you have any help in kicking the habit?'

'No, I did not.'

'None?'

'None.'

'Not Drugs Anonymous? No hospital treatment? No methadone?'

Selma shook her head and then remembered to say no.

'I have to be honest with you, Miss Richards. I find that remarkable, to say the least. The statistics on beating drug addiction are very grim. How exactly did you do it?'

'One day I stopped.'

'One day you stopped. Just like that?'

'Just like that.'

'And you didn't suffer any withdrawal symptoms? My understanding is that some people *die* from withdrawal.'

'I suffered,' Selma said evenly.

'Was there some event that prompted you to stop?'

'No, no event.'

'Were you unable to *buy* drugs at the time?'

'That wasn't it.'

'Then what was it?' the lawyer half-shouted.

Selma felt something unhinge inside her and the truth just popped out. 'I had a vision.'

'Excuse me, Miss Richards, I didn't catch that,' said the lawyer, who most certainly had caught it.

'I said I had a vision.'

She saw Arthur Golderson's head sag closer to his chest. There was just no pleasing anybody today, Selma thought.

To her dismay, David Elliot pursued the subject of her vision, a half-smile swimming across his face. 'What type of vision, Miss Richards?'

She thought about this for a few seconds. She'd never shared this with anyone else, never planned to. She didn't even think about it much, it was just something that had happened, and good thing it had. 'More like a voice,' she said at length.

'A voice,' the lawyer exclaimed. 'A vision *and* a voice.'

'Objection,' said Arthur, rising somewhat dispiritedly to his feet. 'We've submitted tests to prove that my client is totally drug free.'

'Your honor,' answered David Elliot, 'if we do one thing here, we must establish whether Miss Richards is indeed free of drugs or if she is just in temporary remission. How she kicked the habit – or claims she did – is completely relevant.'

'Overruled,' said the judge without hesitation.

235

During this brief interchange, Selma had determined to describe the vision for the court before David Elliot dragged it out of her. 'I heard a voice telling me to stop taking drugs. The voice told me that the drugs was killing me, and that I was sinning against the Lord.'

'Sinning against the Lord?' David Elliot repeated this through clenched teeth, as if stifling a big laugh.

'That's right,' Selma said, lifting her chin. 'The voice said that it would give me the strength to stop taking drugs if I used my own strength, too.'

'You said "it" would give you the strength. Who, or what, was "it"?'

'The Lord, I guess.' Selma thought this was obvious.

'The Lord. So the Lord told you to stop taking drugs, and you stopped. Just like that.'

'I was sick afterwards, but I never went back.'

'Frankly, Miss Richards, I find that hard to believe. Our government and our foundations spend billions to lick the drug problem, and you manage to lick it with a vision. No, I'm sorry. A voice.'

'The Lord has the power to cure,' Selma said evenly. She saw the entire courtroom squirm: the Lewins, Arthur Golderson, the spectators, even the judge. But there it was: that was how it happened, and that was the truth.

'No further questions,' said David Elliot. He cast a satisfied glance at Arthur Golderson before returning to his seat.

'You never told me about this vision you had,' Arthur whispered to her as they left the courtroom.

'You never asked me about it.'

'They're going to try and paint you as some religious nut.'

'It's not crazy to believe in the Lord.'

'Maybe. Maybe not. But voices and visions? That hurt.'

'I was only telling the truth.'

Arthur ignored this. 'Well, they've painted me in a corner, so there's only one way out of it.'

'What's that?'

'Well, if you're a religious nut, they're godless, atheistic, irreligious infidels. I wasn't going to bring up the subject of how they were going to raise Isaiah, you know, in what religion, but I have to now. I have no choice.'

Chapter 32

It was an awful night for Selma, a night of loneliness so extreme, sometimes it felt like terror, sometimes like rage, sometimes like insanity. Her apartment had become a cage, alien and uncomfortable, and she felt a fierce desire to leave it. But where would she go? This was as close to home as any place she knew, even if it felt like prison.

Testifying had made her feel vulnerable, unprotected. It wasn't just the judge who was judging her, it was the Lewins, their lawyer, her own lawyer who she knew she'd let down that day, though why she should feel the need to impress *him* she didn't know, the man from the newspaper, the whole world. And who was on her side? Calvin she'd cut loose, on orders. She had no family she knew of, and the son she was fighting for didn't even know she existed. She had no one, nobody, on her side. And on the other side was – everyone.

She waited until she felt tired before getting into bed, but sleep never happened. Midnight passed, then one o'clock, two o'clock. Still alert, edgy, as if she were waiting for a phone call, a knock on the door.

The part about giving up drugs was the part that gave her the worst pain when she recalled it, which was about every two minutes. She'd never told a soul about that, no one. It wasn't that she was afraid they'd think she was nuts. It was just that she didn't really understand it herself. When she did remember it, sometimes *she* thought she was nuts, so she'd put it out of her mind as much as possible. Church visits were the only tribute she paid to the cause of her renewal.

But now that night came back to her in waves of memory that made her head feel like it was filling up with something, getting heavy, wobbly. A face came back to her, a man's face she didn't even know she'd stored away. A narrow face, with a thin moustache, a face out of an earlier time, like from an old black and white movie. The face was on top of her, looking down into her. But it wasn't seeing anything, it was looking through her, beyond her. What was there to see? Then she felt something at the other end,

237

and she realized, dimly, what was happening. The man was fucking her, this man with the thin face and the watery eyes that crossed when he got excited.

The odd thing was, she didn't feel anything. Here was this face, not two inches from her own, at the end of a long body that was pumping up and down on her, and she couldn't feel a thing. It was like when she gave birth. They gave her a shot of something down on her spine (they didn't bother asking if she wanted to push or nothing) and then they pulled the baby out. She remembered hearing it cry off in the distance somewhere, but she couldn't feel anything. It wasn't as if her body was numb, it was like the whole world ended at her neck, like it was all just a void beyond that. The baby's harsh cries echoed out there in the emptiness somewhere, grew dimmer and dimmer, then disappeared.

The thin man rolled off her and she felt a coolness come over her, a relief. So maybe she'd felt something after all. Crack was funny that way, sometimes you remembered things you didn't think you'd thought of in the first place. She might have passed out, or she might not have woken up, who could tell? But at some point she was aware that the thin man was leaving. She heard him rustling out in the void beyond the haze she was in.

She sat up in the dark, viscous air of her bedroom, got her bearings, then went out into the hallway to find him. You owe me, she told him. He put his coat on like a snake, slithering into the sleeves. You was like fucking a corpse, he said. He said it as if this was the worst thing you could say about a person, and maybe it was, she didn't care. You owe me, she repeated. Her head was ringing so bad, she wondered if he could hear her. She couldn't think of anything else to say, not even the amount they'd agreed on. She felt a tingling in her arms, and down by her feet, like an electric current was juicing through her. You owe me, she repeated more desperately. She felt her shoulder hit the wall, then her head. You doped up, he said. You be like a corpse for real you don't go easy on the stuff. He opened her door and left her standing there, the current in her veins throbbing now. She followed him out into the hallway and started screaming at him as he shambled down the stairway, in no hurry.

Pay me, fucker, she called after him. You owe me.

Bad off as she was, she heard her words die after one flight.

She tried again. You owe me, she shrieked as loud as she could, holding on to the banister for support. God damn you. Again the words sounded too weak to make it all the way down to him. She felt like a whistle with an extra hole in it, all she could do was wheeze. So she went back into her apartment and back to her bed and sat down on it.

Only way to get some stuff was to get some money, and there was only one way to get money. But she just didn't have it in her to get dressed and go down to the street. Her head felt heavier than the rest of her combined, and if she didn't concentrate it started wobbling. Now she felt like she was on fire, but an invisible fire that was burning her up from the inside out. Her muscles were pulling and pinching like they wanted her to dance and on top of that she felt nauseous. A couple of times she gagged but she knew nothing was coming up, she hadn't eaten in . . . how long? Time had collapsed into this one moment; trying to think of the past, even an hour ago, made her head start to throb worse than it already was. She put her head on her pillow but it was like all the fire rushed up to it, so she sat up again and felt something happening in her chest. A fluttering, like something was alive in there, rotating. A fluttering that pained her. I'm dying, she thought, my heart's giving out. But she was too addled just then to figure out if dying was a comfort or not.

The night passed, or maybe it didn't. Once Selma found herself on the floor of the bathroom down the hallway and later she was out in the hallway, crawling back to her apartment. She barely managed to get herself back inside, close the door, when she just let herself collapse on the floor. It felt hard and cool and steady and when she closed her eyes the fire didn't get worse. But a terror overtook her and she opened them. I'm dying, she thought. This is what's happening. I'm dying. Death is waiting behind my eyelids. So she kept them open despite the throbbing pain, terrified and agonized and trying to find something on the hard, bare floor to hang on to. She found a crack in the linoleum and dug in her nails as if she were hanging on a cliff, holding on for life. The floor started to slide by her. She was climbing the floor.

That's when she heard it. A whisper in her ear, the one that wasn't pressed into the linoleum. Close your eyes, the voice said. She felt the warm, dusky breath in her ear. Sleep. I'll watch you.

Who's that? she asked, but she knew the words hadn't left her lips. Who's that?

The voice came back to her. Sleep. You will be all right. Sleep. It was a deep, patient voice, a voice you could believe. She felt the juice inside her slow down a little, felt herself unwind just a bit. Sleep, Selma. Sleep.

Her name! The voice blanketed her, there on the linoleum, like a cool breeze in summer. Still nervous, she closed her eyes. Sure enough, death was not waiting for her behind her eyelids like she'd thought. Just a black and purple swirling that was familiar and safe.

Sleep, Selma, the voice said. Sleep.

She dreamed she was in an airplane as big as the Empire State

Building lying on its side. As far as she could see there were rows and rows of seats. Through her window she saw the world, round and blue, just like a globe. It was turning, slowly and gently, as it grew smaller and smaller. She felt pressed back into her seat as the giant plane sped away from the earth.

Suddenly the plane started to shudder. It was gentle at first, and she ignored it, keeping her eyes closed. Then the shaking got more and more violent until she had to open her eyes, see what was happening. She looked around to see if anyone else was concerned, but the plane was empty now, no heads poked above the seats. She stood up, holding onto the seat in front for stability. The vast plane was empty. She looked outside. The earth was gone now, the sky was dark and murky. The wings were flapping like birds' wings. She heard a loud, creaky noise, like the whole plane was ready to snap. Panic seized her. She left her seat and walked up the long aisle, past row after row of empty seats. She walked for hours and hours but still couldn't get to the front of the plane. She could see the front, but she couldn't get there, no matter how long she walked.

The plane continued to shake and shudder, the creaking grew louder and louder. She passed hundreds of rows of empty seats, thousands. Her legs were tired but she continued until her feet wouldn't leave the floor. She took a last look toward the front of the plane, still too distant to see, then lay down on the carpeted floor.

The rocking continued, but lying on the floor, rolling from side to side, it didn't feel so dangerous. Then she felt a huge, final thump and waited for the plane to blow apart, her with it. But it didn't blow apart. In fact, the shuddering had stopped. Cautiously she stood up. The plane was full again, she even recognized some of the people. She saw her mother a few rows up, talking to a man, but decided not to disturb her. She saw her son, way up toward the front of the plane. He turned to look at her, a boy of about eight or nine, and smiled. She smiled back at him, a wave of warmth coming over her as she realized that he was all right. To her surprise there was an exit door right next to her that she hadn't noticed before. She opened it and stepped out . . .

Selma's eyes opened to a glaring morning sun. The light was unfamiliar to her, it was falling in unlikely places, and for a moment she didn't know where she was. She got up slowly, and only when she was upright did she realize that she'd spent the night on the floor. She walked unsteadily to the bathroom, then back to the tiny kitchen with its miniature refrigerator and two-burner stove. She filled the kettle, placed it on the stove top, lit the flame, and then it hit her: today was the beginning, a new life.

What surprised her was not the resolution itself – it had come to her during her sleep, and already felt familiar. What surprised her

240

was that she wasn't afraid. Just yesterday the thought of an hour without crack inside her made her more terrified than seeing a knife raised over her head, which had happened once, when she had gone up to 145th Street to score. She wasn't afraid. She knew she was in for a rough time, but she knew she'd get through it.

Maybe if she'd known how bad it was going to be she would have been afraid. But that first day she felt the strength of a new resolve. She drank coffee with trembling hands, got dressed slowly, then went over to 127th Street to the Baptist Church. She hadn't been to church in New York, only down in Winfield. But this morning it felt like the only thing to do. There, for the first time in her adult life, Selma knelt down and prayed. She didn't know what to say, at first. It was like standing in front of a large audience, her body started to sweat but her mouth went dry. She tried to think what her grandmother would say. She wouldn't ask for anything, Selma decided. Neither would she. She found the words. Thank you for getting me through the night. Thank you for getting me through what's coming. Only after she stopped did she realize that she'd been talking out loud. But there was no one in the church to hear her, and somehow talking out loud felt right to her. Thank you, she whispered one last time before standing up.

The next few weeks were hell, and she couldn't even manage to get herself back to the church. She'd heard it said that cocaine was the mind's addiction, heroin the body's. And it was true enough that crack worked the head like a magician, lifting you up real fast, then dropping you back down just as quick, only leaving you a step or two beneath where you started out from in the first place, making you want a second hit even more than the first, a third even more than the second. But cocaine had got hold of Selma's mind *and* body, pitted them against each other. Once she'd set her mind against the drugs, her body fought the decision, begging and pleading for drugs in horrible spasms, nausea that felt like it was eating her up from the inside out, headaches so bad they squeezed tears from her eyes. Some days she held on to the leg of a chair just to reassure herself that she wasn't flying away, other days she ran around her small apartment like a mad woman, crazy to do something but unable to do anything except keep moving. Once in a while she thought about checking herself into a hospital, but a voice (from inside her, this time) told her to trust the Lord, not doctors.

Time had ceased to exist for her; some hours lasted days, some flashed by in a second. Her body was keeping time, not her mind. She figured it was a week or two before she felt a little better. The third week she began taking little walks, started to eat like a regular person. In the mirror she saw a shriveled, hollowed-out version of herself, but this too got better over time. In the fourth week she got her hair cut and bought herself some make-up. Some weeks after that she felt strong enough to walk into an employment agency and ask for a job. She lied about her experience – what else could she do? – and was sent on an interview to the Fredricks. Mrs Fredricks wasn't even pregnant then. She was looking for someone to clean for her once a week. Selma had to laugh, thinking how much Mrs Fredricks reminded her of herself just a month ago, all frazzled and frantic. She got the job at the Fredricks, and a few others besides. Cleaning people's apartments when they weren't there suited Selma fine. Just a few months off drugs, she didn't feel up to communicating with people; dusting their *things* was as close as Selma wanted to get.

Then, about six months later, Selma was surprised to find Mrs Fredricks at home when she arrived to clean. 'I'm not feeling well,' she said, and a moment later ran to the bathroom to throw up. Selma followed her, unsure what to do – she'd only met the woman once before, at the interview.

'I'm pregnant,' Mrs Fredricks said, sounding none too pleased.

Selma left her and walked to the kitchen, returning a minute later with a handful of saltines. 'Try these,' she said. Mrs Fredricks looked at the offered crackers like she was being handed a dead rodent. 'These'll help,' Selma said; she didn't add that every drug addict kept a supply of saltines for cases of the heaves. Mrs Fredricks took a saltine, ate it, then took another. Later, Selma made her some broth and took it to her in the bedroom.

That afternoon, Mrs Fredricks found Selma in the guest bathroom, wiping down the shower. 'Selma, have you ever taken care of children?' she asked, sounding and looking much better.

Selma nodded. Growing up, she'd watched any number of children now and then. Babysat for my mother, she might have added.

'Perhaps you'd like to work for us full-time when the baby's born. I'll be lucky if I get three weeks' maternity leave. It'll be a comfort knowing someone's lined up.'

Selma took the job. The money was better than she was earning cleaning, and she figured watching a newborn would be a good way to ease her way back into human society.

Dana was born seven months later, and Selma quit her other jobs to watch her full-time. Not long after that she heard, through another babysitter she met in the park, about this woman in Brooklyn who was looking for a boarder. A week later she packed a suitcase, left her scant furniture behind, and took the D train to Livonia Avenue. After a month she signed up for the literacy program and wrote her first sentence ever:

I want my boy back.

Chapter 33

Tuesday was hot and humid, a delinquent August day in September. The air-conditioning system hadn't been cranked up in time, so the courtroom was stifling, and a stale, close to rotting smell permeated the entire building, as if something had died in the basement a few nights ago.

On the stand, Selma felt as if the sun was shining directly, exclusively, on her. Sweat formed on her forehead; every once in a while she had to wipe it away. Usually you could do this when no one was looking, but here someone was looking all the time. This thought made her sweat more.

Arthur had been waiting for her when she arrived that morning. 'D'you see it?' he'd asked, sliding a newspaper over to her. She hadn't seen it. 'It's about us,' he said. 'You know, about the case.' She looked down at the paper. No pictures this time, thank God. She asked if she could take it. 'Sure,' he answered. 'I called my secretary and asked her to pick up six extra copies. Martin Vandenberg's in the back row. Recognize him? And can you believe this crowd? I counted over fifty spectators today, and they're still pouring in. Nothing like a little publicity. I don't know why the *Post* hasn't picked up this story. Or the *News*. Though our market's really the *Times*.'

'How much do you earn each week, Miss Richards?' David Elliot asked her.

'Two hundred dollars.'

'Two hundred a week?'

'Yes.'

'How much of that do you pay in taxes?'

Selma looked at Arthur. He stared back.

'How much of that do you pay in taxes?'

Arthur finally stood up and objected, but the judge overruled him right away.

'I get paid in cash.'

'In cash. And how much of that cash do you pay in taxes?'

Arthur rose to his feet again. 'Your honor, I have to advise my client to take the Fifth. Counsel is asking my client to incriminate herself.'

'Nonsense, Mr Golderson,' the judge replied in a disdainful tone that made Arthur grimace. 'This is not a criminal proceeding. It is, however, important that we understand Ms Richards' financial situation in order to make a determination about her ability to raise a child.' She turned to David Elliot and nodded.

'How much of your two hundred dollars in cash do you pay in taxes, Miss Richards?'

'None,' she said firmly, emboldened somewhat by the judge's saying that this wasn't a criminal case.

'Does that include federal as well as state—'

'You've made your point, Mr Elliot,' interrupted the judge.

'So you take home eight hundred dollars a month, is that correct?' Selma said it was.

'And out of that eight hundred, how much is for rent?'

'Two hundred and fifty.'

'Leaving you five hundred and fifty to live on, am I correct?'

Selma was too addled to check his math. So she just said yes.

'So, your plan, your *expectation*, is to support your son and yourself on five hundred and fifty dollars a month, is that correct? Assuming you don't have a change of heart and begin paying taxes.'

'That's correct.'

'Who will take care of him while you are working, Miss Richards? Obviously you won't be able to afford a nanny.' He smiled at the irony of this.

'I'll put him in day care,' Selma said.

'Day care,' he repeated, loudly, as if this were a novel idea. 'Day care. So you propose to gain custody of Isaiah Lewin only to place him in—'

'I object,' Arthur said. 'This is badgering the witness.'

'Sustained. Please, Mr Elliot, there's no need for this kind of display.'

'I'm sorry, your honor. I was simply expressing my surprise at the fact that—'

'You've expressed it already. Please continue.'

David Elliot seemed taken aback by the judge's sternness, and after a few moments said, 'No further questions.'

Selma hurried to the tutoring center that evening clutching the newspaper article to her side. She was too nervous to try reading it. When Lizzie saw her she made a face. 'Do I look that bad?' Selma asked her.

'Like you've been through the wringer.'

'That's the truth. Here.' She handed the paper to Lizzie.

244

'I don't suppose you want to try reading it?'

'You suppose right.'

Lizzie opened it and read the headline: 'Two Worlds Clash In Courtroom Custody Fight.'

'Sounds like a sci-fi movie,' Selma said mirthlessly. Lizzie smiled, equally mirthless, and read the article.

Two worlds are clashing in a Manhattan courtroom while a judge tries to determine which one would be a better place for a two-year-old boy to grow up in. The tension was almost palpable.

Selma Richards, a 29-year-old black woman, is suing for custody of the son she gave up for adoption over two years ago to Charles and Margaret Lewin. Ms Richards and her attorney, Arthur Golderson, are contending that the adoption was illegal.

In testimony yesterday morning, Ms Richards described how she took crack while pregnant. Though Ms Richards testified that she stopped taking cocaine after she learned she was pregnant, her son, Isaiah, was born addicted to the drug, and spent several weeks in a neo-natal intensive care unit.

Ms Richards also described for the court the circumstances of the adoption. Margaret Lewin, a 36-year-old photographers' representative, apparently met the child while volunteering at Manhattan Hospital. She continued to visit the child after it was released, and eventually offered $25,000 to Ms Richards for custody.

'We will not attempt to excuse the behavior of my client while pregnant,' Mr Golderson said in an opening statement. 'We will, however, show how [the Lewins] preyed upon her desperation and her inherent love for her child to cause her to act in a way that was counter to her own best interests and those of her child.'

Mr Golderson also hinted at additional damaging revelations about the Lewins to come. 'I will further demonstrate how that first act of turpitude, that $25,000 payment, was just the first in a succession of illegal, even immoral acts perpetrated by the Lewins, thus rendering them unfit as parents to Isaiah.'

The Lewins' attorney, David Elliot, countered in his opening remarks: 'We will not deny that the adoption was not legal. But we will maintain *and prove* that it was undertaken for the right reasons, to rescue a child born to a drug addict from a life of misery and poverty and suffering.'

When asked yesterday afternoon to read a medical chart of her son's stay in intensive care, Ms Richards was forced to reveal that she was unable to read.

Also sparking controversy were revelations that Ms Richards had foresworn crack without the aid of a treatment program. Instead, she testified to hearing 'voices' that urged her to trust the Lord to help her give up drugs. The Lewins' attorney attempted to cast doubt in the judge's mind whether Ms Richards, who works as a babysitter, was in fact permanently off drugs.

'That's the way it happened,' Selma said when Lizzie finished reading the article. 'I can't complain on that account.'

Later, she carefully clipped the article, folded it, and mailed it to Calvin Hughes in Boston.

Chapter 34

The courtroom looked different viewed from the witness stand, larger and more austere. Margaret spent a few moments getting her bearings – it didn't feel as if she were in the same room. Even Charles looked distant, remote. She glanced up at the judge and noticed a cross-hatching of wrinkles on her powdered cheeks. She looked back at the visitors' section, at the fifty or so people already seated, drawn by the second *Times* article. One of the visitors was the reporter, of course. She easily guessed who that was – the one Arthur Golderson was always sidling up to. She stole a quick look at Selma Richards, who seemed to grow handsomer every day; the more dirt David Elliot threw at her, the better she looked, somehow; nothing really stuck to her. The more he talked about her drug addiction, the healthier she appeared, making their lawyer seem like a liar.

David Elliot took his time approaching her, as if he were preparing his questions for the first time. We should have gone with someone less high-powered, Margaret thought for the thousandth time that week. Someone less white-shoe, not to mention less expensive. 'Mrs Lewin, perhaps you could describe for the court your family life.'

The question struck her as terribly unspecific, but Margaret reminded herself that David Elliot was on their side and struggled to fashion a response.

'There's my husband Charles,' she began. Her voice sounded tinny and distant in the large, hard-surfaced courtroom. She cleared her throat and continued. 'Our daughter, Hannah, who's twelve. And, of course, Isaiah.'

He next asked her about their work; she answered as plainly as she could. David had warned them that he'd ask her about salaries, so she was prepared. 'Our household income is approximately one hundred and ten thousand dollars a year,' she said. 'My husband makes about sixty-five thousand, I make about forty, and we have five thousand dollars of income from our savings.' She'd rehearsed this part at home, with Charles, but she still felt uncomfortable saying it in so public a place, particularly in front of Selma Richards,

247

whose income was a tenth of theirs. Most of the time they lamented the meagerness of their incomes, dreaming of the day when their businesses would start to spin off *real* money. But here, in court, the sums involved sounded huge, gross.

She was asked to describe her apartment, the vacations they took, Hannah's school. 'Would you describe this as a *superior* private school?' David Elliot asked her, practically leering over the adjective.

'It's very competitive, yes,' she answered, shying from the word. Then he asked about Isaiah.

'He goes to the Children's Center five days a week,' she told the court.

'Would you call this an *enrichment* program?'

Margaret hated the way this was making her sound, especially in front of Selma Richards. 'Yes,' she said as evenly as she could.

He asked her about her own educational background, and Charles's. He asked about trips to the Museum of Natural History, the library, the Bronx Zoo. He probed her views on health and nutrition, and even elicited from her that Isaiah had been toilet trained rather early for a boy.

'Do you read him stories at night?' he asked her.

'I tell him stories, yes,' Margaret answered. 'I make up stories, from books I've read.' Then, from the gleam in his eye, she saw what he was after. 'And I read to him, yes,' she added hastily.

'So you *read* to him regularly?'

'Yes, almost every night, and sometimes in the afternoon.' She forced herself not to look at Selma Richards.

'No further questions.'

Arthur Golderson rose quickly and scurried to the witness stand with the determined, anxious expression of a shopper racing to a bargain table. 'Who watches Isaiah when he's not at his "enrichment" program?' he asked. His tone was impatient, as if he already knew the answer.

'We have a nanny.'

'A nanny,' he repeated, but twice as loud and with a hint of sarcasm. 'Is this an *English* nanny? Are we talking starched uniform and little white cap here?'

'Mr Golderson,' the judge interjected. 'Please.'

'She's from Denmark. Maybe au pair is the more accurate term.'

'*Au pair*. I see. And basically she watches Isaiah during the day while you and your husband are at work.'

'That's right.'

'How much do you pay her, Mrs Lewin?'

'One hundred and fifty dollars a week.'

248

'How do you pay her?'

Margaret sensed what was coming. 'I'm not sure I know what—'

'Do you pay her in cash?'

'Yes.'

'Do you withhold for Social Security?'

'No.'

'Are you aware that as her employer you are legally responsible for this?'

Margaret looked at Charles and at David Elliot, but no rescue was forthcoming. 'She's not a citizen,' she said, forcing herself to speak loudly.

'Of course she isn't. Does she have a work visa?'

Margaret cast another hopeless glance at her husband and lawyer. 'No.'

'What kind of visa does she have?'

'A tourist visa.'

'Does a tourist visa entitle her to work?'

'Not technically.'

'Could you elaborate on what you mean by *not technically*?'

Margaret took a deep breath. 'She's not entitled to work.'

'So she's working illegally for you, is that correct?'

'I guess so.'

'How long is her visa for?'

'Three months.'

'When is that three-month period up?'

'It's already lapsed.'

'I see. Does she have any plans to return to Denmark, or is she going to remain here, illegally, forever?'

'I'm not sure . . .'

'You're not sure? Frankly, I'm surprised you haven't even discussed so critical an issue before.'

'We've discussed it . . .'

'And?'

'And Liv . . .'

'Liv?'

'Our au pair. She mentioned that she's thinking of going home later this fall.'

'I see. And will you get another *nanny* . . . excuse me, *au pair*, to watch Isaiah at that time?'

'Maybe, I don't know.'

'Well, are you planning to quit your job this fall?'

'No.'

'Then you'll need to find someone else to watch Isaiah, correct?'

'Yes.'

'And so, presumably, you'll get another illegal alien—'

249

'Mr Golderson, really,' interrupted the judge.

'Your honor, I'm trying to establish a pattern of disrespect for the law that began with the illegal adoption and continues to this day with the illegal employment of foreign nationals.' He was panting slightly when he finished.

'I believe you've established that the nanny is not entitled to work in this country given her visa restrictions. Now please move on.'

Arthur allowed himself a few moments before continuing.

'What time do you normally arrive home from your office, Mrs Lewin?' He was leaning an elbow on the witness stand in a pose of false intimacy.

'Around five.'

'Around five. So you leave your office at, what, four thirty?'

'Actually, I leave at five or five fifteen.'

'So you actually arrive home at five thirty or five forty-five.'

'That's correct.'

'And your husband?'

'He arrives home at six or six thirty.'

'So basically Isaiah is with the nanny-slash-au pair from – you didn't mention when you leave for work.'

'Around eight or eight thirty.'

'Thank you. So basically Isaiah is with the nanny from eight to close to six in the evening, is that accurate?'

'More or less,' Margaret said reluctantly.

'Unless you have to work late.'

'I rarely work late.'

'*Rarely* work late. How often, once a week, twice?'

'Once a week.'

'So once a week Isaiah is with the nanny from eight thirty in the morning until, what, seven, seven thirty in the evening?'

'Not often.'

'But this *does* occur.'

'Yes.'

Then, with barely a moment's rest to catch his breath, he asked, 'Mrs Levin, can you describe for us the difficulties Isaiah has been encountering at his playgroup lately.'

She felt her throat contract. 'Difficulties?' she said hoarsely. 'He hasn't had any difficulties.'

'I'm talking about the biting incidents.'

At that moment Margaret knew she was capable of killing Arthur Golderson. She felt fists forming on her lap, and rose a fraction from her chair. 'How did you hear about that?'

'The issue isn't how I heard about Isaiah's biting problem. It's *why* is he behaving this way.'

'It's not a problem. It was a phase.'

'I'm not sure the staff at the center would agree. Wasn't there talk of having him expelled?'

'They don't *expel* children from playgroup.' She forced a deprecatory smile.

'But they did discuss the possibility of withdrawing Isaiah, did they not?'

'Only until the . . . biting stopped.'

'Isn't it true that the other children are afraid of him, Mrs Lewin? Isn't it true that biting is seen by child psychologists as an adjustment problem, a way of asking for something that they're not getting at home?'

Judge Champion actually clapped her hands to interrupt him. 'Mr Golderson, Mrs Levin is not a child psychologist. Please restrict your questions to topics to which she can address herself. If you would like to call a child psychologist, then do so.'

'Maybe I will,' he answered petulantly, walking away from Margaret. When he reached his table he swiveled on one foot. 'In what religion are you planning to raise Isaiah, Mrs Lewin?'

'Religion?' Her recurring nightmare, the one about sitting down for a test and discovering that she'd prepared for the wrong course, was coming true. 'We haven't really discussed that,' she answered weakly. 'Isaiah's not even three, you see.'

'Well then, what religious training does your daughter Hannah receive? I believe you said she's twelve.'

'My husband and I are of different religious backgrounds. We were never interested in organized religion, we—'

'Is Hannah or Isaiah being raised in a religion, organized or disorganized, Mrs Lewin?'

'No.'

'You attend neither church nor synagogue, is that correct?'

'Yes.'

'No further questions.'

That night, driven from her apartment by the inappropriate September heat and her own restlessness, Selma walked the streets and avenues of her new neighborhood, feeling like a visitor, a tourist. That feeling of putting something in motion which she could no longer control had come back to her full force. That afternoon she'd mentioned to Arthur Golderson that perhaps they should talk to the Lewins about a compromise, joint custody or something. His eyes widened like a cornered animal's. We're so close, Selma, he told her. We've got them.

But she didn't want to 'get' anybody. She wanted her son back and she wanted to prove to herself that you could change, that there was such a thing as a second chance. Selma liked the phrase 'born

251

again', she liked to turn it over in her mind, picturing herself dressed in a white robe of some sort, with Isaiah in her arms. She'd never felt born again in a religious sense, even if she had in fact found religion as an adult. She felt that she'd literally given birth to herself, to the person she was now, a person who didn't use drugs and who could read (or was learning to) and who could be a good mother to a little boy. She felt much more responsible for the person she was than her mother had ever been. Born again.

God setteth the solitary in families, she recalled from scripture.

Since moving to Manhattan, Selma hadn't been to church much. Brooklyn was a long way by subway, and she felt a little uncomfortable going to a strange church. But there was another reason. Since this whole process began, Selma was afraid to pray, because if she prayed she'd ask for her son back, and now she was beginning to wonder if this wasn't a selfish request, the kind of thing you're not supposed to pray for. Getting Isaiah back would cause hurt to the Lewins – she hadn't considered this before. How could you pray for something that would hurt other people? So Selma avoided churches and wouldn't even pray on her own, lest selfish thoughts seep into her prayers like a stain spreading on a clean dress. She took what comfort she could from remembered bits of scripture. *God setteth the solitary in families*.

There was tension in the Upper West Side neighborhood where Arthur Golderson had relocated her. Affluent white people were moving in; you could tell which apartments they lived in from the new windows without panes, the shutters and the air conditioners and the window boxes of geraniums and petunias. But the blacks and Puerto Ricans were still there – gauzy curtains billowed out from their open windows – and now crack dealers and crack users, like the rich whites, were beginning to infiltrate. The different worlds rarely interacted, and when they did it was usually something bad happening, a drug deal, a mugging, a murder. Selma didn't know where exactly she fitted in. For her the neighborhood was all strangers – or perhaps only she was an alien, everyone else fitted in.

Driven by heat and agitation from her apartment, she found the streets hotter and more agitated. There seemed no place for her, she concluded when she finally returned to her apartment. But she had at least succeeded in exhausting herself, and not long after she got home she gave into a deep, dreamless sleep.

Chapter 35

The Lewins huddled over the *Times* Wednesday morning, reading about themselves for the second time that week. When Hannah was done she considered asking a question – like why did the article make such a big deal about their incomes, when half the city made more than they did with only one person working? – but wisely decided she'd do better to get herself dressed and off to school as inconspicuously as possible.

When Charles finished reading he went into the kitchen and made himself toast; his expression was grim, and turned grimmer when he burned the toast and had to scrape the charred surface into the wastepaper basket.

'It's worse reading about it than actually testifying,' Margaret told Charles when she finished reading the article. 'I mean, it was bad yesterday, but seeing it in the paper is awful.'

'We're the capitalist pigs,' Charles said through a mouthful of buttered toast, sounding almost satisfied.

'Maybe we should tell David to ask us about expenses. When the judge sees what it costs us to maintain this place, and Hannah's tuition, and the garage—'

'I don't think proving that we can't make ends meet on a hundred and ten thousand a year will make us more sympathetic in the judge's eyes.'

'It's so unfair. They're making us out to be these horrible . . .' She searched for the word. They were too old to be yuppies, too young for fat cats. 'These horrible *materialists*,' she said finally, though the word seemed inadequate. 'And we're not materialistic. You just accumulate *things* as the years go by, and then you have children and you want certain things for them, like good schools and nice vacations and, God forbid, nice clothes.'

'Margaret, you don't have to convince me.'

That's when she realized she was shouting. She stood up to leave and noticed Isaiah standing in the doorway between the dining room and the hallway. He looked fascinated, rapt, the way he always did when he didn't understand something. As she walked over to give him a reassuring hug he smiled in the sly, almost coy way he had and she suddenly saw Selma Richards asserting herself through Isaiah's face. It was like watching a hologram: looked at one way, there was her precious Isaiah; turned the other way, there was Selma Richards, with the same coy smile, the same long, narrow nose, the same flawless brown skin . . .

Margaret scooped Isaiah into her arms and squeezed him. I could lose him, she thought; the possibility descended on her in a downpour of fear that made it momentarily difficult for her to breathe. Worse, when she put Isaiah down she saw, in his face, that he'd felt her clench him too tightly, felt her hold him too long.

Charles took the stand Wednesday morning at ten and answered a series of easy questions from David Elliot about his work, his education, his relationship with Isaiah. He felt almost relieved to be on the stand, talking before the court. Sometimes he felt extraneous to this whole mess, Margaret's ally but not really a key player. Hadn't the *Times* only that morning declared the case 'a contest between two mothers'? To Charles' way of thinking, just the fact that he existed, a father, and an involved, 1980s type of father at that, should have decided the whole issue; of course Isaiah would be better off with the Lewins, a nuclear family, a family *with a father*. But no one seemed particularly interested in this. It was as if he had no contribution to make; the issue was, who was the better *mother*. Maybe if Selma Richards had a husband, there would be an effort to compare qualifications as fathers. Hey, he wanted to shout at the judge, don't you see? Let Isaiah stay with us and he'll have an honest-to-goodness father. Doesn't that count for anything? Doesn't that override every other concern? Aren't fathers *important*?

David Elliot had said that simply putting him on the stand would reinforce the idea that the Lewins were a two-parent family. 'But you have to be careful to avoid attacking her as a single mother,' he'd said. 'That could backfire on us.'

So Charles indulged himself in a sense of vindication, sitting on the stand that morning. He felt gratified that his role in this affair was finally being taken seriously. He answered the questions thoughtfully, in a deep, unwavering voice that he knew made a good impression. Only when David Elliot was finished and he saw Arthur Golderson jump to his feet with almost adolescent eagerness did he sense something bad was going to occur. He was right.

'Who is Susannah Foster?' he asked. For a moment Charles didn't recognize the name; it sounded completely out of place as it circled the courtroom, finding no purchase on the hard, slick surfaces.

'My assistant,' he managed at last.

'Your assistant,' Arthur parroted. 'Nothing more?'

254

The temptation to lie was overwhelming. Charles merely shrugged.

'Are you having an affair with Susannah Foster?'

Charles glanced over at his wife at the very moment that David Elliot did the same thing. 'No,' he answered.

'No? Be careful, Mr Lewin. You're under oath.'

'I am not having an affair,' he repeated, hoping against hope that his careful use of the present tense would disentangle him, *rescue* him.

But Arthur Golderson was no idiot. 'Did you *ever* have an affair with Susannah Foster?'

Charles stole a second look at his wife, who was whispering into their lawyer's ear. 'Yes,' he answered, turning back, frustrated by his inability to find the right tone of voice, the right *attitude* with which to answer such a question; humility would only worsen his position, while confidence might make him seem unrepentant. 'We had an affair, briefly, but it's over,' he said in a voice that he hoped would sound completely neutral.

'How often did you see Susannah Foster?'

'We worked together. Every day.'

'You know what I mean, Mr Lewin.'

'One or two nights a week. At most,' he added hastily.

'Did you spend the entire night with her?'

'Never,' Charles said.

'But you did come home late.'

'Yes.'

'Were your children in bed when you got home on these nights?'

'Yes.'

Arthur turned his back to Charles, as if to a traitor, and took a few steps toward the back of the courtroom. It was a favorite, if not particularly original, technique of his, heightening the drama, emphasizing for all present how he felt about the witness without his having to say anything.

That's when he noticed his father in the back row, behind the still growing crowd of spectators. A rush of emotion came over him, a feeling of success such as he'd never experienced before. It didn't matter, now, what the ultimate decision was: he had won. Abe Golderson, litigator par excellence, had descended from his mid-town office, his *throne*, to watch his son perform in court. Abe Golderson had noticed. Abe Golderson had been impressed (or so Arthur assumed). He gave his father a crisp nod to acknowledge his presence and turned back to Charles Lewin.

'Was Isaiah asleep when you got home?'

'Yes.'

'Did your wife know about the affair?'

'She found out about it.'

'What was her reaction?'

Charles looked puzzled. 'She was upset, of course.'

'Upset,' he echoed. 'Were there arguments. *Scenes*?'

'A few.'

'Was Isaiah present at any of these scenes?'

'Not that I recall.'

'Think hard, Mr Lewin Was Isaiah present at any of these arguments?'

'No,' he answered firmly.

'But there must have been considerable tension in the household during this time, am I correct?'

'I suppose so. We did our best to make things . . . normal for the children.'

'You did your best? Did it ever occur to you that the biting episode at Isaiah's play group could have been caused by the tension he was sensing at home, between you and your wife?'

'That had nothing to do with it.'

'Are you sure about that, Mr Lewin? Are you absolutely positive that Isaiah's hostile behavior towards other children wasn't a reaction to the unbearable situation at home?'

'He wasn't "hostile", he just . . . and it wasn't "unbearable" at home, it was . . .'

Charles Lewin was floundering. Arthur's instinct was to press on, but he knew his father would quit at this moment, leaving his witness flailing on the stand like a beached fish. So he turned and walked slowly back to his table. Only when he got there did he say 'No further questions' in a voice full of manufactured disgust.

'Things are looking good,' he whispered to Selma. But he could tell by looking at her that she took no pleasure in the proceedings. She never did.

So Arthur turned around to seek appreciation from the back of the courtroom. The last row, however, was empty.

Chapter 36

A perceptible feeling of reassurance came over the courtroom when Alicia Smithers took the stand. Here at last was an expert, someone with no stake in the outcome, who would set matters right. Strangely enough, though Alicia Smithers had been called by Arthur Golderson on behalf of his client, even Margaret and Charles felt reassured by her presence. How could this woman, with her superb credentials, fail to help their cause?

Alicia Smithers was the director of the Manhattan Children's Services Association, a private agency that received most of its funding from the city. Children's Services functioned primarily as a clearing house for children in need of foster homes and adoption. It was a highly regarded institution, and it was easy to see why, looking at its director. She was a tall, heavy-set middle-aged black woman who moved at a slow, lumbering pace that bespoke deliberation, caution, sanity. Her voice was smooth as honey but pungent, not sweet, and when she gestured with her large hands, which she did frequently, the eye followed them as if mesmerized.

Arthur asked Alicia Smithers a number of questions about her agency and her own credentials. He'd done his homework and still had a dozen more questions to ask when the judge interrupted him. 'I think we get the point you're trying to make. Ms Smithers is amply qualified to testify here this morning.'

Arthur looked forlornly at the sheet of paper in his left hand, on which were listed the additional questions. After a few seconds he recovered from this setback. 'Ms Smithers, are you familiar with the facts of this situation?'

'I've followed the case in the paper, yes.'

'Then you're familiar with the fact that Charles Lewin,' he turned and, rather histrionically, thrust a finger at Charles, 'carried on an affair with a young woman in his office?'

'I am.'

'Are you also familiar with the fact that Isaiah,' Arthur stopped himself from using the child's last name, 'that Isaiah had a severe problem with biting at his day care center?'

'Your honor,' interrupted David Elliot, 'we have not established that this was a "severe" problem, and in any case, the child is not in a day care center.'

'Withdrawn,' Arthur retorted before Judge Champion could say anything. 'Ms Smithers, the biting incidents occurred at an *enrichment* program.' He waited a moment before continuing, disappointed at not eliciting at least a smirk from his witness. 'Could these two facts, the extra-marital affair and the biting, be related?'

'Most definitely,' she answered, as if this point were obvious. 'One of the key indicators of an unsatisfactory placement is anti-social behavior on behalf of the child. Any tension at home will almost invariably be reflected in the child's behavior towards its peers as well as other family members.'

'Would you characterize biting as anti-social behavior, then?'

'Yes, I would.'

'Is there always a *cause* for the biting?'

'I don't know if I'd say *always*,' she answered in a measured voice.

'Usually, then?'

'Almost always.'

Arthur paused to let this sink in with the judge.

'Ms Smithers, does your agency have a policy regarding cross-racial placements?'

'Yes, we do,' she replied.

'And what is that policy?'

She took a deep breath. 'We discourage them. Our concern is that a black child, and we're almost always talking about black children being adopted by white parents, our concern is that a black child growing up in a white family, in a white neighborhood, will lose a sense of cultural identity. We're concerned that the child won't be accepted by the extended family. We're concerned because adoption is already a burden for a child to bear; the race issue only compounds this.'

'So your agency forbids inter-racial adoptions.'

'We *discourage* them.'

'And is this policy reflective of other children's agencies?'

'There's no uniformity. But I think it's safe to say that most if not all agencies would prefer to place a child with a family of the same racial background.'

'You mention the stress of adoption,' Arthur continued. 'Could you elaborate?'

'Certainly.' She raised the index finger of her right hand. 'I meant that in the best of situations – let's say a white child adopted at birth by a middle-class white family – there are going to be tensions and anxieties on the child's part caused by the fact of the adoption. It's inevitable. Not insurmountable, but inevitable. The child must come to grips with a profound sense of rejection.'

'On balance, then—'

'This doesn't mean, however,' she interrupted, 'that a child is always better off with its birth mother or parents. It's just that, all things being equal, the birth parents should be favored.'

'Given the tensions in the Lewin home, then, the racial issue, the character of the child's birth mother, and so on and so forth, what would your recommendation to the court be?'

Again she stepped in quickly, as if there could be only one conclusion. 'That the child should be returned to his natural mother.'

The judge jumped in here. 'Aren't you concerned about the sense of loss the child would experience?'

'Oh, of course,' Alicia Smithers said, turning to look up at the judge. She was one of the few people who didn't look somewhat ridiculous in this pose. 'There would have to be an accommodation made for visitations to ease the transition. Perhaps the Lewins could function as ongoing godparents. But the important thing is, the child must be raised by its birth mother.'

The judge nodded solemnly and looked at Arthur Golderson. 'No further questions,' he said.

Margaret and Charles dreaded David Elliot's cross-examination of Alicia Smithers. Her credentials were so unassailable, her composure so secure, they feared that attacking her would be futile, and perhaps even counter productive. But her direct testimony had been too damaging to let stand.

'Miss Smithers, you've stated that you are opposed to inter-racial adoptions.'

'My organization is opposed to inter-racial placements.'

'Does this mean that you *never* place black infants with white couples?'

'Oh, no. We do this all the time. There just aren't enough black families willing to take in the children. But these are temporary placements.'

'You mean, foster homes.'

'That's correct.'

'These children stay temporarily with a white family until a suitable black family comes along?'

'Correct.'

'How long does this usually take?'

'It can take years.' A faint crack appeared in her voice.

'And then the child is wrenched from the only home it knows, and placed with strangers.'

'I don't know if "wrenched" is the word I'd use.'

'Don't babies form attachments to the families?'

'It's the long-term interests of the child we're concerned with.'

259

'I repeat. Don't babies form attachments to the families?'

'They do, yes.'

'And yet you – your organization – still persist in putting the child through a wrenching separation because of the belief that a black child is better off with a black family.'

'This is the policy of most child welfare agencies.'

'Miss Smithers, is a black child *always* better off with a black parent, no matter what the circumstances?'

She answered even more slowly than usual, as if aware that she was walking into a trap. 'All things being equal,' she said.

'All things being equal. You used that phrase earlier. Well, let's say that all things are not equal, shall we? Let's say that the white family is a couple, while the potential adoptive black "family" ' – he made quotation marks in the air with his fingers – 'is in fact a single mother. Would your agency still take the child from the white couple and give it to the black woman?'

'By and large, yes.'

'Let's say the white couple is solidly middle-class, while the black woman is at the poverty level.'

Alicia Smithers sat up and leaned forward. 'Mr Elliot, I am sick and tired of this attitude, which I'm sorry to say I hear all the time, that taking poor children out of their environment and placing them with upper- and middle-class homes is always in the best interest of the children. What kind of values does that suggest?'

David Elliot looked away, briefly, as if to avoid having to answer. 'What if the woman were a drug addict?'

'We would never place a child with a drug addict, Mr Elliot.'

'Oh, so you mean a white couple *would* be preferable to a black drug addict.'

'Of course.'

'Which means that there are cases where inter-racial adoptions would be preferable?'

'I suppose so. But in this instance, we're not talking about deciding between two adoptive parents. We're talking about the child's natural mother.'

David Elliot appeared to lose his composure a bit at this point. 'We're talking about a woman who continued to take drugs while pregnant,' he said angrily.

'Selma Richards is a former addict, it is true. But she's been off drugs for—'

'Surely in your professional work you've learned, as I have in my reading, that fewer than ten percent of drug addicts ever get cured.'

'I've never heard that statistic.'

'Really? I'm surprised. It's a well known fact that—'

'Mr Elliot,' Judge Champion broke in, 'if you'd like to call a drug rehabilitation expert, then do so. But I don't believe that Ms Smithers is qualified to talk on this subject, am I correct, Ms Smithers?'

'I *am* capable of determining if an individual is on drugs or not. We don't place children with drug users.'

'With *former* users, then?' David Elliot asked.

'If the former user demonstrates that she has given up drugs, and if she is the child's natural mother, then of course the child stays with the natural mother.'

David Elliot turned away from her. 'I really question the judgment of your organization, Miss Smithers. I really do.'

'I beg your pardon!' retorted Alicia Smithers.

'You're out of line, Mr Elliot,' the judge warned.

'No further questions,' David Elliot said disgustedly.

The room emptied slowly that morning, leaving only the Lewins and their attorney. All three felt the need to talk things over. Charles spoke first. 'We have to call an expert of our own.'

David Elliot shook his head. 'I've called around. I can't get anyone who will testify unconditionally that Isaiah would be better off with you.'

Margaret started to speak.

'Let me finish. I've talked to several psychologists who personally feel that the child should stay put. Unfortunately, under cross-examination they will also testify that the interracial thing, the religion thing, the affair, all cast a doubt. A serious doubt.'

'I don't believe this. I mean, what you're saying is we're going to lose him.' Margaret's voice caught after each word, lending her speech a staccato tone.

'There's one other possibility.'

They both looked at him hopefully.

'We could call your daughter.'

Hannah thought it was pretty funny the way no one even *mentioned* the custody case. Like, her friends' parents never said a word, even though she knew they read the *Times*. Her teachers never brought it up. And Mr Sackman across the hall? He smiled now whenever he saw Hannah, which was something he'd never done before. But he never mentioned the case. Neither did her dentist when she saw him last week. Neither did the doorman. Neither did anybody.

Her friends talked about it only when she brought it up first. Which she didn't do very often. Hannah had this terrible, guilty feeling about the case that she couldn't tell anyone about, not even her best friends. It was a feeling that both sides were right. She knew if she breathed one word of this to her parents they'd have a

261

fit, so she kept it to herself. But still she couldn't help thinking that if she were Selma Richards she'd want Isaiah back. What mother wouldn't want her son back once she was straight? Also, unlike her parents, who thought it was *cool* to have a black kid (not that they'd ever admit this), Hannah could see how hard it was going to be for Isaiah. He wouldn't fit in. He'd always be different. No one wants to be different.

I don't *want* him to leave us, Hannah reassured herself often. I just understand why Selma Richards is doing what she's doing. And I wish this whole thing was over with.

She knew something was up when her parents called her into the dining room. That's where all the really heavy discussions were held. Like when she got a C+ in French that time. Or when her parents wanted to talk about whether she should keep on going to sleep-away camp even though she was eleven.

'Yeah, what's up?' she asked. From their saggy faces she knew this was going to be really heavy.

'Hannah,' her father said, 'our lawyer, David Elliot, thinks it might help our case if you testified before the judge.'

'Testified?'

'Just answered some questions about your relationship with Isaiah.'

She was about to say, sure, if it would help, when her mother broke in. 'We don't want to get you involved, sweetie. We've tried to make things as normal as possible for you.'

'I don't mind.'

'David would go over the questions with you in advance,' her father explained. 'The other lawyer wouldn't do this, of course.'

'I'll just tell the truth, right?'

'Just the truth.'

'Will this be a school day?'

'Tomorrow, actually.'

Hannah ran tomorrow through her mind. She'd miss her flute lesson, which was good, and an algebra quiz, which was even better, though she'd have to make it up. 'No problem.'

'We'll be sitting just a few feet from you,' her mother said.

'I can handle it.' She paused for a moment, wondering how far she should go. 'Even if they ask me about, you know, the affair, like, I'll tell them that I didn't know about it and that there wasn't any tension in the family that I knew about.'

They stared at her, silent.

'Isn't that important?' she asked, unsure herself how sincere she was being. 'I mean, aren't they trying to show how much tension there is around here? I mean, I never felt any tension, I never even knew about it until I read it in the paper.'

262

The day the affair appeared in the *Times*, her parents had kept the paper away from her. She didn't really like reading the *Times*, but when she realized that she wasn't going to get to read about the case that day, she knew something was wrong. So she bought a paper that morning on the way to school and read about her father and Susannah Foster. Did they really think they could fool her?

'Honey, I wish you didn't have to hear about that,' her father told her. Her mother was staring down into the table.

Hannah shrugged. 'You're practically the only married parents in my school. Married to each other, I mean.'

They both looked at her like she'd said something in Swahili.

'I mean, all my friends' parents are divorced or separated or having affairs. It's cool.'

'My . . . affair is over, you realize that, don't you?'

'That's what the article said.' Boy, this was really something, feeling like you had your parents hanging by a string.

'I don't think they'll ask you about . . . this,' her mother said.

'Either way,' she said as casually as she could. She got up to leave. 'Can I go? I have homework.'

'Sure, honey,' her mother said. 'Thank you.'

'No problem,' she said, and left them at the table, defeated.

Chapter 37

Margaret felt fortified with Hannah sitting between her and Charles. Hannah's presence seemed to prove a point of some kind. Perhaps it was only that now there were three of them, a family. She looked slyly across the room at Selma Richards, all by herself.

'Are you nervous, sweetie?' Margaret whispered. Hannah had on the dress she'd worn to the bar mitzvah, earlier that year, of Charles's nephew, the son of his elder brother. It was bright red with a column of large black buttons down the front. Its sophistication was jarring on Hannah, whose face and body still retained a pre-adolescent puffiness, though the contours of her adult self were beginning to emerge. Certain of Hannah's expressions had the same chilling effect on Margaret: the way she affected boredom by arching her eyebrows, the way she showed mild displeasure by raising a corner of her mouth. It was like seeing a very young girl playing dress-up; the sight of a child wearing her mother's lipstick was always more unsettling than amusing. Margaret had wanted to suggest that Hannah wear something less dressy to court, but had backed off. She sensed a confrontation, and didn't want ill will to trail them into the courtroom.

'Your honor, I am calling Hannah Lewin to the stand,' David Elliot announced moments after returning to the courtroom; he'd left to make a call after briefing Hannah on the questions he'd be asking. Hannah jumped to her feet and hurried to the stand, the heels of her patent leather shoes clicking rather ominously, Margaret felt, on the marble floor.

In a gentler tone than he'd used before, David Elliot asked Hannah to tell the court about her school, her friends, her interests. Her voice was small and strained in the large room, and a nervous wavering was easily detectable. Her eyes darted from the lawyer to her parents and occasionally over to Selma Richards and her lawyer.

'Do you remember when your parents adopted Isaiah?' David Elliot asked her, getting to the point at last.

'Yes,' she answered.

'Do you remember how old you were at the time?'

This had been rehearsed. 'I was nine and a half.'

265

'Do you recall your feelings at the time?'

'Yes.'

'What were those feelings?'

'I was happy about it.'

'Can you describe in more depth your feelings at the time?'

'I thought he was real cute. He was tiny but he had these big eyes and this big mouth . . .' She paused, then appeared to have remembered something. 'I was happy to have a little brother.'

'I see. And have you been happy ever since?'

'Yes,' she said emphatically. 'Very happy.'

Selma watched Hannah Lewin through squinted eyes. This was her son's sister? The notion made her want to cry, but her lips formed a smile nonetheless. Next to her, Arthur Golderson leaned forward, hunched over a pad of paper. Once in a while he'd grab his pen and scribble something on it, then drop the pen and resume staring at Hannah. He's like a vulture, Selma thought, ready to pounce on the remains. This thought was not as reassuring as it should have been. She looked back at Hannah Lewin. Selma heard her voice quake and tried to feel sorry for her. She thought of the girl losing Isaiah and tried to feel pity. But a bitterness rose up in her and drowned the pity. This girl looked well taken care of, like she'd survive. She had parents, grandparents. She had a big apartment with a doorman standing guard downstairs. She went to a private school. When it came to survival, money wasn't a guarantee, but it helped. Selma squinted, trying to see something else, something her pity could grab onto, or even something she could like. But all she could see was a twelve-year-old girl who had everything, even a baby brother.

'Hannah, do you think you could describe your parents *as parents*?'

'I don't know what you mean.' She shook her head slightly from side to side, in the gesture that she knew drove her mother crazy.

David Elliot was leaning one elbow on the edge of the railing in front of Hannah. This was doubtless meant to make her feel comfortable, but in fact it made her nuts. A lot of older men, when you looked at them closely, had big, inky pores and hair in unexpected places. She looked away from him as often as she could, but then sometimes her eyes would alight on her parents, which unnerved her, or on Selma Richards, which unnerved her even more.

'What I mean is, what kinds of things do your parents think are important for you?'

'Everything, you know? School.'

'Are they very concerned with homework?'

'Yes.'

'Do they ask you about it make sure you do it that kind of thing?'

'Constantly,' Hannah said truthfully.

'How are you doing in school?'

'Okay, I guess.'

'Isn't it true that you're in the top fourth of your class?'

'I guess.'

Charles was thinking about all the times he'd sat in the audience and watched his daughter on stage. The ballet recitals, the music nights, the school plays. And now this, testifying in family court. His reaction hadn't changed. He still held his breath while she performed.

Poor Hannah. He was aware that to people who didn't know her well, she was not perhaps the most likeable twelve-year-old. Maybe they'd made a mistake bringing her into this. There was this false sophistication about her that was just repulsive. All her friends had it, too, this patina of refinement that was all the more objectionable for its transparency. It probably came from living in Manhattan and going to private school. Sometime in the past two years she'd started getting her hair cut in a blunt, angled style that was years beyond her age; it swung freely around her face, but not in concert with it, as if obeying different laws of gravity. And these mannerisms of hers, the way she flung her hair back from her face, the way she shook her head almost imperceptibly if she didn't understand something and thought it was your fault for not making it clear.

Charles could see through the veneer, but he didn't expect the judge could. She might not even know there was a veneer. He stole a look at Selma Richards. What must she make of Hannah? How could either of them, Selma or the judge, picture this ageing Lolita as the older sister of a black child born of a drug addict?

'Hannah, are you aware that Selma Richards' lawyer is attempting to paint a picture of your household as one filled with tension?'

'I guess.'

'Do you agree with this picture?'

'There's no tension.'

This answer didn't appear to satisfy the lawyer, who grimaced slightly and shifted tack. 'Hannah, tell me, do you spend a lot of time with your brother?'

She knew the answer that was expected to this one. 'Yes.'

'Could you tell us the kinds of things you do together?'

'Well, we watch television, and we eat dinner together.' Hannah racked her brains to think of something else. 'Oh, and there's this game. It's like I throw the ball in the hallway and he catches it. I mean, it's stupid, but Isaiah likes it. And sometimes I read him a story from one of his books.'

'He has a lot of books?' David Elliot interrupted.

'Tons.'

'And he likes to read.'

'Well, he likes when I read to him. He has this one book, it's about animals. Only the animals are hidden in things, like trees and bushes. And when I read it to him I ask him to point to the animals. Can you find the tiger, Isaiah? I ask him. And then he points to it and . . .'

Something flashed in her head, an image of the way Isaiah looked when he'd found the tiger for the fiftieth time, maybe the hundredth time, not a smile but a sly grin of triumph and pleasure, a look that always made her squeeze him with the arm that wasn't holding the book. Good, Isaiah, she'd say. Very good. Then the smile *did* appear, exposing a row of perfect, miniature teeth.

'And then what happens?' David Elliot asked, seizing on her emotion.

Hannah looked up at him and realized she couldn't answer. So she gave him her one-shoulder shrug instead, another thing that drove her mother crazy.

'You said that Isaiah points to the animal and then . . . then what, Hannah?'

Quickly, in one breath, she replied 'Then he gets all proud of himself and I hug him and he smiles. Then we go to the next page.'

'Hannah, why are you crying now?'

I am not, she almost answered. Then, to her alarm, she felt a dampness on her cheeks.

He leaned closer to her, sending a breeze of stale breath. 'Please, Hannah, tell us why you're crying.'

She knew what to say: Because I'll miss Isaiah. But something kept her from answering right away. Maybe it was the look on her parents' faces, the look they used to have at music night when she had a solo and she spotted them, halfway though, leaning forward with this *look* on their faces that made her forget the lyrics or go dry in the throat. Maybe it was Selma Richards, also leaning forward, hanging on her answer. No one had warned her how much this woman was going to look like Isaiah. Selma Richards had the same expression that Isaiah did when she was about to flip to the next page, like everything depended on what was on the next page, like he hadn't already been through this book a thousand times before. Maybe it was just that things were too complicated and too important to depend on what she said.

'I don't know,' she finally answered, drying her face with the cuff of her red dress.

'Think about it for a minute. Please.'

She could see she wouldn't be let off the hook without an answer. So she composed a line in her head and then let her lips speak it in a smooth, flat voice. 'Because I'll miss Isaiah if he leaves us.'

'Thank you, Hannah,' David Elliot said. Then, turning to the judge, he said, 'No further questions.'

Arthur grabbed his notepad and stood up. 'Miss Lewin,' he began, but just then Selma grabbed the hem of his jacket and pulled him back down.

'Let her be,' she whispered.

'But I have to question her,' he protested. 'Those tears just now were very damaging to us, Selma. I have to neutralize them.'

'Some other way.'

'There is no other way,' he hissed.

'No more questions, then. I mean it.'

Chapter 38

Judge Champion asked the attorneys to make their closing arguments Friday morning, one day after Hannah Lewin's testimony. Thursday evening, Arthur holed himself up in his office on Lexington Avenue until long after dark. He made a neat, three-page outline of his thoughts, and then began inserting new items between the numbered headings. Then he inserted still more items, until the pages were a thoroughly unsatisfying clutter. He regretted sending his secretary home at six thirty and briefly considered combing the halls of Golderson, Schaeffer and Pollack for a typist. Instead he copied the outline himself, selecting a gold Mont Blanc cartridge pen, a law school graduation present from an uncle – or was it from a family friend? When he finished he was dismayed to find that it was only eight o'clock. He'd been prepared to stay long past midnight if necessary on the eve of the most important day of his professional life.

He put his notes in a manila folder, which he placed with some ceremony in his briefcase. He stopped at his secretary's desk on the way out and left a note saying that he'd be in court tomorrow but would call in before noon. Rounding the bend toward the reception area, he noticed a faint light from his father's corner office and felt his heart sink. It wasn't fair, it simply wasn't fair that even tonight, on the eve of the most important day of his professional career, his father should be working later than he was. Abe Golderson's stamina was legendary.

Arthur peeked his head into the office. There, at the end of a long, narrow room, sat his father, behind the enormous desk that seemed to protect him as much as provide a writing surface. His father was hunched over it, scribbling on a yellow pad. Arthur stood in the doorway watching him write, unnoticed for several minutes. The office was preternaturally quiet; the distant hum of a Xerox machine seemed to insulate them further from the outside world.

Arthur considered crossing the big room and discussing the Selma Richards case with his father. But he immediately quashed the idea. His father would inevitably offer advice on his closing argument; Arthur was looking for congratulations, approval. His father had

271

never been congratulatory or approving. Arthur walked quietly past the corner office. *When I've won this case, when that boy, Isaiah, is returned to his mother, when the old man reads all about it in the* Times, then *I'll bring it up with him. Perhaps he'll bring it up with me.*

As the elevator descended, Arthur recalled his father's brief presence in the back of the courtroom that day. Surely that counted for something. Arthur couldn't help smiling at the memory. In fact, he felt suddenly so buoyant, he stopped at a pay phone in the lobby and called Lizzie Kaplan. He'd take her to that new Italian place off Fifth, the one that sends a Rolls-Royce for guests.

Lizzie was just leaving the Literacy Center when the phone rang in her apartment. Selma seemed reluctant to leave that evening, she was unusually agitated, and Lizzie, with no plans of her own, decided to wait for Selma to call an end to the session.

She was reading a book called *My Name Is Harriet*. It was written by a student in another city's literacy program and published by a literacy foundation that funded such programs. It was about a woman who as a child was abused by her father. The righthand pages were photographs; on the left was a paragraph or two of text.

Selma read a few pages a night, and another page or two, aloud, with Lizzie. Her reading was improving steadily, though in such imperceptible stages that it was difficult for her to appreciate how far she was progressing. She shrugged off Lizzie's diligently offered encouragement, however, focusing instead on how far she had yet to go.

'Then one day my father . . . hit me so hard I had to go to the h-o-s-p-i-t-a-l . . . *hospital*.'

Abruptly, Selma closed the book without marking her place. 'I don't want to finish this.'

'You only have a few more pages.'

'I don't want to finish it.'

'Okay, there's no point to reading something you're not interested in.'

'Oh, I'm interested all right. People abusing each other. Kids not loved by their parents. Poverty and drugs and now this,' she slapped the cover of the book. 'Hospitals and whatnot. I'm interested but I don't want to read about it. I want to read something I'm not used to. These books here,' she waved to the bookcases that constituted the Center's library, 'they all full of depressing stuff. All about poor people and children nobody loves. How come on the subway I see people reading books with pretty covers of rich people and big cars and airplanes and beaches, and here all we got is ghettoes and slums?'

272

Lizzie stared across the table at her, startled by the anger in her voice. Her face seemed to be pulsing, and her eyes looked fierce. 'I don't know, Selma. Maybe we could find something more, I don't know, romantic.'

'You won't find no romantic books in there,' Selma said. 'We don't deserve romance, us poor illiterates.'

'That's not true and you know it.'

'No? Then how come all those books is about poor folks and drugs and abuse, huh?' She gathered her things into her 'The family that prays together, stays together' book bag and stood up.

Lizzie started to explain that people usually liked reading about what they knew about, and that many people in the literacy program had experienced these things, but it sounded hollow coming off her lips.

Selma waited impatiently until she finished, then said, 'I got to get out of here. I got to . . .' She spread her arms, letting the book bag flop against her hip. 'I got to go somewhere but I don't know where. See you next time.'

She turned and walked quickly out of the room.

Margaret knew there wouldn't be anything truly new in David Elliot's summary. But she eagerly anticipated it nonetheless. Perhaps when all the issues were woven together in a neat, seamless package, the merits of her position – hers and Charles's – would become obvious.

So she was dismayed to discover, Friday morning, that David Elliot had made only a few lines of notes for his remarks, not the detailed, lengthy outline she had been looking forward to. How could those few lines capture all the points in their favor, the dozens and dozens of arguments they had for keeping Isaiah? Where in the notes did it mention that Isaiah, contrary to all the advice in all the child-rearing books, liked his bath water almost scalding? And heaven help you if you added bubble bath – he hated this. Where in the notes did it mention how he refused to wear any shirt that buttoned around the neck, no matter how loosely? Where in the notes did it mention how he liked his back stroked over and over when he woke up screaming in the middle of the night, his body damp, his blanket bunched in a tight ball in the far corner of the crib?

Margaret looked anxiously at Charles, but he looked maddeningly composed. Did you see the notes he brought? she wanted to ask him. For what we're paying him, this is what he's come up with? But she didn't say anything. If she did, Charles would remind her that it was she who had insisted on using David Elliot. Even here, fighting to keep their son, their petty differences would bubble to the surface and pour out. Nothing had changed at home, either. They still danced gingerly around each other, avoiding the issues that smoldered between them. Margaret wondered if things would be different if there were no trial. They'd be worse, she figured; the trial galvanized them to a common purpose, even if it didn't truly unite them.

David Elliot began with a reminder. 'We are here to determine one thing and one thing only: what is best for Isaiah Lewin. All other issues are subsidiary.' He then listed all the ways in which Selma Richards fell short. Her drug addiction – he reminded the court that few addicts ever truly recovered. Her illiteracy – he sympathized with her plight, but wondered whether this wouldn't be a handicap for her child as well. He described her meager economic prospects, the nature of her work – not that money is the most important issue, he added hastily, but it must be a factor. He discussed the issue of raising Isaiah without a father – didn't the boy need, didn't he *deserve*, wasn't he *used* to a man in the house?

Margaret stole glances at Selma during David Elliot's sermon of denunciation. She seemed to repel his attacks, sitting calmly, unemotionally, her hands resting almost primly in her lap. Margaret tried to zero in on her expression, which wasn't nearly as blank as it looked at first glance. In any other circumstance Margaret would have dubbed it smug. Here, where smugness was impossible, it could only be called . . . what? Composed? Dignified? Margaret rejected these words as presumptuous and settled on impervious. She looked impervious.

'But there are two sides to this coin,' David Elliot said. Margaret thought she saw Judge Champion flinch from the cliché. 'Not only must we evaluate Selma Richards's competence as a parent, we must look at the Lewins' competence as well. Here there can be no question. These kind people rescued a child born with a drug addiction and faced with a life of who knows what misery, and offered him a good home, a caring home.' He then enumerated all the reasons why the Lewins were ideal parents. Much as she'd been looking forward to this, Margaret felt herself reddening at David Elliot's idealized depiction of her and Charles. She was almost relieved when he mentioned Charles's affair. 'Yes, this is not a perfect situation – what situation is? Yes, Charles Lewin strayed.' Margaret and Charles both stared resolutely forward. 'But Charles has atoned. His indiscretion has been paraded before this court and before the public in the press and he has paid the price and learned the lesson.'

It's amazing what you can get used to, Charles was thinking. Six

274

months ago, having an affair would have seemed unthinkable. Then, once he'd begun the affair, having Margaret learn about it would have struck terror in his heart. The idea of half the city knowing about it would have seemed worse than humiliating. But each of these things had happened, and each had been absorbed into the porous fabric of his mind. Now he was listening to their two-hundred-and-fifty-dollars-an-hour attorney describe his affair and his 'atonement' before a standing-room-only crowd and it might have been his college grade point average he was detailing for all the distress he felt. The conscience is a marvelously flexible thing, he thought. Just like pride.

'Finally, let's not forget the terrible disruption to Isaiah's life that a separation from his parents would entail. Margaret and Charles Lewin are the only parents the boy has ever known. Hannah the only sister he's ever had. Selma Richards is a stranger to him, a complete stranger. She ceded all maternal rights when she handed him over to the Lewins two years ago. There are decisions that are irrevocable. Giving up your child is one of them. There are some things that can't be undone. Two years of close family love is one of them. For Isaiah's sake, not for the Lewins', not for Selma Richards', for Isaiah's sake, let him stay with the family he loves.'

Charles watched David Elliot pause theatrically before returning to his chair. His square, chiselled face was poorly suited to describing emotion. We should have chosen a less Waspy lawyer, Charles thought for the tenth time that morning. He turned to Margaret, her face frozen in the same grim pose it had held all morning. Even now, locked in battle for their son, he wanted to remind her that he had argued against retaining David Elliot. He had borne an unequal share of blame since this whole custody thing got started, and now he was tempted to cast some of it back at Margaret.

The sound of a chair scraping on the linoleum floor saved him from further unworthy thoughts. Arthur Golderson hoisted his pants under the edge of his vest, which looked to be two sizes too large for his reedy body, and scrambled to the front of the room.

'What we're really talking about here is justice,' he began. Selma thought she saw Judge Champion make a face at this, but couldn't be sure. Certainly *she* cringed inside. Selma didn't care about justice, she just wanted her son back and she wanted reassurance that it was possible to change your life, atone for the past. Justice? If there were justice in the world, none of them would be in this courtroom, except maybe Arthur himself, for whom this seemed a perfect setting.

'This was not a legal adoption,' Arthur was saying, waving his

275

notes before him as if they constituted proof. 'This was exploitation. Charles and Margaret Lewin snatched Isaiah away from his mother when they knew, *they knew*, she would be in no position to protest, to fight for the right to keep her baby.'

Arthur sopped up attention like a dry sponge, allowing Selma opportunities to glance over at the Lewins. It chilled her sometimes that she had almost no memory of them, especially Margaret Lewin, who had visited her repeatedly just a couple of years ago. When she forced herself to remember those awful weeks, all she could bring back was a feeling of being watched, judged, a feeling that she wanted to be alone, *alone*. The woman herself – her face, her body, her clothes – was just a blur, a void in her memory. It was as if she had been blind back then, able to recall only a presence but not an appearance.

She couldn't hate the Lewins, couldn't even resent them. Charles Lewin had a wide-eyed, hunted look, like he was being attacked – and maybe he was. Margaret looked like she was the one on the attack, like she'd *kill* to keep Isaiah. Her face had the alert look of a dog on the scent, and her eyes never rested on one thing for long, always shifting about, watching, waiting, preparing. Selma had to admire this, though it upset her. It upset her not because she thought *she* might be the one to be attacked, but because, much as she wanted Isaiah back, down deep she knew she herself had never felt this way.

'Will there be short-term distress for Isaiah when he is separated from the Lewins? Undoubtedly. That's why my client is prepared to work with the Lewins to develop a series of transitional visits. But the short-term trauma must be weighed against the long-term trauma of this black child being raised in a white home. What is a brief period of unhappiness next to a lifetime of alienation? Selma Richards has been to hell and she's come back. She's prepared to make a loving, caring home for her son, and to provide him with the religious and moral environment he'll need to flourish in today's environment.'

Arthur turned to the Lewins. 'Where is the morality in this family? The husband has a girlfriend, the wife works long hours, leaving the child in the inexperienced hands of a teenager. Both Lewins tell us they "haven't really thought" about religion for their children. The pattern of deceit and corruption that began two years ago with an illegal adoption continues today. I urge the court to follow the precedent set by the city's family service agencies and return Isaiah Richards to his mother.'

Arthur walked crisply, militarily, to his seat. He looked at Selma, trying unsuccessfully to disguise his elation. She turned away, confused and ashamed. That wasn't me you were describing, she wanted to tell him, and that wasn't the Lewins, neither.

For Margaret, the silence that followed Arthur Golderson's summation was a powerful vacuum that threatened to suck her into a deep, textureless void. She gripped the edge of the table and, a moment later, grasped Charles's left hand, but she still felt herself being pulled, wrenched. She looked up at the judge, who seemed to be reviewing some papers on her desk, maddeningly serene, and wanted to shout at her: You can't possibly understand, you haven't heard the whole story, the true story. But she knew her words would be sucked into the emptiness that she felt just at the edge of her consciousness.

'You've presented me with a difficult decision,' Judge Champion said, her voice tired. 'I will review the facts over the weekend and render a decision on Monday at nine in the morning.' The judge rose and left the courtroom by a door behind the bench. This left the attorneys and their clients and the crowd of spectators. No one seemed inclined to move from this place where so many fates were to be decided. Finally, Selma pushed her chair back and stood.

'I'll see you Monday,' she told Arthur. Then, looking neither right nor left, she walked out of the courtroom.

Isaiah dragged the blue crayon across the paper, but he didn't press hard enough to make much of a mark. He never did. Hannah, exasperated, placed her hand over his and traced the outline of a face. 'There, Isaiah, see? A person.'

He looked at the paper, then up at Hannah and smiled proudly.

'You're so easy to please, Isaiah,' Hannah said. The words just popped out, and embarrassed her, for some reason, but it was true: the simplest things made him ecstatic. Like taking all the pots and pans out of the cabinet and lining them up on the kitchen floor. Or emptying the contents of their father's wallet onto a table.

She got up from the dining room floor where they'd been drawing and walked toward the kitchen. He followed her, as she knew he would. She wanted to be alone but she forced herself to turn and smile at him. Her parents would be home from the court in a few minutes, so she might as well make one last effort. 'Want some juice?' she said.

Of course he did. God, the way he looked at her, like she had all the answers. Like she was the only other person in the world.

Hannah put her hand on the refrigerator handle but stopped before opening it.

All those times she'd wished he'd just disappear.

She hoisted Isaiah up and squeezed him. God, he was so heavy, so much heavier than you expected, no matter how many times you lifted him. Like the medicine balls in school, you just never expected the weight. Were all kids like this, like they had a special kind of gravity, all their own, that pushed them down on you?

All those times she'd just wished they could be normal, average.

She set him down on the counter, standing, so that his face was above hers. He had that look he got lately whenever someone held him too long or too hard, like he felt trapped. Sometimes Hannah knew just what he meant by that look. 'I know, Isaiah, let's make some Jello.'

His eyes widened, as she knew they would.

'You're so easy to please, Isaiah,' Hannah said again. She lifted him off the counter and thought about squeezing him one extra time. But she just set him down on the floor next to her.

Chapter 39

Selma had never taken much interest in the places she lived. But most of her rooms eventually took on a character, if only from the clutter of clothes and jewelry, that made her feel welcome and in control.

Her apartment in the West Nineties wouldn't do this. It resisted her personality like a non-stick pan. She didn't feel welcome in it and she didn't feel in control.

The neighborhood wasn't much better. She'd never had many friends or even acquaintances, but the streets in her past, even Livonia Avenue, were full of people who *could* be her friends. It was different here. Everyone she passed seemed nervous, jumpy, which was strange, since this was the safest neighborhood Selma had ever lived in. The neighborhood's getting better every day, Arthur had told her, which Selma interpreted as meaning that the rich were moving in and the poor were moving out. But everyone, those on the way in and those on the way out, seemed suspicious, even angry; change was coming too slow for some, too fast for others.

So her apartment offered no respite from the neighborhood, and the neighborhood no respite from her apartment. Waiting to learn from Judge Champion if she could have her son back, Selma spent Saturday pacing her apartment and pacing the Upper West Side, finding neither comfort nor weariness from the exercise. If I only knew, she thought. Good or bad, it would be better to know.

The Lewins spent the weekend at the Mellors' newly purchased home in Connecticut. 'I couldn't take weekends in the city anymore,' Charlotte told them as she led a tour through the early-eighteenth-century farmhouse. 'Here, I put Emma out the back door after breakfast and she's on her own until lunch.'

'Like a dog,' Charles observed humorlessly. Everyone managed an uneasy laugh. The judge's pending decision about Isaiah was an uninvited guest in what would otherwise have been an idyllic fall weekend. The air was fragrant with moldering leaves, the horizon glowed with late-turning elms and maples. Margaret would stare at the distant hills and remind herself how beautiful they were. How brilliant the reds are, she'd remark silently, unmoved. And the yellow oaks etched on the cloudless blue sky.

Only Isaiah and Emma were unaffected by the gloom. They roamed ceaselessly from one corner of the Mellors' yard to another, seemingly out of breath for hours at a time. Hannah was particularly morose, emerging from her assigned room only for meals. 'Would you like to talk?' Margaret asked her Saturday afternoon, poking her head in the room, where Hannah was lying on the bed, staring blankly at an algebra text.

'About what?' Hannah answered.

'About what's happening,' Margaret replied. 'About the trial.'

Hannah shrugged, her most prolific gesture these days. 'Why bother? It's not up to us.' She returned to the algebra book.

'It can't hurt to talk about feelings,' Margaret offered hopefully. Another shrug.

Margaret resumed her ramble through the mercifully large house, wishing she could simply place herself on a bed and hibernate until Monday, like Hannah. She knew that half her motive for approaching Hannah was selfish; *she* needed to talk, and Hannah seemed like the most appealing partner. Charles offered her little comfort. We have to face the prospect of losing him, he'd tell her. But Margaret couldn't deal with that prospect; she'd simply have to face the blow head on, without preparation – when and if it happened. And the Mellors, though they'd undoubtedly be willing and sympathetic listeners, would never understand what she was going through. All happy families seemed smug to Margaret, so secure in their ordinariness. It was getting so she had a hard time walking down Broadway, with its endless stream of families that no court would ever attempt to pull apart. It was one of the reasons she'd accepted the Mellors' invitation to Connecticut this weekend. But she'd forgotten how happy the Mellors could appear. She reminded herself that Charlotte complained about Rob's long hours and heavy travel schedule, but this didn't help. How could the Mellors know what it feels like to be told that you're unfit as parents, that your child may be taken away from you?

On Sunday, tired of pacing but not tired enough to rest, Selma took the A train out to Bed-Stuy. The mid-morning air was cold and dry; she felt her skin shrink like plastic wrap round her face. On the subway people read huge Sunday papers. Selma thought that maybe when she learned to read, Sundays wouldn't seem so long, so empty. Maybe they won't seem so bad once I have Isaiah back, she thought, but stopped herself from exploring this dangerous conjecture any further. Better not to jinx myself, she decided.

She rang Marie's doorbell twice before she began to worry.

Usually there'd be a stampede of feet after one ring, Raymond followed closely by Josette. Though she'd heard the bell clearly, she knocked on the door a few times, then started to pound.

'Kids gone,' said a voice behind her. Selma turned to find her old neighbor, the same short, elderly black woman who had told Selma about Marie being taken off in an ambulance last spring. Selma knew it wasn't going to be good news this time, either. 'What d'you mean, kids gone?'

'What I said. The city come for them.'

'Where's Marie?'

'She inside, least I think she is. Sleepin'. Sleepin' it off.' The woman chuckled hoarsely, joylessly. 'Said she weren't fit to raise 'em.'

'Who said that?'

'Social worker. Took the kids 'way from her.'

'Where they take them to?'

The woman coughed, engaging her entire body in the effort. 'Guess to a foster home.'

A leaden sadness overcame Selma and she wanted to be outside as soon as possible, away from this place. Unconsciously she pressed the down button for the elevator.

'Can't blame 'em,' she heard the woman say, and Selma knew right away she didn't want to hear what was coming. Where *was* that elevator? 'They found marks on Raymond. Bruises. Weekend they took 'em away, weren't no food in the house, and no money neither for Josette to run out 'n buy some.'

Where *was* that elevator?

'I hear screamin' and fightin' all times of day and night. Kids is better off in a home than here, s'my 'pinion. That Raymond look like he didn't sleep for a week las' time I seen him. Big bags under his eyes.'

The elevator opened and Selma quickly got in.

'Don't care how bad them foster homes is,' she heard the old woman saying as the doors shut. 'Got to be better than what's goin' on here.'

The Mellors suggested an apple-picking expedition and the Lewins did not resist, though only Isaiah was enthusiastic. With his Ghostzapper slung over his shoulder, he was practically panting at the thought. The idea of apples on trees, rather than on shelves in the market, was magical to him.

Scrunched together in the Mellors' Volvo, they were an uncomfortable group in more ways than one. Rob Mellor tried to engage Charles, sitting next to him up front, in a conversation about the graphic arts business, even suggesting that his law firm might be interested in a new graphic identity program. But Charles felt divorced from his work and found it hard to think about it, let alone discuss it, when he wasn't physically in the office. Susannah had left a week ago for a job at an ad agency, and he'd yet to hire a replacement. Work was piling up but Charles couldn't muster the proper concern. LewinArt had taken on an aura of unreality; once it had been his refuge from home, now home was his refuge from the business. It was as if he had sold LewinArt and was staying on only to honor an employment contract. This will change, he reassured himself without conviction. This will change once the custody thing is settled.

Isaiah was literally, and uncharacteristically, speechless when they arrived at the orchard. The sight of branches sagging with red apples was apparently more than he could absorb. He wandered from tree to tree, staring up with his mouth and eyes open, stumbling over the fallen apples. 'I think he thought apples were made in the supermarket,' Margaret told Charlotte.

Each family purchased an empty basket and began filling it. Charles hoisted Isaiah on his shoulders so he could participate. But his wonderment waned quickly and after a few minutes he decided to hunt ghosts instead. Emma happily joined him in this more momentous pursuit.

The adults, including Hannah, moved listlessly from tree to tree. 'I don't know what we'll do with all these apples,' Charlotte said. 'I mean, we can make a pie this afternoon, but we'll still have three dozen left over.'

Margaret suggested cider but no one knew how to make cider without a press, or even if it were possible to do so.

'We could have target practice with them,' Charles offered. He picked an apple from his basket and threw it at a tree several yards away. It exploded on contact. They all looked at him as if he'd just desecrated something. But a moment later Margaret threw the apple she'd just picked at a tree only a few feet from her. To her enormous pleasure it broke up on contact with a satisfying splat. A moment later Rob Mellor threw an apple at the tree Charles had hit. It burst apart, leaving a pale white stain on the bark. Soon all four adults were hurling apples at the tree. Milky splats punctuated the cool fall day, along with the softer thuds of apples hitting the leafy carpet beneath the tree.

To a stranger it may have looked like a frolic, but from her position on the sidelines, Hannah at least recognized it for what it was. No one was saying anything, no one congratulated anyone on a good hit or challenged anyone to hit a more difficult target. It was a silent and mirthless endeavor, and only when the baskets were empty did it finally exhaust itself. By then even Isaiah and Emma were captivated by the spectacle, standing nearby in mute amazement.

That night, Selma dreamed she was driving, which in real life she'd never learned to do. The steering wheel felt enormous between her spread arms, big as a hoola-hoop. At first she enjoyed herself, though throughout the ride she knew she shouldn't be driving without a license and tensed up each time she passed a policeman. The air felt cool and refreshing on her face, the bumps in the road were a constant, gentle massage. A sense of wellbeing flooded over her, a feeling of happiness as pure as ether.

Suddenly she realized that the road was coming at her faster and faster. She had to lean her whole body into negotiating a turn, but each time she managed one curve, another one followed almost immediately. She knew she could handle the curves individually; it was the thought of one coming after another without a break that made her panic. The bumps in the road became jolts, and before long she could feel the car bottoming out each time it lurched off a bump. Then a high-pitched cry from the passenger's seat reminded her that Isaiah was in the car with her. How could she have forgotten this? From the corner of her right eye she saw him tossing about the car, his tiny body limp as a puppet. The curves were coming at her faster and faster, and Isaiah's cries were getting louder, more insistent. She hit a huge bump and felt the car take off. She waited in terror for it to hit the ground. Moments passed and her alarm only intensified. Next to her, Isaiah was silent, his body rigid as he, too, anticipated the crash.

The sensation of careening along a hilly road hadn't completely left her when she woke up. When her eyes opened to the stationary room she felt as if she'd come to a sudden, lurching halt. She took a deep, involuntary breath and actually grabbed hold of a handful of sheets to steady herself. Only after a few minutes, when she felt stable enough to look at the clock, did she discover that it was only midnight. She'd been asleep for just an hour.

Back in New York, Margaret didn't sleep much at all Sunday night. She and Charles read magazines until well after midnight, resolutely avoiding mentioning what was on their mind. Worrying exhausted them more than anything else, and at one o'clock they both turned off their respective bedside lamps and tried to sleep.

A half-hour later neither had fallen asleep and the covers were a heavy jumble in the middle of the large bed. 'I'm going into the living room to read,' Margaret whispered.

Charles grabbed her round the waist. 'Don't,' was all he said. He pulled her to him and hugged her.

283

'I'm scared, Charles.'

He stroked her face, then her back. 'I can't believe the judge would take him away from us. I just can't believe that will happen.'

'Just the thought . . .' Margaret breathed. Charles held her closer and neither spoke for several minutes. Charles's massaging grew more intense, and she felt him growing hard. When he angled his head to kiss her she said no and started to turn away.

'Yes, Margaret. We need to,' Charles answered.

She shook her head.

'It will strengthen us.' His hands massaged her breasts and then moved down to discover that she was already aroused. This embarrassed her, though she didn't say anything. Why did fear and anxiety so often do this to her? She opened herself to him but after a few minutes when he didn't feel her respond he asked her what the matter was. Nothing, she replied. You go ahead. But he waited for her, thrusting and angling and shifting until she had no choice but to respond. She cried out in what could have been taken for agony, and he followed almost immediately with a guttural moan. When, moments later, he tried to roll off her, she held him on top, squeezing him tightly, and felt him withdraw from her in imperceptible stages.

When he finally did move off her, he fell asleep almost immediately. Margaret, too, felt exhausted but knew she still wouldn't sleep. Quietly she got up and put on her robe. She closed the bedroom door silently behind her and walked to Isaiah's room. She stood in the center of his room until her eyes adjusted to the darkness. Then she could make him out, crammed into a corner of his crib. They'd been talking about getting him a 'big boy' bed, as Isaiah called it, for several months now, but had not had the heart to do it while the custody trial loomed. Tonight he looked absurdly large in the crib, as if fashioned from a different scale altogether. She wanted to touch him, pat him, but knew he'd wake up. In Metropolitan Hospital, and even after she'd brought him home, he'd been so sensitive that he'd shriek and flinch at the slightest touch. Just to pick him up from his layette required ten minutes of patient coaxing, first a finger placed gently on his shoulder, then two fingers, then the entire hand, which almost covered his torso. Margaret remembered how he trembled under her hand, all his nerves raw from the drugs his mother had fed him early in her pregnancy. And she remembered how she'd felt when he'd finally stopped shaking and she could feel his regular breathing as she held him to her chest.

Isaiah was still a light sleeper, but now when he was awake she could touch him and hold him without the painstaking preparation. He was hers, her son; they both knew it. She had given him life, not

Selma Richards, though this wasn't what made her tremble with anger and grief at times like this, late at night, in Isaiah's preternaturally quiet room, while, outside, the city held its breath till dawn. Charles felt agonized by the injustice of the situation, but Margaret knew that justice had nothing to do with it. This child was her son and she was his mother. For Margaret, tonight as much as two years ago, it was as simple as that.

PART FOUR

Chapter 40

Winter made a premature appearance on the Thursday following Judge Champion's decision. On television, weathermen crowed about 'record lows' as New Yorkers struggled to retrieve their heavy coats from the recesses of their over-filled closets.

Selma bundled against the cold and against the chilly fear of the future that the judge had laid out for her on Monday morning. All week, waiting for Saturday to come, she'd felt her life hanging in the balance, suspended between what was and what was coming. This made it difficult for her to concentrate on anything, least of all on Dana Fredricks, who had skipped walking, it seemed, and progressed directly to running. Selma didn't think she had the energy to keep up with the child, though tiredness had nothing to do with it. Tuesday afternoon, she gave Dana a bath, dried her off, dressed her, and an hour later she unconsciously started the process all over again. Only Dana's bewildered expression prevented her from bathing the child a second time.

At night she sat primly on the sofa in her living room, as if someone were already there with her. She felt lonelier than ever.

All the people from her past haunted her that week, as if they knew she was going through something and were hanging around to see what she'd do. Her mother, a ghost even when Selma lived with her, appeared in her mind as a gauzy shadow. She hadn't given much thought to her mother recently – she'd died, of an inevitable heart attack, long before Isaiah was born – but this week she couldn't keep her mind off her. What was it her mother was telling her? Her words evaporated just beyond the range of Selma's hearing, but then her mother had never had much to say to her. Isaiah Reptoe made an appearance, and sometimes, for a moment, a warm feeling would come over Selma. But this dissolved quickly into disappointment, leaving a kind of vacuum. The disappointment was as vivid and bitter today as it was then. Faces of men, dimly-lit even in those days, emerged from the darkness of her memory and swirled around her that week. What did *they* want? What had they ever wanted?

Only Isaiah's face refused to come to her, though she tried to summon it often enough. She'd squeeze her eyelids together, trying to conjure him, and still he wouldn't appear. Such failures made her heart beat faster and brought sweat to her forehead. On Saturday I'll have him forever, Selma consoled herself. But it didn't really help.

Arthur had called Monday with the judge's decision. 'We won!' he'd shouted, practically blowing the receiver off her ear. The news made her knees go soft; she grabbed a chair back and waited to catch her breath.

Selma didn't feel victorious, just pleased. Victories needed losers, and she didn't want to sully her joy by thinking about anyone losing. Isaiah was hers; she'd have a lifetime to make up for two and a half years.

Later, inevitably, waves of panic and misgiving washed over her, engulfing her. At these moments, Selma wished she had a picture of Isaiah, something to remind her that she needed to be strong, committed. She'd walk quietly over to his bed, as if he were already sleeping there, and smooth out the little blanket she'd bought – an actual bed, now. She'd try to imagine her boy sleeping there, but couldn't.

Isaiah knew something was wrong. Whenever he looked up at his mother, it was like her eyes were seeing something behind him, a monster or . . . a ghost. When she held him to her, which she did all the time now, he could feel her trembling the way his car seat did when they were stopped at a red light. His father was different too, quieter. Once he even picked Isaiah up at playgroup and brought him to McDonald's for lunch. Hannah played the bouncing ball game with him and didn't make him stop until he was ready to, which he didn't think would ever happen, he loved to play it so much, but which did happen, after a long, long time.

None of this was all that bad, but Isaiah wasn't happy about any of it. Something was wrong, and he kept to his room as much as he could, until he'd run through his toys and had no choice but to emerge. Then he'd feel his mother's red, frightened eyes looking just over his shoulder, or feel his father scoop him up and toss him in the air, which he actually liked, only he usually had to *ask* his father to do it – uppie, uppie, over and over – he'd feel these things and hurry back to his room, wishing he knew what was going on. Wishing, too, he had more toys to keep him company.

Selma's new book was about a short-order cook. It was just about the only book in the Center's library that wasn't about drugs, alcoholism, abuse of one kind or another, or crime. There were books about history, especially black history, but they were too advanced for her, according to Lizzie.

Actually, the book wasn't too bad. Selma had no interest in cooking, let alone short-order cooking, but it was a pleasure to read a book with so many long words she recognized. Hamburger. French fries. Pancakes. Coffee. These words were like faces she recognized but couldn't place for a few seconds. Then she'd figure them out and a feeling of success would flood over her. At home this week, waiting, she'd puzzle out a few pages a night, feeling strengthened as she turned the pages.

Thursday night Lizzie had on a blue print dress instead of her usual suit. Selma complimented her on it, said she should wear more dresses.

'I know I should,' Lizzie answered her. 'Suits are a habit with me, though.'

'Saturday I pick up Isaiah,' Selma said. Lizzie nodded. 'Just for the day and night. Sunday he goes back to the Lewins. After a month of this, we switch. I have him six days, they have him on the weekends. After five months, he's mine for good.' Selma actually felt breathless after this recitation.

'How do you feel about this?'

Selma felt her back go up. 'About him bein bein' mine for good?'

'No, about seeing your son on Saturday for the first time.'

'Oh, that.' Selma chuckled. Then, softly, she said, 'Scared.'

'I don't blame you.'

'In all this trouble, I never stopped to wonder if he and I would get along. I figured we was family, we oughta be together.'

'It might take a while before he warms up to you.'

'That's what I keep on reminding myself. Treat him like Dana at first, is what I tell myself. Be nice but not too close. But I just miss him so bad, I know I'll want to keep my arms around him the moment I lay eyes on him. I never feel that way with Dana.'

Lizzie smiled and nodded.

'I know it sounds strange, my missing him when I don't even know him . . .'

'It's not strange,' Lizzie said quickly.

'But it is strange, Lizzie. I ain't even sure I could pick him out from a line-up.'

They both laughed at the image.

'I miss him like it was just yesterday I gave him up. Like he's a habit I just gave up, that's how bad I miss him. My arms . . .' she raised her elbows above the table, 'my arms vibrate when I think about holding him.'

'You'll do the right thing on Saturday,' Lizzie said quietly. 'Your instincts are right.'

'Instincts,' Selma repeated. 'I don't know about instincts. Last night Calvin called.'

Lizzie looked so pleased, Selma hated to disappoint her.

'He wanted to know about Isaiah.'

'And?'

'And nothing. I still can't see him. If the Lewins was to ever see me with him, they'd go right back to court. Probably get Isaiah back. And I told Calvin, no way I'm going to sneak around with him.' Selma knew her voice sounded more sure than she felt. The sound of Calvin's voice on the phone had given her a boost. Having to put him off had deflated her. The way crack leaves you just a hair below where it took you from in the first place. That's how she felt hanging up on Calvin.

'There's something else we gotta discuss. Once I have Isaiah permanent, I don't know how I'm gonna continue on here. I gotta pick him up at the day care center by six.'

'It would be a shame to stop now. You're making such great progress.'

'I know. Makes me sick to think of stopping. But I don't have a choice.'

'Maybe I could get you permission to bring Isaiah here with you,' Lizzie offered.

Selma looked around. 'He'd disrupt everything and you know it.'

Both were silent for a bit, contemplating an end to their relationship.

'Always gotta compromise on something,' Selma said. 'You get one thing, you give up another. It's the way it works.'

'Maybe we can work something out, like meeting at lunchtime.'

'You think I get a lunch break?'

Lizzie rolled her eyes 'Stupid.'

'I'm lucky I still got a job at all. I can tell by the way Mrs Fredricks looks at me, she wishes I'd disappear. Hates the idea that I got a distraction. That's her word, distraction. Probably thinks I'm still on drugs, too. But she's afraid of all the bad publicity if she fires me.' Selma chuckled.

Lizzie smiled and shook her head. 'Anyway,' she said, 'we have a month to think about it, let's get some reading done now.'

Selma opened her book to the page where she'd left off It was lunchtime, the short-order cook was deep into hamburgers and BLTs. She read, surprising herself and Lizzie with her ability, but then reading was like dancing and sewing and a lot of other things; you did it better sometimes when you were concentrating on something else.

Charles insisted on accompanying Margaret and Isaiah up to Selma

Richards' apartment. She appreciated the offer and she didn't resist, but the truth was, she'd rather have gone without him. She wanted the pain of this day, the day on which she began the hideous process of giving up her son, to be undiluted, pure. She had no need of soothing words or calming gestures; she didn't need these because she knew they wouldn't work. But Charles wanted to come and she knew he should.

'We're going to see a lady,' Margaret told Isaiah as she stuffed him into his winter coat.

He smiled in anticipation; there was little in life that Isaiah didn't look forward to.

'You'll spend the day and night with her and then you'll come back here tomorrow afternoon. Does that sound like fun?'

He nodded. The thick down jacket forced his arms out from his body; he looked like a plump angel.

'Why don't you get any toys you want to bring,' she told him. He returned a minute later with his Ghostzapper. 'That's all?'

'Ghostbusters!' he screamed.

'Do you think there'll be ghosts at the lady's house?' Margaret whispered.

'Yes,' he whispered back conspiratorially, trying, despite the down padding, to manoeuver the gun into position.

They had talked about running away, to Mexico, perhaps, or South America. They'd even talked to David Elliot about which countries were legally suitable for hiding out in. But there was Hannah to consider. And they'd never be able to hide anyway; they were easily identifiable, as they'd always been: three white people and a black child – something odd there, wouldn't you say? What will Isaiah think in ten years, Charles asked, when he finds out that we kept him from his birth mother by moving to Mexico? Hard enough for him grow up black in a white family. But think about it: black in a white family in a Spanish country? It's almost comical. We couldn't do that to him.

They thought about filing an appeal, but David Elliot told him you really couldn't appeal this type of dispute unless the circumstances changed materially. If you learn that Selma Richards is back on drugs, yes, then you can appeal. But only if something changes.

So Margaret packed a bag for Isaiah and felt the injustice of the world choking her like a gas. She pictured Selma Richards unpacking his tiny things, then repacking them on Sunday. Life had turned ugly for her; she was constantly buffeted from one ugliness to another. Everywhere she opened her eyes, ugliness. And bitterness. What an ugly city this is, she concluded lately, even before she got to the corner of their street. Ugliness and bitterness.

Hannah broke her self-imposed isolation to say goodbye to

Isaiah. She hoisted him up, barely making a dent in his down casing, and kissed him on the cheek. He clearly enjoyed the attention, smiling in a self-important way that squeezed reluctant smiles out of all of them.

A cold rain was falling, making it impossible for them to get a cab. So they waited, shivering, for a bus up Broadway. When it arrived they lifted Isaiah up onto it. He raced to the back of the bus but had difficulty hoisting himself onto a seat; he was small for his age, and the slippery jacket made it worse. By the time his parents joined him in the back he was panting from the effort. 'You look like an Eskimo,' Charles told him. Isaiah's face lit up with puzzled delight. 'Eskimo,' he shouted, waving his hands. Charles lifted him onto a seat, arms still akimbo. Margaret sat on Isaiah's right, Charles on his left. Neither parent said anything, and after a few blocks even Isaiah caught the gloom and became unusually quiet.

They got off the bus at 98th Street. Both Lewins were familiar with the Upper Nineties where Selma Richards lived, but all of their friends lived west of Broadway, not east of it, like Selma. Up here, Broadway was a kind of Mason-Dixon line between the gentrified strip to the west, leading down to Riverside Drive, and the modern, effectless projects that lined Amsterdam Avenue to the east. Selma Richards' building was very close to Broadway and so was able to turn its back on the projects nearby. Margaret, who couldn't help recalling the squalid apartment where she'd tracked down Selma and Isaiah, was relieved to see that Selma's present building had been renovated not too long ago; new windows and an occasional window box promised well-maintained, neatly-kept apartments within.

If either woman could have managed to hate the other, their first meeting without lawyers present might have been less difficult. Hate is a relatively uncomplicated emotion, and thus both easy to bear and hard to let go of. But as their eyes met over Isaiah's head, each knew that the other had done just what she would have done in her position. Each had fought for her son. Unfortunately, there were two mothers and only one son.

And Selma had won.

As for Charles, he felt, once again, left out of this drama of women. He had a momentary but satisfying fantasy of grabbing Isaiah and running off with him – there was only one father involved, after all.

Isaiah clutched his mother's leg and looked up at the tall black woman who had opened her apartment door to them. He could feel his mother's tension, though he didn't understand it. It made him nervous just to feel the extra hardness of her leg, the slight, barely distinguishable trembling.

For her part, Selma couldn't even bring herself to look at her son. She'd wanted him so badly for so long, it seemed almost risky to gaze on him, as if reality might dissolve back into fantasy. So she stared over his head at the Lewins, standing awkwardly in her doorway. Selma felt guilt start to rise up in her but fought it back. I did nothing they wouldn't have done, she told herself, not for the first time. I just wanted my son back.

Margaret Lewin handed Selma a card. 'This is our phone number and address, in case you need us.' Her voice faltered over this. 'He likes apple juice, so I put a few cartons in his bag. He goes to sleep around eight or nine. Sometimes later.' She smiled nervously. 'He likes a little light on, maybe a night light? For dinner he likes anything with—'

'Margaret, let's go.'

Her face reddened. She looked at Selma. 'He's never spent the night away from us. Never.'

'Please don't cry in front of him,' Charles whispered. 'It'll only make it harder.'

Selma was tempted to say something reassuring but thought better of it. What could she say?

Margaret bent down and unzipped Isaiah's coat. 'Guess what?' she said brightly. 'You're going to spend the night with this lady . . .' She didn't know what he was supposed to call Selma. The possibility of 'mother' appalled her. 'Her name is Selma, Isaiah. And you're going to do lots of fun things together.' Margaret looked up at Selma, as if to confirm this. Then she kissed Isaiah and stood up. Charles lifted the boy to face level and kissed him, then replaced him in front of Selma.

'I'll bring him to your place tomorrow before dinnertime,' Selma said.

Margaret could only nod, and even Charles had to turn away. He took his wife's elbow and led her back down the stairs. As they descended they heard Isaiah begin to cry. It started off as a whimper but quickly crescendoed into hysterical sobbing. Equally unsettling for both of them, however, was the sound of Selma trying to comfort him. The pain and bewilderment in her voice rivalled that in Isaiah's.

Chapter 41

Selma tried to usher Isaiah into her apartment but each time she touched him he shrieked even louder. She strained to hear the front door of the building open and close, but it seemed an eternity before the Lewins were gone. Were they waiting downstairs to see if she could quiet Isaiah?

'Come on now, let's get inside before we catch cold,' Selma said quietly, feeling a bit silly, since the hallway wasn't, in fact, much colder than her apartment. 'Come on now, Isaiah. You'll see your parents tomorrow.' Saying this gave Selma pause; would he ever be weaned off the Lewins?

He stood rooted to the floor outside her apartment. After a few minutes she scooped him up, a mass of slippery down jacket, and planted him in her living room. She shut the front door and then tried to unzip his jacket. He wouldn't let her, spinning around whenever she came near him until she felt dizzy and foolish.

'Isaiah, don't you want to have fun this weekend?' she offered. His answer was a deep sob, followed by a series of sounds somewhere between a hiccup and a moan. 'Maybe you want some apple juice.'

Selma didn't wait for an answer but went directly into her small kitchen and got a glass. Then she retrieved one of the little cartons from Isaiah's bag. It occurred to her that he might prefer to drink it from the carton, using the plastic straw that came with it. 'Do you want a glass or just the box?' she asked him, holding one in each hand. He didn't respond, just continued with the staccato sobbing. So she opened the carton and poured the juice into the glass. But when she held it out to Isaiah he looked at it in horror and returned to shrieking. He even took a swipe at the glass, spilling a few drops on the floor. Selma placed the glass on the coffee table and went to the kitchen for a paper towel. She realized, once in the kitchen, that she was out of breath. Calm down, she told herself. This won't last.

But Isaiah seemed to have an incredible capacity for noise. The periods of moaning were like rests for him, restoring his strength for the shrieking. He stood in the center of the living room, frozen, and the more hysterical he became, the less steady Selma felt. 'I'm going to wait you out, Isaiah,' Selma told him. 'Sooner or later you going to have to stop crying. Might as well be sooner.'

But he took this as a signal to wail even louder. Selma sat on the couch and crossed her arms on her chest, but she couldn't sit still. She stood and went into her bedroom, where she leaned against the wall and fought back tears. We can't both be crying, she told herself; this brought a smile to her face. Isaiah's sobbing was more rhythmic now, but muted by the thick walls of the apartment. Still, the sound cut through her, rebuked her. Just wait him out, she told herself. Just wait him out.

Isaiah eventually exhausted himself, and Selma took advantage of the first quiet moment to re-offer the glass of apple juice. Isaiah looked at it suspiciously at first, but Selma kept it in front of him and eventually he reached out and took it. He drank quickly, greedily. Must be dried out from all the crying, Selma thought. When he was done, Selma offered to take the glass but he flinched from her outstretched hand and placed it on a table instead. 'You know how to hurt a person,' Selma said. His face glowed from the exertion of crying. There was a crust of dried tears round his eyes. Selma had to remind herself not to stare at him too much. Having him with her, here, in her apartment, still seemed hard to believe. And he was so beautiful! Just the sight of him, perfectly formed, healthy, reassured her that she'd done no lasting damage. It was all she could do to keep from grabbing him, running her palm over his smooth cheeks, his hair.

Isaiah sat and stared at his lap while these thoughts crowded Selma's mind. When she woke up from them she realized she needed to do something with him, keep him occupied. 'There's a toy store not far from here,' she told him. 'How about we go look for a toy?'

His eyes widened at this prospect, though they never lost their wariness. But he stood up and let her put his down jacket back on. Selma had some trouble with the zipper, and as she fussed with it, she felt Isaiah begin to lose his cool. 'It's all right, Isaiah, I'm just not used to this either,' she said as soothingly as she could.

He refused to take her hand as they walked downstairs. Instead he gripped the metal railing and took the steps one at a time. Selma nervously preceded him, in case he stumbled. When they reached the street she insisted on holding his hand. He resisted but she grabbed him and started walking. 'Maybe I shoulda brought your stroller,' Selma told him. 'But I have a feeling you'da said no to that too.' He whimpered as they walked, and dragged behind her.

Selma wondered if people would think that she was kidnapping Isaiah. The child looked so *unwilling*. But then they passed a drugstore on Broadway whose front window was lined with mirrors, and when she spotted her reflection, and Isaiah's, she knew there was no mistaking them for what they were: mother and son.

Isaiah perked up in the toy store at least. At first he walked cautiously through the aisles, touching something now and then. But after a while he surrendered to the abundance and began cruising the aisles like a hungry shark. It wasn't long before he found the Ghostbusters section. He eagerly felt all the items here, finally holding up for Selma's inspection a collection of ugly figures that looked to be made of Day-glo-painted rubber. 'This is what you want?' Selma asked. He nodded solemnly. She checked the price and was astonished to see it was $12.95. But she said nothing, only hoped she had enough in her pocketbook for the toys and for lunch at McDonalds.

At the restaurant it took her five long minutes to coax out of Isaiah what he wanted. 'Isaiah, listen to me, do you want a hamburger, a Chicken McNuggets, or a McFish? Just choose one.' He clutched his new toy and said nothing. 'Isaiah, I'm having a Whopper and fries. That sound good to you? You want a milk-shake, too?' To her disappointment he shook his head. 'Then what *do* you want, child?' She saw his eyes go all dewy at this and made herself calm down. 'When we get to the head of the line, will you tell the lady behind the counter what you want?' Slowly, reluctantly, he nodded. 'Okay then.' Sure enough, when it was their turn to order she lifted him up and he practically whispered, 'Hamburger . . . and milkshake.'

'Chocolate or vanilla, honey?' the lady asked him.

''Nilla,' he said, putting his whole body into it.

Selma gave her order and then waited. She tried to put Isaiah down but he protested. So she held him until her arms started to ache while he watched the lady assemble their lunches.

'How old is your son?' the lady asked as she loaded up their tray.

'Two and a half,' Selma answered, hoping Isaiah hadn't caught the word 'son' – too early for that.

'Looks just like you,' the lady said. She handed Isaiah a pointed hat with Ronald McDonald on it. 'A present,' she said, then shouted, 'Next.'

Selma was too nervous to enjoy her meal, but at least Isaiah managed to eat. Or at least she *thought* he was eating. After ten minutes his tray was a jumble of scrunched hamburger bun, smeared mayonnaise and ketchup, and scattered pickles; Selma hoped some of the mess had found its way into Isaiah's mouth.

Selma wasn't sure how you started a conversation with a two-and-a-half-year-old. But she found the silence between them awkward, even if Isaiah was unaware of it. 'How's your burger?' she asked him. But he only nodded in response, and nothing happened after that. Isaiah rescued her after a while, though not in a way she found very inspiring.

'Hannah go to park?' he piped between bites of mush.

'You want to go to the park?' Selma answered.

'With Hannah,' he said emphatically.

'I'll take you to the park this afternoon if you want.'

'Hannah,' Isaiah said. 'Hannah park.'

'But today you're with me, Isaiah. I'm taking you to the park.'

Isaiah sat back in his chair and Selma saw tears beginning to form around his eyes. 'Please, Isaiah, don't cry. I'll take you to the park.'

But he started to cry anyway, and Selma felt herself having to fight back a sob. Like when someone yawns and you have to yawn too, she thought – crying is contagious.

Isaiah moped on the way to Riverside Park, and he moped on the way back. At least in the park itself he managed to look happy now and then. Selma had some difficulty getting him into the swing seat, his legs kept getting caught, then she couldn't get the safety strap over his head. This swing was different from the one she took Dana to in Central Park, but then, no two kids are the same, either. You have to learn how each one folds into a swing seat, how each one likes to be carried, how each one likes to be coaxed out of crying. My mistake, Selma considered as she pushed Isaiah on the swing, was that I thought knowing one kid would help with knowing another. She watched Isaiah swing away from her, then swing back, away and back. With his face turned away from her, he could be just a child she was paid to take care of. But she'd never feel this nervous, this *frantic* about someone else's child. No way. Only her own flesh and blood could make her feel this miserable.

No one said anything, no one made any specific plans. But that Saturday the Lewins – Margaret, Charles, and Hannah – stayed close to home, close to each other. Each, in their own way, sensed that to plan something, some *diversion*, would be a travesty, as if the loss of Isaiah could be offset by a visit to a museum, a matinee. So they kept pretty much inside that day, though the bright, unusually warm weather might ordinarily have beckoned them onto the streets, the parks.

'I keep thinking I'm forgetting something,' Margaret said at one point in the early afternoon.

Charles knew precisely what she meant. It was too quiet in the apartment; usually such a silence signalled that Isaiah was up to something he shouldn't be, and one of them would have to venture through the apartment to find out what it was. Sitting in their bedroom in their peaceful apartment, both parents felt neglectful, remiss.

'Another thing,' Margaret said a few minutes later. 'I keep running through all the things I forgot to tell . . . her. About Isaiah. About brushing his teeth. Changing him in the morning. The songs he likes at bedtime.'

'One thing about Isaiah, he'll let her know what he wants.'

Margaret nodded. 'I used to think you learn how to be a parent from instinct, plus maybe a little advice from friends and relatives. But you learn to be a parent from your kids. There's not a lot of decision-making involved. You do what you have to, what they demand of you.'

'Somehow that doesn't sound as positive as it should.'

'It depresses the hell out of me. It means that after two and a half years with Isaiah, this other woman can just step in and . . .'

'Succeed,' Charles said quietly.

'I know I should be happy about that . . .' She couldn't finish.

The day after the judge's decision, Charles had called David Elliot with a question that had plagued him from the very beginning of the whole mess. 'If I hadn't had an affair, would the decision have been different?'

He got the answer he'd been hoping for, more or less. 'It didn't help. But the inter-racial thing was the clincher. I'm getting another call, Charles. Anything else I can do for you?'

Later that Saturday, their first without Isaiah, Charles needed to talk about it with Margaret. He didn't want absolution so much as clarity, and closure. 'About my thing with Susannah,' he began.

'Your thing,' Margaret snorted.

He forced himself to continue. 'I never loved her. I'm not sure I even liked her. I had this intense need at the time to break away, to do something completely unconnected to you and the kids and this . . . life.'

'Something selfish, you mean.' She sounded so hostile, he was beginning to regret raising the issue. But he knew he had to get through the bitterness.

'Yeah, you could say that.'

'*I* never felt the need to break away.'

Charles knew this was true. The pressures of raising a family and making a living weighed equally on both of them, but Margaret couldn't separate herself from her family, her life, the way he could, or thought he could. If she had an affair, it would have to be all-consuming; anything less would simply intrude.

'I wish I could find a way to say how sorry I am . . .'

Margaret shook her head, cutting him off.

'I talked to David. He didn't seem to think it made much of an impact on the judge's—'

'What difference does it make now?' she interrupted, turning

301

away from him. 'You had an affair. We lost our son.'

'It makes a difference because we're still here. We have to find a way to live together.'

Margaret said nothing.

'We have to find a way, Margaret. I don't think I can go on like this.' He waited, then asked, 'Can you?'

She turned and buried her head in his chest, as if fearful that he'd see her face. He put his arms round her. 'I'm not asking you to forgive me. I don't expect that.' She shook her head against him and he had to smile; even in moments like this, she rarely gave an inch. 'Just promise me that you'll help me try to find a way to move on.' She nodded into his chest. He pulled her closer.

They stood that way for a few moments, until Charles realized that Hannah had entered the room. He forced a smile. 'We're having a love-in. Want to join?'

She gave them that cockeyed smile, that tilt of the head that she knew they hated. 'A love-in?' she said.

'Come on,' Charles said, gesturing for her to join them.

'I have homework?' she said feebly.

Charles gestured again and, reluctantly, she shambled over. As soon as he could reach her he pulled her towards them, then put one arm round his wife, the other around his daughter. A second later he felt Hannah's arm around his back.

And there they stood, rocking slightly, as if to a dimly heard melody. Three of them, again. The Lewin family.

Sometime later, Hannah broke the silence, and the spell. 'This is too weird,' she said after a while, and disengaged herself from the trio.

Isaiah was calm that afternoon, though he refused to take a nap. Then Selma started fixing dinner and he became uneasy, probably because he had expected to go home for dinner. But exhaustion won out over uneasiness once dinner was over, and he gave Selma no trouble when she put on his pajamas. She wanted to give him a bath but knew better than to push her luck. She tucked him into what had been her bed (that night would be her first on the sofa bed in the living room) and then suggested a book. He seemed happy about this idea, which pleased her, since she'd gone over the book that week with Lizzie to make sure she understood it.

'This book is called *Robbie the Rabbit*, Isaiah. Look, here's Robbie right on the cover.'

Isaiah looked at the cover and pointed at the rabbit.

Selma opened the book and skipped to where the illustrations began (in her own books she often had trouble skipping over the stuff in the front, like the contents and whatnot; she never knew if she was going to miss something important). 'Robbie the Rabbit lives in a . . .' Damn, she was in trouble on the first page, and she'd rehearsed this a hundred times. '. . . in a field,' she said after a short pause, though she knew the word – m-e-a-d-o-w – wasn't field but something that started with the m sound.

She turned the page. 'He lives with his mother and father. Can you see the mother and father, Isaiah?' He leaned over and pointed to the two larger rabbits.

'That's right.' She turned to the next page. 'All day long Robbie hops around the . . . field.'

Selma read a few more pages and felt her confidence growing. But then Isaiah, whose eyes were half closed already, suddenly jerked his whole body, as if waking from a nightmare, and cried, 'Mommy!' This so surprised Selma that she turned round, half expecting to see Margaret Lewin. When she turned back Isaiah had a wide-eyed look of terror and was breathing heavily, as if he'd just stopped running. Feeling defeated, she put down the book and placed a hand on his shoulder. But Isaiah recoiled from her, rolling over to face the wall. 'It's okay, Isaiah,' Selma whispered, feeling helpless. 'It's okay.' A moment later she noticed his breathing had normalized; then it grew steady and she knew he was asleep.

Sleep was more elusive for Selma. The thin mattress of the sofa bed was only part of the reason, as was the insistent, chemical light of the street lamps through the living room's uncovered windows. Mostly it was worry that kept Selma from sleeping. She worried that Isaiah would never accept her, let alone love her as his mother. She worried about what the separation from the Lewins would do to him. She worried about whether taking him back from the Lewins was the right thing to do. Why did I start this whole thing? she asked herself over and over that Saturday night. For me? To prove *to me* that I could make up for a past mistake, that I could start over, from scratch? Or did I do it for Isaiah, because I thought I could really raise him properly?

I did it for Isaiah, she told herself more than once. Because I'm his true and lawful mother. He belongs to me, that's why I did it.

But a voice slithered into her head from somewhere in the night and whispered that she was as selfish now, taking Isaiah from the Lewins, as she had been when she gave him to them two and a half years ago. Selfish. Selfish. It was an ugly snake of a word, hissing and spitting inside her.

Selma got out of bed and walked into the bedroom. It took her a few moments to adjust to the darkness; Isaiah came into focus slowly, like a Polaroid photograph. He had thrown off most of the covers and was lying practically horizontal on the bed. Only his face looked peaceful; his body seemed frozen not by sleep but by exertion, as if he were holding a pose. Selma bent over to touch him, needing the reassurance of the feel of him, but hesitated just an inch from him, afraid that he'd wake up and not recognize her. Quietly she returned to the white-lit living room.

I wish I drank, she thought. I could use a drink right now. This feels like when the drugs were wearing off, when my nerves felt like they were being vacuumed out of me. She angled around the protruding sofa bed and looked out the window. Across the way a large brick building was being renovated. Huge dumpsters had been parked outside it for weeks now, piled up with old sinks and toilets and woodwork. Paned windows had been replaced with the kind Selma's building had, black-rimmed with no panes. This is not where I belong, Selma thought. I have no business living in a place I can't afford. On Friday, Arthur Golderson had called to see if Selma would mind if he arranged to have a photographer take some pictures of her and Isaiah on their first day together. No way, Selma had told him; the thought alone made her want to run and hide. This could be very important for me, Selma, he'd told her. A reminder that we won. No way, she'd repeated, not even bothering to explain herself. Don't forget, Selma, I never got a fee for this case. You got your son back but I never got a fee. Selma had wondered when he'd bring this up. No way I'm lettin' a photographer shoot us, she told him. Selma, it's the least you can do, after all . . . Here comes the part about the cheap rent on the apartment, she thought just before hanging up on him. The phone had rung right after that but she hadn't answered it.

Tomorrow I'm calling Arthur Golderson and telling him I'm vacating this place, Selma decided. The resolution made her feel stronger. I'll find a place in Brooklyn, maybe in a project. Someplace I can afford on my own.

Later, in bed, bathed in shadowless halogen light, she knew what else she had to do tomorrow. Isaiah was happy with the Lewins. He was happy and I was selfish, Selma thought. The Lewins are rich, educated. They're *married*, a real family. Isaiah has a sister at the Lewins, he has more than two years of his life with the Lewins. She thought of Raymond and Josette. Kids who really needed her. She wondered where they had gone to, and if she would ever be able to find them. She'd heard about the hopeless maze of the city's foster care system. I was never Isaiah's mother, not really. I did this to prove something to myself. Well, now I've proved it. Time to set things straight. Really straight.

Twenty blocks to the south, Margaret and Charles Lewin thrashed about in their bed, unable to sleep. It was their first night separated from Isaiah and the feeling they shared was one of having been burglarized. The map of Manhattan reappeared in Margaret's mind, which it never did at home (why should it? At home she always had her children with her), and she saw Selma Richards' apartment up in the Nineties, east of Broadway. She saw their own apartment, further downtown, and she saw the distance that separated the two places, saw it as impenetrable, uncrossable. Thinking about a life without her son made her mind swim, she literally couldn't focus on it. So she concentrated on her mental map of Manhattan Island, on the twenty blocks between her and Isaiah.

Chapter 42

Selma was up before Isaiah, though she wasn't sure she had ever fallen asleep. When Isaiah emerged from his room he looked bewildered, and when he saw Selma he actually looked reassured, which heartened her. He wore a diaper only at night, which she changed now, replacing it with one of the pull-up diapers she'd found in his bag. He'd been toilet trained on the early side, she thought. Another point in the Lewins' favor.

She made him pancakes for breakfast, which he mauled with his fork in between tiny bites. 'We're going home early today, Isaiah,' she told him. 'Back to your parents.'

He smiled at that and drank his milk.

'We'll take a bus down, okay?'

'Okay.' He nodded vigorously.

'First, though, I got to make a call.'

Arthur Golderson sounded groggy when he answered on the fourth ring.

'It's Selma,' she said.

'Anything wrong?' he said anxiously.

'Nothing's wrong. I'm thinking of moving.'

'Moving?' He sounded panicked. 'Moving where?' He coughed, clearing the sleep from his throat.

'Back to Brooklyn. I wanted to give you notice 'fore I started hunting a place.'

'I don't know if the judge will be pleased with this, Selma. One of the conditions of custody is that Isaiah attend the day care center near you.'

'I'm letting him stay with the Lewins,' she said evenly.

At first Arthur was silent. 'What?' he hissed after a while.

'You heard me. He don't belong with me.'

'Selma, you've had him one day. Give yourselves a chance to get reacquainted.'

'We never was acquainted, Arthur.'

He started to say something but stopped himself. 'This is a disaster,' he wailed after a few seconds.

'Why do you say that? You won, didn't you? That's what counts.'

'Selma, think about it. Don't make a rash decision.'

'I been thinking. All night. The child belongs with the Lewins. I belong in Brooklyn.'

Selma was feeling almost high. Making a decision, even a painful one, always made her feel strong and capable. Isaiah seemed to share her high: he squirmed into his clothes and drank a whole glass of orange juice, and when the 104 bus appeared on Broadway he practically flew onto it. His eagerness to get home only strengthened Selma's resolve.

But as the bus made slow progress down Broadway, Selma's high started to fade. She began to think about the trip back uptown, alone. She could already feel the blankness, the empty seat next to her. How quickly she'd become used to having someone with her! Isaiah was sitting on the edge of the seat, kicking his legs against it. The dull thumping noise he produced seemed to upset the woman across from him, who peered at him through eyes squinting with hostility. Selma placed a hand on Isaiah's knee and he stopped and looked up at her.

Maybe if he didn't look so much like me, she thought. Certain expressions of his, like this one, a puzzled look with a half-smile, were heart-stopping mirror images of herself, like seeing a photograph and thinking, That's me? Yep, that's me. Maybe if he didn't look so much like me, losing him wouldn't be so hard.

Dread began swelling up in her as they approached their stop. Exactly the opposite was happening to Isaiah, who jumped down from his seat before the bus stopped. 'Hold on, Isaiah,' Selma told him. He grabbed her hand and, with his other hand, took hold of her knee. Then he looked directly into her face and smiled. 'That's right, Isaiah,' she told him, 'we're almost home.'

She knew the building better than she should have, from her days of spying on him with Dana. But even if she hadn't, Isaiah would have led her to it. She could feel his eagerness in his tiny hands, which seemed to tremble in her own hand as they walked. When they turned the corner to the Lewins' street, Isaiah broke away from her and ran up to the front door.

'Well, look who's back,' the doorman said. He patted the top of Isaiah's head but frowned when he looked up and saw Selma. 'Ninth floor,' he mumbled as Selma walked past. Waiting for the elevator, she heard him say, over the house phone, 'They're back, Mrs Lewin.'

Selma rehearsed in her mind what she was going to say. It wasn't hard to find the right words, there were a million ways to say 'I was wrong.' What she had a hard time thinking about was the look on the Lewins' faces when she told them. Their happiness would be her sadness, their pleasure, her pain. Life was like that, she was learning once more. Only so much pleasure to go around; take more than you're due, and someone's got to suffer. Life's just unfair, Selma thought. Or is it? Wasn't there something basically fair about this system when you really thought about it? Something neat and even, at any rate?

Selma bent down and fixed Isaiah's shirt while the elevator brought them up. For the first time all weekend she gave in to a powerful urge and ran her fingers over the side of his face. She was so nervous doing this she barely touched him, it was like feeling to see if a pot was still hot. But to her considerable relief Isaiah didn't flinch, and a small, sly smile formed at the corners of his mouth.

'I want to do what's right for you Isaiah, understand?'

He looked at her blankly.

'I let you down once . . .' But she felt her eyes begin to fill up and stopped herself. She kissed his forehead and stood up, relieved not to be looking at him any longer. The elevator opened on the ninth floor.

Isaiah ran to the door of the Lewins' apartment and tried to reach the doorknob. Selma rang the bell and was startled when the door was answered almost immediately.

Margaret and Charles Lewin were both at the door, Charles standing just behind his wife. Margaret bent down and hugged Isaiah, then stood up and looked at Selma. That's when something happened inside her, something changed. It was the woman's eyes, seen close up, that did it. Selma was taken back two and a half years to her apartment uptown. She was lying on the bed in her dark, dusky room. In a corner of the room that seemed a thousand miles away a baby was crying. A high, raw, angry sound. The wailing wouldn't stop. *Panic.* Stop crying, stop! Sweat was forming on her forehead. She felt like wailing herself, crying until her throat was raw, but at least she knew how to stop, knew what it would take. And here was this woman with her, hanging over her. This woman who always seemed to be looking down on her with these big, white eyes. Critical eyes. She tried to stand up but couldn't, as if a hurricane wind was blowing her against the bed. I can stop the baby crying, the woman told her. Let me, please. I can stop the baby crying. Yes, yes, Selma said, stop it, stop it crying. The sweat on her forehead was icy cold, menacing, but she was shivering from the heat. Stop the baby crying, yes, stop it.

And then it was quiet.

'Are you okay?'

Selma blinked and saw those same eyes looking at her. They still seemed to be looking down at her, though Margaret Lewin was no taller than she was. They were blue eyes, pale blue, but what Selma fixed on, now as then, were the whites: so clear and smooth, so *white*. Selma looked down at Isaiah, standing quietly between the three of them like a small calf nestled in a herd. Then she looked up at the Lewins and saw it plainer than she'd ever seen it before: these were good people, good parents, but they weren't *Isaiah's* parents.

She took a big, steadying breath. 'I'll see you next Saturday, then, okay?'

On the subway to Brooklyn she kept thinking she had forgotten something. Panicking, she'd clutch for her pocketbook, only to realize that what she was missing was Isaiah. Her son. A sense of wellbeing surged in her, forcing out the dread she'd been feeling. She was on her way to Brooklyn to find a place for her and Isaiah to live. Maybe she could only afford one room, or maybe she'd have to find another situation like the one with Marie. Whatever. Once you know where you're going, once it's fixed in your mind, getting there isn't hard, she thought. Getting there's the easy part.

And she had another mission that Sunday afternoon. She was going to ask around for Raymond and Josette, make sure they were okay. She'd start with Marie, see what she knew. Then she'd talk to the neighbors. Tomorrow, she'd call the foster care people. Maybe Lizzie would help her if she had trouble finding the right number in the phone book. Anything was possible, Selma thought, even second chances: I've proven that, for me and my son. Now I'll try to give Raymond and Josette a second chance. Anything's possible.

The subway clattered onto the Manhattan Bridge and crossed the river to Brooklyn. The afternoon light was startling after the long ride underground, but once her eyes adjusted, Selma looked out over the vast landscape of Brooklyn. Somewhere out there is a place for me and Isaiah, she thought.

The train re-entered the tunnel in Brooklyn, grey darkness once again engulfing it. She thought of Isaiah, back with the Lewins. She thought of Josette and Raymond, together, she hoped, but with foster parents. She even thought of Dana, spending the day with parents she saw just two full days out of seven.

Trouble with this city, she decided, is all the kids with all the wrong people.